## J. J. Connington and The Murder Room

**>>>** This title is part of The Murder Room, our series dedicated to making available out-of-print or hard-to-find titles by classic crime writers.

Crime fiction has always held up a mirror to society. The Victorians were fascinated by sensational murder and the emerging science of detection; now we are obsessed with the forensic detail of violent death. And no other genre has so captivated and enthralled readers.

Vast troves of classic crime writing have for a long time been unavailable to all but the most dedicated frequenters of second-hand bookshops. The advent of digital publishing means that we are now able to bring you the backlists of a huge range of titles by classic and contemporary crime writers, some of which have been out of print for decades.

From the genteel amateur private eyes of the Golden Age and the femmes fatales of pulp fiction, to the morally ambiguous hard-boiled detectives of mid twentieth-century America and their descendants who walk our twenty-first century streets, The Murder Room has it all. **>>>**

## The Murder Room
**Where Criminal Minds Meet**

**themurderroom.com**

T0352424

### J. J. Connington (1880–1947)

Alfred Walter Stewart, who wrote under the pen name J. J. Connington, was born in Glasgow, the youngest of three sons of Reverend Dr Stewart. He graduated from Glasgow University and pursued an academic career as a chemistry professor, working for the Admiralty during the First World War. Known for his ingenious and carefully worked-out puzzles and in-depth character development, he was admired by a host of his better-known contemporaries, including Dorothy L. Sayers and John Dickson Carr, who both paid tribute to his influence on their work. He married Jessie Lily Courts in 1916 and they had one daughter.

*By J. J. Connington*

**Sir Clinton Driffield Mysteries**

Murder in the Maze (1927)

Tragedy at Ravensthorpe
  (1927)

The Case with Nine Solutions
  (1928)

Mystery at Lynden Sands
  (1928)

Nemesis at Raynham Parva
  (1929)

  (a.k.a. *Grim Vengenace*)

The Boathouse Riddle (1931)

The Sweepstake Murders
  (1931)

The Castleford Conundrum
  (1932)

The Ha-Ha Case (1934)

  (a.k.a. *The Brandon Case*)

In Whose Dim Shadow (1935)

  (a.k.a. *The Tau Cross Mystery*)

A Minor Operation (1937)

Murder Will Speak (1938)

Truth Comes Limping (1938)

The Twenty-One Clues (1941)

No Past is Dead (1942)

Jack-in-the-Box (1944)

Common Sense Is All You
  Need (1947)

**Supt Ross Mysteries**

The Eye in the Museum (1929)

The Two Tickets Puzzle (1930)

**Novels**

Death at Swaythling Court
  (1926)

The Dangerfield Talisman
  (1926)

Tom Tiddler's Island (1933)

  (a.k.a. *Gold Brick Island*)

The Counsellor (1939)

The Four Defences (1940)

# No Past is Dead

J. J. Connington

# CONTENTS

# CONTENTS

# Introduction
## by
## Curtis Evans

During the Golden Age of the detective novel, in the 1920s and 1930s, J. J. Connington stood with fellow crime writers R. Austin Freeman, Cecil John Charles Street and Freeman Wills Crofts as the foremost practitioner in British mystery fiction of the science of pure detection. I use the word 'science' advisedly, for the man behind J. J. Connington, Alfred Walter Stewart, was an esteemed Scottish-born scientist. A 'small, unassuming, moustached polymath', Stewart was 'a strikingly effective lecturer with an excellent sense of humour, fertile imagination and fantastically retentive memory', qualities that also served him well in his fiction. He held the Chair of Chemistry at Queens University, Belfast for twenty-five years, from 1919 until his retirement in 1944.

During roughly this period, the busy Professor Stewart found time to author a remarkable apocalyptic science fiction tale, *Nordenholt's Million* (1923), a mainstream novel, *Almighty Gold* (1924), a collection of essays, *Alias J. J. Connington* (1947), and, between 1926 and 1947, twenty-four mysteries (all but one tales of detection), many of them sterling examples of the Golden Age puzzle-oriented detective novel at its considerable best. 'For those who ask first of all in a detective story for exact and mathematical accuracy in the construction of the plot', avowed a contemporary *London Daily Mail* reviewer, 'there is no author to equal the distinguished scientist who writes under the name of J. J. Connington.'[1]

Alfred Stewart's background as a man of science is reflected in his fiction, not only in the impressive puzzle plot mechanics he devised for his mysteries but in his choices of themes and depictions of characters. Along with Stanley Nordenholt of *Nordenholt's Million*, a novel about a plutocrat's pitiless efforts to preserve a ruthlessly remolded remnant of human life after a global environmental calamity, Stewart's most notable character is Chief Constable Sir Clinton Driffield, the detective in seventeen of the twenty-four Connington crime novels. Driffield is one of crime fiction's most highhanded investigators, occasionally taking on the functions of judge and jury as well as chief of police.

Absent from Stewart's fiction is the hail-fellow-well-met quality found in John Street's works or the religious ethos suffusing those of Freeman Wills Crofts, not to mention the effervescent novel-of-manners style of the British Golden Age Crime Queens Dorothy L. Sayers, Margery Allingham and Ngaio Marsh. Instead we see an often disdainful cynicism about the human animal and a marked admiration for detached supermen with superior intellects. For this reason, reading a Connington novel can be a challenging experience for modern readers inculcated in gentler social beliefs. Yet Alfred Stewart produced a classic apocalyptic science fiction tale in *Nordenholt's Million* (justly dubbed 'exciting and terrifying reading' by the *Spectator*) as well as superb detective novels boasting well-wrought puzzles, bracing characterization and an occasional leavening of dry humour. Not long after Stewart's death in 1947, the Connington novels fell entirely out of print. The recent embrace of Stewart's fiction by Orion's Murder Room imprint is a welcome event indeed, correcting as it does over sixty years of underserved neglect of an accomplished genre writer.

Born in Glasgow on 5 September 1880, Alfred Stewart had significant exposure to religion in his earlier life. His father was William Stewart, longtime Professor of Divinity and Biblical Criticism at Glasgow University, and he married Lily Coats, a daughter of the Reverend Jervis Coats and member of one of

Scotland's preeminent Baptist families. Religious sensibility is entirely absent from the Connington corpus, however. A confirmed secularist, Stewart once referred to one of his wife's brothers, the Reverend William Holms Coats (1881–1954), principal of the Scottish Baptist College, as his 'mental and spiritual antithesis', bemusedly adding: 'It's quite an education to see what one would look like if one were turned into one's mirror-image.'

Stewart's J. J. Connington pseudonym was derived from a nineteenth-century Oxford Professor of Latin and translator of Horace, indicating that Stewart's literary interests lay not in pietistic writing but rather in the pre-Christian classics ('I prefer the *Odyssey* to *Paradise Lost*,' the author once avowed). Possessing an inquisitive and expansive mind, Stewart was in fact an uncommonly well-read individual, freely ranging over a variety of literary genres. His deep immersion in French literature and supernatural horror fiction, for example, is documented in his lively correspondence with the noted horologist Rupert Thomas Gould.[2]

It thus is not surprising that in the 1920s the intellectually restless Stewart, having achieved a distinguished middle age as a highly regarded man of science, decided to apply his creative energy to a new endeavour, the writing of fiction. After several years he settled, like other gifted men and women of his generation, on the wildly popular mystery genre. Stewart was modest about his accomplishments in this particular field of light fiction, telling Rupert Gould later in life that 'I write these things [what Stewart called tec yarns] because they amuse me in parts when I am putting them together and because they are the only writings of mine that the public will look at. Also, in a minor degree, because I like to think some people get pleasure out of them.' No doubt Stewart's single most impressive literary accomplishment is *Nordenholt's Million*, yet in their time the two dozen J. J. Connington mysteries did indeed give readers in Great Britain, the United States and other countries much diversionary reading pleasure. Today these works constitute an estimable addition to British crime fiction.

After his 'prentice pastiche mystery, *Death at Swaythling Court* (1926), a rural English country-house tale set in the highly traditional village of Fernhurst Parva, Stewart published another, superior country-house affair, *The Dangerfield Talisman* (1926), a novel about the baffling theft of a precious family heirloom, an ancient, jewel-encrusted armlet. This clever, murderless tale, which likely is the one that the author told Rupert Gould he wrote in under six weeks, was praised in *The Bookman* as 'continuously exciting and interesting' and in the *New York Times Book Review* as 'ingeniously fitted together and, what is more, written with a deal of real literary charm'. Despite its virtues, however, *The Dangerfield Talisman* is not fully characteristic of mature Connington detective fiction. The author needed a memorable series sleuth, more representative of his own forceful personality.

It was the next year, 1927, that saw J. J. Connington make his break to the front of the murdermongerer's pack with a third country-house mystery, *Murder in the Maze*, wherein debuted as the author's great series detective the assertive and acerbic Sir Clinton Driffield, along with Sir Clinton's neighbour and 'Watson', the more genial (if much less astute) Squire Wendover. In this much-praised novel, Stewart's detective duo confronts some truly diabolical doings, including slayings by means of curare-tipped darts in the double-centered hedge maze at a country estate, Whistlefield. No less a fan of the genre than T. S. Eliot praised *Murder in the Maze* for its construction ('we are provided early in the story with all the clues which guide the detective') and its liveliness ('The very idea of murder in a box-hedge labyrinth does the author great credit, and he makes full use of its possibilities'). The delighted Eliot concluded that

*Murder in the Maze* was 'a really first-rate detective story'. For his part, the critic H. C. Harwood declared in *The Outlook* that with the publication of *Murder in the Maze* Connington demanded and deserved 'comparison with the masters'. 'Buy, borrow, or – anyhow – get hold of it', he amusingly advised. Two decades later, in his 1946 critical essay 'The Grandest Game in the World', the great locked-room detective novelist John Dickson Carr echoed Eliot's assessment of the novel's virtuoso setting, writing: 'These 1920s [. . .] thronged with sheer brains. What would be one of the best possible settings for violent death? J. J. Connington found the answer, with *Murder in the Maze*.' Certainly in retrospect *Murder in the Maze* stands as one of the finest English country-house mysteries of the 1920s, cleverly yet fairly clued, imaginatively detailed and often grimly suspenseful. As the great American true-crime writer Edmund Lester Pearson noted in his review of *Murder in the Maze* in *The Outlook*, this Connington novel had everything that one could desire in a detective story: 'A shrubbery maze, a hot day, and somebody potting at you with an air gun loaded with darts covered with a deadly South-American arrow-poison – *there* is a situation to wheedle two dollars out of anybody's pocket.'[3]

Staying with what had worked so well for him to date, Stewart the same year produced yet another country-house mystery, *Tragedy at Ravensthorpe*, an ingenious tale of murders and thefts at the ancestral home of the Chacewaters, old family friends of Sir Clinton Driffield. There is much clever matter in *Ravensthorpe*. Especially fascinating is the author's inspired integration of faerie folklore into his plot. Stewart, who had a lifelong – though skeptical – interest in paranormal phenomena, probably was inspired in this instance by the recent hubbub over the Cottingly Faeries photographs that in the early 1920s had famously duped, among other individuals, Arthur Conan Doyle.[4] As with *Murder in the Maze*, critics raved about this new Connington mystery. In the *Spectator*, for example, a reviewer hailed *Tragedy at Ravensthorpe* in the strongest terms, declaring of the novel: 'This is more than a good detective tale. Alike in plot, characterization, and literary style, it is a work of art.'

In 1928 there appeared two additional Sir Clinton Driffield detective novels, *Mystery at Lynden Sands* and *The Case with Nine Solutions*. Once again there was great praise for the latest Conningtons. H. C. Harwood, the critic who had so much admired *Murder in the Maze*, opined of *Mystery at Lynden Sands* that it 'may just fail of being the detective story of the century', while in the United States author and book reviewer Frederic F. Van de Water expressed nearly as high an opinion of *The Case with Nine Solutions*. 'This book is a thoroughbred of a distinguished lineage that runs back to "The Gold Bug" of [Edgar Allan] Poe,' he avowed. 'It represents the highest type of detective fiction.' In both of these Connington novels, Stewart moved away from his customary country-house milieu, setting *Lynden Sands* at a fashionable beach resort and *Nine Solutions* at a scientific research institute. *Nine Solutions* is of particular interest today, I think, for its relatively frank sexual subject matter and its modern urban setting among science professionals, which rather resembles the locales found in P. D. James' classic detective novels *A Mind to Murder* (1963) and *Shroud for a Nightingale* (1971).

By the end of the 1920s, J. J. Connington's critical reputation had achieved enviable heights indeed. At this time Stewart became one of the charter members of the Detection Club, an assemblage of the finest writers of British detective fiction that included, among other distinguished individuals, Agatha Christie, Dorothy L. Sayers and G. K. Chesterton. Certainly Victor Gollancz, the British publisher of the J. J. Connington mysteries, did not stint praise for the author, informing readers that 'J. J. Connington is now established as, in the opinion of many, the greatest living master of the story of pure detection. He is one of those who, discarding all the superfluities, has made of deductive fiction a genuine minor art, with its own laws and its own conventions.'

Such warm praise for J. J. Connington makes it all the more surprising that at this juncture the esteemed author tinkered with his successful formula by dispensing with his original series detective. In the fifth Clinton Driffield detective novel, *Nemesis at Raynham Parva* (1929), Alfred Walter Stewart, rather like Arthur Conan Doyle before him, seemed with a dramatic dénouement to have devised his popular series detective's permanent exit from the fictional stage (read it and see for yourself). The next two Connington detective novels, *The Eye in the Museum* (1929) and *The Two Tickets Puzzle* (1930), have a different series detective, Superintendent Ross, a rather dull dog of a policeman. While both these mysteries are competently done – the railway material in *The Two Tickets Puzzle* is particularly effective and should have appeal today – the presence of Sir Clinton Driffield (no superfluity he!) is missed.

Probably Stewart detected that the public minded the absence of the brilliant and biting Sir Clinton, for the Chief Constable – accompanied, naturally, by his friend Squire Wendover – triumphantly returned in 1931 in *The Boathouse Riddle*, another well-constructed criminous country-house affair. Later in the year came *The Sweepstake Murders*, which boasts the perennially popular tontine multiple-murder plot, in this case a rapid succession of puzzling suspicious deaths afflicting the members of a sweepstake syndicate that has just won nearly £250,000.[5] Adding piquancy to this plot is the fact that Wendover is one of the imperiled syndicate members. Altogether the novel is, as the late Jacques Barzun and his colleague Wendell Hertig Taylor put it in *A Catalogue of Crime* (1971, 1989), their magisterial survey of detective fiction, 'one of Connington's best conceptions'.

Stewart's productivity as a fiction writer slowed in the 1930s, so that, barring the year 1938, at most only one new Connington appeared annually. However, in 1932 Stewart produced one of the best Connington mysteries, *The Castleford Conundrum*. A classic country-house detective novel, Castleford introduces to readers Stewart's most delightfully unpleasant set of greedy relations and one of his most deserving murderees, Winifred Castleford. Stewart also fashions a wonderfully rich puzzle plot, full of meaty material clues for the reader's delectation. *Castleford* presented critics with no conundrum over its quality. 'In *The Castleford Conundrum* Mr Connington goes to work like an accomplished chess player. The moves in the games his detectives are called on to play are a delight to watch,' raved the reviewer for the *Sunday Times*, adding that 'the clues would have rejoiced Mr. Holmes' heart.' For its part, the *Spectator* concurred in the *Sunday Times*' assessment of the novel's masterfully constructed plot: 'Few detective stories show such sound reasoning as that by which the Chief Constable brings the crime home to the culprit.' Additionally, E. C. Bentley, much admired himself as the author of the landmark detective novel *Trent's Last Case*, took time to praise Connington's purely literary virtues, noting: 'Mr Connington has never written better, or drawn characters more full of life.'

With *Tom Tiddler's Island* in 1933 Stewart produced a different sort of Connington, a criminal-gang mystery in the rather more breathless style of such hugely popular English thriller writers as Sapper, Sax Rohmer, John Buchan and Edgar Wallace (in violation of the strict detective fiction rules of Ronald Knox, there is even a secret passage in the novel). Detailing the startling discoveries made by a newlywed couple honeymooning on a remote Scottish island, *Tom Tiddler's Island* is an atmospheric and entertaining tale, though it is not as mentally stimulating for armchair sleuths as Stewart's true detective novels. The title, incidentally, refers to an ancient British children's game, 'Tom Tiddler's Ground', in which one child tries to hold a height against other children.

After his fictional Scottish excursion into thrillerdom, Stewart returned the next year to his English country-house roots with *The Ha-Ha Case* (1934), his last masterwork in this classic mystery setting (for elucidation of non-British readers, a ha-ha is a sunken wall, placed so as to delineate property boundaries while not obstructing views). Although *The Ha-Ha Case* is not set in Scotland, Stewart drew inspiration for the novel from a notorious Scottish true crime, the 1893 Ardlamont murder case. From the facts of the Ardlamont affair Stewart drew several of the key characters in *The Ha-Ha Case*, as well as the circumstances of the novel's murder (a shooting 'accident' while hunting), though he added complications that take the tale in a new direction.[6]

In newspaper reviews both Dorothy L. Sayers and 'Francis Iles' (crime novelist Anthony Berkeley Cox) highly praised this latest mystery by 'The Clever Mr Connington', as he was now dubbed on book jackets by his new English publisher, Hodder & Stoughton. Sayers particularly noted the effective characterisation in *The Ha-Ha Case*: 'There is no need to say that Mr Connington has given us a sound and interesting plot, very carefully and ingeniously worked out. In addition, there are the three portraits of the three brothers, cleverly and rather subtly characterised, of the [governess], and of Inspector Hinton, whose admirable qualities are counteracted by that besetting sin of the man who has made his own way: a jealousy of delegating responsibility.' The reviewer for the *Times Literary Supplement* detected signs that the sardonic Sir Clinton Driffield had begun mellowing with age: 'Those who have never really liked Sir Clinton's perhaps excessively soldierly manner will be surprised to find that he makes his discovery not only by the pure light of intelligence, but partly as a reward for amiability and tact, qualities in which the Inspector [Hinton] was strikingly deficient.' This is true enough, although the classic Sir Clinton emerges a number of times in the novel, as in his subtly sarcastic recurrent backhanded praise of Inspector Hinton: 'He writes a first class report.'

Clinton Driffield returned the next year in the detective novel *In Whose Dim Shadow* (1935), a tale set in a recently erected English suburb, the denizens of which seem to have committed an impressive number of indiscretions, including sexual ones. The intriguing title of the British edition of the novel is drawn from a poem by the British historian Thomas Babington Macaulay: 'Those trees in whose dim shadow/The ghastly priest doth reign/The priest who slew the slayer/And shall himself be slain.' Stewart's puzzle plot in *In Whose Dim Shadow* is well clued and compelling, the kicker of a closing paragraph is a classic of its kind and, additionally, the author paints some excellent character portraits. I fully concur with the *Sunday Times*' assessment of the tale: 'Quiet domestic murder, full of the neatest detective points [. . .] These are not the detective's stock figures, but fully realised human beings.'[7]

Uncharacteristically for Stewart, nearly twenty months elapsed between the publication of *In Whose Dim Shadow* and his next book, *A Minor Operation* (1937). The reason for the author's delay in production was the onset in 1935–36 of the afflictions of cataracts and heart disease (Stewart ultimately succumbed to heart disease in 1947). Despite these grave health complications, Stewart in late 1936 was able to complete *A Minor Operation*, a first-rate Clinton Driffield story of murder and a most baffling disappearance. A *Times Literary Supplement* reviewer found that *A Minor Operation* treated the reader 'to exactly the right mixture of mystification and clue' and that, in addition to its impressive construction, the novel boasted 'character-drawing above the average' for a detective novel.

Alfred Stewart's final eight mysteries, which appeared between 1938 and 1947, the year of the author's death, are, on the whole, a somewhat weaker group of tales than the sixteen that appeared between 1926 and 1937, yet they are not without interest. In 1938 Stewart for the last time managed to publish two detective novels, *Truth Comes Limping* and *For Murder Will Speak* (also published as *Murder Will Speak*). The latter tale is much the superior of the two, having an interesting suburban setting and a bevy of female characters found to have motives when a contemptible philandering businessman meets with foul play. Sexual neurosis plays a major role in *For Murder Will Speak*, the ever-thorough Stewart obviously having made a study of the subject when writing the novel. The somewhat squeamish reviewer for *Scribner's Magazine* considered the subject matter of *For Murder Will Speak* 'rather unsavoury at times', yet this individual conceded that the novel nevertheless made 'first-class reading for those who enjoy a good puzzle intricately worked out'. 'Judge Lynch' in the *Saturday Review* apparently had no such moral reservations about the latest Clinton Driffield murder case, avowing simply of the novel: 'They don't come any better'.

Over the next couple of years Stewart again sent Sir Clinton Driffield temporarily packing, replacing him with a new series detective, a brash radio personality named Mark Brand, in *The Counsellor* (1939) and *The Four Defences* (1940). The better of these two novels is *The Four Defences*, which Stewart based on another notorious British true-crime case, the Alfred Rouse blazing-car murder. (Rouse is believed to have fabricated his death by murdering an unknown man, placing the dead man's body in his car and setting the car on fire, in the hope that the murdered man's body would be taken for his.) Though admittedly a thinly characterised academic exercise in ratiocination, Stewart's *Four Defences* surely is also one of the most complexly plotted Golden Age detective novels and should delight devotees of classical detection. Taking the Rouse blazing-car affair as his theme, Stewart composes from it a stunning set of diabolically ingenious criminal variations. 'This is in the cold-blooded category which [. . .] excites a crossword puzzle kind of interest,' the reviewer for the *Times Literary Supplement* acutely noted of the novel. 'Nothing in the Rouse case would prepare you for these complications upon complications [. . .] What they prove is that Mr Connington has the power of penetrating into the puzzle-corner of the brain. He leaves it dazedly wondering whether in the records of actual crime there can be any dark deed to equal this in its planned convolutions.'

Sir Clinton Driffield returned to action in the remaining four detective novels in the Connington oeuvre, *The Twenty-One Clues* (1941), *No Past is Dead* (1942), *Jack-in-the-Box* (1944) and *Commonsense is All You Need* (1947), all of which were written as Stewart's heart disease steadily worsened and reflect to some extent his diminishing physical and mental energy. Although *The Twenty-One Clues* was inspired by the notorious Hall-Mills double murder case – probably the most publicised murder case in the United States in the 1920s – and the American critic and novelist Anthony Boucher commended *Jack-in-the-Box*, I believe the best of these later mysteries is *No Past Is Dead*, which Stewart partly based on a bizarre French true-crime affair, the 1891 Achet-Lepine murder case.[8] Besides providing an interesting background for the tale, the ailing author managed some virtuoso plot twists, of the sort most associated today with that ingenious Golden Age Queen of Crime, Agatha Christie.

What Stewart with characteristic bluntness referred to as 'my complete crack-up' forced his retirement from Queen's University in 1944. 'I am afraid,' Stewart wrote a friend, the chemist and forensic scientist F. Gerald Tryhorn, in August 1946, eleven months before his death, 'that I shall never be much use again. Very stupidly, I tried for a session to combine a full course of lecturing with angina pectoris; and ended up by establishing that the two are immiscible.' He added that since retiring in 1944, he had been physically 'limited to my house, since even a fifty-yard crawl brings on the usual cramps'. Stewart completed his essay collection and a final novel before he died at his study desk in his Belfast home on 1 July 1947, at the age of sixty-six. When death came to the author he was busy at work, writing.

More than six decades after Alfred Walter Stewart's death, his J. J. Connington fiction is again available to a wider audience of classic-mystery fans, rather than strictly limited to a select company of rare-book collectors with deep pockets. This is fitting for an individual who was one of the finest writers of British genre fiction between the two world wars. 'Heaven forfend that you should imagine I take myself for anything out of the common in the tec yarn stuff,' Stewart once self-deprecatingly declared in a letter to Rupert Gould. Yet, as contemporary critics recognised, as a writer of detective and science fiction Stewart indeed was something out of the common. Now more modern readers can find this out for themselves. They have much good sleuthing in store.

1. For more on Street, Crofts and particularly Stewart, see Curtis Evans, *Masters of the 'Humdrum' Mystery: Cecil John Charles Street, Freeman Wills Crofts, Alfred Walter Stewart and the British Detective Novel, 1920–1961* (Jefferson, NC: McFarland, 2012). On the academic career of Alfred Walter Stewart, see his entry in *Oxford Dictionary of National Biography* (London and New York: Oxford University Press, 2004), vol. 52, 627–628.
2. The Gould-Stewart correspondence is discussed in considerable detail in *Masters of the 'Humdrum' Mystery*. For more on the life of the fascinating Rupert Thomas Gould, see Jonathan Betts, *Time Restored: The Harrison Timekeepers and R. T. Gould, the*

*Man Who Knew (Almost) Everything* (London and New York: Oxford University Press, 2006) and *Longitude,* the 2000 British film adaptation of Dava Sobel's book *Longitude:The True Story of a Lone Genius Who Solved the Greatest Scientific Problem of His Time* (London: Harper Collins, 1995), which details Gould's restoration of the marine chronometers built by in the eighteenth century by the clockmaker John Harrison.

3. Potential purchasers of *Murder in the Maze* should keep in mind that $2 in 1927 is worth over $26 today.

4. In a 1920 article in *The Strand Magazine,* Arthur Conan Doyle endorsed as real prank photographs of purported fairies taken by two English girls in the garden of a house in the village of Cottingley. In the aftermath of the Great War Doyle had become a fervent believer in Spiritualism and other paranormal phenomena. Especially embarrassing to Doyle's admirers today, he also published *The Coming of the Faeries* (1922), wherein he argued that these mystical creatures genuinely existed. 'When the spirits came in, the common sense oozed out,' Stewart once wrote bluntly to his friend Rupert Gould of the creator of Sherlock Holmes. Like Gould, however, Stewart had an intense interest in the subject of the Loch Ness Monster, believing that he, his wife and daughter had sighted a large marine creature of some sort in Loch Ness in 1935. A year earlier Gould had authored *The Loch Ness Monster and Others*, and it was this book that led Stewart, after he made his 'Nessie' sighting, to initiate correspondence with Gould.

5. A tontine is a financial arrangement wherein shareowners in a common fund receive annuities that increase in value with the death of each participant, with the entire amount of the fund going to the last survivor. The impetus that the tontine provided to the deadly creative imaginations of Golden Age mystery writers should be sufficiently obvious.

6. At Ardlamont, a large country estate in Argyll, Cecil Hambrough died from a gunshot wound while hunting. Cecil's tutor, Alfred John Monson, and another man, both of whom were out hunting with Cecil, claimed that Cecil had accidentally shot himself, but Monson was arrested and tried for Cecil's murder. The verdict delivered was 'not proven', but Monson was then – and is today – considered almost certain to have been guilty of the murder. On the Ardlamont case, see William Roughead, *Classic Crimes* (1951; repr., New York: New York Review Books Classics, 2000), 378–464.

7. For the genesis of the title, see Macaulay's 'The Battle of the Lake

Regillus', from his narrative poem collection *Lays of Ancient Rome*. In this poem Macaulay alludes to the ancient cult of Diana Nemorensis, which elevated its priests through trial by combat. Study of the practices of the Diana Nemorensis cult influenced Sir James George Frazer's cultural interpretation of religion in his most renowned work, *The Golden Bough: A Study in Magic and Religion*. As with *Tom Tiddler's Island* and *The Ha-Ha Case* the title *In Whose Dim Shadow* proved too esoteric for Connington's American publishers, Little, Brown and Co., who altered it to the more prosaic *The Tau Cross Mystery*.

8. Stewart analysed the Achet-Lepine case in detail in 'The Mystery of Chantelle', one of the best essays in his 1947 collection *Alias J. J. Connington*.

# CHAPTER I

## The Hernshaw Thirteen Club

PETER DIAMOND — better known to local newspaper readers by his pseudonym "The Yellow Dwarf" — had two qualities which stood him in good stead in his journalistic work: an insatiable thirst for information and a retentive memory. In addition, he had more than a dash of youthful cynicism, a front of brass, a sense of humour, a friendly manner, and a temper which nothing could ruffle. His complete lack of respect for the opinions of his elders was less of an asset in some quarters. For him, history was sharply divided into two epochs: the pre-Peter Period and the Peterian Age, which began on the day of his birth. The former, as he often averred with conviction, was of interest merely because it had led up to the latter era.

Wendover, on the other hand, had a profound respect for tradition, precedent, and the Good Old Times in general. He was willing to learn new ways, but only so far as they fitted in with the habits of mind of a country squire, rooted in his ancestral acres and playing minor Providence to his tenantry. His long friendship with the Chief Constable had given him a keen interest in criminology, one of the few hobbies which he shared in common with Peter Diamond, who specialized to some extent in crime reporting for his newspaper.

The clash of their temperaments and the oil-and-water nature of their fundamental ideas gave Sir Clinton Driffield some quiet amusement. He liked, from time to time, to invite them to dinner together and to listen to their wrangles, which, though occasionally acrimonious in tone, never left any sting behind. Peter came of a good local family; and Wendover bore with him more, perhaps, on his father's account than on his own. On this particular evening dinner was over, and they had gone into the Chief Constable's study, a big airy room, comfortably furnished, with serried rows of books, mostly criminological, upon its walls.

"You wrote that half-column about the dinner of this newly-founded Thirteen Club, didn't you, Peter?" inquired Sir Clinton as he offered Wendover a cigar. "I thought I recognized bits of your style in it."

Peter Diamond nodded, with a resentful expression on his usually cheerful face. He and his editor never saw eye to eye in the treatment of certain topics.

"You'd have recognized more, if Donnington hadn't blue-pencilled it," he declared ruefully. "That man has no notion of the light touch in journalism. For instance, I was reporting the doings of the local Bench the other day, and tried to make them more interesting by putting some of it into verse. Like this: 'John Smith, a burglar of renown, had recently come into town. To crack a crib was his chief aim, but Sergeant Burford spoiled his game. No diamond stars fell to his lot. A tray of moons was all he got.' I printed it as prose, of course; but Donnington spotted the rhymes, nevertheless and notwithstanding. So he scored it all out and told me to paraphrase it into what he called 'decent English.' Decent English! Well, I ask you. Isn't it a nice poetical fancy to contrast the diamond stars of the jewellery with the tray of moons . . . ?"

"Yes, I remember we gave him three months hard," interjected Wendover, who was a Justice of the Peace. "He ought to have got more. Candidly, though, Diamond, I shouldn't put you in the same class as Shakespeare."

"I should hope not, indeed!" said Peter, indignantly. "Shakespeare? Why, that man couldn't even write grammatically:—

> Hark, hark! the lark at heaven's gate sings,
>   And Phœbus 'gins arise,
> His steeds to water at those springs
>   On chaliced flowers that lies.

"If you can make 'lies' agree with 'that' when it's equivalent to 'springs,' you must be so free from all scruples as to be positively dangerous. Signed, P. Diamond."

"Don't let's go quite so far back as Shakespeare," Sir Clinton suggested, soothingly. "Stick to the point, if you can, Peter; and tell us about this Thirteen Club dinner."

"That was a subject simply crying to be guyed," Peter complained. "So I guyed it. And then Donnington put a blue pencil through all the best bits in my copy. Disheartening, to work with an editor like that. I was ashamed of the stuff, after he'd done with it. No pep, vim, yip, or even fizz, about it. It might have been the description of a Dorcas meeting. Dull as ditchwater. Nobody knows that better than I do. And it was an amusing show, that dinner."

"So I suspected," said the Chief Constable. "That fact glimmered through even your turgid prose, Dwarf. I'd like to hear more about it, so reel off a few extra details while they're fresh in your mind. I gathered that this precious Club is out to fly in the face of every available superstition, regardless of risk, trouble, or expense. A futile business, but quite harmless, I suppose."

"They must be a funny crew," said Wendover, tolerantly.

"They surely are," confirmed Peter, with a reminiscential grin. "A quaint conglomeration of mixed spirits, however you looked at 'em. I got a lot of bright thoughts, though, just by gazing at 'em as they shovelled down the vitamins."

"They held their jamboree at the Black Nag, didn't they?" Sir Clinton observed. "What took them there? It isn't one of the best places for a dinner."

"It's the only place in town that's old-fashioned enough to have stone paving in its corridors," Peter explained. "They began at the very beginning, you see."

"Suppose you copy them," the Chief Constable suggested. "And start now. We shall probably hear better when you take that pipe out of your mouth, I must say."

"Right!" said the reporter. "Well, it began by Donnington handing me an invitation-card they'd sent to the office. Which betrayed to me at once that it wasn't a show of much importance. My esteemed editor collars all the best functions himself, greedy dog. I cast an eye over the exhibit, which read as follows: *The President of the Hernshaw Thirteen Club has the honour to invite you to dinner at 8:30 P.M. on Friday, March 13th, 1936, at the Black Nag Hotel, Tankard Street, to meet Ill Luck. R.S.V.P. to Ambrose Brenthurst, etc.* All nicely printed in green, which they regard as an ominous colour, I gather. To make it more enticing, the word *Complimentary* was scrawled across the face of the card, also in green ink. Well, at that price, one could hardly be done in the eye; so I told Donnington I'd take on the job. I'm not superstitious; and Ill Luck's no stranger to me, so I wasn't shy."

"That last phrase has the ring of truth about it," interjected Wendover, in a sardonic tone.

Peter ignored this and continued:

"On Friday the Thirteenth — note the care shown in selecting a double unlucky date — I turned up at the Black Nag. Jodrell of the *Courier* was there, and Ommaney of the *Argus* came in on my heels. A pure waste, sending Ommaney to report a dinner. He's a chronic dyspeptic, and his worst nightmare is when he dreams he's half-way through a lobster supper. Just then, the worthy President came over and gave us the Left Hand of Fellowship with a dank paw. . . ."

"Ambrose Brenthurst?" interrupted Sir Clinton. "The fellow who advertises *Loans, £20 to £10,000, with or without security?*"

"That's the pippin," Peter confirmed, with a nod.

"What does he look like?" demanded the Chief Constable. "I've never come across him professionally, though I'm not without hopes."

"Hard up, are you?" queried Peter, with mock solicitude. "I can't rise to ten thousand pounds — with or without security — but if half a dollar's any use to you, I'll . . ."

He fumbled ostentatiously in his trouser pocket.

"Don't bother, Dwarf," Sir Clinton reassured him. "I'm not so hard up as to want to take your last penny off you. What I meant was that Brenthurst might need my professional attentions some-time, though I don't suppose he'll come seeking them."

Peter gave the Chief Constable a shrewd glance.

"Oh! So you've heard something, too?" he said with a cock of his eyebrows.

"The 'too' indicating that we're both in the same boat, there? Yes, I've heard various things — unofficially. What have you heard?"

"I don't mind being frank with you, for old sake's sake," Peter returned. "You won't drag my name into it, I know. I've heard that he's apt to put the screw on his debtors when they can't pay up promptly. It's only a rumour. But I can smell smoke as far as the next man can. And smoke means fire, more often than not. If I were a good-looking girl, I don't think I'd yearn to be up to the ears in debt to Brenthurst, unless I saw some chance of finding the cash in full when required."

"That tallies with some information of my own," said Sir Clinton, thoughtfully. "But unless people complain, I've no way of bringing him to book. Anything else, Peter?"

"Men aren't the same as girls, of course," the reporter answered slowly. "Still, if you have a man completely under your thumb, you can often find a use for him. It's handy, say, to have a man of straw who'll sign on the dotted line and ask no questions about what's written above it. That sort of thing, and so forth."

"You don't give him much of a character," said Wendover in disgust. "If all that's true, he must be a repulsive animal."

"I wouldn't back him for the Adonis Stakes, myself," said Peter, in wilful misunderstanding.

"I never expect moral judgements from a reporter," retorted Wendover.

"I'm just going to answer Driffield's question," Peter protested in an injured tone. "He asked what Brenthurst looks like. I can put it in one word: disgusting. I now proceed to amplify. He's a bit over fifty. Six feet high and the same round the stomach. Chest measurement not on the same scale, so he's what you might call pear-shaped. Weighs about seventeen stone, by the look of him. Coarse hair, like a gorilla. Low brow, ditto. Small piggish eyes. No lips to speak of. Complexion, blotchy. Special feature: a tuft of hair on one cheek-bone, as if a bit of rabbit-skin had been grafted on. Congenital, no doubt; but a drawback in a beauty competition. He might get it eradicated, I think, if only to spare the feelings of the man in the street. But he seems to have no thought for other people's comfort. How's that for a *portrait parlé*, Driffield?"

"I might recognize him," Sir Clinton admitted. "From the hair on his face, I mean; for apart from that you've left out nearly every item that goes into the normal *portrait parlé*."

"Then put the lot of 'em down as 'bad,' or even 'worse,' and you won't go far wrong," Peter suggested. "The general effect of him is to produce a slight feeling of *malaise* in the onlooker. I speak from experience."

"Your description does the same," grunted Wendover.

"Well, you asked for it," Peter pointed out mildly. "But to continue. He greeted us, as aforesaid, with a flash of false teeth. Quite on his best behaviour and devilish oily, it seemed to me. Then we surged into the dining-room. I told you the passages in the Black Nag are paved with stone slabs, didn't I? Coming in modestly at the tail-end of the procession, I had the opportunity of seeing the members of the Thirteen Club taking immense pains to step on the cracks between the slabs."

"And did the bears get them?" inquired Sir Clinton, interestedly.

"What bears?" demanded Peter, at a loss.

"Christopher Robin's, of course. Don't you know the classics?

And the little bears growl to each other, 'He's mine,
As soon as he's silly and steps on a line.' "

"Oh, of course it's supposed to be unlucky to step on a line," the reporter agreed. "You see it in Hopscotch and that Peever game the kids play in Scotland. See *The Child's Book of Manly Sports and Pastimes*. I'd forgotten A. A. Milne's verse, for the moment."

"And did they all look proud of themselves for accomplishing this deed of derring-do?" asked Wendover, in a tone of contempt.

"To tell you the truth, some of them didn't," Peter replied, seriously. "And that made me open my eyes a bit. But that's the psychological side of the entertainment, to which I'll return anon. To proceed. We entered the banqueting-hall, as you might expect, under crossed ladders."

"Personally, there's a sound basis for that superstition, I think," commented the Chief Constable. "I never walk under a ladder if I can help it. If it slips, you're apt to get a nasty jolt, especially if there's a twelve-stone man on the ladder."

"These particular ladders didn't slip," Peter explained. "We all got through the door unscathed. One up for the Thirteen Club. There were two tables in the room. One had thirteen chairs at it. That was for members of the Club. The other was a small one, in a corner. It was for us penny-a-liners. Brenthurst led the way, and the Club processed thrice round the big table, walking counter-clockwise. I suppose that's reckoned unlucky?"

"Going widdershins? Against the course of the sun? Yes, it's supposed to bring ill-luck," Sir Clinton confirmed. "What next?"

"After that, they all seated themselves, and we made for our appointed feeding-stalls. Brenthurst was at the top of his table and I noticed that before he sat down he adorned himself with a sort of Lord Mayor's chain. It had a pendant tacked on, with an opal in it. Opals are supposed to be unlucky, you know."

"I do," Wendover assured him.

"Then perhaps you can guess what the opal was set in?" returned Peter, with a grin.

Wendover shook his head, to Peter's delight, but the Chief Constable made a suggestion.

"Onyxes, by any chance?"

"Onyxes they were," Peter admitted with some surprise. "How did you guess that, Driffield?"

"General education. An onyx is supposed to have an imprisoned devil in it, who wakes up at nightfall and terrifies the wearer. He brings bad dreams, too, they say."

"Say you so? But I mustn't forget the zoological side of the show. On one wall there was a big cage with nine magpies in it. I counted them. Why nine? One's enough for most people."

"Probably they were thinking of an old Scots rhyme about magpies," hazarded Wendover. "It starts with *One's for sorrow,* and the last line is *And nine's the Devil, his ain sel'.* They seem to believe in having the worst there is."

"No doubt," Peter agreed. "But to continue the catalogue. They had a speckled hen in a coop. That's supposed to be unlucky. And a rather smelly weasel in a cage. It was the Press who were unlucky there. The cage was quite near our table. I never realized before that weasels were so whiffy. Attar of weasel would not be much run upon, I guess. To complete the zoological curiosities, one of the Thirteen was a cross-eyed man. Unlucky again — especially for him."

"Had they any ceremonies during the dinner?" asked Sir Clinton. "One would expect something of the sort."

"Oh, yes, quite a lot," Peter explained. "First of all, as they sat down, each guest took his table-knives and solemnly crossed them. Then, instead of a Grace before meat, Brenthurst rose and threw a horseshoe into the fireplace, remarking boldly: 'We need no protection of *that* sort!' Between the courses, they all spilled salt. When wine was passed, it went counter-clockwise round the table — widdershins, you called it, didn't you? And in the interval before the dessert, each of them wound up a few feet of black thread on a reel. That's a new one to me."

"It comes from Scotland," Wendover explained. "Winding black thread at night is supposed to be unlucky, in the Highlands."

"Ah!" said Peter, in mock admiration. "You've got this general education, too, have you? Same as Driffield? Much good may it do you, say I. But I proceed. Instead of a Grace after meat, Brenthurst got up, smashed a small mirror with his gavel, and then said: 'I'm sure that every one of us will be alive and happy, this day twelvemonth. And I *don't* touch wood!'"

"Stout fellow!" interjected Sir Clinton, sardonically. "It must take a lot of courage to make oneself so ridiculous. And after that?"

"Oh, after that, when it came to lighting-up time, they used one match for each three cigarettes, one after another."

"That's a parvenu superstition," said Wendover, in some contempt. "Lucifers weren't invented until the days of Trafalgar, so it can't date back beyond that, at the furthest. I believe it started in the last war. If three men used the same match, an enemy sniper had plenty of time to mark down the flame, and the third man was unlucky in consequence."

"Anything more?" asked the Chief Constable, glancing at Peter.

"I've given you the cream. There may have been more, but I don't remember them. And possibly some of their show was esoteric and not comprehended by me," Peter explained. "Still, that's a fair sample of them."

"They certainly seem to be a lot of solemn asses, by your account," commented the Chief Constable. "What did you make of them, Peter?"

The reporter leaned back in his chair and seemed to ponder for a few moments before replying.

"I said they were a quaint conglomeration of mixed spirits," he said, at last, "and that's what they were. Very mixed. And the more I looked at them, sitting round that table, the more I seemed to spot the differences between them. Now take Brenthurst as a start. He impressed me as a rank fanatic. The stuff that militant atheists are made on. He's not content to disbelieve quietly in a corner. He wants to testify to the lack of faith within him, with brass band accompaniment, and he burns to force everyone else to toe the line of his opinion. He was obviously the fellow who's running this weird show. And there was a female edition of him, a Mrs. Lygon — widow, I judge — who talked just the same kind of lingo."

"It seems a queer streak in a usurer," said Wendover. "But it takes all sorts to make a world."

"Or even a Thirteen Club," added the reporter. "But I proceed

9

with my analysis. Listening to their cheery table-talk, I spotted other types. You know how a kid will go into a dark room to 'prove' that he's not afraid, whilst all the time he's quivering with blue funk? Well, one of that Thirteen push was in that very state. *He* believed in Ill Luck, all right; but nobody must guess it. Bravado was his trouble. He made too many jokes about superstition to sound quite genuine to me. Too loud and hearty about it, altogether, I thought."

"Shouting to keep his courage up," interjected Wendover, "like a child passing a cemetery wall in the dusk?"

Peter nodded in agreement, and pursued his analysis.

"Then there were four others of a different breed: the sort of people who'll join any dam' silly Society if you ask them. If you started a Society for the Extermination of Mammoths, they'd join it lest they should be missing a good thing. The only one of them that struck me much was a girl who sat at Brenthurst's right hand, a Miss Diana Teramond. Ommaney said she was a white Creole. She certainly seemed a bit exotic. A good-looking piece beyond all doubt; and fairly dripping with sex attraction, though a bit short in the brain department, I surmise. Well, put down four asses on the tally, for that's what they were. Just silly asses. Drunk or sober, there was nothing in 'em, as Charles II remarked about some relation of his. Extraordinary fellow, Charles. Always went straight to the point and gave you cold common-sense."

"Yes, he kept to the point," agreed the Chief Constable. "Suppose you imitate him, Peter, and get on with your catalogue. We can discuss Charles another time."

"Well, there were three members who seemed ashamed of the whole affair," continued Peter, with perfect good humour. "Two men and a nice-looking girl. I put the men down as Brenthurst's debtors, brought in to make up the magic Thirteen. They had a worried look about them, as if they were doing sums in their heads instead of entering freely into the gaiety of the show and taking leading parts in the chit-chat. Perhaps they *were* doing sums in their heads. Working out their balance sheets, as likely as not. It didn't seem to make them any happier. Morose is the word. Except when Brenthurst spoke to them, and then they displayed a sort of false and temporary interest, painful to witness. But when he was looking elsewhere, they either stared at their plates or glared at him on the sly. Not the kind of looks that would bring him much luck, I imagine."

"And what about the girl?" demanded Wendover.

"Oh, the girl? Brenthurst had her on his left. Onslow's her name, I believe. She's a gymnastic teacher, according to Jodrell. A nice girl by the look of her. Pretty, too. A fine lithe young animal. But a bit worried. Mouth drooping at the corners in repose. Not unbecomingly; but she looks best when she smiles. She seemed to shrink when Brenthurst spoke to her, and looked markedly relieved when he turned to chat to the Creole damsel. I imagine that she wasn't there by her own choice."

"Another debtor, then?" queried Sir Clinton.

"Yes," confirmed Peter, soberly. "I'm only a reporter, but I was sorry for her, though it's no affair of mine. Too much like Beauty and the Beast for my taste. Luckily Brenthurst was a good deal wrapped up in the Teramond and left the Onslow girl alone, most of the time."

# CHAPTER II

# The Red Diamond

"THAT's ten of the party accounted for," said Sir Clinton, who had kept count. "What about the remaining trio?"

"Your arithmetic's right," said Peter, graciously. "I've kept three to the last, the most diverting ones of the lot: a girl, Garfield by name; young Percy Fairfoot; and his mother, Cora Fairfoot. None of them, I'd say, has the least interest in the Thirteen superstition; so it was amusing to guess what brought them to that festive board. You don't know any of the parties?" he concluded, turning to Wendover.

"Never heard of them," was the reply.

"That makes things easier," said Peter, sagely. "I can discuss their characters, histories, and doings without ruffling your sensitive feelings, then. So nice. Well, to start with, take the Garfield girl. She's about thirty, good-looking if you like the rather statuesque brand, nice voice, pretty hands and no rings, harmonious lines, and good eyes. Quite a drawing-room ornament, in fact. I discovered, later, that she and the Creole damsel live together at Fountain Court."

"Fountain Court?" interjected Sir Clinton. "That's out on the Arnprior road, isn't it? A house with a big garden full of hydrangeas in season?"

"That's the place," Peter confirmed. "It belongs to the fair Diana. Of which, more anon. Meanwhile, let's keep to this interesting trio. Miss Garfield was sitting next to Percy Fairfoot. Not having been under the table, I can't swear that the two of them were matching knees or pressing insteps during the proceedings; but I had more than a suspicion that something of the sort was in progress at intervals. No harm in that, is there? Merely a symptom of the attraction which keeps the world going. To put it concisely, they seemed fairly thick with each other. Young Percy has common or garden good looks; so I'm not crabbing the girl's taste, if she likes that sort of thing. Awkward, of course, that he has a bar sinister in his escutcheon. But who cares much about that, nowadays? Besides, the 1926 Act might put it right, any day, if Cora Fairfoot could bring Brenthurst up to the scratch."

"I see what you mean," said Sir Clinton. "Percy is the illegitimate child of Brenthurst and Cora Fairfoot. If they marry, any time in the future, then Percy becomes legitimate under the Legitimacy Act of 1926. Is that it?"

"That's it," said Peter, striking a match to relight his pipe. "And to judge by a look or two which Percy gave his male parent, I inferred that it's rather a sore subject with him. In fact, I'd say he hates his progenitor like the worst kind of poison. A severe case of Œdipus complex. But he does his best to conceal his feelings from that parent. From which I deduce that he hasn't altogether given up hope that justice will eventually be done. Which brings us to the final exhibit: Cora Fairfoot. She's quite a fine-looking woman still. A bit mature for my youthful taste, of course. Somewhere in the late forties, but well-preserved for that advanced age. No double chin or billowy figure; rather taut and slender for her years. As you say, if she could blandish Brenthurst into making her an honest woman, then Percy would be recognizable as the son and heir. And, as both she and Percy are younger than Shylock, they might come into his dibs eventually. Brenthurst's got no other near relations barring his old mother; and she's rolling in rhino herself, and doesn't need any more. But Brenthurst has all the makings of a confirmed bachelor. No matrimony for him. Which naturally might make both Percy and his dam hate the old bird like poison."

"You seem to take a lot for granted," objected Wendover.

"Not at all," contradicted Peter. "I watched 'em and that was quite enough. They were both polite, even slightly effusive, when Brenthurst chose to fling them a word or two. Evidently they've made up their minds to avoid any outward friction, which would be apt to ruin their hopes. But if you'd seen the expression on the good Cora's face while Brenthurst was showing signs of feeling the Creole's charm, you'd have seen something that spoke louder than a talkie. There's always a risk that Brenthurst might suddenly take it into his head to marry somebody else — this Creole say — and that would dish all hope for Cora and Son."

"You seem to take a great interest in other people's private affairs," commented Wendover, not too kindly.

"In my trade," retorted Peter, quite unashamed, "the more one knows about people — even obscure people — the more chance there is of the information turning up useful in unexpected ways. I was adding a sentence to your obituary notice the other day."

"Oh, were you?"

"We have to keep these things filed, all ready for use," Peter explained, with a gesture of deprecation. "One never knows what may happen. 'Thou fool, this night thy soul shall be required of thee.' And if we didn't look ahead, where should we be with people like yourself who haven't got into *Who's Who?* There's a quarter-column about you all ready. A very favourable notice, I'd call it," he ended with a reassuring smile which infuriated Wendover.

"Thanks indeed! If you're taking a hand in its composition, I trust your editor will vet it before it gets into print. Your habit of alliteration would make me turn in my grave."

"Oh, it'll be printed before the funeral," Peter hastened to point out. "Most likely you won't even be in your coffin when it appears, so you'll have plenty of elbow-room if you want to turn. Alliteration? You wouldn't care to be described as a Munificent Magnate of Local Lineage? No? Or Bountiful Benefactor? Oh, very well. I'll cut these out and just give a list of your charities: Fund for the Prevention of Nurses for the Sick Poor, Society for the Provision of Cruelty to Animals, gift of a wing to the Cottage

Hospital. Which last reminds me that things usually fly better with two wings. Suppose you double your donation. I make no charge for the use of this idea."

"We seem to be wandering from the point," interrupted the Chief Constable. "Tell us something more about Brenthurst. I'm interested in him."

"I'm in a generous mood to-night," responded Peter. "I'll do more than that. I'll tell you about his mother as well, just for good measure. An interesting old party, she is. Close on eighty, now. A survivor from the Victorian hey-day cast up on the sands of Time and left gasping. It's a popular error to suppose that these mid-Victorians were a dull lot. Quite hot stuff, some of them; and she was at least tepid. Originally, I'm told, her name was Cotman — Alison Cotman. When she was about nineteen, she married a middle-aged sea-captain, name of Adine. One son, Paul, died in infancy. Meanwhile Adine, who commanded a tramp, went off to the East. And stayed there for three years, gathering apes, ivory, and peacocks, no doubt — or whatever else appealed to a tramp skipper Autolycus in the early eighties of last century. During these three years his young bride found time hanging on her hands. You know what Satan does, then. Enter a snake in the grass, Leo Brenthurst by name. Affluent, sunny-natured, fascinating, and a heavy swell, as they used to say round about that period. In fact, a complete contrast to the dull skipper. To be fair to Leo, he fell genuinely in love with the beauteous Alison and wanted to marry her. She was frail as well as fair. In fact, she tripped over that snake in the grass. Perhaps she had her eye fixed on the main chance. Anyhow, Captain Adine returned home to find himself confronted by young Netta Adine, born only twelve months earlier. A fact which required more explanation than was possible in the circumstances."

"Pardon me," interrupted Wendover, silkily. "Just one question, Diamond. Are you making this up as you go along? I don't see how you know so much about things which must have happened before you were born or thought of."

"I have a great-aunt," said Peter, concisely.

"She has my sympathy," Wendover assured him. "But I don't see how she comes into the story, unless her name was Alison."

"No, you've guessed wrong. It's quite a habit with you, Wendover. I'll explain, though these digressions spoil the run of my narrative. My great-aunt was born about 1860, and was well abreast of all the local news up to about the last war. Especially gossip, scandals, tittle-tattle, and all the tea-table talk in which her contemporaries delighted, having little else to think about. Nowadays, she lives entirely in the past, dwelling fondly on the episode of the curate being caught hugging Miss Priscilla Prune after the Dorcas meeting in 1884, and such-like epoch-making affairs. I visit the old lady, from time to time. She talks lengthily on the subjects which interest her; I hang on her every word. That's a fair division of labour. So I've heard most of the gossip of the town in the eighties and nineties of last century. I've got a retentive memory. Things stick in it, whether I like it or not. Satisfied now, Wendover? Mind quite at ease? Good."

He took out his pouch and refilled his pipe before continuing.

"Change here for the main line," he went on, referring to his digression about his great-aunt. "We'd reached the point where Captain Adine returned to make the acquaintance of Miss Netta Adine, born in 1881. He suffered some natural vexation at the state of affairs. In fact, he sued for divorce. And secured it without difficulty, since the facts were plain and the suit wasn't defended. As a subsidiary bit of work, poor little Miss Netta was declared illegitimate, since the good Captain had been . . . What's the legal phrase, Driffield?"

"I suppose you mean *extra quattuor maria* — outside the four seas when the child was conceived."

"That's it!" said Peter, with a gesture of acknowledgement. "Your general education turning up trumps again, eh? So nice. I continue. Leo Brenthurst paid up some damages, as was but fair. He could well afford them. Then, all legal impediment having been removed by a decree absolute, he took his adored Alison to wife and settled down to be a family man. With some success. A legitimate son, Lionel Brenthurst, was born in 1883, and his

16

brother Ambrose in 1885. Their father died the year after that, and Lionel died in 1894, so we needn't worry any more about them. Nor about Philip Adine, sea-captain, who was drowned in the mid-eighties."

Peter struck a match and lighted his pipe. Then he went on.

"Now the tale becomes of more psychological interest. Somewhere in the last years of the nineteenth century, Alison Brenthurst — as she now was — got caught in a religious revival. It must have had a marked effect on her, for her character altered noticeably as a result. She'd been, as one might guess, a harum-scarum creature, out for any fun that came along and distinctly earthy in texture. Almost within a week, my great-aunt tells me, she changed completely. Grew very pious. Devoted herself to good works among the citizenry of the poorer classes. Talked openly of the advantages of salvation until people fled her neighbourhood. And repented of her past sins.

"It was awkward, of course, to have young Netta about the house. All very well to repent of sins in the abstract; but not so nice to sit down to dinner with their results, especially when you recall that text about the wages of sin. To make matters worse, young Netta in those days was at the age when children often regard their parents as damn' fools, or worse. Altogether, things were a bit unhappy in the Brenthurst circle, what with Netta's little ways and her mater's new-found rigidity. However, a solution appeared. Leo Brenthurst had left the bulk of his cash to his wife; but he'd also bequeathed a few hundreds to Netta and to Ambrose, which they could get their claws on when they came of age. So as soon as she was twenty-one, Netta had one flaring row with her dam, collected her dibs from her trustees, and cleared out to America to live free from maternal shackles. Her Ma never forgave that. And things were made worse when news came that Netta had married a third-class actor, one Reuben Ducane or Duquesne, and had gone on the stage with him. That was in 1904."

"You seem to have got that date very pat," commented Wendover in a suspicious tone. "How do you come to remember it?"

"The same way as my great-aunt does," explained Peter. "She had her silver wedding in 1904, and she linked up the two events when she told me the yarn about the Brenthursts. As she's told me about her silver wedding umpteen times, if not oftener, I've every reason to recall the date of it. Simple, isn't it? Any further comments, Watson? No? Well, that's always a relief.

"I proceed. Old Mrs. Brenthurst, since her conversion, had a perfect phobia against the theatre. So, naturally, when Netta joined her husband on the stage, that was the last straw. The old lady didn't cut Netta out of her will, because she hadn't made a will. But she made no secret of her views about her daughter's doings. The girl was damned, and that was all about it. And the elect could have no dealings with the damned, in any shape or form. So that was that. All communication between mother and daughter ceased, thenceforward. It would have ceased very soon, in any case; for in 1906, news filtered through that Netta, her husband, and a child, had all been killed in some American disaster or other. So that finishes this bit of the story. I mention it because my great-aunt was quite shocked to find that old Mrs. Brenthurst refused to put on any mourning for her offspring. And that, I gather, was a strong step in those days. Alison Brenthurst's a bit of a character, or she'd never have run counter to public opinion on such a question in those days. My great-aunt dwelt on the subject. 'You can understand my feelings, Peter, when I saw her going about in gay colours, after losing her daughter in that dreadful way!' I couldn't understand her feelings, but there was no use telling her that. I like my great-aunt.

"Well, the extinction of Netta and her progeny left old Mrs. Brenthurst with only two relatives in the world: her son Ambrose and a niece, this Cora Fairfoot whom I saw at the Thirteen Club dinner. Cora's the daughter of Mrs. Brenthurst's younger sister, who married a man Fairfoot, a small farmer up in Cumberland. Both the Fairfoots died of typhoid in 1895, when Cora was seven or eight years old; and Mrs. Brenthurst took the child under her roof. Better for Cora if she'd been left to the Fairfoot family, even if they weren't well off. Ambrose took a passing fancy to his young cousin when she grew up. But sometimes these passing fancies have permanent results. Young Percy was the result in this case."

"Without casting a slur on your clarity, Peter, I think a rough family tree would help," said Sir Clinton. "Here's a sheet of paper."

Admitting the justice of this at once, Peter pulled out a pencil, jotted down a table of relationships, and handed it to the Chief Constable who, after examining it, passed it on to Wendover.

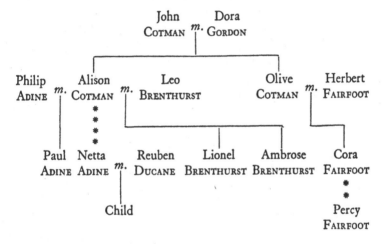

"That's the family tree, so far as I know it," Peter continued. "The asterisks show irregular descent. But let's get back to where I left off. When young Percy began to manifest himself, there was the devil of a row. Both Mrs. Brenthurst and Cora wanted a marriage, naturally. But Ambrose had cooled off completely by that time, and flatly refused to marry his cousin. If he'd been a year younger, his mother might have put on the financial screw; but he came of age just about that time, and got his claws on the money left to him under his father's will, which was enough to set him up in his chosen trade and make him independent of his mother. So she had to make the best of it. She scored Cora off her visiting list, but she made up for that in a way by paying a small pension to her niece and offspring.

"It was a small pension, but even so, it must have rankled in the old lady's mind; for here you come up against another effect of her conversion. In her early days, Mrs. Brenthurst had been pretty fair in the scatter-cash line. After her conversion, she changed over, somehow, and looked on spending as sinful, or next door to it. Her favourite text, in later days, was the one about the love of money being the root of all brands of evil. She developed a queer aversion to even handling money, coupled with the *idée fixe* that everybody was trying to swindle her out of her cash. She was almost touched on that subject, one may reasonably suppose. For instance, she refused point-blank to sign her name to any document which concerned cash even in the most remote way."

"But surely she must have signed cheques?" Wendover interjected.

Peter shook his head decidedly.

"Not even that," he declared. "She put all her fortune into bearer bonds, dumped them in her bank, ordered the manager to clip off the coupons when due, pay her a fixed income — month by month — out of the proceeds, and plank the residue into new bearer bonds. A cheque of any sort was anathema to her. She had all sorts of suspicions about forgery and so forth. She wouldn't even make a will, because that meant signing a paper referring to cash. As I told you, she must be slightly touched in that particular region of the brain, though she's sane enough for all practical purposes. We all have our little fads."

"You say that friend Ambrose started with a few hundreds," said Sir Clinton. "Now he's advertising that he'll lend anything up to ten thousand pounds. Apparently he's prospered."

"There used to be an old music-hall song about money," Wendover mused aloud. "It was popular before your day, Diamond. You can talk about it to your great-aunt.

M-O-N-E-Y! [*it ran*]
That is the stuff to bring you joy.

"Your friend Ambrose can't be a miser, or he wouldn't lend any of his precious cash. So what joy does he get out of it?"

"Power, I think," surmised Peter lightly. "Get some poor bloke well into your debt and you can make him squirm as you please, so long as he's got a social or a commercial position to lose. All the joys of sadism without the dirty work. From what I saw of some of his precious Thirteen Club, I certainly got the idea that he had 'em well under his thumb and could order 'em about very much as he chose. And some minds like power, you know. They get a kick out of seeing some poor devil in a tight corner while they give an extra turn to the screw. Our fellow-citizen has more than a streak of that nature in him, I gauge."

Peter Diamond paused for a moment or two, as if a fresh idea had occurred to him and he was thinking it out before putting it into words. Then he continued:

"Much more than a mere streak of it. The way that girl shrank when he turned to throw a word to her — that told a tale. And there's that affair of Cora Fairfoot and her son. Obviously they still have hopes of getting things legitimized, though personally I wouldn't give a farthing for their chances. Plainly he must be playing cat-and-mouse with them, or they'd have dropped him off their visiting-list long ago, since they so obviously hate him. To my mind, that's just another facet of his sadistic nature coming out. Keep them on the string, encourage their hopes, then give them a drop, then encourage them again, and so on — getting a kick out of it every time he hurts them. I tell you, Driffield, that fellow's a real bad lot, through and through. I'm only a reporter, as Wendover would say; and I'm no moralist or Puritan. But that fellow rouses my dislike, from what I've seen of him."

It was seldom that Peter displayed feelings of this sort, and the Chief Constable gave him a curious glance. Peter caught it; seemed to regret his self-betrayal; and tried to cover it up by a return to his normal flippancy.

"To go back to that Thirteen Club dinner," he went on. "I've kept the cream of the entertainment until the last. It was quite a ceremony. At the tail-end of the proceedings the waiters cleared away all the table-decorations, leaving nothing but the decanters and glasses on the bare board, and putting a clean plate down in front of Brenthurst. They then took up the usual collection and retired. Whereupon Brenthurst got to his feet, fumbled in his pocket and produced a small leather case and also a sheet of paper. We at the Press table augured the worst from that. Evidently he meant to make a speech. So we sighed and reached for our pencils and note-books. After all, it hadn't been a bad dinner, and one must pay for one's little pleasures.

"Well, he started his harangue with a few remarks on superstition in general. Very dull. He hasn't got the airy-fairy touch which goes well in after-dinner oratory. Then he went on to talk about jewels which were supposed to bring bad luck. Of course he dwelt at some length on the classic case of the Queen's Necklace. As you both suffer from a general education, I need only remind you of the sequels to that affair: Cardinal Rohan ruined; Marie Antoinette and her husband guillotined; Cagliostro exiled; Grey, the jeweller, killed in a duel; and the arch-planner of the stunt, Jeanne de Lamotte, flogged and branded, and finally jumping out of a second-floor window at her London lodgings and dying of her injuries. . . ."

"Or of a surfeit of mulberries during her convalescence after the jump," put in Sir Clinton.

"Oh, yes, if you like," conceded Peter. "She died, which is the main point. Quite a nice little catalogue of disasters, and I fancy I could have made it quite a lively tale. Brenthurst merely made it sound like one of these Bills of Parcels we used to get at school: an arid catalogue. As for this train of mishaps pointing to ill luck, he would have none of that at all. Pure coincidence, by his way of it. Most likely he's right, though it asks a lot of dirty work from Mr. Coincidence, to my mind. Then he turned to the blue Hope Diamond, and dragged in coincidence again to account for the troubles which befell some of its owners."

"What was all this leading up to?" demanded Wendover. "It

looks to me as if he was queering his own pitch by doling out these cases."

"It led up to the opening of the leather case and the production of a pendant," Peter explained. "He didn't pass the thing round the party, so I can only tell you that it was a thumping big stone, set in a plain gold disk; and you'll have to take his word for it that it was worth at least five thousand pounds. He said it was a red diamond—"

"That's not very common," interjected Sir Clinton, "though they do exist."

"Well, it's not often one sees a bit of crystallized carbon worth five thousand pounds," continued Peter, "except when one goes to the Tower to see if the Crown Jewels are still in stock. So we all stared at it most interestedly, with eyes like prawns or lobsters. Then some bold fellow—one of the asses, I remember—suggested that it was merely a replica. Which much annoyed Brenthurst, as his looks betrayed. He handed the pendant to another of the party—Sigdon, the fellow who keeps a jeweller's shop in Tamar Street—and asked him to say if it was genuine or paste. I wouldn't call Sigdon an expert mineralogist myself; and all the testing he did was to scratch his wine-glass with the stone. However, he swore it was a genuine diamond, so everybody was quite pleased. Then Brenthurst put it down on the plate, and let the assembly gloat over it. Which we all did, as aforesaid. It's not often one sees concentrated value like that."

"And then?" queried Sir Clinton.

"Oh, then he gave us a sketch of its history. I'm not superstitious myself. A hare can cross my path without giving me a quiver. But undoubtedly some of these jewels are things I'd rather be without. This red diamond, for example. Apparently it originated in India. At least, the first remembered incident in its history is a transaction round about 1750, when Dupleix was in the Carnatic. It came into the hands of a French officer—as the result of some native gent getting his throat cut, I gather. Then this French officer got fatally damaged, in Clive's day; and the red diamond found its way to Haiti, where the officer's cousin had an estate.

When the Haitian slave insurrection came along, his serfs filled the cousin up with gunpowder and blew him to bits. A most untidy death. The diamond came to France after that and one of its owners was shot in the '48 troubles in Paris and another was executed by the Communards in 1871. After that, it wandered to Russia, and its owner was liquidated by the Bolshies later on. Then it came to England, where the Bolshies started to raise the wind by selling looted jewellery. The first buyer lost his money in the post-war slump. And so on. A year ago it was bought by a youngster called Julian Lorrimore. He fell in love with a girl who did a song and dance turn on the Halls between times; and he gave her the red diamond in the engagement gift, as well as other things. One day young Julian took his peri out for a drive, and they had a bad accident. He passed out and she got a devil of a shake which left some after-effects. Need I say that at this point in his tale, Brenthurst made his best bow to the Creole damsel and thanked her for allowing him to display the diamond to the Club on this occasion. So that brought us quite up to date."

"H'm!" said Wendover, reflectively. "I'm not superstitious; but I wouldn't go out of my way to buy that particular stone if it came into the market again. It's got too many unpleasant associations attached to it, quite apart from any idea of ill luck; and one would be too apt to think about them when one saw it."

"Same here," agreed Peter. "Plenty of other rocks in the market, so why buy that particular one? Not that I'm thinking of making a bid for it in any case. I'd have to take advantage of Brenthurst's generous offers — the ones where he wants no security — before I rose to that. She can keep it, for all I care. I'm not really keen on diamonds, anyhow."

"You've missed one point, Peter," said Sir Clinton. "Who was the first to rise from the Thirteen table when the dinner was over?"

"Meaning who's going to die in the next twelvemonth? Oh, Brenthurst has the courage of his convictions, I'll say that for him. He hopped to his feet before anyone else, at the close of the show, without an instant's hesitation."

Wendover glanced down at the family tree which he still held in his hand. Evidently his thoughts had gone back to the tangled relationships among the Brenthurst connection.

"Did you notice how Percy Fairfoot behaved to his mother?" he asked. "She seems to have had a rough deal from Brenthurst. One hopes her son treats her nicely."

"Oh, yes, quite nicely," Peter assured him. "He kept her waiting a minute or two while he chatted with the Garfield girl, when the party was breaking up. But she didn't seem to mind; she obviously adores Percy. Not got much else to admire in the world, perhaps, since Brenthurst spoiled her career. She wasn't a bit jealous of the Garfield girl; I could see that by the way she looked at the pair of them. And they were quite nice to look at. About the same height to within an inch. Percy's a good average height for a man and she's a shade over the average for a girl, but her figure's good and she looks just right. But if she marries him, she may look out for squalls. That young man's got a devil of a temper. I saw him when one of the waiters accidentally jogged his elbow at dinner. That sort of thing really isn't done. A rough streak in Master Percy, I fear."

"How did the Fairfoots behave to Brenthurst?" asked Wendover.

"A bit chilly," said Peter. "I saw Cora look at him as he was fussing over the fair Diana and helping her with her wrap before she got into her car. Cora wasn't pleased. Afraid, perhaps, that the Creole might snap up Brenthurst and so put a period to the hopes of the Fairfoot clan. Anyhow, it was quite a little study in expressions to see them all together."

"This Thirteen Club business seems to me as futile a thing as I've heard about for a while," commented Wendover. "Serve them right if they all had ill luck for a twelvemonth after making such fools of themselves."

# CHAPTER III

# The Hop-picker

THE HOP-PICKING season brings into some country districts a multitude of decent people; but in their train, sometimes, come others less desirable. Mr. William Sprattley — *alias* Leary Bill — belonged to the latter class. A diligent observer, watching him year after year, would have noticed that he seldom attached himself to the same group of pickers in two successive seasons and, from this, might have drawn some interesting inferences.

On the surface, Bill Sprattley was a shabby little man, timid in manner, ingratiating in address, and most obliging in any matters which cost him no particular trouble. He was prepared to work just hard enough not to attract adverse criticism; but he never exceeded this limit; and often, during the day-time, he seemed to be half asleep, interrupting his toil at intervals to yawn openly and noisily. If anyone remarked upon this, he complained bitterly of the insomnia to which he was a martyr. ("I'm that subjec' to it that I can't get a proper sleep, nights. Often and often I've got to go out an' walk about to get over my wakefulness. Come back fit to drop, I do, an' then p'r'aps I manage to get a snooze before it's time to wake up.") This explanation was better than most, for it served three purposes. It excused his slackness in the day-time; it gained him a certain sympathy; and it accounted satisfactorily for his return in the small hours of the morning to the barn which he shared with several other hop-pickers.

His brown, hare-like eyes, magnified by his convex spectacles, seemed mild, and even benignant. They were invariably fixed upon the main chance, and there was very little that they missed as their owner went his way about the world. Hop-picking *per se* he regarded as a mere "mug's game"; but hop-picking served excellently as a cover for his less avowable practices. It gave him a sound excuse for staying temporarily in the country, where otherwise he would have been conspicuous; and once in the country, "with all them villas, bungalows, an' farmhouses positively askin' to be looked into, it 'd be a poor night when a leary cove couldn't earn his bread an' scrape—an' maybe a shade over." Which furnishes an alternative explanation of his perambulations after dark.

Not being a blundering amateur, Bill Sprattley always prepared for his advance by thorough reconnaissance. He liked to know who lived in a house, who sat up late, where they slept when they went to bed, and numerous other details of professional importance which are cheap at the cost of a night or two spent on the watch. Even the times and seasons of the domestic tabby have their importance for such as Bill, since the love-songs of courting toms may disturb the sleep of the house's human inhabitants and rouse them to an irritated wakefulness when normally they should be in dreamland.

The village inn was one of the wells from which Bill drew draughts of general information, and it was there that he heard of a house which seemed to have been planned to suit his purposes. "Fountain Court, they call the house. You'll know it by the rows of pink and blue hydrangeas," his informant had told him, quite unaware of the use to which the intelligence would be turned. "There's a big French window opening on a terrace that overlooks part of the garden."

Further useful details were that the garden was big enough to require two gardeners and a boy and that one of the gardeners lived in a cottage not far from the side gate. Two maids were kept, but they slept out, somewhere in the village. There was no man in the house. Two ladies shared it: one foreign and good-looking, the other not quite so gifted — "Though not bad, at that," Bill's friend explained. Bill had no need to inquire about their financial status; the two gardeners and the boy told their own story. There would be pickings in the place, obviously; and the French window was a gift from the gods.

"Two old maids," he commented, ruminatively. "Then they'll keep a cat, I bet?"

"They're none so old," explained his informant. "Young, they are, as women go in these days — thirty-ish, I'd say. And the foreign one looks frisky enough. French she is, so they say. She calls her cat Mee-mee, I'm told. That's a funny name for a cat, now, ain't it?"

"What kind of cat is it?" Bill Sprattley inquired with an unconcealed yawn which served to mask his real interest in the subject. "Tom or tabby?"

"I never had the curiosity to make sure," was the answer, given with a bucolic grin. "It's a big cat, that's all I say; and I do say that, mister. Would you say it weighed ten pound, Harry?" he asked, turning to a neighbour and giving a slow wink.

"Ten pound, anyway," Harry pronounced with the air of Sir Oracle delivering judgement. "Or even a bit more. Yes, likely a pound or two over the ten would be my guess."

"A tom, then," declared Bill Sprattley, with another yawn. "Tabbies don't run to a weight like that, not in my experience of cats."

His mind was relieved. There would be no trouble with caterwauling suitors. And, having ascertained this, he turned the conversation into other channels.

Several reconnaissances of the house in the garden of red and blue hydrangeas still further reassured him. The household arrangements ran like a smooth piece of clockwork, which was all to the good from Bill Sprattley's point of view. At 8 P.M. the two mistresses had dinner. After this, they went into the drawing-room which had a big French window overlooking the garden. By half-past nine the maids had finished with the after-dinner washing up, and they then left the house by the side door and made their way to the village via the front gate. This gate stood open all day long; but the maids closed it as they went out, and apparently it had a spring lock. Bill had heard one of the maids ask the other: "Have you got your key?" from which he inferred that they were able to unlock the gate for themselves when they arrived in the early morning to get breakfast ready. The other gate to the garden also had a spring lock, Bill ascertained; and it was the duty of the resident gardener to close this entrance at 7 P.M. each night. Like the maids, he had a key for his own use. The garden was entirely surrounded by a ten-foot wall with broken glass atop; and both gates were heavily spiked. But obstacles of this kind merely made Bill Sprattley smile; he could see a dozen ways of surmounting them with the greatest ease. The gardener went to bed early; and as he snored loudly, it was easy to tell when he fell asleep. As for the two women, they also were early birds. They sat in the drawing-room until about eleven usually. The Frenchy — as Bill described her to himself — slept in a ground-floor room next the drawing-room, whilst her companion had a room on the first floor, overlooking the front garden. Unless they had visitors, both of them got to bed by about 11:30 P.M. As for the cat, Bill never caught a glimpse of it during his watches. Apparently it was kept indoors at night; and, whatever its sex was, it seemed to attract no visitors of its own. Bill had made certain, by a few words with the resident gardener, that there was no watch-dog on the premises. Altogether, from Bill Sprattley's standpoint, the house was what he called "a fair gift," and he was optimistic about the value of the "pickings" to be had.

When Bill set out upon his burglarious mission, the harvest moon hung like a huge silver bubble in the heavens, amid slow-sailing clouds, and on its emergence from transitory occultations it gave him all the light he needed. Once inside that high-walled garden, free from espial from outside, the more light he had the easier his task would be. He had explained to his hop-picking mates that he felt "a dose o' that sleeplessness comin' on," which sufficiently accounted for his absence from the barn when the others betook themselves to their rest. Then, in rubber tennis shoes with some necessary tools in his pockets, he had set out along the country roads for the garden with the pink and blue hydrangeas.

Light-hearted at the prospect of the "easy thing" in front of him, he whistled softly as he shambled along, speculating pleasantly on the kind of loot which might fall into his hands. Not that he was fastidious about such things. Whatever found its way into the rolled-up sack under his arm would be well received by his favourite fence, a gentleman with the most catholic taste in stolen goods. Jewellery, Bill hardly counted on. That meant going into the bedrooms; and some women slept, as he put it, "on a hair-trigger." Bill preferred, if possible, to get through his job "without any o' that rough stuff that gets you disliked by the beaks." What he meant to secure was the contents of the plate-basket, and in view of the profusion of flowers in the garden, he had hopes of some silver rose-bowls.

At this stage in his musings, Bill abruptly put aside speculations and turned to more practical matters. Rounding a gentle curve in the road, he reached the high glass-topped wall of the Fountain Court garden; but he shambled on, for he had decided to escalade it farther along, beyond the wicket-gate which gave entrance to the grounds to the rear of the house. Then, as he swung round the arc of the curve, a heartfelt oath rose to his lips at the sight of a four-seater car drawn up, facing him, by the roadside.

Bill's step maintained its tempo, for he was no amateur, to be thrown out of his stride by a hitch of this sort in his plans. If the car held a pair of lovers, he knew more than one way of scaring them off and clearing the decks for his own operations. If it was empty, however, things might be more awkward, for the driver would be somewhere about; and Bill preferred to be sure that his retreat was clear before he started work.

He trudged boldly up to the car and discovered, to his disgust, that it was untenanted. Somebody must be near by. Tough luck! Then an even worse hypothesis crossed his mind: suppose the car belonged to someone who was paying a call at Fountain Court. These women would be still afoot, and it might be long enough before they got to bed and went to sleep. Why should a thing like this happen on the very night when he wanted the house routine to follow its usual course? Enough to make a cat grin on the wrong side of its jaw! He cursed under his breath with a vigour and fluency quite beyond his usual efforts in that field.

The moon slipped behind a cloud and its light was suddenly dimmed. Bill mechanically tried the car's door-handle, but the lock was on. No pickings there. He turned away and shambled on, trying to decide on his best course. A few yards beyond this point, the road made a sharper turn and disclosed a fresh stretch of highway, and as he came round the corner, Bill's eyes caught something which brought him sharply to a halt. Ten yards in front of him, the clouded moon shone dimly upon something in the roadway, a dark shapeless mass, larger than a man, from which a dark patch spread out over the pale concrete surface.

"There's been a —— accident!" was the first thought which passed through Bill's mind; and it was instantly followed by a second one: "This puts the kibosh on my little game to-night!"

Then part of the dark mass before him moved suddenly; he heard a dreadful snarl, the vicious note of some formidable animal, which sent a tremor through him; then came a fearsome tearing sound, followed by another and even more menacing growl. The thing, whatever it was, shifted its position with a litheness which seemed half familiar; and in its new position Bill could see its eyes aflame, two big green disks shining in the half-light of the obscured moon. They vanished as the beast dipped its head, and the horrid sound of tearing began again. Suddenly the cloud-veil passed from the face of the moon, and now Bill could see clearly what was before him: a human body prostrate and dreadfully still, whilst over it crouched a big feline shape with a spotted hide.

Bill Sprattley had not the precise brand of courage needed to face such a situation with coolness. Uttering a brief ejaculation which served him as a prayer, he turned about and ran, his head down, heedless of whither he was going. Anything, anything to get away from that horrid sight and still more horrid sound. He seemed to feel the brute close on his heels; his back quivered in anticipation of the spring which would land the creature on his shoulders and plant its claws in his flesh. In sheer panic, he shut his eyes and stumbled on, his knees almost failing in their action, and every nerve reacting under the shock of that ghastly surprise.

A violent concussion stopped him in his flight and seemed to rob him of his last hope of escape. With a squeal of despair, he recoiled, putting his hand to his temple which had been hurt by his collision with the back of the standing car. A second later he realized that he had the means of safety before him, for he recalled that the ignition-key had been left in place. He broke the glass of the driving-seat window with his jemmy, put his hand inside and opened the door, scrambled into the seat, and worked the self-starter. A glance at the driving-mirror showed the road behind him, white and empty in the moonlight. Evidently that spotted monster had remained to finish its horrid work, disdaining the trouble of pulling down a second victim. Bill gave it no time to change its mind. He got the lever into second, let the clutch slam home, and gave a gasp of relief as the car jerked violently into motion.

"Safe!" he gasped, hardly able to believe that he had escaped unharmed. "But if this —— car had been left standin' t'other way round . . ."

He preferred not to consider the results. His flesh still crept at the recollection of those cruel teeth and pitiless eyes. Not until he had gone half a mile did he feel really out of danger. Then, curiously enough, his mind went back to the evening when in the bar of the local inn he had sought for information.

"A *cat!* That's what that beggar said," he mumbled to himself furiously. " 'Would you say it weighed ten pound, Harry?' An' the other swine grinned, he did, and said it'd likely be a pound or two over the ten. If they'd said ten stone, they'd have been nearer the truth, and then I'd have spotted what they were grinnin' about. Cat! The thing's a leopard, a —— spotted leopard. And dangerous! Ugh! The sound it made, tearing at that poor beggar's throat! Keep me awake o' nights, that will, unless I can forget it. What right have people to keep brutes like that? . . . Well, it's given somebody socks to-night, anyhow. There'll be a bit of a stir over that little do, there will so. And it might have been me, if I'd got there before that unfort'nit geezer, so it might.

Somebody else can 'ave the crackin' o' that crib, now, if he wants it. I'm through with it myself, and damned lucky to have a whole skin at the end of the job, too."

Then it dawned upon Bill that he was not yet "through with it," after all. Here he was, in possession of the car belonging to the brute's victim. If he left it by the wayside and trudged back to his barn, he might get clear. But a gruesome affair like this would be sure to raise a hue and cry. The police would find the car and would want to know how it had managed to trundle itself away after its owner had gone to his death; and once the police started inquiries, no one could tell where they'd stop. If he cut out the burglary scheme and simply told the plain truth about the rest of the affair, his tale would hold water at every point. Probably the boldest course was the safest.

Then he remembered the tools in his pockets. He put on his brakes, got down from his seat, sought about for a temporary hiding place and cached his implements. Then, getting back into the car, he took the shortest way to the nearest police station. Blue lamps over doors had never appealed to him before; but that night he was almost glad to see one as he pulled up the car before it.

# CHAPTER IV

## Mimi

In charge of the station that night was Sergeant Burford, an official who owed his promotion to his diligence rather than to any special brilliance. Knowing that his mind worked slowly, he tried to conceal this defect by speaking measuredly in a kind of telegraphese which he hoped would give the impression that he thought too quickly to waste time over superfluous words. Bill Sprattley, still badly shaken by his recent adventure, was able to give only a confused account of his recent experiences, and the Sergeant was at first inclined to treat him summarily as "drunk, in charge of motor-car." Further questioning, however, made it clear to Burford that Bill's trouble was due to nerves and not to drink; and he then dealt with the matter seriously.

"Fountain Court, eh? Now I know what your beast was. A tame cheetah. They keep one. Never given any trouble before, though. I've seen Miss Teramond with it, once or twice. Leads it round the garden on a string. Quite tame. Purring like a big cat. No complaints about it from anyone. So no business of ours. Different now, though. Serious affair."

He considered for a moment before going on.

"This man you saw. Dead? Didn't move, you say. Nasty business. Very nasty."

"If 'e wasn't dead, 'e must be tough," declared Bill, with a shudder. "It was at 'is throat and tearin', tearin' at 'im. . . . Like this!"

He gave a rather unsuccessful imitation of the sounds he had

34

heard. Sergeant Burford was an unimaginative man, and seemed unimpressed by Bill's efforts.

"That'll do! Sounds like somebody gargling, the way you do it. You'd make no fortune on the Halls as an animal imitator. That's plain. Well, we'll look into this. You'll come along with us. We'll take that car. And an ambulance. I've some telephoning to do. Wait here."

The Sergeant retired for a few minutes. When he came back he was accompanied by three armed constables and he carried a revolver himself.

"No use trusting you with one," he decided, with a glance of unveiled contempt at Bill's trembling hands. "You've got the wind up, proper. Put a bullet into one of us, likely, first time you pulled a trigger. Not used to pistols?"

"Never 'ad one in my 'and," asseverated Bill.

Which was true enough. Bill, as a professional burglar, had a horror of fire-arms. An armed householder was his nightmare; whilst to be caught with a gun in his own possession would mean a stiff addition to the normal sentence.

"The ambulance follows on," Burford explained.

He ordered Bill and two constables into the back seats of the car. He himself took the wheel, with a third constable beside him. They reached Fountain Court by the road Sprattley had taken when he approached it earlier in the night; and before they came to the end of the garden wall, Burford slowed down to a walking-pace.

"Point out where you found the car," he ordered, and Bill jerked his finger towards the spot. "Body was just round the corner? Right!"

As they rounded the bend, the rays of the headlights fell on the ghastly group in the road. The cheetah was still busy with its prey. Then it looked up, faced them, its eyes glowing like twin green lamps in the glare of the car lights. Dazzled and intimidated by the approach of the motor, it rose on all fours, snarled with a flash of bare teeth, and then loped off down the road. It stood higher than Bill had expected and the motion of its long slim legs was dog-like rather than wholly feline. Seeing it now, clear of its victim, and noting its true size, Bill breathed one of his favourite ejaculations of thankfulness. Much chance he'd have stood if that thing had got him down!

At the garden gate it turned its head malevolently, as if meditating a stand; then, with a final snarl at its pursuers, it sprang at the bars, scrambled over the spikes, and vanished. The Sergeant pulled up the car just short of the body. As he did so, a motor-ambulance swung round the corner and drew up behind him. Burford reflected for a moment or two before giving his orders.

"You, Jennings, go to the gate. Keep your pistol ready. Shoot if that brute shows its nose. I've no fancy for it jumping on our backs while we're examining this fellow. Wilks and Medhurst, you come with me. Keep pistols ready. Get that stretcher out," he concluded, turning to the men who had descended from the ambulance.

Bill Sprattley hesitated for a moment; then, calculating that he would be safer with the armed men than alone in the car, he got out and kept close to the others. The moon had gone behind a cloud, but Burford had left the motor in such a position that its headlights lit up the body. As Bill came near enough to see its horrible disarray and the pool of blood in which it lay, he hurriedly turned away and went over to the road-side.

"Feeling sick?" asked Burford, unsympathetically. "You wouldn't be much good in the Force."

He knelt beside the body and switched on his torch.

"'Strewth!" commented one of the constables, leaning over to see better. "It's fair played Old Harry with him, hasn't it? It's lucky our patrol didn't come along in the middle of its little game. He wouldn't have stood a dog's chance against the brute."

"It seemed tame enough, any time I saw it," said the second constable. "Like a big pussy-cat. She used to call to it — 'Mimi! Mimi!' — and it'd run up to her, purring and as good as gold."

Burford completed his cursory examination and rose to his feet.

"Dead as a door-nail," was his verdict. "Throat all torn by the brute. Lost any amount of blood, too. No point in taking him to hospital. Mortuary will do, by and by. Must go through his pockets first. Find out who he is."

He knelt down again by the light of a torch held by one of the constables, and searched the dead man, making remarks on each object as he found it.

"Cigar-case, five cigars in it. Petrol lighter. Key-ring with some Yales on it. Two other keys loose in vest pocket. One of them'll be the key of the car door, likely. Pocket-knife. Note-case with some notes . . . three fives, four one-pound notes and a ten-bob one. Odd change in trouser pockets, six and four. Handkerchief, no initials, but a laundry mark. Fountain-pen. Ah! Here's an envelope . . . addressed to Ambrose Brenthurst, Oakley Lodge, Darlington Drive. Outside our district; no wonder we didn't recognize him. Could pick him out of a thousand, if one ever had met him, with that tuft of hair. That's the lot. . . . No, here's a ticket pocket. . . . Hullo! What's this?"

He held up in the beam of the flash-lamp a gold pendant in which was set a large stone which scintillated as he turned it.

"Looks valuable," Burford commented. "Now that's all he has in his pockets. Better be sure he *is* Brenthurst, though. Look in the car pockets for his driving-licence, Wilks."

"It's in the name of Brenthurst, Oakley Lodge," the constable reported after examining the booklet which he found in the car.

"Good! Now we'll get him into the ambulance. He's no sort of sight to leave about in the road. Not that anyone's likely to pass by at this time of night. Still, best to have things shipshape."

When Brenthurst's body had been put into the ambulance the Sergeant ordered the driver to stand by.

"Wait here. I phoned the Chief. Be along shortly, I expect. He'll want to see it, likely. Now we'll have a look round. And there's that cheetah. Need to keep our eyes skinned. Shoot it if it shows fight. I'll take the responsibility. Can't have dangerous brutes like that wandering on the loose. You men stay here. Patrol the road. Keep your eye on the wall and the gate, in case it breaks back. And turn back any traffic that happens along."

Switching on his torch again, the Sergeant noticed a trail of blood spots which led towards the gate. He followed it up and found that it turned into the garden. Constable Jennings, it seemed, had already observed this.

"I saw the marks myself when the moon came out from behind the clouds for a moment," he explained to Burford. "That cheetah must be a powerful brute if it dragged him all that distance, for he's a good twelve or fourteen stone, by the look of him. A man of that size takes a bit of dragging."

"Keep your revolver handy," advised the Sergeant. "And what do *you* want?" he demanded, turning to Sprattley, who had come up.

"To get 'ome to my bed, o' course. 'Ave I got to stay 'ere all night, watchin' you doin' what you're paid for?"

"You wait here. There may be more questions to ask you."

"Ho? Indeed? All right, since you're so pressin'. But I ain't armed to the teeth, like you, so nat'rally I don't feel so brave. My kind regards to the cheater, an' I sincerely 'opes you'll all 'ave a real pleasant time when you meet. . . . Why, see! There it goes!"

He pointed eagerly at the lithe slinking shape which appeared for a moment among the hydrangeas and then vanished again.

"Come along, Jennings," said Burford. "We'll need to get after it and fix it, somehow."

"The gate's locked," Jennings objected. "I tried it. There's a spring lock on it that catches when the gate slams."

"Then how did the cheetah get the body through?" demanded Burford, incredulously. "It couldn't have hauled that weight over the gate."

"Perhaps it had its latch-key in its vest pocket," suggested Jennings, ironically. "Or it took and closed the gate after it. All I know is that I've been on patrol duty along here and the gardener has orders to see that gate's locked every night."

"What gardener?"

"The one that lives on the premises. He's got a little cottage along to the left there, just inside the wall. There's the path that leads to it."

The Sergeant's slow mind was still working upon Jennings'

ironical suggestion about a latch-key. It recalled the second key which he had found in Brenthurst's pocket. He took this out, tried it on the gate lock, and found that it fitted.

"Come on!" he ordered, pushing the gate open and following Jennings through. "We'll shut the gate behind us, just in case that brute breaks back."

He stepped on the grass border, motioning to Jennings to do the same.

"That's a rum idea," he commented, examining the path in the light of the moon which had emerged from the clouds and now shone clear in the sky. "Quite a layer of sand on that path. Must be some foreign notion. Never saw it before. Makes for soft walking, certainly."

"And should leave nice clean tracks," added Jennings, practically. "I say! This is a rum start!"

"What is?" demanded Burford, crossly.

"There ain't no tracks on that sand," Jennings pointed out excitedly. "So how did that cheetah get to the gate? And where's the trail of the body it was dragging?"

Burford was continually being outvied by quicker-minded subordinates, and he resented it.

"It must have dragged the body along the grass strip beside the path," he announced after some silent pondering.

"Then how did it get across here?" demanded Jennings, pointing to the semicircle of sanded surface which extended round the gate and cut it off from the turf.

Jennings delighted in putting his superior in the wrong, and he proceeded to elaborate the difficulty.

"It couldn't have jumped that ten yards, not with a twelve-stone man in its mouth. . . . Good Lord!"

From not far off came a snarl of menace from the unseen cheetah, lurking somewhere in the cover of the hydrangeas.

"That's our first job," said Burford, relieved from the need to meet Jennings' arguments. "Can't leave that beast to make more trouble while we're doing a Sherlock Holmes act, Jennings. First things first. Come along!"

A straight, broad, grass-flanked walk, about a hundred and fifty yards in length, led from the gate towards the house, which stood on a low bank surmounted by a balustraded terrace. Rows of pink and blue hydrangeas, their colours etiolated in the moonlight, made the pathway into a little avenue and concealed the rest of the grounds. Half-way between gate and terrace the avenue widened into a *rond-point* about a curious little erection imitating the architecture of a Chinese pagoda with its up-turned eaves. Beyond this, the avenue continued until it ended in a flight of broad stone steps leading up to the level of the terrace. The house behind showed no sign of moving life. Its window-panes, here and there, shone with reflected moonbeams. But the central French window stood open and uncurtained, giving a glimpse into the tenantless room behind it where sprays of electric lamps were alight. Not a zephyr stirred in the garden. Over the whole brooded a stillness broken only by the soft splash of an unseen fountain in another part of the grounds.

Then, as the two men moved forward, there came from the cheetah a discontented whine which jarred on the tranquillity of that night peace. Followed by the constable, Sergeant Burford advanced cautiously along the grass border towards the pagoda, keeping his revolver ready. Once again the big feline shape showed itself among the bushes, its eyes glowing balefully in the moonlight. But it was too far off for easy shooting; and before the Sergeant could make up his mind to fire, it vanished again into cover.

"Like the old fairy-tale, ain't it?" said Jennings, thoughtfully. "The Palace of the Sleeping Beauty, and all that sort of thing, it reminds me of, somehow."

Sergeant Burford was surprised and slightly shocked by this flight of fancy on the part of his subordinate.

"The beauty *we*'re likely to come up against won't be sleeping. Take my word for that," he said, severely. "And it won't want no kissing neither, Jennings. So don't you go for to be romantical. Keep your pistol ready."

Thus recalled to reality, Jennings offended his superior in another way. He peered down at the grass, then stooped and stroked his hand over one spot.

"That's blood, that is," he declared, showing a discoloured palm.

"Well, didn't I tell you it hauled him along the grass?" retorted Burford. "Now you see I was right. But don't you go staring at the ground, d'you hear? We're hunting for a cheetah just now, not for a clue. Just you mind that, and keep your pistol handy."

They reached the pagoda without mishap. From this point alleys curved away to various parts of the gardens, and down one of them they could see the top of the high-wired enclosure framing a tennis-court. Burford halted for a moment and glanced round in search of the cheetah. Then he set off again towards the house, crossing a sanded alley. Jennings was about to follow, when suddenly he halted as the moon came out of a slight cloud.

"Look you here, Sergeant!" he said, impulsively. "There's a set of footprints down here, a man's. And they begin nowhere, just as if he'd jumped down from the sky. And there's some blood-spots beside them, but nothing like the amount that there was on the grass back there."

He switched on his torch and examined the marks.

"The cheetah's been down that alley, too," he announced. "After him, no doubt."

"Rum!" admitted Burford coming back to look. "What was he doing down that path? I took it he'd been up at the house. . . ."

"See!" Jennings interrupted in some excitement. "There it goes!"

He gripped the Sergeant's arm and pointed to the sinister shape which loped across a lawn to their right, evidently making for the steps leading up to the terrace. The sight acted like a spur on the two men, and they ran towards the stairway in an attempt to cut the beast off ere it reached the house. But at the sound of their steps it turned its head, saw them, and bounded more swiftly, so that it gained the terrace ere they had reached the foot of the steps. There, swinging round, it confronted them, teeth bared, eyes glaring, and switching its tail like an infuriated cat. The Sergeant, who was foremost, lifted his revolver and fired; and on the heels of the report came a yelp of pain. The cheetah drew back from the stair-head and took refuge under cover of the balustrade, snarling its defiance as it retreated.

"You stand there," ordered Burford, who had no intention of letting Jennings play the chief role. "I'll go up this side. Gives you a clear line of fire if it jumps at me. If it gets me down, see you blow its brains out, quick time."

And without hesitation he began to climb the steps. But as his head came level with the terrace and he could see round the balustrade, he gave an involuntary ejaculation. The cheetah was waiting for him; but there was a second figure there, over which it stood: a woman in disordered night attire over which a red kimono had been thrown. She was lying face upward, apparently in a faint, with one arm out-thrown on the terrace pavement; and not far from her lay a small automatic pistol which seemed to have been jerked from her hand. Over her crouched the cheetah, lambent-eyed, with lips retracted in a vicious snarl and menace in every line of its body.

Burford fired just as it sprang, and almost simultaneously he heard the report of Jennings' revolver. The weight of the brute landed on his chest and shoulders, driving him headlong backward down the staircase. He lay there, helpless, half stunned by the crash of his head on the stone paving, with the cheetah on top of him, tearing at the collar of his tunic in its effort to get at his throat. But that was its last effort. Before it could do real harm, Jennings sprang forward, clapped his revolver to its head, and fired. It rolled over, clawing the air in a last convulsion, and then relaxed.

"Hurt?" demanded the constable, anxiously, as he put out a hand to help Burford to his feet. "I thought it had got you, when the pair of you came trundling down the steps. Your face is all right," he added, reassuringly, as the Sergeant put his hand to his head instinctively.

"I'm O.K.," Burford declared after a second or two. "Got a knock on the head on these stones, that's all. Thought I was for it, though, when I found the brute on top of me and my pistol knocked out of my hand."

"We do seem to be having a pleasant evening," said Jennings, sardonically. "And what's next?"

"There's a woman's body up there on the terrace," said Burford in a rather unsteady voice, since he was still suffering from the blow on his head. "I suppose the damned cheetah got her before we turned up. Go up and have a look."

He sat down on the lowest step of the stairway to recover from his shock. Jennings, running up the steps, got his first glimpse of the woman, who had hitherto been hidden from him by the balustrade.

"It's Miss Teramond," he reported. "I know her by sight."

He knelt down and felt her pulse.

"She's alive, all right," he announced after a while. "I can feel her heart beating. And she doesn't seem to have been clawed or bitten. Just fainted, most likely. Wait a jiffy till I get something to cover her. She mightn't like it if she came out of her faint like this, with her nightie all torn, the way it is, and only men to look after her. Funny there ain't any claw marks, though, with her night-gear in rags like that."

"Go and see if there isn't some woman in the house," ordered Burford.

"The maids go home after they've washed up the dinner-dishes," Jennings told him, "but there's a Miss Garfield lives here. I'll fetch her."

He disappeared into the house, but returned alone after a few minutes.

"There's nobody at all in the house," he announced. "I've been over the whole place. There's only one bed been used to-night, and that's in the room next to this drawing-room. Maybe we could get her in there before she wakes up. And get her a hot-water bottle, since she's got a shock."

Diana Teramond stirred slightly, muttered some incomprehensible words, and then showed symptoms which perturbed both watchers.

"Here!" ordered the Sergeant. "Shove something between her teeth. Quick! or she'll be biting her tongue. She's in a fit of some sort. You look after her while I ring up a doctor and a nurse. No job for us, this."

By the time he returned the symptoms had died down and Diana seemed to have fallen into a coma.

"She'll get her death of cold if we let her lie out here till the sawbones comes," said Jennings, anxiously. "After a shock like this, she'd get a chill in no time. We'd best carry her to her bed, and I'll see about a hot-water bottle."

Together they carried Diana into the bedroom and put her to bed. Then, while Jennings went in search of a hot-water bottle, Burford began an examination of the premises, starting with the drawing-room. Now that he had leisure to look about him, he saw plain signs of a struggle: an upset chair, some knick-knacks swept off an occasional table, and a tear in one of the curtains at the side of the French window.

"That cheetah?" he queried to himself.

But this idea he dismissed instantly when his eye fell on a man's cloth cap which lay on the carpet, half concealed by one of the chairs. He picked it up and read the initials "A.B." in marking-ink on the lining.

" 'A.B.,' " he mused. "Ambrose Brenthurst was the name on that driving-licence. Must have been up here, in this house. Visiting her at this time of night. And there was a row, and a bit of a struggle. That's how her nightie got all ripped open. No claw-marks on her skin. Of course not. That cheetah was a pet of hers. Wouldn't hurt her. Maybe it came to her help and gave Brenthurst what-for. Drawing-room door was open when we came in. Cheetah might have been here when the scrap started. Or she may have called to it to come and help. I'll see where it lived, anyhow."

He went and examined various rooms on the ground floor. One of them, a house-maid's pantry originally, had been converted into a den for the cheetah. Burford found its bed, a large platter, a dish of water on the floor, whilst heavy bars on the window had plainly been fixed to prevent it escaping once it had been shut in for the night. Burford turned into the scullery, where Jennings was waiting for two kettles to boil on the gas-stove.

"You saw the room they kept the cheetah in?" he demanded. "Did you open the door when you were hunting about?"

"Never touched it," declared Jennings. "I didn't need to. It was open and I just had to look in."

"Then if that cheetah was in its den, it could get out into the hall," said the Sergeant, working out the sequence of events with meticulous care. "And if the drawing-room door was open, it could get in there, if it was called. And, seeing the French window was open, it could get out into the garden."

"Well, it *was* in the garden, wasn't it?" retorted Jennings, impatiently. "And out on the road as well, so the garden gate must have been wide open, too."

"I was just going on to that, when you burst in," Burford declared in an aggrieved tone. "We've got to reconstruct this crime, step by step. . . ."

At this moment, with a brisk rattling of their lids, the kettles came to the boil, and Jennings filled two rubber hot-water bags which he had discovered. When they took these to Diana Teramond's bedroom, they found her conscious, but apparently not very clear in her mind after the shock. She showed no surprise at finding her room invaded by two uniformed men.

"Did I kill him?" she asked, faintly. "I remember shooting him with my pistol, after he took the diamond . . . and after he caught hold of me. . . . He ran off when I fired . . . and I ran after him . . . and I called Mimi . . ."

The Sergeant, always a stickler for rules, was about to interrupt her with the usual cautionary phrase when her voice died away in an inarticulate murmur and she seemed to relapse into drowsiness. Burford packed the hot-water bags into the bed, made her as comfortable as he could without rousing her, and then he and Jennings tiptoed out of the room.

"So she shot him?" mused the Sergeant aloud. "And she called up the cheetah — if its name's Mimi. There's not another living creature on the premises to call, anyhow. And it went after Brenthurst. Tore the throat out of him. Then it came back to stand guard over her. And we shot it, poor brute. . . ."

He was silent for a moment or two. Then he continued in a remorseful tone:—

"Sounds like some poetry-stuff I learned at school, about a dog called Gelert. His master came home one day. Found the dog all bloody. Thought it had killed his child. Gave it what-for with his spear. Finished it. Then he found it had got the blood on it by doing in a wolf that had attacked his young son. Touching, I used to think, when I was a kiddie. Drew tears from my eyes, I remember, first time I read it. And now we've done the very same trick. Blown out the brains of a faithful defender, all under what you might call a misapprehension. Well, well. . . ."

Jennings was still smarting under the Sergeant's treatment of his remarks about the Sleeping Beauty, and felt unimpressed by the tale of Beth-Gelert.

"It's done now, anyway," he pointed out. "After all, it was a real dangerous beast, and better dead, 'fore it did any more harm."

Burford abandoned the faithful hound theme as his audience was so obviously unappreciative.

"That doctor and nurse ought to be here almost any minute," he said, briskly. "We'd better take a look round. See if we can spot anything in the way of a clue. There's that pistol, to start with."

He walked on to the terrace and picked up the little weapon, handling it gingerly on account of possible fingerprints. A sniff at its muzzle satisfied him that it had been fired only a short time before.

"No better than a toy," he said, disparagingly, as he showed it to Jennings. "A .22, I'd say. Or perhaps a .25. About as dangerous as a rook-rifle. Not but that a rook-rifle can't do nasty work if it hits the right place."

"Um," said Jennings, indifferently.

Using caution, Burford slipped the magazine out of the butt and counted the cartridges.

"Holds six when it's full," he commented. "Two left in the

magazine. There'll be one in the breech. Three shots fired, then. We'll need to find the empty cases. Come on and hunt for them."

After some minutes they had examined the floor minutely and had discovered two empty cases under some of the furniture. The third one they could not recover, either on the drawing-room carpet or on the paving of the terrace.

"Rum, that," declared the Sergeant. "But we'll find it in daylight."

He examined the pistol again.

"Just a toy. Vest-pocket size. Couldn't do much harm to anyone. And the noise it'd make wouldn't raise a panic in a village street. No use even to bring help, if you loosed it off. So it don't hurt and it's no good as an alarm, so what earthly use is it, anyway?"

"I dunno," confessed Jennings, in a detached tone.

Sergeant Burford was inclined to expiate still further on the obvious, when he was interrupted by a sharp trill from an electric bell in the house. Then a motor-horn sounded at the front gate.

"That's the doctor, likely. I'll go and let him in."

A few minutes later he was sorry that he had not delegated the task to Jennings, for the doctor was in a bad temper at being called up for a night visit. He had a nurse in the car with him, and as they drove round to the other gate he demanded information from the Sergeant about the case. Burford did his best, but obviously the medico was not inclined to give him full marks on the results of the examination.

"Sounds like Jacksonian epilepsy," he declared finally, with a contemptuous sniff. "But from all you've told me, Sergeant, it might be diabetic coma, or slight concussion, or almost anything barring a cold in the head. Do you know if she's had similar attacks before? You don't? Well, then, we'll do without your help, thanks, and just see for ourselves. Where's the patient?"

He and the nurse went into Diana's room, leaving the police to continue their investigations. Sergeant Burford, glaring at the doctor's retreating back, made a grimace as if he had swallowed some quinine, and entered up a black mark against Dr. Winthorpe's name in his mental ledger. Upsetting beggar, this fellow, with his superior airs! What did he suppose they called him in for, if they could have diagnosed the case for themselves without his help? Not their job. It was some relief to turn back to his own proper work.

"We've got to find that third cartridge-case," Burford announced when he returned to the drawing-room after leaving the doctor.

"S'pose we hunt along that path, then," suggested Jennings. "She ran after him, she said, and he must have gone that way."

The Sergeant was obviously vexed that he had not thought of this course himself.

"Something in that, mebbe," he conceded, grudgingly. "Give it a chance, anyhow. Not that I think there's much in it, mind you. No more light outside there than would make a blind man's holiday. More by chance than anything, if you find much. Still, come along and we'll try. Keep on the grass."

The moon had come out from behind a cloud-bank, and the expanses of the garden lay bathed in dim light. The quaint architecture of the storied pagoda threw its many-horned shadow on the sand of the *rond-point*. Not a zephyr stirred among the long lines of hydrangeas, ash-tinted under the cold illumination of the moon. From the height of the terrace the tip of the slim silver jet of a fountain shone among the greenery, and the plashing of waters came intermittently through the stillness which brooded over the lawns. The searchers descended the stairway and threw the questing beams of their electric torches hither and thither on the path and its grassy borders.

"A lot of tracks there," pointed out Jennings, undepressed by his superior's faint praise. "There's the spoor of the cheetah, plain enough. And a man's shoes. And these must be the prints of her bedroom slippers."

"One thing at a time," snapped the Sergeant. "It's a cartridge-case we're looking for, isn't it? These tracks won't run away. Easier to see them properly when dawn comes up. No use bothering about them just now."

"And there's no blood-drippings here," concluded Jennings, determined to put his observations on record.

Still keeping to the grass edging, they moved along the avenue of hydrangeas. Suddenly Jennings stooped to pick up something which had caught his eye.

"Here's your extra cartridge-case," he announced triumphantly. "So she must have followed him this length, anyway, if a shot was fired here."

"Mark the spot where you found it," ordered the Sergeant, "and then come along. We'll have a look down that side-alley. I want to know why he blundered down there."

As they neared the *rond-point*, Jennings gave an exclamation of surprise.

"Well, what is it *now?*" demanded Burford, impatiently.

"Look there," said Jennings, who had thrown the beam of his torch farther ahead. "The whole bunch of these tracks stop dead —a regular blank end to them. Somebody's been here and raked the sand. Well, *that*'s a rum start, that is!"

Sergeant Burford liked to make his own discoveries and then parade them. He began to wish that he had brought Wilks along with him instead of Jennings. He stood silent for a moment or two, staring at the place where the sand had been disturbed.

"There's only two people could have done that," he opined at last, "either Miss Teramond or else this gardener we haven't seen yet. They're the only two living human beings about the place now. And why leave the job like this? It's only half done, with all these tracks left untouched up to the stairway. This raking-over only starts at the round-about. . . ."

Jennings had moved farther forward while the Sergeant was pondering. He had changed over to the grass border of the side-alley and was examining the ground with the help of his torch.

"That's why Brenthurst's tracks seemed to start all of a sudden, when we looked at them before," he declared. "All the prints between here and the round-about have been raked over. But here they are quite plain, and here's the spoor of the cheetah, too. It came up after him, because here's one of its prints right on top of one of his foot-marks. But what made him turn off the straight road? If the cheetah was after him, his best game would be to get inside this pagoda-thing and slam the door after him, or else bunk for the gate, straight ahead, where his car was waiting."

"Perhaps there's better shelter down this alley," suggested the Sergeant, though without much conviction. "Come along. We'll have a look and see."

Twenty paces farther on, out of sight of the pagoda, Brenthurst's tracks left the path, and a few yards beyond this point the two investigators came upon a broad dark patch upon the turf.

"Blood — and lots of it," pronounced Burford when he had rubbed his finger in the liquid and examined the tip by the light of his torch. "This is where the cheetah got him. He must have been trying to escape through these hydrangeas when he left the path. Clean off his rocker with funk, it seems to me."

"One *could* bust one's way through," commented Jennings. "These hydrangeas aren't like a box hedge."

Burford disdained to answer this. Motioning Jennings to follow, he walked past the high wire cage of the tennis-court and continued along the alley until it ended in a walled garden, in the sunken centre of which lay the fountain whose jet they had seen from the stairway. There was no shelter of any sort in the enclosure.

"He might have had the notion of scrambling up that wall with the help of the stems of these nectarines," mused Burford, gazing at the plant-decked brickwork. "A poor chance, though, with the cheetah close behind. Far better to have kept straight for the gate. Blind panic was his trouble, if you ask me. We'll go back, now."

Flanked by Jennings, he retraced his steps, obviously puzzling over the problem which had presented itself. As they passed the tennis-court, Jennings surreptitiously tried the handle of the wire gate and glanced at the little pavilion which overlooked the nets.

"Take it that he started from the terrace," Burford resumed, after a spell of silence which lasted until they had passed the *rond-point* and turned towards the gate. "She was after him with that toy pistol. What would you do yourself, Jennings, if you had a woman after you with a pistol in her hand?"

"Take it from her," said Jennings, concisely.

"Well, *he* didn't," objected Burford. "So what else would you do instead?"

"Run like hell," was the constable's terse solution.

"*Pre*-cisely," pursued the Sergeant, evidently delighted to reason things out, step by step. "There's the gate at the end of the path. There's your car waiting for you on the road. Wouldn't you run for them? What would you swing off into that alley for, at all? It stops short in that walled-in place with the fountain. It's what the French call a cue-de-sack, meaning that you're bagged if you get into it."

Jennings had another of his bright ideas.

"He may have been trying to get into that wired-in tennis-court and slam the gate behind him to keep off the cheetah."

"A fat lot of good that would do," retorted Burford, scornfully. "The cheetah could have shinned up that wire fence as easy."

"I don't know whether cheetahs can climb or not," admitted Jennings. "But no doubt with the cheetah after him, he was a bit more flustered nor what we are just now, thinking things out all nice and quiet. He mayn't have had time to run over his natural-history knowledge and see things clear. Any port in a storm."

"Maybe. *Maybe*," said Burford, weightily. "I don't think much of that notion."

"Well, then, try another," suggested Jennings, undiscouraged. "The garden gate was shut when we came to it. P'r'aps it was shut when Brenthurst was pushing off. He wouldn't have time to open it, with the cheetah at his heels. It would get him while he was fumbling about. So he may have thought he could do better in the side-alley."

"Ingenious," admitted the Sergeant, with heavy irony. "Very smart indeed, Jennings. *But*, if that gate was shut, how did the cheetah manage to drag the body outside? No, you've made what the French call a fox pass, meaning a false step or a bloomer. Unless the cheetah had its latch-key in its vest pocket, same as you suggested a while back, in your humorous way. But unless it had, how did it get the body out on to the road? Answer me that."

"Well, the gate must have been open," Jennings admitted. "It couldn't have lugged a fourteen-stone man over that, spikes and all."

"Gate open, eh? Then why didn't Brenthurst go straight for it, instead of turning down this alley? Choose either way, you run into a cue-de-sack, same as he did himself."

They had reached the point where the blood stained the turf. The Sergeant paused here and expounded his ideas further.

"Now, Jennings, if you had a cheetah jump on your back just here, what would you do?"

"Yell for help," said Jennings, laconically.

"Precisely. *Pre*-cisely," agreed Burford. "That sounds well, don't it? But that gardener's cottage is within a hundred yards. And he didn't hear any yells for help, or he'd be up and about, wouldn't he? How do you fit *that* in?"

"Then he didn't yell, if you like that best," conceded Jennings, placably. "The cheetah got his throat before he could say 'Squeak!'"

"Maybe so. Maybe not, p'r'aps," said the Sergeant, broadmindedly. "Main thing is, we've got the bones of it, now. Like this. The man Brenthurst comes here in his car which he leaves down the road. Shows he didn't want to attract attention, or he'd have gone round to the other gate and left his car at the front door. He didn't want any chat about his paying visits to Miss T. That's plain enough. He let himself in by that gate down there with the key we found in his pocket. He left the gate open behind him. Up he went to the house and met Miss T. If he came by appointment . . . Well, there she was in bed in her nightie, and you can draw your own conclusions, Jennings. Though it's possible that he came unexpected-like, and she got up out of bed in her daisy-beel, as the French say. But his having the key of that gate certainly looks like a special appointment. And on that basis, her daisy-beel gives one furiously to think, as the French say. Be that as it may. They were in the drawing-room when they had a row, a real nasty bit of brass-rag parting. He attacked her, and she fished out that toy pistol and chased him off, following him up, just as she told us."

"You talk like a book," declared Jennings, with an air of admiration which was perhaps not wholly genuine. "Tell us the rest, now."

"She fired a couple of shots in the room up there, for we found the cartridge-cases," Burford continued. "And near the pagoda, she fired again, for there was the third case. Now come to the cheetah. It must have lain in its little bed, good as gold, so long as the talk between those two was friendly. When Brenthurst started the rough stuff, it waked up and popped out. Or else she called to it. So it flew out after the two of them, eager to defend its loved mistress. I'm downright sorry we shot that beast, Jennings, downright sorry indeed. It sticks in my throat that we had to kill it."

"If we hadn't killed it, you wouldn't have a throat for anything to stick in, at this moment," Jennings pointed out. "Brenthurst hadn't, by the time it had done with him."

"Well, I was always fond of animals," protested Burford, "and it was doing its best, poor thing, not understanding how the land lay. Anyhow, it came tearing down here after those two, and jumped on Brenthurst. A horrible sight, that, I expect. Miss T. wouldn't stay to watch it. She'd run back to the house. And then, most like, her nerves gave out and she fainted on the terrace, where we found her. And then the cheetah dragged Brenthurst's body out of the garden to the road."

"It must have had a tidy mind," commented Jennings. "'No Rubbish Must Be Shot Here,' eh? Cats are tidy beasts, I admit. But by your way of it, the bigger the cat, the tidier it is in its ideas. The truth is, I expect, that it dragged him outside so as not to be interrupted."

"Not being in its confidence, I can't say," said the Sergeant, with heavy sarcasm. "If it explained its motives to you, well *and* good. It dragged the body out, and we can leave it at that. When we turned up, I expect it thought: 'Hallo! More people come to hurt my mistress? We'll see about that!' That's what its attitude suggested, when I saw it standing over her."

"You saw it, I didn't. Not till after it put its paws round your neck. If it was just kissing you, then I made a mistake. But you've left out one or two little things in this sy-nop-sis of yours, Sergeant. Who raked over the sand? And why? And what about the pendant we found in his pocket? Was it a sort of left-handed wedding-present? And another thing. When we were in her bedroom, I noticed a small safe with the door open. Was Brenthurst up here to do a spot of burglary, and she woke up and caught him at it? That seems as good a tale as your one."

They had almost reached the gate when the Chief Constable entered through it, and the two men sprang sharply to attention.

# CHAPTER V

## Diana Teramond

Sir Clinton acknowledged the Sergeant's salute and listened to his report without comment. When Burford had finished, he put a question.

"Brenthurst was quite dead when you picked him up?"

"Oh, quite, sir. You've seen the body, out there in the ambulance? Look how his throat was torn by that cheetah."

"Yes, the cheetah did its share, certainly," the Chief Constable admitted. "You formed no idea of how long he'd been dead?"

"No, sir. The body was still warm."

"It can go to the mortuary now for the police surgeon to examine. Inspector Sandrock's out there with some extra men. Just tell him what I've said and ask him to put a man on to watch the gardener's cottage, in case he slips away before we've seen him. The rest of the men are to picket the grounds."

When the Sergeant had gone upon his errand, Sir Clinton turned to Jennings.

"You saw an open safe in Miss Teramond's bedroom? Did you notice if her window was open?"

"Yes, sir. It's a sash window — you can't see it from here because of that pagoda-thing. The lower sash had been lifted about a foot."

"Brenthurst was a bulky fellow," commented Sir Clinton. "Was the window wide enough open for him to crawl through?"

Jennings was obviously disconcerted by this question.

"No, sir," he admitted, reluctantly. "Come to think of it, the sash was only about eight inches up. Not enough for him to have squirmed through. She may have had it open just for fresh air," he ended, rather disconsolately.

"People usually open the top sash of the window if they want fresh air in a bedroom," Sir Clinton pointed out. "But she may have had her own methods. You'd better come with me up to the house."

He set off along the grass edging, halting once or twice to examine the blood-spots which Jennings pointed out to him. At the cross-alley beside the *rond-point* he halted and made a rough measurement of Brenthurst's footprints in the sandy surface. Then he went farther on and made similar measurements of the tracks which his subordinates had put down to Diana Teramond's bedroom slippers.

"That path hasn't been raked," he pointed out. "The obliteration of the tracks was done with a birch besom, by the look of the sand. The gardener will be able to tell us where they keep their gardening tools."

He paused for a while, scanning the house-front which was now brightly lit up by the moon. As he stood there, Inspector Sandrock and the Sergeant joined the party. The Inspector was a dry, taciturn man, coldly efficient and not given to betraying his thoughts. In his speech he inclined as far as possible to a monosyllabic vocabulary.

"Where did you find that third cartridge-case?" asked the Chief Constable, turning to Burford.

"Just there, sir," explained the Sergeant. "You can see where Jennings marked the spot with a page of his note-book fixed down with a twig."

Sir Clinton nodded and walked on towards the stairway. But instead of ascending the steps, he turned to the left, rounded the end of the terrace, and moved cautiously over the flower-bed which lay under Diana Teramond's bedroom window, using his flash-lamp to light up the ground. When he had found what he was looking for, he made a gesture summoning the Inspector to his side, and another cautioning him to make no noise which might arouse the patient within the room. Obediently, Sandrock stooped and examined the soil to which Sir Clinton's torch-beam was directed; and after a few seconds the Chief Constable withdrew to a distance where they could talk freely.

"You saw the marks, Inspector? Evidently a heavy man came up to the window and stood there for a while, for the prints under the window are deeper than those that he made in walking up to it. You noticed that the window is open at both top and bottom? As I read it, she had her window open at the top for fresh air. Then Brenthurst came along and attracted her attention. She lifted the lower sash a few inches and spoke to him through the gap for a while. After that, he went round to the French window, for you saw the prints of his shoes as he went away. That proves he didn't go into the bedroom through the window. When he got on to the terrace she must have let him into the drawing-room. From the way she was dressed, when Sergeant Burford found her, it looks as if she had been in bed when Brenthurst turned up."

"Waiting for him?" queried the Inspector, cynically.

Sir Clinton shook his head.

"I doubt it," he answered. "If she'd been expecting him, she'd have left the French window open so that he could walk straight in. Also, to judge by the depth of these prints in the soil, they talked for quite a little while at the window. There would be no point in that, on your assumption, would there?"

"No, sir, perhaps not. You seem to have the right end of the stick."

"It doesn't amount to much in itself," said the Chief Constable. "But it may help to check one part of her story when we hear it."

He led the way round to the stairway again and went up to the terrace and the drawing-room. The doctor had gone away, but had left a note for the police. Sir Clinton picked it up and glanced through it.

"Dr. Winthorpe says his patient seems to be suffering from Jacksonian epilepsy, whatever that is," he explained. "He says there's nothing very dangerous in it, and she'll probably be quite fit to tell us her tale in a little while. Unfortunately, the doctor thinks she might suffer from the same kind of black-out that one sees in the ordinary epileptics after a fit. She may not remember things which happened just before the attack; and it's just these things we want to know about, worse luck."

"She did remember something, sir," Burford ventured to put in. "She muttered a word or two as we were shifting her to her bed: about shooting, and running after Brenthurst, and calling to the cheetah. A bit incoherent, she was, but she did remember something."

"You've searched this room?"

"Only looking for cartridge-cases, sir. We'd no time for more."

Sir Clinton glanced round the room, noting the disturbance of the furniture, some burnt paper in the fire-place, a spatter of cigar-ash on the hearth, left by a half-smoked cigar which had evidently been thrown down carelessly.

"There's not much upset," he commented. "It must have been short and sharp. Brenthurst was a big heavy fellow. What's Miss Teramond like?" he demanded, turning to the Sergeant.

"Good-looking, sir, above the average. Nice figure, as we saw when we were taking her to her room. Rather under average height for a woman. Slim, small-boned, neatly made, sir."

"Not the Amazon style, then? Not the sort of woman who could cope with a big man?"

"Oh, no, sir. I could hold her with one hand, myself, by the look of her. But she had the pistol to fall back on, of course."

"Yes," agreed Sir Clinton, "she hit him thrice. One shot, from the front, seemed to have got him in the left lung. There was blood and froth on his lips. Another bullet got him in the left shoulder. And the third one, so far as I could see by rough inspection, hit him near the spine, rather low down. It must have been fired from the back, probably as he was running away."

He stepped over to the fire-place and gingerly examined the bits of burnt paper in it.

"Not much to be made out of this stuff," he reported. "It's almost all burned away and broken up. From the few words left legible, it looks as if the original papers had something to do with cash transactions. I could read a word or two on the top one, and it mentions one thousand pounds. Another one seemed to be an

IOU by what's left of it. I could just read 'IO . . .' and a pound sign. I'm afraid there's nothing much to be made out of this stuff, but you might preserve it as well as you can."

"I'll see to that, sir," said Sandrock.

Sir Clinton picked up the cigar-butt.

"You found a cigar-case in his pocket?" he asked, turning to the Sergeant. "You have it? Ah, thanks."

He took a cigar from the case and compared it with the half-smoked fragment.

"I've never read Sherlock Holmes's pamphlet on cigar-ash," he confessed, "but we hardly need it here. These two seem to be the same brand. We can get an expert on to it if we need him. The point is that this cigar was only smoked half-way; and from the dent on the side of the burned tip and the splash of the ash yonder, I'd say it was flung into the fire-place, pretty hard, while it was still burning. It looks as if Brenthurst argued with Miss Teramond for a while, smoking during their talk; and then he decided to brusque matters, pitched away his cigar, and got to grips with her."

"That would be when her night-dress got torn to rags," commented the Inspector, who had extracted some facts from the Sergeant on the way up to the house. "The cheetah had nothing to do with that, or else she'd have had the marks of its claws on her skin."

"Cheetahs are queer beasts," said Sir Clinton, reflectively. "Like cats in most things, but like dogs in their toe-nails. Their claws don't retract like the ordinary feline's. So you can't reckon the cheetah out, merely because she had no talon-marks on her skin. But I agree with you on the main point, Inspector. It wasn't the cheetah that tore her night-dress. Now let's have a look at this pendant you found in Brenthurst's pocket, please."

Burford produced it and handed it over to the Chief Constable, who examined it with care. A slightly contemptuous expression crossed his face as he handed it to the Inspector.

"A schlenter," he pronounced, curtly. "Just a fake, and not a very good fake at that, either."

"Are you sure of that, sir?" asked Sandrock, obviously surprised by the certainty in his chief's tone. "It looks all right to me."

"Quite sure," Sir Clinton declared positively. "In my young days, Inspector, I held a post on the diamond fields; and I haven't forgotten what I learned there. That's a very poor specimen. Good enough to take in the ordinary person, of course."

"I wonder what Brenthurst wanted with it," Sandrock said in a puzzled tone. "A phony bit of jewellery wouldn't be much good to a money-lender as security."

"Of course not," said the Chief Constable. "But I've heard a story that Miss Teramond had a real diamond, just like this snide affair, and that makes me inclined to wonder a bit. Did she palm off this dud to Brenthurst as the real thing? Or had the two of them cooked up some scheme for diddling an insurance company? Or did he mean to ring the changes, swap this paste affair for her real diamond on the sly? He hadn't a nice reputation, and a game of that sort would be just what one might expect. Her story may throw some light on the point, and we'd better get it now. Just tap on the door of her room, Inspector, if you please, and ask the nurse if her patient's fit to talk."

In a few seconds Inspector Sandrock returned.

"Nurse Canning says you can speak to Miss Teramond now, sir, if you don't excite her and don't stay too long with her. She's still a bit queer, it seems."

"Very well. Let's go in now."

The nurse had evidently prepared Diana for the interview. A new diaphanous night-dress replaced the torn one, which lay across one of the chairs; and the patient, wearing a dainty and obviously expensive bed-jacket, was propped up with pillows in the big double bed. Sir Clinton greeted the nurse with a smile, and then turned to Diana.

"I'm sorry to trouble you, just after this shock," he said kindly. "But we need some information, and I'm sure you won't mind answering a question or two. May we sit down? Thanks."

He drew a chair to the side of the bed and seated himself, using the pause to examine her inoffensively. Peter Diamond had not been far out in his estimate of Diana's sex-attraction. She had that gift in a lavish degree by nature; and evidently she was accustomed to exert it consciously. Even now, shaken as she was, Sir Clinton could see her pulling herself together, settling herself into a provocative attitude, and glancing from him to the Inspector as though to gauge the effect she was making on them.

"She's what Peter, in his crude way, would call 'hot stuff,' obviously," was Sir Clinton's unspoken comment. "She's even making Sandrock sit up and take notice, and he's not an excitable animal. On Brenthurst, her effect must have been devastating. She could move him in that way, easily enough. But as for dragging his body about, she simply doesn't seem to have the physique for the job."

Diana glanced at him with a brave attempt at archness.

"And what is it that you would wish to hear?" she asked.

Sir Clinton suspected that her peculiar little locutions were not altogether unstudied. They gave a faint exotic tinge to her speech, which she heightened occasionally by a slight mispronunciation. Evidently she found that a suggestion of her Creole ancestry lent her an additional attraction for some men, and she employed it without scruple.

"I'd like to know how Mr. Brenthurst came to be in your garden last night."

"Ah! But was he hurt? Did I hit him when I fired my pistol? I can recall almost nothing of what happened. That sounds strange to you, without doubt, but I shall explain, later."

"He was wounded," Sir Clinton admitted, with apparent frankness. "But let's take things in the proper order, please. How did he come to be here at all?"

Diana shifted her position slightly, as if to make herself more comfortable, though the Chief Constable suspected that she was merely anxious to render herself more attractive to her listeners. She turned her eyes towards Sandrock and seemed rather dashed to find that he had taken out a note-book and was preparing to jot down notes.

"*That* I can explain to you," she said, after a pause. "I remember all that, clearly enough. But I must go back further in order to make it plain. I shall make it short, as short as possible; but I cannot just begin with yesterday, if you are to understand."

She paused again, evidently trying to gather her memories into some order. Sir Clinton noticed that her original foreign accent was overlaid with a faint American twang which added to her rather languid manner of speaking.

"I must be quite clear," she went on, as though this phrase were addressed to herself as much as to her hearers. "I have known this Mr. Brenthurst for some time. I did not like him — indeed, who could like such a man, hideous, brutal, and hard-hearted? But he was useful to me. Why not? It is my business to make men useful to me, you see? This Brenthurst is not the man to do one a favour for nothing. And he was paid, well paid in good money, for anything he did. But the fact is — I am quite frank about it — I am extravagant. I have never possessed what one calls 'the money-sense.' And one lives but once, *hein?* One must enjoy while one can, is it not so? And to get enjoyment, one must spend, spend with both hands. One must have fine clothes, dainty underwear, pretty jewellery, all sorts of nice things, which cost one money and still more money. And then, when the money is finished, one must get more. Not so very difficult, that, if one has good looks, a nice figure, attractive manners, and some knowledge of the world. I know all about that. I make no pretences. I am an actress; and not the actress who is a good little girl, no. Men are there to give me money, eager to give me money, and I take it. Why not, indeed?"

Sir Clinton, rather bored by this exposition of Diana's philosophy of life, interrupted her gently.

"I don't want you to over-tire yourself, Miss Teramond. Perhaps it would save your strength, after this shock that you've had, if you tell us your story very shortly."

Evidently this displeased her, for she pouted a little; but as this failed in its effect, she recovered herself almost immediately and, with an arch glance at Sir Clinton's face, continued her story.

"I understand! Business is business, with you just as it is with me, *hein?* Very well, I shall be ever so concise. To please you. As I told you, I am a spendthrift" — she seemed rather proud of this — "and one runs short of money from time to time. This

Brenthurst is a money-lender. One applies to him when one needs to be tided over for a while, is it not so? I do not keep an exact account of these things; it is my way, with my lack of money-sense. One borrows, and one borrows again. One pays no attention, and the sums mount up, it appears. The rate of interest is high, one learns. It is like breeding rabbits; there seems no end to it. I do not understand figures at all. In fine, he told me I had reached the limit of the security I had given him. Something further must be arranged before he would lend any more."

"What security had you given him?" asked Sir Clinton.

"Oh, this house of mine. One would have thought that a good security for quite a large loan, *hein*? I was surprised, but I have no money-sense, and perhaps he was right. And meanwhile, he had been attracted by my person. He dropped hints not at all difficult to understand. Not at all difficult, for he was an ill-bred man who does not know how to put such things gracefully. And he is hideous, repulsive, not the right sort of man, you understand? So I thought of something else. I have a diamond, a red diamond, very valuable, given me by a man who was fond of me. And this Brenthurst, I knew, had taken a great fancy for it. He got me once to show it at some stupid Club. And he spoke to me about it, and I could see greed in his little pig's eyes when he looked at it. So I wrote a letter to him, not saying too much, you understand? Just to whet his interest. 'Come and discuss our affairs; we shall find some way out!' That sort of thing. One did not mention the diamond. That would have given him time to think and consider and fix a price, coolly, beforehand."

"Quite so," agreed the Chief Constable. "You meant to make him put a figure on it, then and there?"

"Exactly. And he was to bring back to me all the contracts of indebtedness up to that stage, so that we could start afresh from a new beginning, with my diamond as the only security. I had had it valued, for insurance, at the suggestion of a friend. There was no difficulty on that score. And I had had all this about the interest explained to me by another friend, a man of affairs. I did not understand it — not altogether. I have no head for that kind of thing.

But I knew what rate of interest I was to pay in this new bargain, something much lower than in the earlier affairs. And I was secure in my mind that I could bring him to agree. A pretty woman can always get the better of a man like that, if she uses her own weapons. And laugh at him, also, which is the best part of it."

She laughed herself at the thought, a delightful little trill of merriment.

"So that was all arranged, and the letter was sent to him. He was to come here last night, and to bring all the papers. Then, in this new bargain, I would see that he was more reasonable and that I got a good further advance. He was to bring notes for that. I waited for him in the room next door. He did not come. Ah, thought I, he imagines he can play with me. He wishes to disappoint me and so make me ready to give him better terms. That does not take with me, my friend. I know a little about men and their ways. Still, I waited for him until midnight, and then I retired to my room, here, and got into bed for the night. It did not worry me, that he had not appeared to keep his appointment."

She paused in her narrative, took a cigarette from a case on the table by the bedside, lighted it, and then continued her tale.

"I fall asleep almost at once, when I go to bed, and I sleep sound. All at once, I was awaked. Someone was rapping on the window, over there. I sat up. I was afraid, terrified, even. Quite natural, is it not? My maids had gone away after dinner. My friend, Miss Garfield, who stays with me, was away for the night, by some ill chance. Figure to yourself the feelings of a woman, alone in an isolated house, who wakes up to hear someone rapping on her window! My heart beat till it made me uncomfortable, and I was all nervous. But I am courageous, after all. I sat up. I put on a kimono. I keep a little pistol always beside me at night. That is quite sensible, isn't it, when one is alone in a house like this, far away from neighbours?"

"Quite reasonable," Sir Clinton conceded.

"I slipped the pistol into the pocket of my kimono and went over to the window. I remember these things quite clearly; it is only later that I find myself forgetting. I had switched on the lights, and now I drew back the curtains. And there, outside, was that Brenthurst with his hideous face, smiling like some dreadful gargoyle through the glass. He cried out something or other. I could hear him through the opening at the top of the window; but I had no desire to have him shouting like that outside my bedroom at that time of night. The road is not so far off, and one does not care to have one's private business cried abroad for any passer-by to hear. I opened the lower sash a little and told him to be quiet. If he would go round to the French window of the drawing-room, I would let him in and he could talk quietly."

"Yes," said Sir Clinton, as she paused again.

"Perhaps it was foolish of me to let him into the house at all," Diana continued, "but I had my pistol, you see? Besides, as I was going through the hall towards the drawing-room I thought of Mimi . . ."

"The cheetah?" asked the Chief Constable.

"Yes, my cheetah. She lives in the house at night, in a little room off the hall. She is very fond of me, just like a big kitten. So, as I passed through the hall, I opened the door of her room, oh, so gently, so as not to rouse her. She knows my step. But she would wake up at my call, if I had need of her; and that made me quite brave enough to let that man in. I went into the drawing-room and closed the door behind me, so that the sound of voices should not disturb Mimi. I could always throw it open and call, you see? Brenthurst was waiting on the terrace outside. I let him in; and I left the leaves of the French window wide open, for it was a warm night."

"You switched off the lights in this room when you left it?" interjected Sir Clinton, recalling that Burford and Jennings had seen only the drawing-room lights on when they came up to the house.

"Did I? It is very probable. One does that without thinking. It is not important, as you will see. He came into the drawing-room and sat down. I had forgotten how I was clad, but I remembered it when I saw the look on his face, and I was not sorry that I had Mimi within call. But at the beginning he kept to business. No doubt he said to himself: 'Business first and pleasure afterwards.' He did not get much pleasure!"

She began to laugh, but in her overwrought state the first trills passed into spasmodic peals interspersed with gasps. The nurse stepped swiftly over to the bedside and soothed her with cool, professional skill.

"I am all right now, quite all right," Diana said at last, when her hysteria passed off. "That was foolish of me. But I have had a bad time, a rough passage, you know. Now I shall go on, quite quietly, and not laugh again. We talked business, though it is not so easy to talk business with a man who looks at you all the time like that."

"About what time was it then?" demanded Sir Clinton, partly for information, partly to avert any further attack of hysteria.

"It was not long after one in the morning," Diana explained in a more collected tone. "I had looked at my watch when I switched on the light in my room. We discussed business. Everything arranged itself to my satisfaction. He handed me back my promises to pay, and I burned them on the hearth. I wanted them finished with. Then he gave me bank-notes for a further loan. All that remained was for me to give him my diamond as security and for him to draw up a fresh paper for me to sign. I brought the notes in here, where I have my little safe, which you can see there with its door open. I put the notes into it and took out the pendant in its leather case. That leather case had some tender associations for me, something to do with the man who gave me the diamond. It has a sentimental value, you understand? And, besides, it has our initials intertwined on it, and I did not wish it to be in Brenthurst's hands. He might have lost it. It was just sentiment, but I took the pendant out and put the case back into the safe. Then I went back to the drawing-room. You asked about the light here. It is most likely that I switched it off as I went out of the room, without thinking of it. I did not need a light in the hall, because the moon was shining brightly through the windows of the staircase, so that I could see my way about almost as if it were day.

"I went back into the drawing-room, and I did not close the door

66

of it behind me, as I now remember. That Brenthurst was on his feet when I went in, standing waiting; and he gave me a look which did not please me — but far from that, indeed. I held out the pendant to him. He took it without a glance at it — his eyes were on me, devouring me — and stuffed it into his pocket. Then he muttered something, I do not remember his exact words. I was angry and told him to go, to go immediately. Instead, he gripped me with his great hands and grinned, like some great ape. There was a struggle, my garments were torn, and then he swung me off my feet. It is pleasant to be lifted off one's feet and carried by an attractive man. But to be seized by a gorilla, that is not so nice. I screamed as he carried me towards the door. I fumbled desperately amongst my torn garments for my pistol, and by good fortune I got my hand on it in the pocket of the kimono I was wearing, and I pulled the trigger at random. There was a report. . . ."

Sir Clinton caught the Inspector's eye, and Sandrock, putting down his note-book, went over and picked up the night-dress and the red kimono which were lying across a chair. He held them up, one after the other, outspread; and the rents in the fabrics testified to the truth of Diana's tale of the struggle.

"There's a bullet-hole at the right-hand pocket, sir," Sandrock reported, nodding towards the place. "A shot's been fired through the fabric. There's nothing in the pockets."

He held the garment out to Sir Clinton, who examined it carefully.

"That is as I said," continued Diana. "I must have torn the pocket in trying to wrench the pistol out of it while he had me in his arms. The pistol went off, and I called to Mimi. I am not the sort of woman to be taken by force by such an uncouth monster. He cried out when the pistol exploded, and then as he loosed his hold on me in the surprise of the moment, there came a rush and a snarl and Mimi was on him. I called to her again, to come to heel, for it was plain there was no more to be feared from Brenthurst. He turned to run . . ."

She stopped short with a puzzled expression on her face. It was several seconds before she spoke again.

"And that is all I can remember," she said, haltingly. "Strange, is it not? But after that, things are a complete blank in my mind; I can recall nothing until I woke up again here in bed. I try. . . . No, it is no good. I remember nothing."

"Not even whether you fired other shots or not?" demanded the Chief Constable.

"Nothing, nothing at all."

"Have you ever had any experience like this before?" asked Sir Clinton. "Any temporary failures of your memory?"

Diana seemed relieved by the underlying suggestion.

"Why, yes," she answered, quite frankly. "I am subject to that kind of thing—ever since that dreadful motor accident when my friend was killed and I was unconscious for a long time. It is not often, but sometimes I seem to forget things completely, I cannot recall what I have been doing. It was a bad accident, that. I have never been able to write properly with a pen since that time. Some strange trouble, which I do not understand. The doctors had a name for it. . . ."

"Agraphia?" suggested Sir Clinton.

"A . . . ? Agraphia? Yes, that is it. I have suffered from agraphia since that disaster. I am learning to write again, but, oh, so slowly. I can just write my own name, now, and it is never twice the same, though I am improving as time goes on."

"Did you suffer any other injury in that accident—a broken limb, or anything of that sort?"

"Oh, no, nothing, except the injury to my head. But that is not disfiguring because it is hidden by my hair."

"You can read?"

"Oh, quite well. But writing is different. I manage best with a typewriter. I can write with it, but slowly. One letter at a time with one finger only."

"You signed nothing for Brenthurst?"

"Oh, no. He attacked me at once when I went back into the room."

Sir Clinton nodded sympathetically.

"Now, I think we have bothered you enough for the present,"

he said. "Just lie down — the nurse will rearrange your pillows — and Inspector Sandrock and I can take a look through your safe, just to see that everything is all right. We may have to take a paper or two, but they will be kept carefully and you need not worry about them."

It was evident that Diana had begun to feel the strain of the interview. She gladly allowed the nurse to rearrange the pillows and take off her bed-jacket and let her lie down. Then, with a little sigh, half weary, half contented, she turned her face away from them and snuggled down with a graceful movement.

Sir Clinton went over to the safe and began to remove its contents, item by item, handing a selection to the Inspector as he went along. At last he finished his examination, and then, as the Inspector withdrew, turned to the nurse, whom he beckoned out into the hall.

"I suppose this state of affairs is the result of what Dr. Winthorpe called Jacksonian epilepsy?" he asked. "Could it be brought on by a physical shock: striking her head on the stone of the terrace or something like that?"

"Dr. Winthorpe thought so, sir," the nurse explained. "The original accident — I mean the motor accident — may have led to pressure of some bone on the brain; and that pressure might be accentuated by a blow on the head. That might bring on symptoms rather like a slight epileptic attack."

"Then she might forget the events immediately before the blow on her head — immediately before it?"

"That's what happens in epilepsy, certainly," the nurse admitted.

"Or she might wake up, recall something that happened, and forget it immediately afterwards and not be able to recall it later? That's what seems to have happened."

"It's quite possible, sir. I had a case once rather like this one; and the patient in it did act more or less as you suggest. But Dr. Winthorpe could give you a better opinion than I can."

"Ah, thanks. I'll ask him, later on. Just one more question, nurse. When you took charge of her, did you wash her face and hands? Or did you just strip off these torn things and put a fresh night-dress on her?"

"No, I didn't give her a wash, sir. She was drowsy, and Dr. Winthorpe thought it was best not to do anything to rouse her, just then. I put her into a fresh night-dress and rubbed some eau-de-Cologne on her forehead. That was all. Would there be any harm in giving her a wash when she wakes up again? It would freshen her up and make her more comfortable, you know."

"Oh, no, there's no harm in that, nurse," Sir Clinton assured her. "Do just what seems best to you. That's all I wanted, thanks."

# CHAPTER VI

# The Gardener

LEAVING THE NURSE to return to her patient, Sir Clinton rang up the police surgeon and then went back to the drawing-room where Sandrock had laid out on the table various things which he had taken from the safe.

"You didn't caution her, sir," said the Inspector, glancing up as the Chief Constable came in. "You're not going to charge her, then? Not that one could look for a conviction, if her tale's true. A jury would call it justifiable homicide, and I don't think they'd be wrong."

"It's early yet to talk about charges," returned Sir Clinton, lightly. "Let's get on with our work. What about this stuff?"

Sandrock put his finger on a packet of bank-notes.

"These should go back into the safe, I think, sir. I've noted their numbers. Ten hundreds and four fifties — £1,200 in all."

"Yes, they may as well go back. We've no claim on them."

"And the title-deeds of this house, sir?"

"Oh, put them back, too. There's nothing to prove that they don't belong to her. And I see they're in an envelope with Brenthurst's name stamped on the flap. That certainly helps to confirm her tale to some extent. He must have had them in his possession. I'm inclined to agree with her that she's got no money-sense, or she'd have got an overdraft at the bank on the strength of these deeds, instead of applying to a money-lender and paying his idea of proper interest."

"Very good, sir," agreed the Inspector. "I'll put them back. Here's another bit of evidence that fits her yarn, sir."

71

He picked up a red leather case and handed it to Sir Clinton.

"H'm! It's got initials in gold on it, just as she said. A 'D' and a 'J' intertwined. 'Diana' and 'Julian.' That's correct."

"Why 'Julian,' sir? It might be John or James."

"I happen to know that she was engaged to a Julian Lorrimore. He was killed in that motor accident she told us about. Have you got that snide pendant that was found in Brenthurst's pocket? Thanks. Yes, it fits into this case neatly enough. That seems all right. Whether she told us the whole truth or not, I don't know; but so far things seem to hold together. What else have you got? Oh, yes, that letter our men found in his pocket. Let's have a glance at it."

Sandrock picked up a paper and gave it to Sir Clinton, handling it gingerly.

"We may want to get the finger-prints on it, sir," he suggested.

"To confirm that Brenthurst has actually received it? I've no doubt about that. But you're quite right. We may as well be certain. Now let's see what it says. It's dated the day before yesterday. Typed by somebody who's not much of an expert, to judge from some overprinting of letters here and there. The signature's very scrawly, just like a child's. That fits her story also."

He read out the letter in a deliberate voice: —

"DEAR MR. BRENTHURST,

"I cannot pay what you ask just now. I am short of money again and want you to lend me some more. Come here at one o'clock tomorrow night to discuss things and I am sure we shall find a way out which will satisfy you. Miss G will be away that night so I shall be all alone. The maids leave here after dinner, but I enclose the key of the back entrance so that you can get into the garden. Don't tell anyone you are coming here as I don't want anyone to get to know that I am hard up. I am sure we can come to some arrangement which will satisfy you *in every way* and give you something I know you have been wanting for a long time. Bring about £1,200 in notes of £50 and £100 and bring also all my notes of hand and the things you took as security before, as I want to start afresh.

"Yours,

"D. TERAMOND."

"Whatever she had in mind when she wrote that, sir, it's plain what Brenthurst read into it," commented the Inspector. "After getting a note like that, it's no wonder he played the game he did."

"Injudiciously worded, certainly," Sir Clinton agreed. "She has only herself to thank if people say nasty things. But, if she meant what you're suggesting, why all this Wild West gun-play?"

"Many a man's been lured into a trap by that bait, sir," declared the Inspector in a weighty tone. "She was getting hard-up, and she owed Brenthurst a good fat sum, to judge from these burnt papers in the fire-place. That's a strong motive. She tempted him up here in the small hours. That's down in this note, and she admits she wrote it. Put my gloss on it, and she hoped to drive a bargain with him for payment in kind. She's an attractive little piece, stuffed full of S.A. and ready to use every scrap of it if it serves her ends. Even in the state she's in just now, she was doing her best to put the come-hither on the two of us with her eyes and her twists and squirms and all the rest of it. But for all her S.A., I don't think Brenthurst would have paid as high a price as all that. So her scheme must have fallen through if she tried it. But she had another string to her bow, and that was to play the hand out on the lines of the tale she laid off to us just now. She could turn the cheetah loose on him, and if it killed him . . . well, that was a pity, of course, but no blame of hers. The pistol-play would make it seem more likely."

"Then why wasn't his body found in the garden?"

"You have me there, sir," confessed Sandrock, frankly. "But maybe she thought that if it was found on the road, we'd not be able to bring anything home to her. *Could* we have proved that she'd anything to do with it at all, if it hadn't been for the cheetah?"

"It might have been difficult," Sir Clinton conceded easily. "But the cheetah was there, so there's no good supposing what things might have looked like if it hadn't been there."

"I can't think why she didn't call it off and bring it into the house again," said the Inspector. "That would have been the sensible thing to do."

"Evidently you haven't studied cheetahs," said the Chief Constable. "When I was a youngster, I was told that when cheetahs are used for hunting in India, the only way to get them away from their prey is to offer them a nice bowl of fresh blood. Probably Miss Teramond hadn't such a thing handy at the moment."

"But she may not have known it would be so hard to call off, sir."

"More than likely," Sir Clinton admitted. "But, even so, I don't see why the cheetah should have dragged Brenthurst out on to the road at all, if it pounced on him in that side-alley. But there's something else. How do you fit that sham pendant into the affair?"

"You have me there, sir," the Inspector admitted frankly. "I don't know what to make of that. The likeliest notion is that she palmed it off on him instead of the real one. He'd know no better. He wasn't an expert in jewels, I suppose. I'd have been in the same boat myself, if she'd played that game on me."

"But why not have given him the real pendant and told some tale about how he had robbed her of it? Then she'd have got it back with no trouble, after all this business was squared up — assuming that she isn't hanged. No one could deny that it was her property. It was a well-known stone, in a small way. And, remember, there isn't a scrap of paper to prove that he made a fresh loan, if by any chance she chooses to deny what she'd said to us in the other room."

"I give it up, sir," said Sandrock, ruffling his hair with an air of perplexity. "Unless it was some stunt to pretend that the real stone had been stolen, somehow, and so getting the insurance people to pay up for it. It was insured, I suppose? It must have been. No one would keep a thing of that value without insuring it."

"It *was* insured, I believe. At any rate, it was valued for insurance purposes. But we needn't bother about that for the present. What concerns us now is how Brenthurst came by his end. I've just been ringing up our surgeon. He's made a rough examination of the body and he agrees with me that the bullet in the lung wouldn't cause immediate death. In fact, Brenthurst might have recovered from that, with good luck."

"I had a look at the body myself, sir, while it was out there in the ambulance. There's not much doubt about how he died, so far as I can see. That cheetah fairly tore his throat out."

Sir Clinton made a very slight gesture of impatience.

"Do you know, Inspector, I think that cheetah has been a very over-worked animal. Just consider what we're expected to believe about it. First of all, it rescues Miss Teramond from Brenthurst's clutches. Then it pursues him into that side-alley, and mauls him severely, if one may judge from the quantity of blood the Sergeant found there. It then, for no conceivable reason, drags the body out of the garden to the road, thoughtfully closing the gate behind it. Then it settles down to tear out Brenthurst's gizzard, *after neatly cutting his throat with a knife of some sort.* Really, it sounds too good to be true."

"Cutting his throat with a knife, sir?" ejaculated the Inspector in amazement.

"Just so. You didn't examine the wound closely, did you? Took it for granted that he died from the cheetah's teeth? It certainly did make a terrible mess of his throat. But when I looked at it, I found one incision — the police surgeon agrees with me; I've rung him up — just beyond the area of tearing. It wasn't more than half an inch long, but no teeth ever made a cut like that. You may take it from me, Inspector, that Brenthurst's throat was cut with a knife or a razor. That was what killed him. It was after that that the cheetah got in its work and concealed the throat-cutting by all the tearing it did. Cheetahs can be trained to do tricks, I believe; but I never heard of one that could use a knife so neatly as all that."

Sandrock was silent for a moment or two, evidently turning this fresh idea over in his mind.

"Then you think he was killed down in the side-alley, sir?"

"It seems possible," said Sir Clinton, cautiously. "There's other evidence pointing in the same direction, but we needn't bother about it just now. Just pass me the letter of invitation, please."

Sandrock handed it over; and the Chief Constable held up the paper between his eyes and the electric light pendant.

"That's not very clever," he commented, passing the sheet back to the Inspector, who held it up in his turn. "Look at the sentence beginning: 'Come here . . .' See anything peculiar?"

"There's been an erasure, hasn't there, sir? The paper's a shade thinner at the word 'one.' I didn't notice it before. It doesn't show up by reflected light; but it's clear when you look through it."

"And the rubbing-out was done with an eraser-shield, because it doesn't extend beyond the three letters. What do you make of that?"

"Somebody's altered it, sir, or else the typist made a slip and had to put it right."

"Assuming that it's a deliberate alteration, does it suggest anything to you?"

"Well, sir," said the Inspector, evidently not catching Sir Clinton's drift, "I suppose somebody wanted to change the hour."

"How many hours have only three letters in their names? One, two, six, and ten: that's the lot. Six o'clock won't fit, for the context shows that the hour was after dinner. So far as Mrs. Grundy goes, there's not much difference between one and two o'clock in the morning. One's as bad as the other, as a calling-hour for a man on a lone damsel. It wouldn't have been worth rubbing out 'two' just to put 'one' in its place. My reading is that originally it read 'ten,' which fits 'after dinner' in the context. And you remember she told us that she'd waited for him until midnight and then given up hope of his coming. Now let's compare the type. That's her machine over yonder."

He sat down before the typewriter, slipped a sheet of paper into it, and wrote the sentence beginning with "Come here . . ." He made a rapid comparison between the type of the original and that of his own copy, which he then handed to Sandrock.

"Same type in both, so far as cursory inspection goes," he pointed out.

"It may have been just a slip," suggested the Inspector. "She told us she wasn't very good at typing."

"There's no evidence, one way or the other," admitted Sir Clinton, cheerfully. "Now I think we'd better have a chat with this resident gardener."

He stepped out on the terrace. The sky was almost cloudless, and the moon, though sinking in the west, still threw its light over the garden. Sir Clinton halted and looked at the landscape.

"Very pretty," he commented, "with those cornfields and that little lake down yonder, overshadowed by the trees. We'll lose sight of all that when we go down from this terrace, I suppose."

He stooped and examined the body of the cheetah at the head of the stairway.

"Jennings evidently did a good bit of shooting there," he said, after a short inspection. "If he hadn't, we'd probably have been a Sergeant short this morning. It's a powerful brute, by the look of it. And yet, somehow, I can't see it dragging Brenthurst's body all that distance."

"Then you don't think Miss Teramond could have done that, either, sir?" queried Sandrock. "She's no Amazon."

"You never can tell what a human being is capable of," retorted the Chief Constable. "Given sufficient stimulation of the nerves, some people can do physical feats that would make one open one's eyes. It's as well not to be too ready to shut out possibilities, even if they don't seem over-probable. Now, we'll go along and see this gardener. You'll do most of the talking, Inspector, if you please. He ought to be able to tell us something."

"I'm not keen on hearing about other people's dreams, sir," said Sandrock, sardonically. "And he must have been in Dreamland — and pretty far in, too — if he slept through all that's gone on here the last hour or two."

Near the gate, they turned off the main walk into the side-path which led past the gardener's cottage. It was built against the wall of the garden, so that none of the windows commanded the road. Sandrock beat a resounding tattoo on the door. There was a long pause, and he was about to repeat his performance when they heard a nervous voice on the other side of the door.

"Who's there, at this time o' night?" it demanded, rather quaveringly.

"Police!" said the Inspector. "Open that door."

Reluctantly, the door was opened an inch or two so that the gardener could examine his visitors; but evidently he had kept the chain on. The sight of two men in plain clothes apparently did not reassure him.

"How do I know you're police?" he queried, regarding them with unconcealed suspicion through the aperture.

"I'm Inspector Sandrock. Do as you're told."

The tone of authority gained the Inspector's point, and the door was opened wide enough to reveal a man of about fifty, dressed in pyjamas, and with tousled hair.

"What are you coming here bothering for, at this time of night?" he asked, aggrievedly. "And how did you get in? The gate's locked."

"We've come to ask you a thing or two," returned the Inspector unamiably. "Have you heard anything unusual to-night? You aren't deaf, anyhow."

The gardener glanced from one to the other with elusive eyes before making a reply. He seemed to be perturbed, and in doubt as to what he should say.

"I've been asleep," he said, at last. "How would I hear anything?"

The Inspector made a sound which blended impatience and contempt.

"Have you been asleep all night? When did you go to bed?"

"It would be about ten o'clock," answered the gardener, in a doubtful tone. "I've been asleep most of the time."

"What's your name?"

"Henry Sperling."

"Are you alone in this place?"

"Yes, there's no one here but me."

"You were asleep 'most of the time,'" Sandrock pursued. "That means you were awake sometime in the night. Did you hear anything rum when you *were* awake? Come on! Don't dress it up. Out with it!"

Sperling's fingers went up to his neck and he buttoned up the throat of his pyjamas, shivering a little as if he found the night air cold. He seemed to be using the pause for consideration.

"I think I heard voices," he said, reluctantly.

"When was that?"

"I don't just rightly know," declared the gardener, sullenly. "I don't look at my watch when I wake up in the night."

"You've no idea of the time?"

Sperling shook his head doggedly.

"Were they men's voices, or a man and a woman, or what?" demanded the Inspector.

Sperling considered again before replying, but his manner suggested that he was thinking what he should say rather than consulting his memory. Sandrock grew impatient.

"Come on! You're wasting our time, man."

"Well, I was just thinking," protested Sperling. "It was the sound of the voices that woke me up. Leastways, I think it must have been. And when I wake up in the night I'm always a bit muzzy. I don't take things in all at once. And I'd just had a dream. . . ."

"I don't want to hear about your dreams," said the Inspector, with a glance at Sir Clinton.

"But it was a bad dream, the kind of thing you wake up out of in a queer state. . . . I'm trying to explain it to you, if you wouldn't jump down my throat the way you're doing. . . ."

Inspector Sandrock knew that he had a bad temper, but he prided himself on keeping it under control.

"Answer a plain question," he said, with a slight quiver in his voice which spoke as clearly as any expletive could have done. "Was it men you heard? Or what?"

"It sounded like a woman, first of all," Sperling declared,

though in an obviously guarded tone. "She seemed all worked up, as if she was on the edge of highsterricks, so I thought. She said: 'Go! Go at once! Oh, *please* go!' And then a man's voice said, a bit angrily, as if he was giving in against his will: 'Oh, all right!' Like that, you know: 'Oh, all *right!*' "

"Did you recognize either voice?"

Again Sperling seemed to consider before replying.

"No, I don't think so," he admitted at last. "No, I couldn't swear to either of 'em. I was muzzy, with being waked up, just as I said, and I didn't pay much attention, anyhow. And after that I must have gone asleep again."

"You heard nothing more until we came and knocked you up?"

"No," declared the gardener, after an even longer pause for thought. "I heard nothing at all beyond what I've told you."

Sir Clinton had been looking the man up and down very deliberately; and the Inspector, who had seen that kind of examination made before, drew the inference that the Chief Constable was no more friendly to this witness than the Inspector was himself.

"You'd better be careful, my good fellow," said Sir Clinton, with scepticism written large on his face. "You'll be on oath, later on, and it won't pay you to shuffle then, I warn you. Just think again."

They waited for half a minute, but Sperling maintained his silence.

"Nervous, aren't you?" said the Chief Constable, abruptly. "I see your left knee quivering. You're not a courageous person, it seems. Now I'm going to suggest to you that you *did* hear something in the night, but you decided it was no business of yours, so you put your head under the blankets instead of getting up. Is that correct? If not, then we'll want to know the real reason for this quivering-frog performance of yours. Better be careful, Sperling. We can see you're not exactly brave, by the look of you. If you *did* hear something more, and acted out of cowardice, you'd better own up to that. You'll not surprise us. But it *would* surprise me very much indeed if I were asked to believe this tale of yours. Now tell us the plain truth for a change."

Sperling looked helplessly to and fro, as if seeking inspiration but finding none. At last he evidently decided to take the Chief Constable's advice.

"I did hear some shots," he confessed, shifting nervously from one foot to the other and evading the eyes of his questioners. "But what good would it have done anybody if I'd gone out asking for trouble?"

"None whatever, I imagine," said Sir Clinton, icily. "So we're getting the truth at last, after all this shuffling. Don't try any more of it, please. It wastes my time. You heard shots, you say. Now tell us exactly what happened, stage by stage. I've no doubt it made a strong impression on you."

"I couldn't help it, sir," Sperling protested, almost whimpering with the disgrace of his confession. "I'm built that way, sir. I've not got the . . . the . . ."

"Guts," interjected the Inspector, helpfully. "Cut that out. Tell us your tale."

"Well, the first thing I heard was Miss Teramond giving a kind of a scream, if you could call it that. . . ."

"Perhaps I could," Sir Clinton assured him, courteously, "but I'd like to hear more about it first. Was it a long scream or a short one, or what?"

"It was shortish," returned Sperling, gravely. "Sort of angry and surprised-like. Then I heard a couple of bangs. Not very loud, they were, and they seemed to me to come from the house."

"Two reports? No more?"

"There may have been three or four, sir. I didn't count. I was all shook up, being awakened up out of a dream with that."

"H'm! You knew Miss Teramond was alone?"

Sperling made no pretence of misunderstanding the underlying meaning.

"Yes, I did," he retorted, angrily. "But I'm paid as a gardener and not for doing copper's work. Burglary's for the police, isn't it?"

"Precisely," admitted the Chief Constable. "That's why we're asking these questions. What happened next?"

"I really can't remember, sir," Sperling admitted, frankly. "It's all getting a bit mixed up in my memory. I wouldn't swear to the order of things. It's like a bad dream, all muddled up."

"Very sad," said the Chief Constable, unsympathetically. "We quite understand. You were in a blue funk. Still, you can tell us what you heard, even if you can't put it into proper sequence. The bedclothes can't have shut out everything."

"I heard some bangs," Sperling admitted. "Louder than the first lot, they were, by a long way."

"And the cheetah?"

"Yes, I heard it snarling, somewhere close by, very ferocious-like. I never trusted that beast, for all it went about as if butter wouldn't melt in its mouth. But these snarls made my flesh creep, they were so wicked."

"Did you hear it once only, or twice, or what?"

Sperling rubbed his hand on his brow in evident perplexity. His recollections were evidently completely disordered.

"I really can't remember which things came first, sir," he pleaded. "I know they all happened, all the ones I've told you about; but when I try to put them in the right order it just beats me. I did hear the cheetah more than once. And I do remember, too, that I heard voices at the gate. That must have been the police, from some of the words I caught. It's not that I'm trying to hide anything, sir. It's just what I tell you; I don't remember what order things happened in."

"Well, let's get what we can," said Sir Clinton, patiently. "You heard the following noises which you're quite sure about. Miss Teramond crying out. Some shots from a small pistol. More shots, louder than the others . . ."

"The loud ones were after the first lot," interrupted Sperling. "I do remember that, sir."

"You're improving," said the Chief Constable. "Then voices which you took to be the police at the gate. The cheetah snarling at intervals. You didn't hear any steps? No, these sanded paths muffle the sound. And a woman's voice saying 'Go' and so forth, and a man answering her. That's all? No, one more point. You say the first shots weren't loud. Have you heard anything like them before?"

"Oh, yes, I have, sir," Sperling affirmed, evidently glad to answer. "They were like the noise that Miss Teramond's pistol makes. I've heard her and Miss Garfield shooting with it in the garden now and again, just for fun. It was it that I heard, now I come to think of it."

"Ah! Then they did a little pistol-practice now and again, did they?"

"Yes, sir. They used to put up a cardboard target in one of the alleys and fire at it. I didn't like that myself. I always used to take care to be somewhere else, when they started that game. Miss Garfield was pretty good, but Miss Teramond put her shots all over the place. Dangerous, it was, for anyone near about."

"Then I don't blame you for keeping out of the way," confessed the Chief Constable. "Now another question, Sperling. When did you lock this gate last night?"

"Seven o'clock, sir. That's the time I always lock up. If I have to go out myself after that, I take my key with me."

"You'd better hand over that key to me," interjected Sandrock. "Get it now."

Sperling went into the cottage and returned with his key which he handed to the Inspector.

"I noticed a garage attached to the house," said Sir Clinton. "Does Miss Teramond keep a chauffeur?"

"No, sir."

"Who cleans her car?"

"I do, sir. It's part of my job. I don't drive, though. Miss Teramond can drive, sir; but after that motor accident she had, she doesn't care about it, and generally it's Miss Garfield that does any driving that's wanted."

"Is the car there just now? What's the make?"

"No, sir. Miss Garfield's away for the night, and she took the car with her. She told me to be sure to fill up the tank and she left me to feed her white rabbits, too. It's a Riley car."

"When did she leave?" demanded Sir Clinton.

"I couldn't rightly say, sir, not to a minute. All I know is that the car was gone when I happened to pass the garage about four in the afternoon, so she must have gone before then."

"Miss Garfield's fond of animals?"

"Yes, sir. She was in a rare bait about one of her pet rabbits that came to a bad end; very put out indeed, she was. The cheetah got it. I saw it eating the carcase, making a nasty purring noise over it, too. I kept out of its way, it looked so cross at being disturbed. Yesterday morning, that was."

"Where do you keep your gardening tools?" demanded Sir Clinton, dismissing the rabbit question.

"In the pagoda, up the garden, sir. It's central, and nobody uses it for anything else."

"Miss Teramond's fond of gardening?"

"Not gardening really, sir. Neither of them care much for that. But Miss Teramond's fond of flowers. She cuts all she wants for the house herself. Does it every day."

"You'd better dress yourself," said the Chief Constable. "Don't leave the premises. We may want you again."

Much to Sperling's relief, he gave a curt nod of dismissal and moved away, followed by the Inspector. When they were out of earshot of the cottage, Sir Clinton turned to Sandrock.

"Rather hopeless as a witness, I'm afraid," he commented. "No good blaming him for that. Evidently he was in a blue funk last night, and that doesn't tend to make one observe carefully or remember properly. But he's a shifty customer at the best."

"He's all that," agreed the Inspector, who did not share Sir Clinton's latitude of judgement.

"I wonder what he's keeping back," mused the Chief Constable. "Something that's important to him, I imagine, from his general make-up. Whether it's important to us is another question. We'll come across it later on, no doubt; and then we can screw it out of him."

# CHAPTER VII

## The Pagoda

"What do you make of these voices that Sperling says he heard, sir?" queried the Inspector. "The man and the woman arguing, I mean."

"Not much," answered the Chief Constable, frankly. "Or perhaps too much. Perhaps the woman was Miss Teramond. Perhaps she wasn't. Possibly the man was Brenthurst. Or again, it may have been somebody else. That doesn't take us much further forward, does it?"

"It doesn't, sir," admitted the Inspector with a faint grin. "But it sounds like Brenthurst and the Teramond woman. All that stuff about: 'Go, please go!' is just what she might have said if she was trying to get rid of him."

"But if Sperling heard it, they must have been near the cottage when they spoke; and that hardly tallies with her story," objected Sir Clinton.

"Sperling was all mixed up about the order in which things happened, sir," countered Sandrock. "That bit of dialogue may have come on before the shooting began at all. He and she may have taken a turn in the garden before they got down to business. Her memory's just as much a dud as Sperling's is, if it comes to that."

"Then you think it was some other woman's voice, sir?"

"I don't think anything about it at all, just now," retorted Sir Clinton. "Let's gather a few more facts, first. The light's growing brighter. We can have a look at the tracks in that sanded valley."

Starting with their backs to the pagoda, they moved on towards the terrace, and soon came to the frontier of the swept area of the avenue.

"This is more interesting," commented Sir Clinton, as they reached the uneffaced zone. "Here's Brenthurst, first of all, going up to the house on his arrival. Then here are his tracks in the reverse direction, with a longer stride. Evidently he was on the run when he made those prints. There's the spoor of the cheetah, running towards us. No marks of its return journey, of course, because Burford and Jennings saw it slinking about amongst the bushes and not on the path. Then there's another set of tracks, evidently Miss Teramond in her bedroom slippers. She came out and then went back again to the terrace, where our men found her. That's plain enough. Notice anything else, Inspector? No? Nor do I. We seem to have seen all the sights here. Now let's cast back to the pagoda and see what happened to Brenthurst."

They turned about and regained the *rond-point*. Brenthurst's tracks were obliterated there, but started afresh along the side-alley.

"Only his trail, and the cheetah's," Sir Clinton pointed out. "Ah! here's the place where his throat was cut, evidently, to judge from the pool of blood. You'd notice that there was no blood-trail up to this point. These shots didn't lead to any violent gush, obviously. Probably any flow from the wounds was only enough to soak his clothes and not drip down to the ground. But there's no mistake about bloodshed here. Plenty of gore on the grass."

"Whoever did it must have walked on the grass, sir," said Sandrock, who had no false shame in discovering the obvious.

"Probably whoever it was walked on the path first of all," Sir Clinton pointed out. "Because the sweeping-up operation has been continued for a yard or two down this alley, if you notice. I think I begin to see what may have happened, Inspector. But I'm not going to risk my reputation on it, at present. Let's have a look at this pagoda, since it's handy."

They returned to the cleared space, crossed it, and entered the door of the pagoda, which faced towards the gate. It was a mere toy building, exiguous in floor-space, with windows on the house side and the door opposite, facing the gate. Various gardening implements were stacked in the corners and also under the cramped little staircase which led to the upper story. A table occupied the centre of the room. The tiny windows admitted only a dim light at that hour in the morning, and Sir Clinton switched on his flash-lamp. Its beam fell first across the table-top strewn with odds and ends: a small gardening basket, a brass syringe, some seed envelopes, a pruning-knife, a ball of tarred twine, some raffia, and a pair of leather gardening-gloves. Then, travelling farther, it lit up a couple of birch besoms resting against the wall in one corner.

"There you are, sir," said the Inspector, pointing at them.

Sir Clinton nodded and continued to swing his light hither and thither. Finally he turned the beam on the table-top and began to examine the objects lying there. He picked up the pruning-knife very gingerly and examined it with the lamp close up. Then he rubbed his finger-tip cautiously on the haft and held his digit in the light of the lamp for the Inspector to see.

"Blood, sir?" ejaculated Sandrock, staring at the cruel-looking curved blade. "Why, then, that must be the thing that cut Brenthurst's throat!"

"Wait a little, wait a little," advised Sir Clinton. "Don't let's be too hasty, Inspector. First of all, we must be sure that it *is* blood. One of the hospital pathologists will be able to tell us about that. Second, from what I saw of Brenthurst's throat, it was cut with a very sharp knife. A gardening-knife like this, if it's been much in use lately, might well be too blunt to make a clean cut. Let's try it on a bit of paper."

Handling the tool with care to avoid finger-prints, he made the experiment, and found that the blade was almost razor-sharp.

He put down the knife and picked up one of the gardening-gloves.

"This looks like blood, too," he reported. "This glove's soaked with it."

"Oh!" ejaculated Sandrock, suddenly enlightened. "Now I see why you asked the nurse if she'd washed that woman's hands. I heard you through the open door, sir. Of course, if she had these gloves on, there might be no blood on her hands at all, even after the throat-cutting. Was that what you had in mind, sir?"

"I knew someone had cut his throat," answered Sir Clinton. "When I looked at her hands, there was no blood on them, not even round the edges of the nails, where anything of that sort sticks, even after a rough wash. Still, it was on the cards that the nurse had given her a thorough wash, so I asked about that, just to make sure. And there's another bit of evidence, but we needn't bother about that for the moment. We may not have come to the end of our discoveries here, yet. Let's hunt about and see if anything more turns up. Just poke round and see what you can find."

They set to work, shifting the gardening implements and peering into corners with the help of their flash-lamps. Suddenly Sandrock gave an exclamation of triumph.

"Got it! Look here, sir! Here's something."

He came to the table and laid on it a crumpled scrap of cambric stained ominously red. Opening it out, he disclosed a small embroidered monogram in one corner.

"There's a 'T' on it," he pointed out, bringing his lamp closer. "That'll be for Teramond, sir."

"The other letter's a 'D,'" said the Chief Constable. "I happen to know that her first name's Diana. That seems to fit, nicely. Spread it out flat, Inspector, please."

Sandrock obeyed, and the Chief Constable examined the scrap of fabric minutely.

"Useful enough for a nose-drip, but no good if you had a streaming cold, sir," commented Sandrock rather disdainfully. "I can't think why women carry rags like these."

"I don't think she had even a nose-drip, as you describe it," said Sir Clinton with a smile. "The folds are quite sharp still. And if she'd got a blow that made her nose bleed, there would be a good deal more blood on the fabric. What do you make of the blood-stain?"

"Might be the portrait of a wood-louse, sir, and quite a good likeness, too," said the Inspector, sardonically. "But I guess it came from somebody wiping the blade of that knife, and not making a good job of it."

"A very poor job, I agree," returned Sir Clinton, with a glance at the steel. "But you can't expect thoroughness from somebody who's just committed a murder, can you? Some slight agitation must be natural in such circumstances. Well, never mind. It's always an exhibit to show to the jury, if we get that length. Keep it flat, Inspector, please. The fluid's still moist and we don't want the markings to get overlaid with fresh ones due to refolding. Here's a paper bag that will serve. Meanwhile, I'll have a look round upstairs, just in case there's something there; though I don't expect it."

He returned in a moment or two.

"Nobody on the premises," he reported.

"But the brooms are there in the corner," objected Sandrock, "and all the space round this shanty has been brushed smooth. How did a man get away, sir, after putting the broom back in place? He'd have to leave his prints on the sand in going over it."

"Why assume that Miss Teramond could afford only two birch besoms? My own gardener buys them for a shilling or less, I believe. Obviously our departed friend took a third broom with him and swept up his tracks tidily from outside the circle. If we can find his besom, we'll have an idea which way he went. We may as well set about it now, if you've finished."

For a time they searched the formal gardens without result, until the Inspector was lucky enough to discover the missing besom thrust in among some bushes beside one of the paths. With that as a guide, they went farther in the same direction and ended up in a little orchard which bounded the Fountain Court grounds near Sperling's cottage.

"Nobody here, evidently," said the Chief Constable, after a rapid survey. "But here's something suggestive."

He pointed to a garden ladder which stood propped against the wall of the grounds not far from the cottage.

"He's got away, then!" ejaculated Sandrock in a disappointed tone.

"Not necessarily," objected the Chief Constable. "Certainly not since Burford came on the scene. That road outside has been patrolled by our men ever since then. And before that, the cheetah was there; and you know what kind of reception it gave Sprattley. I doubt if anyone would have cared to drop down from the top of that wall in front of it. No, Inspector, that ladder belongs to another part of the story, unless I'm much mistaken. We'll see in good time. Meanwhile, I think we'll have another little chat with Sperling. I've thought of a question or two more for him."

The gardener was dressed by this time, but he had not troubled to shave. He seemed still very nervous and was obviously perturbed by this second visit from the police.

"I noticed a pruning-knife lying on the table in that pagoda," Sir Clinton began. "Do you use it?"

"Me? No, sir. It's one that Miss Teramond keeps for herself, to cut flowers with. She comes out every morning after breakfast and cuts them for the house. You'd notice the basket she puts them in. It's on the table, too."

"These things get blunted. Who sharpens that knife when it loses its edge?"

"I do, sir. I've got a little grindstone for that kind of work."

"When did you sharpen it last?"

"Yesterday morning, sir. Miss Teramond brought it to me and complained that I'd forgotten to put an edge on it. That wasn't so. I'd sharpened it just a couple of days before that. She must have been mishandling it, or something; for when she brought it to me yesterday morning, it wouldn't have cut cheese. As blunt as blunt, it was. I tried it, just to see; for I thought she must be making a fuss about nothing, seeing I'd sharpened it already. But it was blunt enough when she handed it over to me."

"Now about that cheetah, you don't seem to have liked it. Had it any spite against you particularly?"

"No, sir. But it was an unreliable beast and I never liked it. It had its likes and dislikes, I know that. Some people seemed to get friendly with it, straight off. Others, it couldn't bear. Just the way dogs are, sir."

"Have you managed to remember anything more about last night?"

"Well, sir, I do seem to remember something more. At one time I heard a man's voice. In a bit of a state, he was, calling for help. But that stopped, all of a sudden, just as if you'd turned off a tap."

"You can't remember exactly where that fitted into the rest of the sounds?"

"No, sir, not exactly, except that it was after the first set of shots. I do remember that."

"Can you tell me anything about any strangers who were about the premises last night?"

The gardener evaded Sir Clinton's eye, and he hesitated for some seconds before answering.

"No, sir. I don't know anything about strangers being here, except what I've told you about voices. I was in bed, you see."

"There's a ladder propped up against the wall over yonder. Do you know anything about it? Were you using it yesterday?"

"No, sir."

"Where's it kept, usually?"

"Up alongside the greenhouses, sir. You can see the roofs of them over yonder."

"What's grown in them?"

"Grapes, mainly, sir. Tomatoes, too. And some flowers."

"Quite a lot of glass," said the Chief Constable. "You must get more grapes than they can use in the house here. What happens to the rest?"

"Miss Teramond sells them to the shops, sir."

"Apples, too? I see you've got quite a decent orchard."

"Yes, sir, she sells the extra apples."

"When do the maids come back in the morning?"

"About seven o'clock, sir, usually. They ought to be here quite soon, now."

"Well, stay indoors, Sperling. And don't try to talk to anyone in the meanwhile. When do your mates turn up?"

"Half-past eight, sir. May I talk to them?"

"No, not to them either. I'll see you're not disturbed. By the way, Sperling, have you any family? Anyone living here with you?"

"No, sir. I'm a widower, and my daughter's in service. She's housemaid to old Mrs. Brenthurst, over at Sunnyhill on the Hindon road. I don't see much of her."

"Inspector Sandrock will jot down some notes about what you've told us. You can sign them later on, when he's shown them to you. That's all for the present."

The two officials moved away towards the hydrangea avenue. Sir Clinton glanced at the sky and then over the grounds.

"It's light enough now to have a thorough search of these gardens," he decided, turning to the Inspector. "No one can have got away, with our patrols all round the place. You'd better give the orders."

Sandrock walked down to the gate and gave instructions to Sergeant Burford. But as he returned to rejoin the Chief Constable, he was surprised to see, approaching down the path between the hydrangeas, the figure of a woman.

# CHAPTER VIII

# The Woman in the Garden

"Know her?" asked Sir Clinton, with his eyes on the woman.

"No, sir, I don't recognize her."

"Nor do I. You'd better do the talking, I think."

"Very good, sir," agreed Sandrock.

He glanced at the approaching figure as though measuring the quality of an antagonist; and as she drew nearer he docketed in his mind her outward characteristics. Just a shade over the average height for a woman, and with a litheness in her walk which spoke of muscles in good condition and well under control. Mature, evidently; might be in the late forties or early fifties, but no middle-aged spread about her waist. Coat and skirt, walking shoes, gauntlet gloves. Hair still dark, marked eyebrows, aquiline features, good teeth, and strong chin. Must have been uncommon-looking when she was young; and still handsome, with character written clearly on her face. Not easy to upset, by the look of her. A cool card, in fact. Just as well they had gone over those tracks in the sand before she turned up, for she was walking down the middle of the path as if the place belonged to her.

She came up to them and was about to pass by with the indifference she might have shown on meeting two strangers in her way while walking in a public park, when Sandrock stepped forward with a gesture.

"I'm afraid you can't pass, madam," he explained. "We have to ask everyone for an account of themselves."

"Really? And who are you, please?"

93

She seemed perfectly composed, rather too composed, the Inspector thought. He noted mentally that she had a pleasant, soft voice, and a nice intonation. That meant nothing. Plenty of criminals spoke nicely with good accents.

"The police are in charge here, madam. These are my orders and I've got to carry them out."

"But who are you?" she repeated, with a faintly ironical look. "I never saw you before. You may be a policeman, but you're not in uniform."

"My men down at the gate are in uniform," Sandrock pointed out. "I'm Inspector Sandrock."

"And . . . ?" she queried, glancing at Sir Clinton.

"And the Chief Constable," Sandrock explained, curtly.

"But what are you doing in my friend's garden?"

Sandrock's temper, never of the best, was fraying under these delays. One might think that it was she who was setting up to cross-examine *him*, no less! The initial good impression of her faded out of his mind.

"I must ask what you're doing here, in a private garden, at this hour in the morning," he said in a minatory tone.

"Surely that's a matter for Miss Teramond, since it's her garden," retorted the stranger, coolly. "Has she made any complaint?"

Sandrock realized that he had been manœuvred into a false position. Obviously he was not shining; and the Chief Constable was looking on. That rubbed away a little more of his temper. Why couldn't this woman answer a plain question? Suspicious, that seemed. Then it occurred to him that the waste of time might not be accidental but deliberate on her part, though he could not guess why she should be procrastinating in that manner.

"What's your name, please?" he demanded, with a certain roughness.

"Fairfoot is my name, and I live at 81 Acacia Drive."

"Christian name?"

"Cora. Do you wish to detain me? Or is that sufficient?"

"I'm afraid it isn't," said Sandrock, irritably. "You must tell us what you're doing here at this time in the morning. It's hardly a usual calling hour," he ended, sarcastically.

Something in the last sentence seemed to amuse her, for she smiled. A rather thin-lipped smile, the Inspector thought.

"The calling hours at Miss Teramond's *are* rather strange," she commented, cynically. Then, with an apparent access of frankness, she continued, "You want to know why I'm here? I don't mind telling you. I came here to watch a man who was paying a visit to Miss Teramond at one of these peculiar calling hours. He's my cousin; Brenthurst is his name. I've my own reasons for being interested in his doings. Does that satisfy you?"

"Hardly, I'm afraid," said the Inspector, bluntly. "You see, Mrs. Fairfoot, there's been some rather bad trouble here, in the night; and if you were on the spot, you must know a good deal more than you've told us. You'll need to give us the whole story. Nothing less is any use to us."

Cora Fairfoot gave him a calculating glance. Then she looked at her wrist-watch.

"It won't keep until later in the day?" she asked. "I've been awake all night and I'm feeling rather tired and sleepy."

"No," returned Sandrock. "I'd rather have it now, before you have a chance to forget the details. Some of them may be important."

"There's something in that," Cora Fairfoot conceded, sensibly. "I don't mind, then. But I'd rather sit down. There are seats in the tennis-pavilion, or we could go up to the house, if you like. The pavilion's nearest. Shall we go there?"

"Very good," the Inspector acquiesced.

They made their way to the pavilion in silence. Sandrock drew up three chairs round a little table on the verandah overlooking the courts, placed his note-book before him, and began his questioning.

"First of all, how did you come to know that Mr. Brenthurst would be coming here last night?" he demanded, screwing down the lead of his pencil.

Cora Fairfoot put her hand into the pocket of her coat and drew out a piece of paper which she handed to Sandrock. For the benefit of Sir Clinton, he read out the contents of the note: —

*"Brenthurst is coming to Fountain Court at 1 A.M. He has the key of the garden gate. Susan is going away for the night. Will you come over and wait in the pagoda just in case your help is needed?* There's no signature, sir," he added, passing the paper to Sir Clinton.

The Chief Constable studied it for a moment or two, then compared it with another paper which he took from his pocket.

"It's written with that typewriter we saw," he said, though with no show of interest. "There's a spot of dirt in the loop of the 'a' and another in the 'e,' and that's good enough to go on with." He passed the note back to the Inspector, and then turned to Cora Fairfoot. "Have you any idea who wrote that note?"

"Miss Teramond, I believe."

"It's not signed," Sir Clinton reminded her.

"No, it isn't. But quite often she forgot to sign her notes, or else she couldn't. She can use a typewriter, I know; but she can't do much with a pen since she had that motor accident. The doctors have some special name for that trouble . . . agg-something-or-other. But I know the look of her typescript, so I'd no difficulty in guessing who wrote the thing."

"I understand," the Chief Constable said. "Now, how did this note reach you? By post, or handed in, or how?"

"By post," Cora Fairfoot explained. "It came yesterday afternoon."

Sir Clinton, with a glance, brought the Inspector again into play.

"Why didn't Miss Teramond ring you up about it, instead of writing?" he demanded. "Are you on the phone?"

"Oh, of course. But how can I tell why she wrote instead of phoning? Wouldn't it be easier to ask her instead of me? Perhaps she felt that it was hardly the kind of thing she wanted to talk about over the wire."

"Humph!" said Sandrock, with an air of scepticism which was

not quite convincing. "Let's get on. Now, how long have you known Miss Teramond?"

"Since she settled down here. Say eighteen months or so."

"How did you make her acquaintance?"

Cora Fairfoot glanced at him rather wearily, as if to suggest that surely this was hardly necessary.

"My son introduced us. He's a house-agent and had Fountain Court on his books when it was taken. Miss Teramond knew no one in the neighbourhood when she settled down here, and I did my best to be of use to her."

"You got to know her well," said the Inspector, "else she wouldn't have sent you a note like this. Now, can you tell me anything about her, who she is, where she came from, and so forth? She must have told you something about herself."

Cora Fairfoot did not reply immediately. She seemed to be turning things over in her mind before answering the Inspector's questions.

"She did talk, pretty freely, from time to time," she began, "but I paid very little attention to most of it and I've forgotten a good deal, I'm afraid. I think she's French originally, West Indian French. Is there a place called Guadeloupe? Well, I've heard her mention it when she was talking about her childhood. Later on, she was in the States. I've heard her mention New Orleans, Santa Fe, and San Francisco, and some other places in America. Her father and mother died, and she went on the stage. At least, so she said; but I got an impression that she was more of a music-hall turn than a real actress. Then she came over to England with Miss Garfield. They played together in sketches and that kind of thing, always in the cheaper places, suburban halls and so on. I never heard her mention the name of any of the big Halls. Then she got engaged to some young fool with plenty of money, Lorrimore, I think his name was. They bought Fountain Court and were going to settle down here when he was killed in an accident."

"She was hurt, too?" interjected the Inspector. "Did that leave any effects that you could notice?"

"If you mean scars, no. She got some nervous trouble, though.

She has queer fits of forgetfulness about some things. And she can't write very well, I know. Generally she uses a typewriter."

Cora Fairfoot made a slight gesture towards the typewritten note on the table in illustration of this.

"Just so," the Inspector agreed. "Now what about money? Had she made a fortune on the Halls? Not very likely."

"Not a fortune, certainly," Cora Fairfoot declared. "And she's rather extravagant in some ways. But she's attractive, you know. And an attractive woman needn't be short of money if she knows her way about," she added, cynically.

Up to this point the Inspector had been trying to throw his witness off her guard by putting questions on matters which concerned her only indirectly; but now he judged it time to come to the immediate issue.

"You got this note by post last night," he began, fixing his eyes on Cora Fairfoot's face. "Tell us, please, just what you made of it when you read it."

She smiled with evident amusement before answering.

"I hadn't the slightest doubt about what it meant," she replied. "Mr. Brenthurst happens to be my cousin. I know his reputation where women are concerned. So, apparently, does Miss Teramond. Naturally she would feel . . . well, shall we say happier? . . . if she knew that a third party was within call when her visitor turned up. In her shoes I'd have felt much the same, I know. But why she asked him to come at that hour I simply cannot make out," she concluded, with obvious frankness.

"So you were prepared to put yourself to some trouble in the matter, though she's not an old friend of yours?"

"It certainly amused me to put a spoke in his wheel, if necessary," Cora Fairfoot admitted without hesitation. "I don't owe him anything, either financially or otherwise."

The obvious sneer in this last sentence caught the Inspector's attention.

"You owe him a grudge, perhaps?" he suggested.

"He hasn't treated me well," Cora Fairfoot affirmed. "But has that anything to do with this present affair?"

"You'll have to tell us what you mean," said Sandrock, firmly.

He expected some opposition, but to his surprise she made none.

"It's a matter of common knowledge, and you could find it out for yourself in a very short time," she said, coolly. "So there's no point in my trying to beat about the bush. My cousin seduced me when I was just a girl and then he refused to marry me. Do you suppose it pleases me to see him running after other women? It doesn't. And if I can put a spoke in his wheel, it's only natural that I should do so."

The Inspector glanced at the Chief Constable and was surprised to find that this revelation had produced no effect, so far as he could see. Sir Clinton had picked up the typewritten note and was examining it minutely, as though he had been paying no attention to the dialogue. Inspector Sandrock reflected sourly that Driffield often seemed to know more than he admitted. Probably this was another case of the sort. As for this woman, the job was going to be easier than he had feared when he had found her so damnably cool. "Hell hath no fury . . ." and so on. "Jealousy is as cruel as the grave"; he'd heard that once in church when he was a youngster and had made a note of it. With an urge like that she'd soon part with all the information he wanted. On with the good work.

"So you came over to keep an eye on him?" he asked.

"Just so."

"You live a good way off. How did you get here?"

"On a bicycle."

"Don't you keep a car?"

"When you set out to spy on people, do you send a brass band on in front? Surely not. I wanted something I could hide behind the nearest hedge, and you can't do that with a car, usually. You'll find my bicycle near the gate of the cornfield over there."

Very sensible, Sandrock reflected. Just a shade *too* sensible, though, when one came to think of it. But she was a cool card; no doubt about that.

"You arrived here, then. How did you get into the garden?"

"I came rather ahead of time and waited till Mr. Brenthurst

turned up. I knew the garden gate was kept locked and that he had a key. It said so in that note. If he left it open behind him, I had only to walk in. If not, I'd have got in somehow."

"I don't want to ask one question after another," Sandrock explained. "Perhaps you could go on now and tell me your tale in your own words."

"Certainly, if you wish. I watched Mr. Brenthurst arrive. I was hidden behind the hedge, some distance down the road. I noticed that he didn't lock the gate behind him; and as soon as I'd given him a fair time to get out of my way, I came into the garden myself. He'd left the gate on the latch — closed, but not locked, you know — and I did the same. Then I walked up to the pagoda. I walked on the grass, I think, except where I crossed over to the turf at the start. I suppose I was thinking of going quietly, forgetting that I'd make no sound on the sand, anyhow. When I got to the pagoda, I went inside and closed the door behind me. I was rather afraid of that cheetah which Miss Teramond keeps. I've got a nervous horror of any kind of cat, and it always scared me. Besides, it didn't like me. Miss Teramond always kept it shut up in its den when I came to pay her a visit. So I shut the pagoda door in case it might be prowling about. Then I went over and posted myself at the window that overlooks the terrace. It was a bright moonlight night, you know. I could see things quite clearly, except when a cloud came along."

Inspector Sandrock was very pleased with his change in tactics. This Fairfoot woman was an excellent witness, good pair of eyes, good memory, perfectly cool. Much the best way to let her tell her own tale instead of dragging it out of her bit by bit.

"Yes?" he encouraged her.

"When I got to the window, I saw a light in Miss Teramond's room, and against it the figure of a man, which I took to be Mr. Brenthurst. Miss Teramond was inside the window, stooping down, talking to him through the open sash, I thought. They talked for a few minutes, and then he went along and up on to the terrace, where the French window is. After a minute or two, the light went up in the drawing-room and Miss Teramond let him in through the French window. She was wearing a kimono. That part of the business struck me as . . . well . . . a bit queer. I couldn't quite see why I had been invited there, if you understand me."

"You mean about her being in bed and getting up in her night things to let him in?"

"Well, what do you think yourself about it?" demanded Cora Fairfoot. "Why ask me to come and look at a peep-show of that sort? I couldn't make head or tail of it. Then I began to think it over, and I thought I saw what it meant. Mr. Brenthurst isn't a nice character. He takes a perfect delight in hurting people, if he can do it without any risks. I know that very well. He's done it to me in my time. And this little bit of stage-management might well have been one of his tricks. To get me there, you know, and make me see him making up to another woman. I've still got some pride. I've needed it, at times. And I guessed that this was just a game of his to wound me. She's much younger than I am now, and better-looking, of course. You can guess for yourself how I felt, standing there at the window. I'm not going to make a song about it. I've said enough."

Inspector Sandrock inwardly agreed with her. His interest lay in the domain of events rather than in that of thoughts. The description of Cora Fairfoot's emotions cut no ice with him, as he would have said in his monosyllabic way. All lies, as like as not. She hated Brenthurst. That was clear enough. No need to make a song about it, just as she said herself. Facts were what was wanted here.

"What did you see next?" he demanded in a business-like tone.

"The two of them sat down for a while and talked," Cora Fairfoot continued. "After that Miss Teramond went into her own room for a minute, and came back again. Mr. Brenthurst had got up and was pacing to and fro. When she came in again, he pounced on her. There was a struggle and she screamed as he caught her. Then I heard a pistol go off. . . ."

"How many shots did you hear?" interrupted Sandrock.

"I don't know," Cora Fairfoot admitted frankly. "I didn't count.

Two or three, anyhow. She must have hit Mr. Brenthurst, for he gave a cry or a groan — some kind of noise, anyhow. I was taken aback, for that was the last thing I expected; and I just stood there without thinking of moving. Then I pulled myself together and was going to her assistance, when Mr. Brenthurst let her go and ran out on to the terrace, with her after him. Then the cheetah dashed through the drawing-room, and I stopped where I was. I couldn't bring myself to go into the open with that beast about. It looked terrible, and I was afraid of it. Mr. Brenthurst was running down the path towards the pagoda and I was afraid he'd try to take refuge in it and bring the cheetah in on top of me, so I ran to the door and leaned against it to hold it against anyone forcing their way in. That took me away from the window, and I didn't see what happened next."

"And did he try to get into the pagoda?" interjected Sandrock.

"Yes, he did," answered Cora Fairfoot. "Just when I hoped that he had gone past, I felt the handle turning and rattling, and I had to brace myself hard against the door to keep him out. He cried: 'Let me in! For God's sake, let me in!' I was so terrified of the cheetah that I held fast. And then he must have given up and run away, for the push against the door slackened. Then, almost at once, I heard the cheetah outside. And in a moment or two Mr. Brenthurst gave a horrible gurgling cry. Then I heard the cheetah again, making a sort of purring noise. I didn't dare to go near the windows for fear it might see me; and the sound of it terrified me. So I put my back to the door and covered up my ears and hoped for the best. I knew it was somewhere about. Then I heard it quite close, and the noise it made gradually died away in the distance. So I made up my mind that this was my chance to get away. There was no use staying in the pagoda, because it could have burst in through the window if it wanted to get at me. So I opened the door, looked about me, and slipped out."

"How long did you stay in the pagoda?" asked Sir Clinton.

"I really can't say. It seemed a long time to me; but you know how time seems to drag and ever so much happens when one's in a state of panic. I never thought of looking at my watch, of course. Who would, in a case like that?"

"Please go on," said Sir Clinton.

"I got away quite safely," Cora Fairfoot continued. "I'd remembered a shed near the orchard where I thought I could shut myself in and be out of danger until daylight came, so I made my way towards it."

"You didn't think of going up to the house and shutting yourself up in one of the upper rooms?" asked the Inspector.

"No, indeed I did not," retorted the witness. "For all I knew, the cheetah might have gone back to its den, and it would be ready to pounce on me if I went past its door. I still had some wits about me, you see," she added, with a faint return of her ironical tone.

"And you saw no sign of Miss Teramond?"

"I didn't bother about Miss Teramond," said Cora Fairfoot, candidly. "The cheetah would never harm her; it was fond of her. And she hadn't bothered about me, although she knew it wasn't fond of me and I might be in danger from it. I'm not going to pretend that I cared twopence about her skin, just at that time. She'd landed me into this mess, and my only idea was to get out of it as best I could. I've no desire to pose as a heroine, I assure you."

"You got away, then, towards the orchard?"

"Yes, and I saw nothing of the cheetah after that. But as I came into the orchard I saw two rough-looking men stooping over something on the ground. I couldn't see very well, for a cloud had come over the moon. I was going forward, quite glad to have come across some people who would protect me from that beast. Then I saw they were looking down at the thing that lay between them. I couldn't see it clearly, for the grass is fairly high in that part of the orchard, but it was big and bulky. Then they began to talk. One of them said: 'We'll leave it here.' Then the other one objected and said: 'Not much. Let's get it over the wall. The wheelbarrow's handy and we can get it away all right.' 'Somebody might come along,' said the first one. 'We'd be spotted.' And then the second one gave a nasty laugh, rather low, and said: 'If anyone does come along, I'll out him. That'll teach him to mind his own business.' Then the first man said something about the cheetah, and the second one said: 'Well, we'll go and see if the coast's clear, since you're in such a funk.' And they went away towards the wall of the orchard. These weren't exactly the words they used, but that was the sense of what they said. And I was scared, as much by the manner of one of them — the one who talked about 'outing' anyone interfering with them — as by what he actually said. He evidently meant business; I could guess that from his tone. So I crept away out of the orchard and went to one of the greenhouses. I knew it had a small furnace-room attached to it, and I thought I could take refuge in that, if the cheetah came after me."

"You didn't recognize either of these men?" asked the Inspector.

"No, as I told you, there was a cloud over the moon just then. I could only see them faintly."

"Would you know their voices if you heard them again?"

"I might. I can't say for certain. You see they weren't talking in their ordinary tones. They spoke in a growly undertone; and unless I heard them speaking in the same way I don't think I could identify them."

"Very well. What happened after that?"

"I thought I heard the cheetah again, and that made me hurry off to the greenhouse. I sat down there and waited. I didn't dare to stir out, because of that beast. After hearing it from the orchard, I knew it was wandering about somewhere in the grounds, and I was terrified of it. I'd heard it catch Mr. Brenthurst, remember, and that had given me a dreadful shock. I'm not a policeman, you know, who takes on any risk that he meets."

This compliment did not seem to move the Inspector.

"And what happened next?"

"A good long time passed, I don't know exactly how long. Then I heard men's voices in the garden. Two men, at least, there were.

And the cheetah was snarling as if it was angry. Then I heard some shooting, several shots. I didn't count them. And after that there was quiet. I was too far from the house to hear anything except loud noises, and I couldn't see anything except the upper windows. Once they were lit up, one by one, as if somebody was going round the premises. But I made up my mind I wasn't going to budge until daylight came. I just stayed in that hothouse, wishing that I were safe at home and wishing that the sun would come up, and let me get away."

"Anything else you call to mind?" demanded the Inspector.

Cora Fairfoot thought for some seconds before answering.

"I think — I can't be absolutely sure — that I heard the noise of cars. I heard a horn at the front of the house, once. I do remember that, because of the non-hooting regulation, you know. No one should have been sounding a horn at that time in the morning."

"You've given us all this in its right order?" asked Sandrock. "You haven't got mixed up and put one thing in front of another?"

"I think I've given you the story just as the things happened," Cora Fairfoot declared, knitting her brows as if trying to force her memory.

The Inspector glanced at Sir Clinton as though asking for directions, but the Chief Constable evidently had no desire to interfere.

"Well," said Sandrock, rising to his feet and shutting his notebook, "there's just one thing more. Will you show us the place where you saw these two men in the orchard?"

"Certainly, if you wish," Cora Fairfoot agreed, with no sign of hesitation. "Shall we go now? I'd like to get home. It's been a trying night," she added, with the first sign of strain which she had betrayed up to that moment.

She led them to the orchard, where the dew lay thick on the grass, and after a short search she was able to find the spot where she had seen the two men. As they came up to it, they saw the long grass pressed down as though some heavy and bulky object had rested on the place for a while.

"We may as well have a record of this," Sir Clinton said to the Inspector. "Get it photographed, please, before these grass blades straighten themselves out again."

He made a careful survey of the depressed zone; then, rising erect again, he turned his attention to a track which led away from the spot, clearly visible owing to the disturbance of the dew.

"That seems to run towards the ladder we noticed," he pointed out to Sandrock. "Let's follow it up, just to make sure. These other trails in the grass seem to wander about in all directions. We needn't trouble about them for the present."

The track wound among the trees of the orchard and ended up on a hard-rolled path not far from where the ladder still stood propped against the wall of the grounds. The Chief Constable walked over to the foot of the ladder and, kneeling down, tested the firmness of the soil with his finger.

"Just shift that ladder, if you please," he directed. "Lift the foot of it straight up for an inch or two, first, and don't disturb the earth. It's fairly soft. Now prop the ladder against the wall again — over here, say — at just about the same angle as it was before. That'll do. Thanks."

He knelt down again, drew a little ivory scale from his pocket, and measured the depth of the hole left by the removal of the leg of the ladder.

"Now, let's see, Inspector. You're about twelve stone, aren't you?"

"Twelve-seven, sir."

"Good. Now would you be good enough to run up and down that ladder two or three times, please?"

The Inspector grasped the Chief Constable's idea immediately. He went up and down the ladder several times, glancing over the top of the wall as he did so, and then descended to the ground.

"Shall I shift it now, sir?"

"If you please."

Again Sir Clinton knelt down, and measured the depth of the new impression left by the ladder's foot.

"The first one's a good deal deeper than this one," he explained.

"You're a reasonable weight for a man, Inspector. Evidently something pretty heavy went up that ladder."

"That would be the thing they had in the orchard, sir? Plus the weight of the men who were handling it, perhaps." He broke off to examine the holes made by the ladder legs, and then continued, "It must have been pretty heavy — the weight of a man, anyhow, I'd guess from the depths of these holes. . . ." He broke off sharply, with a glance at Cora Fairfoot, who was listening intently. Evidently Sandrock felt he was letting his tongue run away with him, for he changed the subject immediately and went on: "I had a look round from the top of the ladder, sir. It's not far from where the Sergeant came across the cheetah, out on the road."

"That's interesting," said Sir Clinton.

From his tone the Inspector guessed that this new information had fitted in with something else in the Chief Constable's mind, but he did not care to ask any questions with Cora Fairfoot at his elbow. Sir Clinton seemed to remember her presence also, for he turned to her with an air of apology.

"I'm sorry we've detained you while we looked into this. We'll go up to the house, now, and perhaps you'll be good enough to listen while the Inspector reads over to you the notes that he made of your evidence. Then, if they're correct, you might sign in his book. It's only a formality, but we like to have things shipshape. It saves trouble later."

"Certainly, if you wish it," she acquiesced at once. Then a thought seemed to strike her. "But where's the cheetah? I'm nervous about it, you know, even with you two people here."

"The cheetah won't trouble you," said Sir Clinton, rather grimly. "Miss Teramond's lost her pet. My men had to shoot it last night. You'll see its body on the terrace."

"Oh, then I don't mind going to the house. Is Miss Teramond there? Shall I see her?"

"No, I'm afraid she's had an even bigger shock than you got last night," Sir Clinton explained. "She's under the care of a doctor just now."

"I'm sorry," Cora Fairfoot replied, tersely.

They made their way up to the terrace, where Cora Fairfoot halted for a moment beside the body of the cheetah.

"A dreadful creature, isn't it?" she said, gazing down at its savage mask. "It gave me some awkward moments last night."

Sir Clinton led the way into the drawing-room, found her a chair, and set the Inspector to read out the notes he had made. When they had been gone through without emendation, Sir Clinton produced a thick-barrelled fountain-pen. As he glanced at it before handing it over to Cora Fairfoot, a frown of vexation crossed his face and he rubbed his fingers together.

"I'm afraid I've made my hands dirty by poking about in that earth by the ladder," he explained, taking out his handkerchief and wiping the pen carefully. "There! That's all right now. Please put your name at the foot of the page — your usual signature. I'm afraid you'll have to take your glove off."

Cora Fairfoot mechanically stripped off her right glove, and, as she did so, the Inspector started and opened his lips as if about to say something. Sir Clinton's quick frown stopped him. Cora Fairfoot signed the notes, and then a look of dismay showed itself on her face as she stared at her hand.

"Looks as if you'd come across some wet paint," said the Chief Constable. "May I see?"

He took the pen from her and examined the red smears on her palm.

"I don't remember how it came there," Cora Fairfoot declared, composedly. "I suppose I must have touched something in the dark."

"I think you'd better think carefully," said the Chief Constable in a changed tone. "It's blood, you see? Not paint. Now tell us how you got that on your hand."

"I don't know," retorted Cora Fairfoot, sullenly. "I suppose I must have scratched myself and not noticed it."

"I don't see any sign of a cut or a scratch," the Inspector interjected.

"It may be on the other hand," suggested the Chief Constable. "Will you take off your other glove, please."

Cora Fairfoot hesitated for a moment; then, apparently seeing no way out, she drew off her left glove and disclosed a second palm which looked as though it had been smeared with blood.

"H'm!" said Sir Clinton, ominously. "Just see if you can find a cut to account for that, Inspector."

Sandrock scrutinized the whole surface of the hand, back and front.

"There's no damage to the skin anywhere, sir," he reported. "That blood came from elsewhere."

"Had you your gloves off at any time since you came into this garden?" demanded the Chief Constable, with a new sternness in his tone. "I'm going to warn you, now, that this is a serious affair. I'm not going to charge you with anything — not yet. But you'd better be very careful in what you say."

Cora Fairfoot evidently recognized the gravity in his tone, for she remained silent for quite a long interval, with an expressionless face. At last she decided to reply.

"You can't force me to answer, can you?"

"No, if you don't choose to do so. But it might be better for you if you did."

Cora Fairfoot broke into a rather harsh laugh.

"Ah! Now I see what you were after with that fountain-pen of yours. My finger-prints? That was it, wasn't it?"

Sir Clinton looked at her with a certain admiration.

"You're really very clever," he replied, without the least irony. "But cleverness sometimes defeats itself, Mrs. Fairfoot. If you persist in this course, we shall have to detain you."

"Arrest me, you mean?" she demanded, anxiously.

"No, not exactly that," Sir Clinton said quietly. "Detention and arrest are not quite the same thing. Now, I'm going to ask another question. You're quite acute enough to see that by answering it you'll save us some trouble, and if you won't answer we can easily find out from other people. Are you left-handed, by any chance?"

Cora Fairfoot evidently meant to consider the situation in all its bearings. She knitted her brows, fixed her eyes on the carpet, and remained silent for a couple of minutes. At last she looked up and met Sir Clinton's gaze fully.

"Not one person in a hundred will notice whether a woman's right- or left-handed," she declared. "You couldn't get your evidence. But I'll save you trouble. I *am* left-handed."

"Thanks. Now just another question. When you were in the pagoda, you told us, you were in terror of the cheetah. Did you not think of looking about for some weapon to defend yourself with? A hoe, say, or a digging fork, or a pair of garden shears? I noticed several of these stacked about the place. Or even a pruning-knife. I noticed an open one on the table."

Cora Fairfoot gave this question a longer consideration than her answer seemed to warrant.

"I think I did pick up the pruning-knife," she admitted, reluctantly.

"You can't remember definitely?"

"No, I can't. I was in a state of nerves, as I told you; and I really can't remember exactly what I did, not in detail."

"Ah! I can imagine that. Now, do you wish to revise your statements in any way, Mrs. Fairfoot? I'm going to warn you that if you stick to this story of yours, I've no alternative but to detain you. Think carefully before you make up your mind."

Once again Cora Fairfoot evidently considered the problem in all its bearings before answering.

"I don't see any reason for altering anything I've said," she declared at last.

"Then you leave me no alternative," said the Chief Constable. He turned to Sandrock.

"You might put Mrs. Fairfoot in the charge of one of the constables," he said. "And phone down to the station to see that proper arrangements are made for her, please. After that, I've a word or two to say to you."

# CHAPTER IX

## Olive Hatcham

"THERE ARE a few things to fix," said Sir Clinton, when the Inspector reappeared after handing Cora Fairfoot over to the Sergeant. "I left word at the station that they were to inform the coroner, so you needn't trouble about that. But ring up Dr. Stangate. I want him to deal with the various samples of blood. Ask him to examine that pair of gloves — " he nodded towards the gauntlets which Mrs. Fairfoot had put down, after stripping them off — "and also the blood-stains on that woman's hands. See that she doesn't get a chance of washing, before Stangate sees her. Then there's blood from that place in the alley by the tennis-court, and some from the spots on the grass border. And the stuff on the pruning-knife and the gardening-gloves. And cut a square inch out of the fabric of that handkerchief and give it to him; but don't handle the handkerchief more than you can help, and keep it carefully. The blood on the terrace is the cheetah's, probably, but he'd better sample it also. And, of course, he'll want some blood from Brenthurst's body. What I want to know is the type of blood, you understand?"

"Very good, sir. Anything else?"

"Put our finger-print ferret on to the handles of the pruning-knife and the birch besom. And the inside of the pagoda door. And get our photographic expert up here to photograph these paths — general views — and also some close-ups of the tracks and of that work with the besom. Juries like to see pictures. And get him, while he's at it, to take a picture of that patch of down-

111

pressed grass in the orchard and the ladder against the wall — you can easily fix it in its original position again. And get our surveyor to make a scale plan of the house and garden, of course. The usual routine, in fact."

"I'll look after all that, sir. And I suppose I may take your pen, for her finger-prints? I see she left it there."

"Yes, of course," agreed Sir Clinton. "I've got another one."

"Oh?" said the Inspector, enlightened. "Do you carry that big one specially, sir?"

"Yes," admitted the Chief Constable, with a smile. "I chose it on purpose; the big smooth barrel takes finger-prints nicely. One never knows when it will come in handy."

"That's an idea," said the Inspector, admiringly. "I never thought of that, sir. I must get one myself. One can always get a witness to sign notes. I'll order one straight off. By the way, sir, what made you ask if she was left-handed?"

"Curiosity. There was quite a lot of blood on her left hand, but only a few smears on her right."

"I see, sir," declared Sandrock. "You mean she cut his throat with the knife in her left hand, and the blood spurted out. . . ."

"Gruesome imagination you have, Inspector," said the Chief Constable, reproachfully. "No, I just wondered where all that blood came from. You remember those gardening-gloves in the pagoda? They were blood-soaked, too. And the knife, of course, had its share, and that handkerchief. There seems to have been more dabbling in gore than was called for, really. But that doesn't strike me as the rummiest part of the business."

"Then what was that, sir?"

"Didn't it strike you as queer that Mrs. Fairfoot never showed the slightest curiosity as to what happened to Brenthurst? All that flood of narrative, and not one breath wasted on saying: 'Is he badly hurt?' or 'Did the cheetah kill him?'"

"She wasn't fond of Brenthurst, sir," the Inspector pointed out. "Far from it. As like as not, she'll be quite glad that he's done in."

"Then why not ask about it?" retorted the Chief Constable. "And she has a good sound reason to be interested, I may tell you.

I happen to know that Brenthurst's death may make a considerable difference to her, financially, if things remain as they are."

"Oh!" ejaculated the Inspector, with a faint whistle. "That puts it in a new light to me, sir. Can you tell me how things stand?"

"I haven't checked my information," Sir Clinton warned him. "But unless I've been led astray, the facts are simple enough. The cash belongs to Brenthurst's mother, who's likely to die intestate, from all I hear about her. In that case, Brenthurst would have inherited the lot under the Birkenhead Act. Failing him, it goes to his mother's sister or her issue, as the case may be. That sister is dead; and Mrs. Fairfoot is her only daughter, so she'll inherit the money now, unless her aunt makes a will — which seems most improbable."

"She won't inherit it if she's convicted of killing Brenthurst," declared the Inspector. "A murderer — or a murderess either — can't make any profit out of the murder. That's a principle in law."

"Quite true," agreed Sir Clinton. "But do you think she's aware of that? It's common knowledge to people like ourselves, but I doubt if the general public is so well-informed. And most murderers count on getting off scot-free, you know. In which case the provision doesn't apply."

"Humph!" said the Inspector, rather disappointedly. "Still, sir, there's a motive without that, isn't there? Brenthurst treated her badly, by her own account. And she must have been angry when she found him chasing after this Teramond woman, right in front of her eyes. Some women do lose their wig, in a case like that. Especially a woman who sees somebody younger being put in her shoes. I suppose you think the yarn she told us was a pack of lies?"

"Oh, not altogether," said Sir Clinton, with a slight gesture of mock protest. "Some of it seemed to be true enough. She showed us that place in the orchard, remember. You're not suggesting that she faked those tracks? 'Merely corroborative detail, intended to give artistic verisimilitude to a bald and unconvincing narrative'? No, it doesn't strike me as likely. I don't think her talents run to faking tracks and lying down on wet grass to make a mark. There was some truth in her tale. For one thing, I believed her when she told us that she was in a blue funk of the cheetah. That had quite a genuine ring about it."

There came the sound of voices in the hall.

"That'll be the maids turning up, I expect, sir," said the Inspector, glancing at his watch. "You'll want to see them?"

"Yes, you might bring them in, one at a time. And just make a note of what they say, please."

The Inspector went out into the hall, where he found the two maids arguing with a constable.

"Quiet, please," he said, sternly. "You'll be waking Miss Teramond with all this noise. Which of you's the housemaid? You? All right, we'll take you first. Come here."

He ushered her into the drawing-room.

"This is the housemaid, sir," he explained. "What's your name?"

"Olive Hatcham."

Sir Clinton examined the pretty, rather pert-looking girl and gave her a reassuring smile, which put her completely at her ease, apparently.

"I want to ask you a question or two, and give you a bit of advice," he said kindly. "The advice is simple enough. Don't talk too much to your friends about this business. If you do, you're sure to get your recollections all mixed up, and that we do *not* want. The less you say, the better. You understand?"

"Yes, sir. But they're sure to ask me all sorts of things."

"I dare say they will. But don't start embroidering your story. Now for my questions. Of course you understand that you're not under any suspicion, so you can tell the plain truth. In fact, the plainer it is, the better, so far as we are concerned."

"Yes, sir. And can I say what you asked me, if anyone wants to know that?"

"I can't prevent you," Sir Clinton admitted with a twinkle in his eye. "But you'd probably get a better mark from us if you say as little as possible. Now, first of all, how long have you been in service here?"

"I've been here ever since Miss Teramond set up house, sir. More than a year. Just over a year. Before that, I was parlour-maid with a Mrs. Hyde in Ambledown. I left there because I didn't get on with the housekeeper. She was a bit too old-fashioned for me."

"I suppose you saw all the visitors who came to the house here?"

"Most of them, sir. I wouldn't like to say all, because some of them came in by the garden gate at times and not to the front door. And, of course, there may have been visitors who came after cook and I left at night."

A sly glance invited the Chief Constable to follow up the line of inquiry suggested by this last sentence; but he ignored it for the moment.

"Tell me the names of the visitors you remember, please."

Olive considered for a moment or two, as though drawing up a list in her mind.

"There weren't many lady visitors, sir," she began, with a suggestive look at the Chief Constable. "One or two did call at the start, but when they found the sort of house it was, they didn't come back, and I expect word went round, and nobody else came. There's a Mrs. Dorset, though. She comes quite often. But she's been divorced by her husband, so she doesn't need to be too particular. And a Miss Leyton comes now and again, a silly sort of young woman, always talking about living her own life and not bothering about conventions. I think she amused Miss Teramond and Miss Garfield, for they used to smile at each other behind her back and sometimes make jokes about her when they were alone. She isn't a beauty, and I don't think she'd have come to much harm if you'd left her alone with a man on a desert island. And there was Mrs. Fairfoot. She came pretty often, for afternoon tea, generally, but sometimes for dinner. Of course, *her* coming here was what you might expect. Birds of a feather, as they say. She's no more Mrs. than I am, really. People just give her the Mrs. as

115

you might give anyone a complimentary ticket. She was a bit old for Miss Teramond and Miss Garfield, I thought; but they seemed to get on well enough. . . . That's about all the regular women visitors I can call to mind just now, sir."

"What about others?" inquired Sir Clinton.

"Men, sir? Oh, there were quite a lot of them, sir. Some of them just came once or twice, dropped in at intervals, as one might say. They came to dinner, usually, not in the day-time. Some of them were quite young; others were a good bit older. They all seemed to be well off, with big cars, and when they tipped me, they did it well. I got quite a lot in tips, one way or another. They used to stay for dinner and then pass the evening. I don't know how late they stayed, because cook and I left the house before they thought of moving."

"You can write down a list of their names, by and by," said Sir Clinton. "These were people from a distance, weren't they? Were there any local people?"

"There was Mr. Brenthurst, sir. The money-lender, I mean. He used to come now and again. I didn't like him much. Ugly, he is, with a patch of hair on his cheek. And can't keep his hands to himself. He told me he'd taken quite a fancy to me — ugly old thing! — and he offered to lend me money if ever I ran short. 'I don't need any security from *you*,' says he. 'Your face is good enough for me.' And all that sort of thing. You know. I told him my face wasn't that kind of security, and he just laughed. 'I've got a loose fiver or two,' he says, 'and if you ever need it, just come up and see me, and ask for it nicely. It's waiting for you.' He's a nasty old man, that."

"Which of the two did he come to see?" asked Sir Clinton.

"Oh, Miss Teramond was his fancy, anyone could spot that at a glance. He hadn't much use for Miss Garfield. It used to make me laugh the way he was always trying to hit on some time when he hoped she'd be out of the road. Not that he got much good by that. All Miss Teramond wanted was to borrow money from him, I'll say that for her. I used to hear her talking to Miss Garfield

116

sometimes at dinner, when they were alone, and neither of them liked Mr. Brenthurst; one could see that, plain enough."

"Did Mr. Brenthurst come often?" asked Sir Clinton.

"Now and again. He'd have come oftener if he'd been asked."

"Did he ever walk in the garden?"

"Oh, yes, I've seen him there with the two of them, wandering round. And sometimes they gave him tea out there on one of the lawns, which was a nuisance to me, carrying a tray away out yonder when they could just as well have had it on the terrace and no trouble."

"Then he knew the lie of the land pretty well?"

"Yes, he did. He'd been all over the place, one time or another. I know that."

"Now I want to know something about Miss Teramond. Did you ever notice anything peculiar about her? I mean anything queer in her manner?"

"Well, sometimes she forgot things, if that's what you mean. I noticed that she'd do something, and never remember she'd done it. It didn't happen often. There was a case of it, just yesterday, over a rabbit. . . ."

"I'll come to that later," Sir Clinton interrupted. "How do she and Miss Garfield get on together?"

"Oh, not badly," Olive assured him. "They've been hunting in couples for years, now. They were on the stage together. I know that from things they've dropped at meal-times when I could hear them talking. Not the theatre. Music-hall hacks they'd been, and hacks they remained, after they left the Halls," she added vindictively. "They may think I can't see the length of my nose, but I had them sized up well enough."

"This house belongs to Miss Teramond?"

"Yes, it does; but it's Miss Garfield that looks after the running of it and gives the orders. Miss Teramond's no good at that sort of thing. She's got no head for it. All she does about the house is to go out in the mornings and cut flowers. She's fond of flowers, and she arranges them well, I'll say that for her. She's got an eye for colour, and that kind of thing. Animals are Miss Garfield's fancy. She's fond of dogs; but of course you can't keep a dog here with that cheetah about the place."

"How did you get on with the cheetah yourself?" demanded Sir Clinton.

"Oh, it never gave me any trouble, sir. Rather fond of me, it was. I've got a way with animals, people tell me. I'm sorry it's been shot. It was an affectionate beast. At least, with people it took a fancy to."

"How did it get on with the gardeners?"

"It didn't like Sperling, sir. Not to any extent. But it was quite fond of Shirbutt, the other gardener. And it didn't worry the boy."

"How did it get on with visitors?"

"It had its fancies, sir. It couldn't bear Mr. Brenthurst any more than I could myself. Usually, when he came, Miss Garfield shut it up in its den. It would do anything for Miss Garfield. She taught it a lot of tricks, just like a dog. I've seen her turn a lot of the chickens loose on one of the lawns and then set it to round them up, the way a collie rounds up sheep. But the cheetah had to be muzzled for that sort of play, sir."

"Was it fond of Mrs. Fairfoot?" asked Sir Clinton.

"Indeed it wasn't, sir. But it got on well with her son. Used to rear up and try to lick his face at times, as I've seen, purring so that you'd hear it ever so far off."

"So Mrs. Fairfoot's son used to come here, too? With his mother, or alone?"

"Sometimes with her, sir, but mostly alone. He was about the place pretty constant. When I came here first, I thought he was going to click with Miss Garfield. As thick as thieves, they were, sitting about in the arbours after dinner, in the twilight, and all that. But later on he cooled off and began to run Miss Teramond instead, and pretty hard, too. If I'd been Miss Garfield, I'd have been annoyed, having my nose put out of joint like that. But she didn't mind much. In fact, she rather seemed to encourage him there. He's got a terrible quick temper, and sometimes it led to his getting cross with Miss Teramond, and then Miss Garfield would step in and smooth things over, laughing at the two of them as if they'd been a pair of babies. Not that she hasn't got the spice of the devil, herself, when she's crossed."

"Give me an instance, if you can remember one," said Sir Clinton.

"Well, sir, there was that business about the rabbit, just yesterday. Miss Teramond had been out in the morning, as usual, cutting flowers for the house. That usually takes her quite a while, for she chooses them carefully. After that, she came in, and began to arrange them in glasses for the rooms. Then, a bit later, Miss Garfield went out into the garden and came back, very red and angry. It seems Miss Teramond had one of her queer fits that morning, and she'd killed one of Miss Garfield's white rabbits and given it to Mimi. Mimi's the cheetah, sir. There was a bit of a row between Miss Garfield and Miss Teramond about it, just as you'd expect. But I really believe it happened in one of these queer turns Miss Teramond gets. She'd clean forgotten all about it, so she said; though it's my impression she'd done it, all right. Anyhow, in the end she said she was sorry about the bunny and Miss Garfield cooled down a bit. But there was what you'd call a slight coldness in the air for the rest of the day. Miss Garfield was very fond of these rabbits of hers, and this was a buck she thought a lot of. I don't wonder she was cross."

"How did they pass their time? Reading, sewing, or what?"

"They didn't read, sir, except fashion papers and a picture newspaper or two. There isn't a book in the house. Miss Garfield sometimes worked embroidery, for she was quite clever with her hands. Miss Teramond just loafed about and spent a lot of her time dressing herself up. In the evenings they played cards, some game or other for two; unless they had visitors, and then they used to gamble after dinner. There's a roulette wheel in one of the cupboards; I can show you it if you like. And they played other gambling games, too. That was Miss Teramond's hobby — gambling. She used to go abroad pretty often and it was always to some gambling place — like Le Tookie or Monty. Much good it did her! She always seemed to come home broke. The visitors would turn up and it would all come right again. It was Miss Teramond that was the gambler. I've often heard Miss Garfield telling her off about the foolishness of it; but that never did any good. It's in her blood, as one might say."

"Had Miss Teramond much in the way of jewellery?" asked Sir Clinton.

"She had, and she hadn't, sir. What I mean is, that she had a fair amount, but she was always pawning some of it to raise the wind. So I picked up from things they said to each other. The only thing she stuck to, through thick and thin, was a diamond pendant. She thought a lot of it. It seemed a bit off-colour to me, a bit red-looking for a diamond, I used to think, and it was so big that as like as not it was just a sham, really, if one knew the truth. She wore it oftener than anything else."

"You were never in the house at night?"

"No, sir, never. We haven't even got rooms made up, Cook and I. We live down in the village. Miss Teramond wanted it so, when we took the place. We leave here after dinner and come back before breakfast. But once or twice I've forgotten something and come back when she had visitors. That's how I know about the gambling and so on."

"I see. Miss Garfield is away, at present? When did she make up her mind to go?"

"On the spur of the moment, sir, or less. I mean the first I heard about it was yesterday morning, after the rabbit got killed. She came to me and told me to pack a suit-case for her, just enough for the night. And she went off in the afternoon in the car."

"Is she often away on visits?"

"She does go away for a night or two, now and again."

"Are you quite satisfied with this place?"

"Not now, sir. I'm going to give notice at once. I don't like this kind of thing. Once the police come in, it's time to have a change — not meaning anything against the police, sir, of course. But it does one no good to be mixed up in any police business. It goes against one, no matter how clean one's hands are."

"I quite see your point," said Sir Clinton, with a faint smile. "Well, that seems to be all I have to ask you just now. Please tell the cook that I'd like to see her for a few moments now."

Olive seemed rather sorry to find she was no longer wanted. Evidently she had almost enjoyed the interview, with the chance it had given her of venting her spite against her employers.

"There's nothing good about that girl, barring her looks, sir," said the Inspector after the door had closed. "She's a nasty little piece and can't help showing it."

"Not particularly loyal to her employers," agreed Sir Clinton. "But there aren't many old family retainers knocking about, nowadays, you know. And I suppose people get the kind of maids that they deserve. It seems to be a peculiar household. Some maids would have found it a shade trying, perhaps."

The cook, when she appeared, was able to contribute little evidence of any value. She had seen less of her employers than her colleague, and quite obviously she had a much poorer nose for scandal. In fact, she had done her work, drawn her pay, and paid no attention to anything beyond. Sir Clinton soon satisfied himself that she had nothing useful to tell and dismissed her.

"I think you and I have earned breakfast," he said, glancing at his watch after the cook had retired. "We'd better get it. After that I'll come down to my office."

# CHAPTER X

# Peter Diamond

"WELL, WHAT do *you* want?" demanded the Chief Constable, impatiently, when Peter Diamond intruded on him at breakfast.

"Some grub, as a starter," responded Peter, promptly. "I'll ring the bell, and you can give the order. I've come to lodge a complaint, so you'd better get me into a good temper as quick as you can."

"What's your trouble?" asked Sir Clinton, pouring out his coffee. "Lost your wits, as usual, and expect us to find them for you?"

Peter drew out a chair and sat down at the table.

"The Socratic method is the best," he declared. "I'll ask questions. And to save time I'll give you the answers, too. Are the police expected to prevent crime? The answer is in the affirmative, in case you didn't know it. But do they? The answer is No, in two letters. Enough of Socrates. Here's Brenthurst (Ambrose) been murdered. I don't object to that. He's quite a suitable subject, and I don't mind a bit. But if you couldn't prevent the murder — though it's your job — you might at least have arranged for it to be done at a reasonable time. Why should I be dragged from my bed at unearthly hours because of your slackness? Disgusting. I don't mind what I have for breakfast, so long as you give me eggs and bacon. But see that the bacon's crisp."

The maid appeared in answer to Peter's summons, and Sir Clinton gave his orders. When she had gone, he turned to Peter.

"Who told you that Brenthurst had been murdered?"

"A little bird squeaked," said Peter, who seldom betrayed the source of his information if it was likely to get anyone into trouble.

"You're a bit too thick with some of my men," Sir Clinton pointed out in an ominous tone. "I don't want them to be accused of favouritism because you've got a wheedling way with you, Peter. Your competitors are apt to get jealous, if they think they're not having a square deal."

"I never said a word about your men," said the reporter indignantly. "These things come to me without asking. It's genius, or something like that."

"Is it?" said Sir Clinton, with unconcealed derision. "Well, no harm's been done . . . yet. We'll be giving your colleagues all the news, shortly. You'll be able to read it in the papers, Peter."

"I dare say," agreed Peter, unmoved by the sarcasm. "That'll be about a stick and a half, if you tell them absolutely all you know. 'Further investigations are being initiated' — and all that sort of stuff."

"I'm entertaining you now," the Chief Constable admitted candidly, "simply because I think you may be of some use to us. There's no denying that you've got a lot of miscellaneous local information which helps a bit, at times. And I can trust you to play the game. After which preliminary we can get down to business. I want to know something more about Miss Teramond and Miss Garfield, if you've anything in stock."

Peter nodded thoughtfully, and evidently searched his memory for information.

"What, particularly, are you after?" he asked, after a pause.

"You told me a while ago how they came to settle down here," Sir Clinton reminded him. "I'd like to go back a bit further than that, if you can dig anything up. But to start with, what about that cheetah? Queer kind of pet for a woman, it seems to me."

"Oh, the cheetah? I can tell you something about it, all right. It dates from her music-hall period. What you might call her Miocene Age. From the Greek. *Meion,* meaning less, and *kainos,* meaning new. You know how some audiences love animals. Witness the donkey in *Véronique*. I saw it in a revival, once, when I was young. . . ."

"And had no sense," interjected Sir Clinton, completing the quotation. "I remember. Your Eocene Age, Peter, since you like geological terms."

"Say what you like," said Peter, unruffled, "you can't deny that a second-rate turn, plus an animal, is more amusing than a second-rate turn *solus*. You can always look at the animal, if you don't like the vocalist. The fair Diana grasped this simple but profound truth. Hence the cheetah. I don't know where she got the beast; but she used to lead it on to the stage, and the audience loved it. She had a song about it. Something like this:

> You should see the people staring,
> You should see the policemen frown,
> When Nita,
> With her cheetah,
> Takes a walk through London Town.

The music was rather catchy and covered up the poverty of the verse, which was mostly concerned with the people she picked up and how they were all dealt with by the cheetah when she got tired of them. Most amusing to those who like that sort of stuff. Anyhow, I guess she covered the cost of the cheetah and a bit over, in her engagements. It was still going strong when she retired, so I suppose she had got fond of it and gave it a permanent berth in her household."

"So that accounts for it," said Sir Clinton. "Anything else?"

"Oh, she did one or two other things. I've seen her in something she called her 'Flitterbat Dance' — one of these affairs with a revolving sector in the lime-light which makes a dancer's movements seem jerky, in the manner of the original films. And I remember her doing a Moth and Candle Dance, which really wasn't so bad. She's quite graceful. Her singing wasn't up to much; but if you put on a French accent it covers a lot of defects, apparently. She was quite taking, really, but she never was a bill-topper or near it."

"And what about Miss Garfield?"

"They usually hunted in couples — or a trio, if you count in the cheetah. The Garfield dame has quite a good contralto voice, just a shade deep for my fancy. And they used to do sketches together, some not bad, some half-and-half. You know the kind of thing. There's a screen on the stage, and first one character goes behind it and comes out as something different and then the other one follows suit, until you think you've seen about three men and two women in the cast, when really it's only a couple of females in all. French farce stuff as a basis."

"Now, another point," said Sir Clinton. "You saw a big red diamond once, at the meeting of that silly Club. I suppose you've no notion whether it was a real one or not?"

Peter shook his head decidedly.

"I only saw it from thirty feet or so. And if you'd put it into my paw, I wouldn't know paste from the genuine. Even I have my limits. Why? What's wrong with it?"

"It's a schlenter," Sir Clinton explained. "I just wondered if there ever was a real one."

"No use asking me," declared Peter candidly. "Brenthurst seemed to take it for genuine, that's all I know. And he had a long history of it written down in his notes when he made his speech, as I told you before. It never occurred to me that it was anything but the real McCoy. And now it turns out that we wasted all that good envy on it. H'm! That's the worst of this world. You can't take a single thing for granted. Never mind, I'll make one of my special articles out of it by and by. 'Jewels of Jeopardy,' I'll call it, or else 'Diamonds of Doom.' Then my worthy editor will object to the alliteration and put 'Unlucky Gems,' or something like that, at the head of it. He's got no soul to speak of."

"Then don't discuss it," interrupted the Chief Constable. "What about Cora Fairfoot? For instance, what's her social position?"

"You haven't got the art of transition," Peter complained. "Your style's far too jerky, hopping about from one subject to another like a canary in a cage. Cora Fairfoot? Well, socially she was a bit isolated for a time. That unwanted child Percy stuck in the throats of a good many people. My great-aunt was one of them; she wouldn't look at the fair Cora except to stare through her when they met in the street. And Cora's Aunt Alison was just as bad. Which was a bit thick, I always thought, considering her own career. But she'd reformed by that time, and was busy damning anyone who committed the sins she'd been inclined to herself in earlier years. Apart from paying a subsistence allowance to Cora, she ignored her completely. There were quite a lot like those two in Good Queen Victoria's day. Result was that Cora got amongst the not-quites, socially, with a marked tendency towards the also-rans. Unplaced, if you take my meaning. *Déclassée,* as the French say. Of course people are more tolerant, nowadays, about little side-slips from virtue. But once you fall off your social perch, it's not so easy to hop up again. You've made your place in a fresh stratum, and it's hardly worth while struggling out of it again."

"She fell among publicans and sinners, then?"

"No, not exactly," Peter qualified. "You'd be a bit astray if you looked for her amongst the *skim de la skim*. But you'd be just as far out if you hunted amongst the *demi-monde*. Somewhere on the coast of Bohemia would be the place, if you can find any Bohemians in this town. . . . Ah! My breakfast!" he broke off, with a smile to the maid who came in with a laden tray. "I do like fragrant coffee. My landlady, poor thing, hasn't got the Continental touch. And she's a poor hand at scorching a rasher, very poor. I must join you at breakfast much oftener, I see."

"I'll have skilly made for you next time," said Sir Clinton, hospitably. "As you're bound to end in prison or in the workhouse, Peter, you may as well get a taste for it as soon as possible. That's by way of a gentle hint that I don't yearn for your company at breakfast as a rule. I'd much rather read my *Times* in peace."

Peter began his meal, but evidently felt that he ought to earn it; for he continued his analysis of Cora Fairfoot.

"She tried her hand at writing, I'm told. Everybody thinks they can write, nowadays, even if they can't spell properly. I've heard about some of her efforts. Wild, melodramatic stuff, I believe, with murders and seductions on every second page. No good to anyone, not even the gifted authoress — financially. A friend of mine was asked to vet it. That's how I know about it. It probably acted as a safety-valve to her subconscious mind, which must be in a queer state, to judge by the escaping steam. So my friend averred."

"What about this son of hers?" interrupted Sir Clinton.

"Percy? Oh, she fairly dotes on him. She'd do anything for Percy, I'm told. She pinched herself considerably to give him a passable education. She has her points, you know. Quite a strong character, in some ways, and most of it goes in mother-love. And he seems to reciprocate. In his early days he nearly got into bad trouble by half killing a little playmate who had the tactlessness to disparage Cora. Rather a violent fellow, Percy, by all accounts. An ugly customer to get across. Sullen, bad-tempered, knows what he wants and means to get it. Likely to get on, I think. More than a spice of Brenthurst in him. Gets his callousness from his Pa, probably, as well as his financial cuteness."

"How much do you know about this affair last night, Peter?"

"Everything, and perhaps a bit more," retorted the reporter, helping himself to toast. "Brenthurst a corpse; cheetah in the Happy Hunting Grounds; blood all over the place; the fair Diana in a fit; her boon companion absent on private business; valuable diamond a dud; your police playing Deadwood Dick parts, holding up the citizenry and squibbing off pistols all round the town; Cora Fairfoot under arrest. . . ."

"No, only detained," corrected the Chief Constable. "H'm! You seem to know more than I expected, Peter."

"Oh, we have our methods. . . ."

"Evidently," said Sir Clinton, dryly. "Now I've no objection to your using all the facts you've just mentioned. You've got them, and I'll not ask how. But I'm going to give you the rest of the tale, because I can trust you not to use it until I give you leave or until it's sent out to your competitors as well as yourself."

Thereupon the Chief Constable outlined the case, so far as it had gone.

"What do you make of it all?" he ended.

"Ah! Trying to pick my brains, are you?" Peter retorted with a grin. "Police Puzzled. Reporter Renders Requisite First Aid. That's it, is it? Well, as I said before, I owe you something for this breakfast. I was next door to starving, and far from home. But why ask me?"

"Because sometimes you're useful; and I'm not above using amateur assistants. My job is to get to the bottom of this business, and I don't mind using any spade that comes to hand. You happen to look like a useful tool. So I propose to use you. I want to hear what you make of it all, now you've got the facts."

"Well, I don't make much," Peter admitted, with unusual modesty. "Or, to be accurate, I make much too much. Like adding two and two and getting five for the answer. This business seems to be like some of Shakespeare's plays, with all sorts of sub-plots pullulating around the main stem. But to my mind, the central core of the affair is the fact that Brenthurst got the Teramond girl into his financial clutches. We know what that sort of thing led to in other cases."

"Yes," agreed the Chief Constable. "But in this case the girl wasn't a poor innocent, but somebody with a very extensive and peculiar experience of men and their ways."

"True, O King. I'm bearing that in mind. Also some Continental cases like the Gouffé affair towards the end of last century. That suggests a trap or ambuscade. As thus. She invites Brenthurst to pay her a visit at black midnight. She arranges a time when she knows her house-mate would be off the premises. Why? Well, it suggests to me that she meant to cut the Gordian knot of her financial problem — and the vital thread of Brenthurst, at the same time. Naturally she had no use for a witness."

"Let that pass," said the Chief Constable. "What next?"

"The next, I imagine," said Peter, "is an accomplice. One of her old lovers, most likely. She must have had a wide choice, there; and no doubt she knew of a suitable party amongst the bunch.

You see, Driffield, you've got to account for Brenthurst's body being taken out on to the road. The Teramond couldn't have managed that alone. I've seen her, and I've seen Brenthurst; and his corpse would have been too much for her to handle, let alone that her kimono would have been considerably bedabbled in gore if she'd tackled the job. But a man of sturdy physique could have hauled the late Brenthurst outside the gate, though he'd have got a bit messed up in the process. So I plump for a male accomplice. And by so doing, I clear up another bit of the mystery, *videlicet* the fact that Brenthurst turned aside at the pagoda instead of continuing straight on to the gate. Obviously, while he was streaking away from the terrace, somebody arose in his path unexpectedlike, and caused him to run down the side-alley. That somebody was the accomplice; and he'd been hiding behind the pagoda and only came into sight at the last moment. That's my explanation, and you can either like it or not, just as you please."

"I don't believe in forming likes or dislikes on such a short acquaintance," said Sir Clinton. "I'll have to live with it a little longer, before I make up my mind. Just at this moment, I see its defects looming bigger than its virtues, unfortunately."

"Oh, you do, do you?" queried Peter, vexedly. "And what are its defects, pray, since they bulk so large?"

"Well, in the first place, your tale hardly accounts for Diana Teramond being in bed when Brenthurst called."

"Oh, that was intentional," declared Peter, airily. "A mere dodge to stoke up the fires of passion. Given the Brenthurst temperament, there's no doubt about his reaction at the sight of a pretty girl in a nightie, a kimono, and naught else. Resurgence of the cave man. And the results of that would excuse any slight mishaps with fire-arms. Juries look leniently on any girl who squibs off a pistol in defence of her honour. Justifiable homicide is a likely enough verdict in such a case."

"Then why bother about an accomplice?"

"Because she's a poor shot," retorted Peter. "The results prove it. So she couldn't be sure of finishing Brenthurst with her pistol and had her accomplice in reserve if she happened to miss."

"Ingenious," the Chief Constable confessed, with a twinkle in his eye which offended Peter's vanity. "But there are other defects still in reserve. For instance, there's that sham diamond we found in Brenthurst's pocket. How does it fit in?"

"Oh, she palmed it off on him instead of the real one," declared Peter, easily. "Her tale was true, up to a point, I expect."

"I'm not going to quarrel with that," conceded Sir Clinton. "But she might as well have recovered the schlenter when she was at it, and suppressed that part of her story altogether. As it stands, by your way of it, she's left us clear proof that she was swindling Brenthurst, and that doesn't look too well. It rather takes the gilt off the gingerbread of her case and might have a poor effect on the jury."

"Every criminal makes a little mistake, now and again," said Peter, with an air of sagacity. "I see no reason to suppose that the Teramond damsel was any better than the rest of them. Any more of these looming defects?"

"You don't seem to have accounted for her calling in Cora Fairfoot to witness the performance," Sir Clinton pointed out.

"Every artist wants an audience," declared the reporter, with a grin. "Even you do, Driffield, or you wouldn't be chatting to me in this fashion, you know. And the need of an audience is especially strong in an actress. There's your explanation. No good? Then we'll try again. On closer inspection by a clear intelligence — mine, I mean — the difficulty fades away. Though I admit I'll need to modify my original draft a bit. Suppose we wash out my original *male* accomplice and substitute your friend Cora instead. Then the story goes like this. Cora and Diana put their heads together beforehand and decide to eliminate Brenthurst. They have all their plans cut and dried. That letter to Cora was merely a sort of code signal, telling her that everything was O.K. and that Brenthurst had fallen into the trap and would come up for treatment at 1 A.M. last night. Cora turns up according to plan. Between them they scrag Brenthurst. Between them they carry him out on to the road. And if they were moderately careful they wouldn't get soaked in blood during the passage. They could carry him by his hands and feet, you know, and then they wouldn't risk any gore falling on them. Once they got him outside the garden, they could loose the cheetah, with the idea that it would tear his throat about sufficiently to conceal the original wounds. Then they'd have to do a bit of crossing-sweeping to hide the tracks they'd made. How's that, umpire?"

"Worse and worse," said Sir Clinton bluntly, much to Peter's annoyance. "In the first place, throat-cutting is a messy business. Even if it's done from behind, a lot of blood spurts about. I don't say it's impossible for the cutthroat to come off unspotted, but it's rather improbable, to say the least. Second, you're implying that they carried Brenthurst out on to the road with the idea of suggesting that the cheetah killed him. But the cheetah didn't carry a pistol, and Brenthurst had three bullets at least in him. If all this business had been planned and thought over in cold blood, that error would never have passed muster for a moment."

"Oh, indeed?" said Peter, huffily. "And are there any more of these captious criticisms in stock?"

"Plenty," the Chief Constable assured him cheerfully. "But one will be enough for the present. You've forgotten that little dialogue, overheard by the gardener, between a man and a woman. It ended up with the woman saying: 'Go! . . . *please* go!' So you've landed between two stools, my poor Peter. Stick to your original hypothesis, and these two people were Diana and her male accomplice — but that fails to explain how Cora was on the scene. Take your second version, and you've no male present to play his part in that dialogue."

"Well, it was a three-ball match, then," said Peter, in desperation. "The characters in the sketch were Diana, Cora, and a male accomplice unknown."

"That sounds more like a mass meeting than an ordinary murder," said the Chief Constable, critically. "You may be right. On the other hand, you may be wrong. I think that covers the ground fully. But I rather like these airy hypotheses, Peter. Give us some more, now. What about the motives behind all this ponderous machinery of yours?"

"Motives?" echoed Peter, sullenly. "They stick out all over the business. I've no trouble about motives."

"But suppose I have," suggested the Chief Constable, suavely. "I'm anxious to hear your views."

"Well, anyone can see Diana Teramond's motive," said the reporter, with assurance. "She's a gambler. She's frittered away all her cash in hand. She's got heavily into debt with Brenthurst. She wants to clear her feet at one stroke by putting her creditor off the map. What more do you want?"

"And she picks up two friendly souls who're kind enough to help her out of pure altruism? It makes one think better of humanity."

"No," retorted Peter. "Cora Fairfoot had her own grudge against Brenthurst. We know all about that. She hated him like poison. He'd spoiled her life for her. And there was another thing in the background. Cash. Old Mrs. Brenthurst hasn't made a will, although she's got a tidy fortune tucked away, if all tales be true. A week ago, if she'd died, it would have gone to Ambrose *en bloc,* and Cora would have got nix, since she's only a niece of old Mrs. B. But suppose the old lady dies *now,* intestate, Ambrose is out of the way. Who's the next heir? Her sister, Olive Cotman or her issue. But Olive Cotman's dead. And her issue is Cora Fairfoot. So if Cora Fairfoot lent a hand in this murder of her cousin Ambrose, she's done herself quite a good turn, financially. That's a non-negligible factor in the situation, Driffield."

"Your reasoning's quite right, Peter," conceded the Chief Constable, graciously. "I'm glad you've mastered the Birkenhead Act. It's part of a general education, of course. But unfortunately in your survey you've omitted another non-negligible factor. If it so happens that Cora Fairfoot gets hanged as an accessory in the Brenthurst murder, she can't inherit. No one's allowed to profit by any murder that they do. So if she did lend a hand in the murder of Brenthurst then I was quite right in describing it as a matter of pure altruism. She couldn't profit by the job. 'Nohow,' as Tweedledum remarked."

"Perhaps she hadn't a general education," pleaded Peter.

"If she was bright enough to look up the 1925 Act, she was quite smart enough to find out about the accessory catch," Sir Clinton declared. "And she's a clever woman, as I found this morning; quick-witted above the average, I'd say."

"Which means, no doubt, that she tried to diddle you, and you caught her out," said Peter with a tinge of sarcasm in his tone.

"It's wonderful how you manage to hit the nail on the head — sometimes," said the Chief Constable, politely. "But I suppose you withdraw your second motive now. What else have you in stock? You haven't accounted for the two men with the burden — whatever it was — that Mrs. Fairfoot described to me."

"You grumbled about a mass-meeting not so long ago," complained Peter. "And yet now you're dragging in two more to swell the mob scene. If you ask me, they were figments of Cora's imagination."

"She must have a very active one, then, since it made a crushed area in the grass of the orchard," Sir Clinton pointed out.

"Probably she lay down there herself to flatten the grass and produce a mark fit to take in the police."

"If she had done that, her dress would have been wet with dew. But it wasn't, for I looked carefully at it, just to make sure. And something quite heavy *did* go up the ladder that was left propped up against the wall; which is further confirmation of Mrs. Fairfoot's story. No, Peter, it wasn't just a pure feat of imagination on her part; you can take that from me. Some of it was quite sound."

Peter helped himself to a second cup of coffee before speaking again. The interruption gave him time for thought, but the results seemed unsatisfactory, as his face betrayed.

"I simply can't understand it," he confessed at last, in a puzzled tone. "Why, the place must have been stiff with people last night. A regular garden-party, less the waiters and refreshments. Let's count 'em up. Diana, one; Brenthurst, two; the cheetah, three;

Cora Fairfoot, four; the two men in the orchard, six; the man and woman talking at the gate, eight; that hop-picker, nine; and the gardener, of course, ten. Ten! Good Lord alive! And usually the difficulty is to find witnesses in a murder case."

"I doubt if the cast was quite as big as you make out," said Sir Clinton. "Some of them doubled their parts, I think."

Peter's mind had gone off on a fresh scent.

"That gardener seems a queer fish. Admitting that he's chicken-hearted and lily-livered, with a yellow streak through the rest of his anatomy, still one would think he'd have some curiosity in his make-up. He might have gone and had a look-see, even if he made up his mind not to interfere in any vulgar brawls. I'm no Lancelot myself, but I think I'd have had grit enough to look out of the window, at least. He must have a very shy and retiring nature, that man."

"Rashness isn't his failing," Sir Clinton admitted. "Nor is the love of truth, so far as I saw. He was keeping something back; and that something meant a good deal to him. There's a subject for you, Peter: The Temptations of a Gardener. Write it up some-time. I can see possibilities in it."

But Peter had other matters in his mind and passed on to them.

"Bit of a nuisance, isn't it, that the fair Diana has these lapses of memory? Are they genuine, think you?"

"They seem to be, according to the doctor," said the Chief Constable, cautiously. "And that maid, Olive Hatcham, gave me an-other instance of them — the case of the pet rabbit that came to a sad end. My own impression was that the amnesia was genuine enough, so far as last night's doings were concerned."

"H'm!" said Peter, rather sceptically. "Let it go at that, then. On that basis she may have been the one who swept up the sand on the paths."

"Possibly, though I can't quite swallow it," said the Chief Constable. "She remembered enough to tell us that she ran after Brenthurst; and if she did the sweeping, she left her own tracks alone, which seems curious. And, remember, the broom came from the pagoda, and Mrs. Fairfoot, according to her own story, was in the pagoda all through the main performance. But she didn't mention Miss Teramond bursting in on her."

"She and the fair Diana were in collusion over the business," Peter pointed out. "The letter you saw is enough to prove that. So you can't trust Cora's yarn. She may have left out that bit."

"I don't trust it completely," admitted Sir Clinton. "But if your version's correct, then Mrs. Fairfoot must have come away from the pagoda with Miss Teramond, because she'd have left tracks on the smoothed sand, otherwise. But why drag in unnecessary characters? Mrs. Fairfoot may have done the sweeping-up herself, though she was too modest to mention it. I'm inclined to think she did, and that she swept up her own tracks as she left the pagoda as well as the others."

"But what did she sweep over the tracks for at all?" demanded Peter, ruffling his hair. "Why didn't she scoot for safety while she had time, after brushing over her own foot-marks? She'd heaps of time to make a getaway."

"The cheetah was at the gate, and the cheetah didn't like her," Sir Clinton pointed out. "I can quite understand her staying where she was, rather than risking it."

"Then why did she go to the trouble of sweeping up the tracks down towards the gate?" Peter demanded.

"Because there were some prints amongst them which she wanted to efface at all costs," retorted Sir Clinton. "That's obvious, since she took the risk of going near the cheetah, just outside the gate. She wouldn't have done that unless she felt some desperate need to remove those traces before anyone else saw them. I've got a suspicion whose tracks they were," he added.

Peter raised his hand to check Sir Clinton.

"Hold on a jiff," he interrupted. "I can guess that myself. What about Percy?"

"I had him in mind," admitted Sir Clinton. "From all I've heard, he's the one person for whom Mrs. Fairfoot would run a big risk — and there's no doubt she was afraid of that cheetah turning on her. Also, I gather that Percy Fairfoot was enamoured of Miss Teramond, which seems suggestive. Further, if Percy Fairfoot was on the spot, you get an explanation of that scrap of talk at the gate: 'Go! . . . *please* go!' That might have been Mrs. Fairfoot urging her son to escape while he could."

"Yes," agreed Peter in a thoughtful tone. "That seems to fit well enough. And . . ."

"And if he was mixed up in the murder and his mother wasn't, it might be safe for her to stay behind and obliterate the tracks. That's what you're thinking, isn't it?"

"Something of the sort," Peter admitted. "But by bringing in Percy, you've made the throng in the mob scene bigger than ever. That garden last night must have been just about as congested as the Wood near Athens in 'A Midsummer Night's Dream.' Even the moon was present, to complete the parallel. Well, I liked that breakfast. Many thanks, hospitable sir."

He rose to his feet, but as he did so there came a sound of voices in the hall outside, evidently raised in argument. In a moment or two the maid opened the door and came in, with a visiting-card in her hand. But the visitor did not wait to be ushered in. He followed on her heels: a heavily built man of middle height, with a pugnacious expression on his face, who seemed hardly able to contain himself. Sir Clinton, always fastidious in his own dress, noticed that Fairfoot was one of those men who seldom look tidy. His jacket was rumpled, and the creases in his trousers were so old that they were almost invisible through wear.

# CHAPTER XI

## Percy Fairfoot

SIR CLINTON glanced at the visiting-card as he rose from his chair. At the sight of the name on it, all trace of his recent flippancy passed in an instant, and it was as a pure official that he faced the newcomer.

"Mr. Percy Fairfoot? What can I do for you?" he asked stiffly.

The visitor had been excited when he came in, but the Chief Constable's formality seemed to exasperate him to such a degree that he lost all thought for courtesy.

"What can you do? You can tell me what the hell you mean by arresting my mother and locking her up in your infernal police station. That's one thing you can do. And you can tell me what you mean by sending your underlings to invade my house with a search-warrant and poke about in it in spite of my forbidding them. That's just to start with. I'll have more to say, though, by and by. I'm not the sort of person to take this kind of thing without getting my own back. Now explain."

"I shall, when you drop this bullying business. It's silly, Mr. Fairfoot," said Sir Clinton, contemptuously. "I'm not amenable to that treatment, I may tell you."

His manner, more than his words, seemed to impress Percy Fairfoot, though he still remained truculent.

"Well, go on," he said, rancorously.

"Mrs. Fairfoot was found, in suspicious circumstances, at an early hour this morning," explained Sir Clinton, icily. "The account she gave of herself was unsatisfactory. I ordered her to be detained until further inquiry has been made into the matter. That answers your first question."

"Can I see her?" demanded Percy Fairfoot, with a shade less vehemence in his tone.

"Not at present," said the Chief Constable, definitely.

"Are you charging her with anything?"

"Not at present," repeated Sir Clinton. "She's not under arrest, if that's what you mean."

"The result seems much the same," retorted Percy, but again there was a falling-off in his truculence.

"As to your second question," Sir Clinton went on, ignoring this, "I've no doubt that the Inspector in charge of the matter went to her house — it's her house, isn't it, not yours? — with the idea of getting his inquiries pushed through as quickly as possible. Did you help him much?"

Percy Fairfoot evidently thought it better not to answer this. He contented himself with shrugging his shoulders.

"Well, what do you expect?" demanded Sir Clinton. "Inspector Sandrock has his duty as an official. You've a duty as a member of the public. He seems to have done his. You've not been doing yours, I gather. In fact, it looks as if you'd been putting difficulties in his way. That's not going to get Mrs. Fairfoot released any quicker. Frankly, Mr. Fairfoot, you seem to be putting sand in the bearings, instead of oiling them; and yet you come and complain because the machine doesn't work quick enough to please you."

Peter Diamond leaned his elbows on the table and put up his hand to hide his smile. The change in Percy Fairfoot's bearing was unmistakable. He was still angry, but he evidently felt that he had been manœuvred into a false position and that he would gain nothing by any further display of truculence.

"Something in that, perhaps," he acknowledged, crossly. "But I'm naturally disturbed about my mother. It was a nasty surprise when your fellows arrived with the news, and they didn't break it too tactfully, I may tell you. Their manners would do with a bit of polishing and be none the worse."

"I'll take the responsibility for their doings," said the Chief Constable, with a marked reversion to chilliness in his tone, for he never failed to support his subordinates.

"Oh, very well, very well," Percy responded, surlily. "Let it pass. I don't want to raise trouble."

"Probably the best thing will be for us to go along now and see whether my men have finished," Sir Clinton suggested. "Have you a car outside? You have? Then I'll get mine, and you can drive on ahead and show me the way, if you please. Good-bye for the present, Peter."

"Oh, my car's outside, too," said Peter, cheerfully. "I'll just come along with you."

Percy Fairfoot seemed for the first time to notice that there was a third person in the room. He stared at Peter resentfully.

"And who are you, anyway?" he demanded, rudely.

"Me?" answered Peter, innocently. "Oh, just one of these reporter fellows. Autolycus is my other name. A snapper-up of unconsidered trifles in the way of local gossip, and all that sort of thing."

"You needn't come along," Percy Fairfoot warned him, uncivilly. "You won't get in. I can at least keep people like *you* off the doorstep."

"It's a free country," said Peter. "You can't keep me off the pavement, and I'll pick up quite a lot by peering through the windows. Ever study lip-reading, Mr. Fairfoot?"

"I think we'll get along without you, Peter," said Sir Clinton.

Peter was quite satisfied. He had played up for this answer, knowing that it would improve the relations between the Chief Constable and Fairfoot. He had already guessed that Sir Clinton wished to throw Fairfoot off his guard if possible, and he was not unwilling to lend a hand.

"Oh, if *you* say so, then it goes," he returned contentedly. "Just a notion of mine. Bye-bye, Mr. Fairfoot. Ta-ta, Driffield. That seems to be everybody."

He glanced round the room as if in hopes of extending his farewells, and then took his departure.

"If you'll go out to your car and wait for a moment or two, I'll bring mine round from the garage," Sir Clinton said, indicating the door.

They started, with Fairfoot leading; but before they had gone far, he swung his car to the side of the road and halted. Sir Clinton in his turn pulled up.

"What's wrong?" he asked.

"Puncture in the near front wheel," grumbled Fairfoot.

"Well, you can put on the spare in five minutes," said Sir Clinton. "I'll wait and lend a hand if you need it."

"The spare wheel's gone, too," Fairfoot explained, sulkily. "It got punctured last night and I haven't had time to get it fixed."

"Well, that doesn't matter," said Sir Clinton. "Unship the spare and stow it in behind me. Then you can lock the car and come along with me. We'll drop your wheel at the first garage, and they can send for your car when they've got the wheel ready."

"All right," agreed Fairfoot, ungraciously. "There's nothing else for it."

He got out his spare wheel, and as he was stowing it in the back of the Chief Constable's car, Sir Clinton noticed a well-defined white splash on the rubber of the tyre. He made no remark about it, and Fairfoot took his place in the front. The Chief Constable stopped at the first garage they came to, and Fairfoot arranged about the repair, after which he came back to the car again. A short distance farther on, they reached a police station. Sir Clinton, with a word of apology to his passenger, got out and went inside, where he remained for a few minutes. When he had finished his business, they drove on again and at last reached their destination under Fairfoot's guidance. A constable on the doorstep saluted Sir Clinton as they passed into the house. Evidently he had notified the Inspector of his Chief's arrival, for Sandrock appeared in the hall almost at once. Fairfoot glowered at him without speaking.

"Now, let's get the facts," said Sir Clinton, cheerfully. "The sooner we're through with that, the quicker you'll be rid of us, Mr. Fairfoot. Shall we go in here?"

He indicated an open door, through which could be seen a room which was evidently half office, half sitting-room. Its most bulky piece of furniture was an open roll-top desk, littered with an untidy mass of papers. Evidently Percy Fairfoot had no talent for neatness, in either clothes or business.

"Now, first of all," continued the Chief Constable, when they had found seats and Sandrock had pulled out his note-book and pencil, "when did you see your mother last?"

"Last night," Fairfoot replied. "About half-past eleven or so. She said good night, then."

Evidently he had realized that further fencing would do no good.

"That's her usual hour for going to bed?"

"About it."

"Did she seem disturbed in any way?"

"No, she didn't. Nothing out of the common."

"And you heard or saw nothing more of her until Inspector Sandrock told you that she was being detained?"

"No, nothing. Nice surprise packet for a man to get," retorted Fairfoot, with more than a trace of renewed irascibility. "And your men scared my maid almost out of her wits."

"You had no knowledge of any appointment which Mrs. Fairfoot might have made?"

"At that time of night?" said Fairfoot, scornfully. "No."

"Did you hear Mrs. Fairfoot leave the house after she had said good night?"

There was just an instant's hesitation before Fairfoot answered the question.

"No, I didn't."

"When did you yourself go to bed?" pursued the Chief Constable, casually.

Again Sandrock noticed the momentary hesitation before the answer came.

"I didn't go to bed till well on in the small hours."

"Then you were down here, I suppose? You didn't hear her coming downstairs?"

"Two of the treads on the stair creak loudly, sir," interjected Sandrock, swiftly, as Fairfoot again showed that curious hesitancy. "You can't help hearing them in here, even with the door shut. I tested that myself."

"Well, Mr. Fairfoot?" demanded the Chief Constable.

"I didn't hear anything," Fairfoot declared, definitely. "You're a bit too clever," he added, turning on Sandrock with an ugly look. "As it happens, I wasn't here. So naturally I heard nothing of the sort."

Sandrock contented himself with making an elaborate note. (Inwardly, his comment was: I wonder he didn't say: "Yah!" at the end of it. He might just as well have done, so far as the tone goes. But he's made a slip, he has. One can see it in his face.)

"You were out?" continued the Chief Constable, suavely. "Can you tell us what took you abroad at that time of night?"

"As it happens, I can," retorted Fairfoot, with a certain relish at this apparent defeat of the police. "I'm keen on photography. Not the ordinary amateur stuff. Out-of-the-way effects. Lately, I've been taking views by moonlight."

"Ah! That explains it, of course," admitted Sir Clinton, innocently. "It was full moon or near it, last night, and a fairly clear sky part of the time. Naturally you would take advantage of that. Did you have any luck?"

"I took one or two shots."

"Not snapshots, of course?" queried the Chief Constable, as if displaying his knowledge. "Time exposures? Fairly long exposures, I suppose, since moonlight isn't very actinic?"

"Yes, time exposures."

"This is interesting," pursued Sir Clinton, with a faintly fussy air which was new to the Inspector. "I suppose you have a tripod. Do you use plates or films, Mr. Fairfoot?"

"Plates."

"I used to do a little photography myself, at one time," Sir Clinton went on. "I'd like to have a look at your camera, if I may. Oh, that's it over there, is it?"

He had followed Fairfoot's unconscious glance round to where the camera's leather case lay in a corner of the room with the folded up tripod beside it. Sandrock had at first fidgeted slightly during this interlude, but soon changed his view. "Putting the beggar off his guard," was his mental comment. "Quite neat." Fairfoot had nodded an affirmative answer to the Chief Constable.

"Well, I'll look at it by and by," Sir Clinton went on. "Let's get business over first, as quickly as possible. You were out last night with your camera and you took several photographs. We've got that. Now, tell us, when did you get home again?"

"I don't know. About three in the morning, perhaps. I didn't look at my watch."

Sandrock noted that there was no particular hesitation before this answer, and he gave Sir Clinton a good mark for diplomacy.

"Of course, you didn't drag a heavy camera by hand," the Chief Constable went on, still with the air of one amateur talking to another. "You went in your car. What views did you take?"

"I took some on the banks of the lakelet on Hawkover Common."

"Twenty miles is nothing in a car, of course," said Sir Clinton, amiably. "I'd like to see the results. You do your own developing, I suppose? One doesn't trust to the nearest chemist when it's a matter of artistic work. By the way, did you ever try the old carbon process? The bichromated gelatine one, I mean? No? You might give it a trial. It's gone out, nowadays, but I used it when I was a youngster. For artistic work it was unbeatable in some ways. But I'm afraid I'm wasting our time," he said, pulling up suddenly and changing the subject. "Let's get on. There's this business of Miss Teramond. . . ."

"Miss Teramond?" echoed Fairfoot, with an unsuccessful effort to counterfeit complete surprise.

"Yes," continued the Chief Constable. "We know that you're a friend of hers. She's in trouble, I'm afraid, rather serious trouble. And, unfortunately, she's ill and can't tell us much at the moment. I don't want to worry her more than is absolutely necessary, but we must have some information about the state of things at Fountain Court — social relations, and so forth. Now it seems to me, Mr. Fairfoot, that as a friend of hers you might tell us a few things which would save us from bothering her about them."

This line of attack evidently puzzled Fairfoot.

"Have you got *her* under arrest, too?" he demanded.

"I haven't got anyone 'under arrest,'" said Sir Clinton. "But I'm not going to conceal the fact that Miss Teramond might find herself in the dock, sooner or later, unless we can get this business made a bit clearer than it is at present. You're quite entitled, at present, to say nothing at all. I'm not trying to bluff you. But I put it to you that by telling me a few things you'll be sparing Miss Teramond from a lot of questioning which might not do her much good in her present condition."

Percy Fairfoot clasped his hands and rubbed one thumb with the other with a quick, nervous motion: the only sign of agitation which he had shown since his own conduct came under review. He knitted his brows and evidently pondered carefully before committing himself, for it was only after the lapse of a full minute that he spoke again.

"You want to know how I got friendly with Miss Teramond? I'll tell you. I'm a house-agent. The late owner of Fountain Court employed me to sell the place. It was bought by a Mr. Julian Lorrimore. He settled it on Miss Teramond. They were going to be married almost immediately. Naturally, he, she, and I met from time to time to make various necessary arrangements about the place. That's how I came across Miss Teramond. Then Lorrimore was killed in an accident. After that, Miss Teramond settled down at Fountain Court. She brought Miss Garfield as a sort of companion. So I assumed at the time. They knew no one hereabouts. I introduced them to my mother. We all became quite friendly. My mother and I were often over at Fountain Court, as visitors."

He paused here and seemed to think carefully before resuming his tale.

"At that time, I imagined that Miss Teramond had plenty of cash and that Miss Garfield was a sort of poor relation. A dependent of some sort, anyhow. I flirted with her a bit, on this basis. It was just a bit of fun on my part, really. Nothing serious, so far as I was concerned. Then I began to put two and two together. Miss Teramond wasn't rolling in money, after all. Then it turned out that both of them had been on the Halls. By that time, I'd got keen on Miss Teramond. She's more my style. And from one thing and another I gathered that she wasn't . . . well, she wasn't so much out of my reach as I'd supposed at first. Miss Garfield didn't mind my change-over. In fact, she was rather decent about it. She made things easy for me. Left us together pretty often and didn't seem a bit jealous. She's not a violently passionate type. A bit cynical in some ways. Neither of them pretended to be anything except what they were."

"You got to know, in fact, that they were . . . women of the world, shall we say?" interjected the Chief Constable.

"Yes, that puts it in a nutshell," agreed Fairfoot. "They'd knocked about a good bit, both here and in America. They came from the States originally. San Francisco, I believe. I've heard Miss Garfield mention the earthquake there. She'd been through it when she was a baby. I remember her saying that, because I was curious about her age. I looked up the earthquake. It was 1906. If she was a baby then, that made her thirty-one, or so. She doesn't look it. And Miss Teramond looks younger, if anything."

"Was Miss Teramond in the earthquake also?" asked Sir Clinton.

"No. She wasn't born then. She happened to mention that. The two of them didn't meet until four or five years ago. They joined forces and went on the Halls out there. Then they came to England."

"What about other visitors to Fountain Court, apart from yourself and your mother?" Sir Clinton inquired.

"A couple of women turned up occasionally when I happened to be over there. A Mrs. Dorset and a Miss Leyton. Apart from them, I don't remember any women about the place. The music-hall business got out in the neighbourhood. I don't suppose that would have meant much, alone. But they had men visitors, some of them pretty rowdy. People didn't like that."

"Which of the two did the men come for?" asked Sir Clinton, bluntly.

"Miss Teramond," snapped Fairfoot, angrily.

"Had Miss Garfield no male friends, then?"

"I never met anyone who came on her account. But I didn't see much of any of these men. I kept away when they were due. In fact, I was rather given to understand that I wasn't wanted when they were on the premises. They were old friends of the girls. That sort of thing."

"I understand," said the Chief Constable, evidently guessing that this line of inquiry was more than distasteful to Fairfoot. "Now can you think of anyone else in this Fountain Court circle?"

The run of his narrative had temporarily put Fairfoot off his guard, but now, apparently, his suspicions came back in full force, and it was with a very sullen expression that he answered the question.

"There was Ambrose Brenthurst, the money-lender."

Sir Clinton noted that Fairfoot made no reference to the relationship between himself and Brenthurst, though it was common knowledge.

"What took him *there*, do you know?"

"Cash, to begin with," snarled Fairfoot. "These girls were always in funds or else nearly broke. When they were broke, Brenthurst got his chance."

" 'To begin with,' " echoed Sir Clinton. "You mean that later on he went there apart from business?"

"He went there to get hold of Diana," said Fairfoot, savagely. "Nobody would look at him on the strength of his face. But he had other ways of getting what he wanted. She laughed at him behind his back. But she was afraid of him, too. I knew that from some things she dropped now and again. If she could have got clear of her debts to him, she wouldn't have let him inside the gate. But his money gave him a grip on her. She was growing frightened of him. She liked her life nowadays. It suited her. And he could have pulled it about her ears by selling her up. That's the sort of man Ambrose Brenthurst was."

Sir Clinton pricked up his ears, but avoided an immediate reference to the tense of Fairfoot's last word. Instead, he turned to what seemed a less delicate subject.

"I suppose you came across the cheetah at Fountain Court?"

"Mimi? Oh, yes."

"You never had any trouble with it? A friendly beast, was it?"

"It liked me," said Fairfoot. "Some people it couldn't stand. But it used to come to me, purring. Rubbed itself up against one just like a big cat. All over me, for some reason or other. Perhaps because I was never afraid of it."

"It didn't like some people, you say?"

"No, it scared my mother badly. She's different from me. Hates cats, for one thing. I suppose that had something to do with it. Diana used to shut it up in its den when my mother paid a visit. No harm in the beast, really. Still, it was better to have it out of the road."

"Now, another question. Were you just a friend of Miss Teramond's, or were you anything more?"

Fairfoot flushed hotly at this blunt inquiry.

"What business is it of yours?"

"Thanks, that's enough," said the Chief Constable. "I needn't press it. But I want a plain answer to *this* question. Were you concerned, directly or indirectly, in the killing of Ambrose Brenthurst?"

An evil smile flickered over Fairfoot's face and then vanished.

"Barking up that tree, are you?" he asked. "Well, I'm not going to answer. You can't force me to say anything."

"And you can't prevent me from thinking, Mr. Fairfoot. I'll give you one more chance. I'd like to see these photographs of yours, the ones you took on Hawkover Common. Will you be good enough to develop them — now — so that we can have a look at them?"

"No, I won't," said Fairfoot, viciously. "And *you* won't, either."

He made a dash towards the camera-case. Instantly, Sir Clinton pounced on him and gripped him in a common ju-jitsu hold. Sandrock sprang to the Chief Constable's assistance.

"I'll break your wrist, if you give me trouble," said Sir Clinton,

147

coolly. "Have some sense, man. A couple of constables are out in the hall. You can't escape; and there's no need to give the neighbours the sight of a frog's march."

Fairfoot was breathing deeply, between exertion and excitement. He evidently recognized the hopelessness of his position.

"All right. I'll be quiet," he decided.

"That's sensible," said the Chief Constable. "I've no taste for brawls."

"I suppose this means I'm under arrest?" Fairfoot asked.

"No, we're merely detaining you for the present until we get some points cleared up. Do you want to make any further statement? No? Well, you can always change your mind, later on, if you choose." He turned to the constables. "Take him into the next room, please, and keep an eye on him."

When Fairfoot had been removed, the Chief Constable opened the leather camera-case and removed from it three large double dark-slides which he laid upon the desk.

"I suppose he was trying to get at these, sir? To open them and fog the plates?" asked Sandrock.

"Obviously," said the Chief Constable, with a touch of impatience. "Is there a phone on the premises? I want to speak to some people."

"It's in the cloakroom, sir."

"Thanks. I shan't take more than a few minutes."

He went out, and was absent for a little while. When he returned, the Inspector noticed that the trace of anxiety seemed to have faded out of his expression.

"Now we can develop these things," he said. "We can use Fairfoot's dark-room, out at the back of the house. It's rather like seething a kid in its mother's milk, using the man's own equipment; but he's given me a bit of anxiety, and I don't want to be kept on pins and needles longer than I can help. Not that I've any real doubt about the result."

"What do you expect to find, sir?"

"Nothing," said Sir Clinton, concisely.

"You mean he never exposed the plates at all? Then why was

he in such a state to spoil them, sir? . . . Oh, of course. Silly of me. You mean he wanted to prevent us proving that he'd never taken those photos that he said he'd taken."

"Exactly. That was a definite lie. And innocent people don't need to lie about their doings. Now we'll develop these things."

As Sir Clinton had predicted, the plates were completely blank. He fixed them and put them in to wash. Then he and the Inspector returned to the semi-office.

"You can take charge of these plates," the Chief Constable directed. "Our pencilled initials on them won't wash off. Have them dried and put among the rest of the exhibits, please. . . . Phew! I hadn't the slightest doubt about them being blank, but it's a relief, all the same. And my telephone calls were satisfactory, also. I don't mind confessing, Inspector, that I feel a good deal happier than I did, half an hour ago, when I told you to detain him. It might have been a bad break if things hadn't come out properly. But it's all right, now."

"I don't quite get the idea of your phone calls, sir," ventured Sandrock. "That is, if they have anything to do with this affair."

"No, you'd hardly guess that, without knowing what went before," explained Sir Clinton. "Here it is. Fairfoot disturbed me at breakfast-time, to complain about your intrusion here. He had his car with him, so I let him go ahead as pilot; and he got a puncture. Then it turned out that his spare wheel was already punctured — last night. Anything that happened last night is of interest to us just now; so I persuaded him to leave his car by the roadside, and we took his spare along with us to the nearest garage. That gave me a chance to look at it, and I noticed a splash of white on the rubber and also on the rim."

"Ah!" interjected Sandrock. "Now I see what you're after, sir. Before he got his puncture last night he must have run his wheel through a puddle of whitewash or something, and if we can find that puddle on the road, it tells something about where he was last night."

"That was what crossed my mind when I noticed that the white splash on his wheel was quite fresh. It hadn't run far after getting splashed, so he must have had his puncture almost immediately after. Puddles of whitewash aren't so common on the road. Obviously somebody had been whitewashing a wall or a cottage and had emptied out the surplus whitewash from his pail into the gutter after the job was done. So after leaving his wheel at the garage, I stopped at the first police station we came to and I phoned the garage people to keep the wheel safe and not to handle it."

"That'll be useful, sir," commented the Inspector.

"There's more in it than that," continued Sir Clinton. "I asked the garage people to tell me what had caused the puncture. Broken glass, probably a bit of a bottle. So if we find a broken bottle on the road near a place where some whitewashing has been done, we've got not only the fact that his car passed that way last night, but we can also tell which way he was going, which may be useful."

"And your phone call from here, sir?"

"I rang up Headquarters and told them to make inquiries about any whitewashing that our patrols had happened to notice yesterday. And I told them to search for broken glass near the whitewash. That will take a little time. But the weather's fine and there's been no rain to wash the white stuff into a drain, which is lucky. They'll photograph it when they find it, just to give us a permanent record. I'll be much surprised if the place is on the road to Hawkover Common. As a matter of fact, I think we've got the place already. One of our men at Headquarters had been out on his motor-cycle lately and happened to remember he'd seen a cottage being whitewashed only a mile or so from Fountain Court and on the road between this house and the Court. That seems the likely spot. Some of our people have gone out already to hunt for broken glass."

"That's fine, sir," declared the Inspector, delighted with the news. "So he was at Fountain Court all right, last night."

"Yes, I suppose so. And that seems to clear up another bit of the tangle. At any rate, it gives one a hint about Mrs. Fairfoot's position. She was shielding somebody at her own expense. That stuck out all over the yarn she told us. Now Miss Teramond hadn't much claim on her, and I didn't believe she was risking herself on Miss Teramond's account. But if her son was on the spot, that's a different pair of shoes altogether. We know enough for that. Further, there's that scrap of talk that the gardener heard: 'Go! Go at once! Oh, *please* go!' That was Mrs. Fairfoot begging her son to clear out while there was still time. And the gardener heard his reply, too. 'Oh, all *right!*' So we seem to be getting some bits of the jig-saw fitting together nicely. By the way, I suppose you've questioned the maid here. Did she hear anything unusual last night? When did she go to bed?"

"She went up to her room about 10 P.M., sir. But she sleeps like a log, it seems, and she heard nothing at all in the night."

"One can't always be lucky," Sir Clinton commented lightly. "And we've no reason to complain, after that whitewash. It's a pure gift from the gods."

He glanced about the room and his eyes finally rested on the desk.

"For a business man, Fairfoot seems a most untidy devil. Look at these papers, higgledy-piggledy. I want to have a look at them."

He seated himself in the desk chair and began a methodical hunt through the documents. At last he stopped and turned to the Inspector with an envelope in his hand.

"Have a look at that," he suggested, handing it over.

"It's an empty envelope, sir. . . . Address typed. . . . Postmark quite illegible — as usual," he grumbled. "Oh, I see what you mean, sir. The type's very like Miss Teramond's machine, isn't it?"

"It's identical. There's the same spot of dirt in the loop of the 'a' in 'Fairfoot' and in the loop of the 'e' in 'Drive.' "

"It's addressed to Percy Fairfoot, Esq.," noted the Inspector.

"Yes," said Sir Clinton. "And that's interesting. . . . Ah! there's the phone. That may be Headquarters. I'll answer it."

He left the room for a short time, and when he came back the Inspector could see from his expression that the news had been good.

"They've found the remains of that broken bottle," he announced. "It's a beer-bottle, or one that held stout, perhaps. Coloured glass, anyhow. The garage people told me there was a bit of glass still embedded in the rubber of the tyre, so a comparison ought to clinch the thing beyond doubt."

"Very satisfactory, sir," said Sandrock, greatly pleased.

"You can send Fairfoot down to the station and put him in a cell. He may talk, or he mayn't. If he does, the sergeant in charge can take his statement. And send down also that camera, with its case, and the slides, and the developed plates, too. I'll keep this envelope for the present. By the way, what happened when you got Mrs. Fairfoot to the station?"

"She asked to be searched at once, sir. So we got a woman searcher in. We found absolutely nothing."

"That's why she asked to be searched, no doubt. You didn't find a key to the garden gate?"

"No, sir. Absolutely nothing of the slightest interest."

"Well, I want you to come up to Fountain Court with me just now. We've one or two things to clear up there still. You'd better phone the station to send up someone to take charge here in the meanwhile."

# CHAPTER XII

# Susan Garfield

WHEN HE and the Inspector reached Fountain Court, Sir Clinton's first inquiry was about Diana Teramond's condition. The nurse was able to tell him that her patient was sleeping, and that there seemed to be no grounds for special uneasiness about her. Dr. Winthorpe was coming round, later in the day. In the meanwhile, the invalid had better be left undisturbed, unless it was essential to question her further. If a night-nurse were needed, Dr. Winthorpe would arrange about it after he had paid his visit.

"In any case," added the nurse, "Miss Garfield has come back, and she's anxious to give any help she can. Besides, I suppose one of the maids could stay overnight in the house and do anything that was needed while Miss Garfield got some sleep."

"Oh, Miss Garfield's here, is she?" said Sir Clinton. "Has she been back long? I'd like to have a few minutes' talk with her."

"She's upstairs in her room, unpacking, I think," explained the nurse. "She should be finished with that, now. She came home about half an hour ago."

"Thanks," said Sir Clinton. "Will you go upstairs, please, Inspector, and ask her if she can see me for a short time?"

Sandrock did so, and returned immediately to say that Miss Garfield would be with them in a few minutes.

She did not keep them waiting long. In fact, she made her appearance at the head of the stairs almost before the Inspector had delivered her message. Peter Diamond had described her as "good-looking, if you like the rather statuesque brand," and Sir Clinton admitted to himself, at the first glance, that here Peter had hit the mark. Susan Garfield was a shade over the average height for a woman, finely built, with a graceful walk. But in terming her "quite a drawing-room ornament," Peter had given the impression of a mere human lay-figure, content to depend on good looks alone, and here he had gone astray by leaving out the humour and intelligence which could be read in her mouth and eyes. She had none of Diana Teramond's cheap emphasis on her sex and physique, though her rather lazy movements had an appeal of their own, of which she appeared entirely unconscious. She had the gift of a perfectly natural manner, and, as she came forward to greet the two officials, she showed just the right amount of interest and no more. When she spoke, it was in a pleasant, rather deep contralto voice, which in some way seemed to harmonize with her appearance.

"You're Sir Clinton Driffield, aren't you? A dreadful business, this, I'm afraid."

The Chief Constable was pleasantly surprised to find that she had no trace of an alien accent. Evidently she had a good ear and an aptitude for intonation, for she spoke just as any well-educated Englishwoman might do.

"It must have been a nasty shock, when you came home and found my men on the premises," said Sir Clinton, sympathetically. "If we had known where you were, I'd have seen that you were forewarned. You haven't seen Miss Teramond? She's suffering from the results of her experience last night, but I hope that there's nothing seriously wrong."

"Has she been able to tell you what happened?" asked Miss Garfield.

"Very little," Sir Clinton admitted. "She's in a rather queer state. But that's a point I want to ask you about later on."

Miss Garfield nodded, with a look of intelligence which showed she had understood what he wanted.

"There's just one thing I'd like to make clear at the start," she said. "You questioned the maids about Miss Teramond, I believe? I've no idea what they said to you, but it's only fair to tell you that one of them — the girl Hatcham — is under notice. Miss Teramond has missed two or three little things from time to time; and when I actually caught Hatcham trying to open a locked drawer in the tallboy in my bedroom, we decided to dismiss her. I'm telling you this because I don't think she'd be quite fair, as a witness."

"That's very good of you," said Sir Clinton, recalling the obvious animus which the maid had shown when she gave her evidence. "We'll bear that in mind, of course. Now, if you've no objection, I'd like to ask a question or two."

"Ask anything you wish," said Miss Garfield willingly. "I'm as much puzzled as you can be by the whole affair. That is, so far as I know about it. But I'm quite certain of one thing. If Miss Teramond shot this man Brenthurst, she did it in self-defence. Isn't that what's called justifiable homicide?"

"When homicide is committed to prevent a forcible and atrocious crime," Sir Clinton admitted, "then it may be regarded by a jury as justifiable. But that depends on the crime, the circumstances, and the jury. I shouldn't care to offer an opinion about it. It's not in my department, you see."

"I thought it was plainer than that," confessed Miss Garfield. "But I got my idea from the newspapers. You know how the thing actually stands, of course. Now what would you like me to tell you?"

"First of all, I'd like to hear how you and Miss Teramond came into contact with Brenthurst. You didn't know him before you settled down here, I suppose?"

"Oh, no. But I can't explain in a sentence; it's too long for that. The fact is, Miss Teramond is something of a gambler. She likes to play cards for fairly high stakes — I mean stakes that are high compared with her resources. And she plays roulette, too, when she gets a chance, and chemmy — *chemin de fer,* you know."

"I know," said Sir Clinton with a faint smile.

"I don't suppose I should say that she plays these here," said Miss Garfield, smiling in her turn, "but she goes to Ostend fairly often, and occasionally to Monte. I'm not much of a gambler myself. It's not a matter of morals with me. Neither she nor I are very moral people, by conventional standards. Gambling simply doesn't give me much of a thrill, so I only play when I have to play. But she has a regular gambling fever, and consequently she's often short of cash. That's where Brenthurst came on the scene. He was a money-lender, you know, and Miss Teramond fell into the habit of tiding herself over temporarily by borrowing from him. I warned her again and again. I know pretty well what happens if you fall into the clutches of people like that. But she has no sense of money. In fact, she rather boasts that she hasn't got a trace of it in her make-up. Naturally, she fell deeper and deeper into debt to Brenthurst. I began to get rather worried about the state of affairs. You see, I'm fond of her, and I saw rocks ahead. I didn't trust Brenthurst much. And at last she began to see the kind of hole she had landed herself into, and she got rather frightened. She hated the look of the man, you know. One of these physical repulsions that one simply can't get over. And he began hinting about this and that, ways of paying off debts that cost nothing, stuff of that sort. And she got more frightened still, for by that time she was so much in debt that no ordinary paying-off could bring her out square. I couldn't help in a practical way. I haven't so much money as all that."

Miss Garfield began to interest Sir Clinton apart from the case in hand. There was a kindly toleration in the tone in which she spoke about Diana Teramond, almost as though an elder and wiser sister were discussing and excusing the failings of her junior, whom she would be ready to defend vigorously against anyone else if necessary. "She has her faults, but can you really blame her for them, poor girl?" It seemed a curious attitude, for the difference in age between the two could not, from their looks, be more than four or five years, if that; but Sir Clinton admitted to himself that Miss Garfield seemed to have learned a good deal more about life than Diana would ever pick up.

"She had some fairly solid assets, though, I understand," he said casually.

"She had this house, for one thing," agreed Miss Garfield. "And she had some good jewellery, too."

"There's a valuable diamond amongst her jewellery, isn't there?" Miss Garfield nodded.

"Yes. It was priced at about five thousand pounds when Miss Teramond insured her things. I arranged that for her. She's quite hopeless in business matters. It had to be listed separately. I know about that, because the insurance people brought in a valuer, a diamond expert, to put a figure on it. Naturally, they wouldn't take anybody's word when the value was as high as that."

"Did you ever hear her speak about raising money on this diamond, when her debts grew large?"

"I did, from time to time. She always had it in her mind as a sort of financial sheet-anchor."

"Now there's another point," said Sir Clinton. "Miss Teramond seems to suffer from some peculiar trouble — Dr. Winthorpe called it Jacksonian epilepsy — and after one of these slight fits she forgets things. You've noticed that?"

"Yes, she has had these attacks ever since a motor accident. She had one yesterday, as it happens. She did something, and forgot about it completely, immediately afterwards."

"What was that?" asked Sir Clinton.

"Well, it was rather unpleasant. Must I speak about it?" asked Miss Garfield, reluctantly.

"Your tame rabbit, was it?"

"Oh, you know about it?" Miss Garfield said, in a tone which suggested that she had been fencing, but now recognized that the truth must come out. "Who told you? . . . Oh, Hatcham, of course. It's the sort of thing she would be glad to advertise. Yes, it's quite true. She did go to the hutch and give one of my rabbits to Mimi — the cheetah, I mean. But when I spoke to her about it, she'd completely forgotten that she'd ever done such a thing. I was very angry, of course, at the time. I hate cruelty of any sort. But one just has to recognize that she did it without really knowing what she was doing. I got hold of her ten minutes later, and she denied it most convincingly, although she still had the poor little beast's blood on her hands. But she was perfectly unconscious of having done anything of the sort. She'd forgotten. What could one say?" she ended, with a gesture of resignation.

"You take it better than most people would do," commented the Chief Constable.

"Well, I'm fond of her," said Miss Garfield, defensively. "And although I was fond of my rabbit, there's no good crying over its death and bearing a grudge on account of something which couldn't be helped, is there?"

"You've known Miss Teramond for quite a long time, haven't you?"

"Yes, for four or five years at least. We're very close friends, and we've always moved about together. She and I were on the stage, you know. Not the legitimate, only on the Halls."

"How did you come across her to start with?"

"My mother kept theatrical lodgings," explained Miss Garfield, frankly. "She was a widow, and had to do something to make ends meet. Miss Teramond took rooms with her, once when she was resting — between engagements, you know. And she and I saw a lot of each other in that way, and we became great friends. She was younger than I was, about four years younger. Somehow, she took to me and treated me as if I were a sort of elder sister. I liked it, for I hadn't any brothers or sisters of my own."

"Where did Miss Teramond come from, originally?"

"The West Indies, I believe," Miss Garfield explained. "She spoke about Haiti at times. You know the place; run by blacks in those days, and riddled with all sorts of queer creepy affairs like Voodoo and Obi-worship. But I don't think Miss Teramond had any Negro blood in her. I gathered that her people were French. Not that I troubled much about that. I take people as I find them, and I've met worse whites than Negroes at times. But I never bothered to ask her about her early days. They didn't interest me."

"Where did you meet her first?" asked Sir Clinton.

"In San Francisco," answered Miss Garfield.

"You won't remember the earthquake; you're too young for that," commented Sir Clinton.

"Is that a compliment?" asked Miss Garfield, with a smile. "I'm thirty-one, so I do remember the earthquake."

"I'd have guessed twenty-five," Sir Clinton confessed, candidly.

"I really thought that you and Miss Teramond were about the same age. Then you do remember the earthquake? A nasty experience, surely."

"Well, I always claim to remember it," said Miss Garfield, "but I was only about a year old at the time, so you needn't ask for any thrilling details. To be honest, I don't recall much about it. At that age, one doesn't register one's memories. I expect that a good deal of what I think I remember is really got from talk that I heard about the thing, later on, when I was a little older."

"Very likely," agreed Sir Clinton. "Now, tell me, how did you and Miss Teramond come to join company?"

"That's a rather sore point," said Miss Garfield, gravely. "The fact is, I was growing bored with the kind of life I was leading. A theatrical lodging-house isn't the best environment for a girl. The company's too mixed, and one hears too many stories about easy money in the theatrical line. And about other things, as well. My mother is a queer sort of woman. She made an income out of these people, but she never approved of them, somehow. She did her best for them, just as I do my best for my pet rabbits. She was quite a popular landlady. But she despised them all the same. She'd come down in the world when my father died, and she resented that. You may not quite believe it, but she was a bit strait-laced in many ways. She'd been well-educated, as things went in her day, and she hated slang and all that sort of thing. She brought me up with a good vocabulary and a nice accent and quite passable manners."

"I noticed how you speak," Sir Clinton interjected, candidly, "and I couldn't quite place you. Now I understand better. Please go on. I'd like to know how you came to take up your present line."

"I more or less drifted into it owing to Miss Teramond," Miss Garfield explained, frankly. "She and I talked a lot about it together, and we began to see that we might join forces. I was quite a good dancer, good enough for all we needed on the Halls, anyhow; and we found that I had a turn for acting of a sort. I'd never make much on the legitimate stage, of course. I'm not near that standard. But I was quite good enough to act in sketches with Miss Teramond. There's not much boasting in saying that, as you can imagine. So the upshot was that I told my mother I meant to go on the stage. This is the sore point. She was violently against the idea, wouldn't hear of it at any price. We're both stubborn, and I was determined to go my own way. To cut the thing short, we ended up with a regular bitter quarrel, and I went off to join Miss Teramond with what used to be called 'a parent's curse' on my head. My mother was very fond of me, up till then. But I was quite old enough to know my own mind, and I wasn't going to let her run my life for me. I'm sorry, in a way, but there's no going back, now."

"You haven't written to her, to make things up?"

"I did, once. But she'd heard a thing or two about me through some of the profession who stayed with her, from time to time. Not much good, I'm afraid. There's no use pretending that Miss Teramond and I drew enormous salaries. We live by our looks and not by our stage talents. So, naturally, stories drifted back to my mother about the sort of life we were leading. Anyhow, she wrote me a letter which quite cured me of any notion about a reconciliation. I was mixed up with a man, just then, and she'd heard all about that, and she threw it in my teeth in an unforgivable way. I see him from time to time still, so he's stuck to me better than my mother did. Not a bad sort, Cecil, after all," she ended, in a tone which suggested kindly recollections.

"Did Miss Teramond know him?" asked the Chief Constable.

"Cecil? Oh, no. He was a private affair of my own. I may as well be quite frank about these things. Miss Teramond is prettier than I am, and more attractive to men. Anyone can see that by looking at the two of us. Quite often a man has taken a fancy to me, but Miss Teramond cut me out when she appeared on the scene. Percy Fairfoot is the latest example. That sort of thing never makes me jealous, because she doesn't wilfully put my nose out of joint. It's simply that she's more attractive. And I'm not very keen on men. I've seen too many of them and too much of them, as you can imagine. They don't mean much to me apart from what can be got out of them. I've looked after Miss Teramond in that way and kept her out of the hands of a good many men who'd have done her no good; for she has no judgement at all in matters of that kind, none whatever, so long as the man's fairly good-looking. But Cecil was different. I didn't want him to turn me down and go over to her. So, naturally enough, I took care that they never got to know each other. Why run an obvious risk?"

Miss Garfield was evidently completely a-moral in some ways; but her frankness made her interesting. That curious "elder sister" touch had come out again during her last speech, with its suggestion that she played a helpful part in Miss Teramond's affairs and kept her out of bad hands so far as possible. There seemed to be no doubt as to which of the two women was the dominant partner in their association.

"I suppose you haven't seen your friend — Cecil — for some time?" Sir Clinton asked, idly. "He's in America? In the profession, perhaps?"

"You're astray each time," said Miss Garfield, with a pleasant little laugh. "He's not in the profession, and never was. To tell the truth, he seems to be in some fresh line every time I meet him. He never sticks at anything, and so he never seems to be a great success in any particular line. He makes enough to keep him going, and perhaps a little more; but that's all. A bit of a rolling stone. And as it happens, he's rolled over into Europe now. And I *have* seen him lately. I saw him last night. That's what I went away for. I met him at the Duke's Head, in Trendon."

Sir Clinton nodded, without comment. Trendon was a big junction town some forty miles away, and the Duke's Head was a five-star caravanserai with a floating population of visitors who seldom stayed more than a night. It was just the kind of place which would suit a rendezvous of that sort. Miss Garfield certainly had an engaging frankness about herself, whatever might be her other failings.

"Did you wire to him to make this appointment?" asked Sir Clinton.

"No, he wrote to me, and I wrote to the Duke's Head to book a room."

"Did you post the letter yourself, or did someone take it out for you?"

"I really don't remember. Usually, we put our letters on the table in the hall and one of the maids takes them out and posts them on her way home at night, if they haven't been posted before then. Or I take them to the pillar myself, if I happen to go out. I can't remember whether I posted that letter myself or not. It was ten days or so ago."

"What's your friend's present address?" inquired Sir Clinton.

Miss Garfield's graceful gesture indicated that she could not answer the question.

"I never know his address," she explained. "He shifts about so much, and I don't believe he has any permanent address at all. And he's a very poor hand at letter-writing, so often I don't hear from him for months at a time. When there's a chance of our meeting, he drops me a line or two to fix it up."

"What's his surname?" inquired Sir Clinton. "You haven't mentioned it."

"Ducane — Cecil Ducane's his full name."

The words roused some faint memory in Sir Clinton, but he did not trouble about it at that moment, as he had other questions still to ask.

"You've told me something about Ambrose Brenthurst and his dealings with Miss Teramond," he went on. "She was afraid of him, you said. Now, apart from yourself, was there anyone to whom she could have turned for support in that affair, anyone who might have been called in to protect her?"

Miss Garfield gave no immediate answer. She seemed to be running over some list in her mind and giving it careful consideration. At last she spoke.

"I've tried to recall anyone likely," she said, "but honestly I can't remember anyone who could have been depended on at a pinch. Of course, she has plenty of men friends; quite a number of them come and pay visits here. Not local people. But they're not the sort to take a risk on her account. Far from it. The last thing they'd want is to have their names trumpeted abroad in connection with either of us. They're very discreet," she ended, with a faintly cynical smile. "I don't blame them for that. No, the only man who was really keen on her — for keeps, if you see what I mean — was Julian Lorrimore. He was genuinely in love with her, enough in love to want to marry her, although he had a pretty good idea of what she actually was. And I did my best to encourage him and help the thing along, because I felt they'd make a success of the business. And I'd like to see her settled down, with a decent man to look after her. She'd be all right then, and I'd be glad to shuffle off my own responsibility, on to someone else's shoulders. She has absolutely no common sense where cash is concerned; and I often find it wearing, very wearing, when she gets herself into a hole over money."

Again, in her manner, Sir Clinton noticed that curious "elder sister" attitude, that affectionate but half-contemptuous lenity which he had noticed throughout her references to Diana.

"What about Percy Fairfoot?" he asked, abruptly.

"Percy?" echoed Miss Garfield, apparently still pursuing her previous line of thought. "No, I don't think Percy would do. He's not really in love with her, as Julian Lorrimore was. His feelings may be strong enough just now, but they're only a flash in the pan. They'd tire of each other before the honeymoon was over. And he's got no money. I don't want her to marry unless she gets a husband who can give her the sort of things she's grown accustomed to."

"I wasn't thinking of that side of it," Sir Clinton explained. "Is he the sort of man who would come to her help if she was in any danger? Or is he like the others you mentioned a moment or two ago?"

"How should I know?" said Miss Garfield, rather unexpectedly. "He's infatuated with her at the moment, anyone can see that. He's an impulsive man, passionate, quick-tempered, all that sort of thing, and I think he's probably eaten up with jealousy. We kept him away from the house when any of our other friends came to see us because we couldn't afford to have any trouble. You can't tell what a man like that might do, on the spur of the moment."

"What about his mother?" demanded Sir Clinton.

"Oh, she was another drawback," replied Miss Garfield, still intent on her original theme. "These two adore one another, you know. I don't think an adoring son makes much of a husband. There's bound to come a time when he's got to choose between mother-love and the other thing, and one never knows which will come on top. If Percy had shown signs of growing dangerous, I'd have stepped in and done my best to stop the affair."

"You knew his mother fairly well?"

Miss Garfield smiled, without even a touch of bitterness.

"Well, we're all more or less *déclassées,* Miss Teramond, Mrs. Fairfoot, and I. We've got that in common, at least."

"Can you account for her being here, in the garden, in the small hours of this morning?" asked Sir Clinton.

"No, I can't," said Miss Garfield, positively. "I've been puzzling my brains over that very point ever since I heard she'd been here. It seems queer. I mean, how could she know that Brenthurst was coming over here at an hour like that? He wasn't likely to tell her — or anyone else — about his plans. They were hardly suitable for broadcasting, to judge by what's happened."

"What sort of person is this gardener, Sperling?" inquired the Chief Constable.

Miss Garfield did not seem to like the question.

"I don't know that I've much to say about him," she replied, cautiously. "We took him over with the house and grounds, when we came. I don't care to say anything against him. . . ."

"Is he honest?" demanded Sir Clinton, bluntly.

"I haven't caught him doing anything dishonest," retorted Miss Garfield. "I've noticed, though, that some of the best fruit seems to vanish, rather mysteriously. But there's another gardener, and a boy. I've no proof that Sperling is responsible. Obviously, if we had clear proof of any dishonesty, he'd get a week's notice."

Sir Clinton nodded, rather absent-mindedly. He seemed to have secured all the information which he required for the time being.

"Thank you, Miss Garfield," he said. "Now I'll leave you with Inspector Sandrock. He's been taking notes and he'll read them over to you so that you can check them. I'm going to speak to Miss Teramond for a few moments. I want to check whether her memory's working properly, now that she's got over the first shock."

Leaving Sandrock and Miss Garfield, Sir Clinton ascertained from the nurse that Diana Teramond was awake and quite able to speak to him. When he was submitted to her room, he put her at her ease with a few inquiries about how she felt, before beginning his actual questions of importance.

"I'm just going to test your memory a little," he explained, by way of introduction. "If you don't recall the answer to any question, just say so, and we'll try something else. Now, first of all, what's the name of your gardener, the one who lives in the cottage?"

"That, surely, is very easy," said Diana, with a faint smile of relief. "I shall get high marks in this examination, without a doubt. His name is Sperling. I do not know his first name, though. But I do not think I ever knew it, so that it is not my memory which is at fault."

"Good," said the Chief Constable, encouragingly. "Let's try again. When were you born?"

"In 1909. I am just twenty-seven. I look older?"

"No," said Sir Clinton, frankly, "you look a year or two younger than that. By the way, where were you born?"

"At Jacmel, in Haiti. I lived there until I was twelve years of age. Then my parents went to Guadeloupe. They were French, not Haitians, you understand. I am a French Creole; but when I say that, most people seem to think I have some Negro blood. But that is not so."

"And after Guadeloupe you went to . . ."

"To the States; and after that, about four years ago, to England."

"That's very satisfactory," said Sir Clinton, in a tone of satisfaction. "Now, another question. Do you remember a song about 'Nita, with her cheetah'?"

"Oh, yes, of course I remember that. I used to sing it with some little success. I used to take Mimi on to the stage with me, and the audience was always delighted."

"I can imagine so," said Sir Clinton, smiling. "I've met one of your admirers. It was he who told me about the song. Now, another question. Did you ever know anyone called Cecil? Cecil Ducane?"

Diana seemed completely at a loss.

"Cecil Ducane?" she echoed. "No; that I do not remember. Not in the slightest. It means nothing to me. Should I remember it?" she asked, anxiously.

Sir Clinton laughed and shook his head.

"I'm asking you a question here and there which you can't be expected to answer," he explained. "That's part of the test."

"Ah! I see. You are making a game of me? You try to catch me out, *hein*? Well, continue with this catching."

Evidently she bore no malice on account of the Chief Constable's little trap.

"You dined at your usual time, last night?" was the next question.

"Yes. That is eight o'clock, always."

"You see, there's not much wrong with your memory," said Sir Clinton, reassuringly. "Now, let's try further back. Where did you first meet Miss Garfield?"

"That was in San Francisco," answered Diana, readily. "I had a room in her mother's house, Mrs. Garfield's, once when I was resting. When I was out of an engagement, I mean. A very strict lady, Mrs. Garfield, what you call a bit of a dragon in some ways. She would stand no nonsense, I remember. But very kind, too, in her own way. I am sorry that she and Susan quarrelled, in the end. That was a pity."

"Do you remember the address you stayed at?"

Diana paused for a moment before answering this.

"It was in Avenell Street North," she said. "That I remember well. But the number?" She hesitated again for a moment or two. "It was either 1144 or 1153, I think. But it is years ago, you understand? I cannot be quite sure."

"You're doing famously," Sir Clinton assured her. "I hardly expected you to recall the number after all that time, especially as you've been moving about so much, in between. Now, let's take something more up to date. When did you write to Mrs. Fairfoot lately — within the last week, let's say?"

But here he drew a blank. Diana looked at him doubtfully while she apparently racked her memory. At last she seemed to give it up.

"You are catching me again? Yes? I really do not remember that."

"Do you remember writing to Mr. Brenthurst?"

Again there was a peculiar hesitation, but it lasted only a second or two.

"Yes, I remember writing to him. At least, I typed a letter on my machine, because I do not write easily with a pen. It was a letter asking him to come and see me yesterday about some money I owed him. I remember that."

"This is the letter, is it?" asked Sir Clinton, taking it from his pocket and opening it up.

Diana glanced at it casually.

"Yes, that is it. It is on our own note-paper, with the printed address. Oh, yes, that is the letter I sent to him."

Sir Clinton refolded the note and put it back into his pocket.

"You and Miss Garfield used to shoot in the garden sometimes? That was to accustom yourselves to handling the automatic pistol, I suppose?"

"Yes, we used up quite a lot of cartridges at one time or another. But we did not become good shots at all. By no means, indeed."

"You had a fire-arms certificate," said Sir Clinton.

"I really do not remember," said Diana, looking rather puzzled. "I know we had some formalities . . ."

"That's quite all right," the Chief Constable assured her. "I had your name looked up, and you hold a certificate. I remember

167

it was granted because you wanted it for protection against burglars, since you and Miss Garfield are alone at nights, and Fountain Court is so isolated from neighbours. Now, just a few questions more, and then I'll stop bothering you. Who gave you that large diamond?"

"My fiancé, it was; Julian Lorrimore."

"Good. Now, another question. Did you lock up cupboards or places of that sort, as a general rule?"

Diana seemed rather puzzled by this inquiry.

"I have a safe, as you see, and that was always kept locked up, because I have my jewellery in it. And Miss Garfield, she also kept one or two of her jewels in it, not many, for she does not care for jewellery. But, except for my safe, I do not think I lock up anything. Miss Garfield locks one or two drawers in her room, for I remember she complained to me about our maid, Hatcham. She found Hatcham trying to open one of these locked drawers. And we had missed one or two little things, so we gave the girl notice. One cannot have about one's house anyone whom one cannot trust. You, naturally, will understand that."

"Oh, naturally," said the Chief Constable, with a gesture of agreement.

He took from his pocket the letter of invitation which Mrs. Fairfoot had produced in order to explain her presence in the garden, and held it before Diana so that she had no need to touch it.

"Do you remember writing this?" he asked. "It was done on your typewriter, as you can see."

Diana examined it without showing a sign of recognition in her features. Then she shook her head rather despondently.

"No, I cannot remember that I wrote it. No, I have forgotten it completely. . . . Ah! I see! You are catching me again? You write it yourself, and then you come to me, all solemn, and say: 'Did you write this?' Is that it? But I do not remember anything about it."

Sir Clinton laughed, as though admitting her interpretation.

"Now that seems all I have to ask you just now, Miss Teramond. I don't think you need feel worried about your memory. It seems in as good working order as many people's. Thanks for your patience."

Before rejoining the Inspector, Sir Clinton went to the telephone and rang up one of his subordinates to give some instructions. When these had been noted, the sergeant at the phone read out a report which had just come in. Sir Clinton listened to it, gave some further instructions, and then returned to the room where he had left Sandrock. The Inspector was alone, having evidently completed his routine with Miss Garfield.

"Did you get anything, sir?" he inquired.

"She remembers some things and forgets others, much like the rest of us," said the Chief Constable. "Evidently there's still a slight hang-over from that fit she had. Still, I think she's given me all we need for the moment."

"You were on the phone, sir?" asked Sandrock. "I saw you going to it."

"Yes, I was ringing up to ask about the wholesale price of apples," Sir Clinton explained, with something very near a grin on his features. "It's a matter of interest, at this season of the year. And I got a report from Sergeant Vicary which seems of more immediate importance."

He sat down and lighted a cigarette, keeping the Inspector on tenter-hooks until he had finished.

"You know the cross-roads just beyond Staghurst?" he went on. "There's a culvert about a hundred yards or so north of them. Well, it seems that some inquisitive youngster was fishing for tiddlers in the streamlet there, and gradually worked up to the culvert. Under it, he found a suit of clothes — jacket, waist-coat, and trousers, I mean — which were considerably blood-stained down the front. He reported his find to our people, and they've collected the goods. They've just come in to the local station, but no one has had time yet to examine them carefully. An interesting find, I think. By the way, when is Dr. Stangate likely to give us a report on these blood samples?"

"To-morrow, sir, I believe."

"Well, you'd better hand over this blood-stained suit as well, and let him make a clean job of it when he's at it. It may have no connection with the Brenthurst case; but it may fit into the jig-saw somewhere. People don't leave clothes about, as a rule, in that way. Especially blood-stained ones."

"No, sir. Anything else?"

Sir Clinton gave one or two more instructions, and the Inspector jotted them down in his note-book.

"Very good, sir. I'll see about these things and let you have the reports to-morrow."

# CHAPTER XIII

# Blood

Dr. Stangate was a tall sparely built man with an impassive face which faintly suggested the features of one of the Roman emperors. In court, he was a useful witness, for he was terse in all his statements and his professional manner impressed juries by its gloomy certainty. On less formal occasions, he had a looser tongue, which, combined with his complete disregard for other people's feelings, accounted for his slight unpopularity among his medical brethren. He was apt to assume complete ignorance on the part of his audience and to set about the task of enlightenment without respect for age, experience, or intelligence. Dr. Stangate was, in fact, something of a pedant.

When Inspector Sandrock called to get the report on the various blood samples which had been submitted for examination, Dr. Stangate was in one of his instructive moods, as his first words proved.

"Do you know what blood is, Inspector?"

Sandrock groaned internally. He knew from past experience that any attempt to by-pass this preamble would be mere waste of time. As he phrased it to himself, he was for it, and would have to go through it.

"It tastes salt, sir, and I know it when I see it. That's about as far as I go."

"Ah, indeed? You ought to know a little more than that, in your position. I'll tell you one or two facts which will be useful to you. Without this information, it would be difficult for you to understand this report which I am about to hand over to you. Blood is a fluid containing large numbers of red corpuscles, and a smaller number of white corpuscles or leucocytes. The fluid is termed plasma; and it contains a number of chemicals, one of which is named fibrinogen. When blood leaves the body through a wound, this fibrinogen is converted into a stringy substance, fibrin. The fibrin mats together with some red corpuscles, forming a clot which serves to plug the wound and stop the bleeding. You may have noticed the process when you cut yourself in shaving, as I see you did this morning."

"Oh, yes," said Sandrock, resignedly.

"After blood has coagulated in this way, there is some clear fluid left over, which is termed serum," continued Dr. Stangate. "As I see you fidgeting in your chair, I shall condense what I have still to say, if, in return, you will be good enough to restrain your rather discourteous impatience. I have your kind permission to proceed?"

"Oh, yes," repeated the Inspector, with surface politeness, though inwardly he was raging.

"The two most characteristic features in the blood are the corpuscles and the serum," continued Dr. Stangate, mercilessly bent on his self-imposed task of education. "It is on them that we rely when attempting to identify a particular blood submitted to us for examination. There are four distinct kinds of blood, and only four. A human being may be classed into one of four groups according to the way in which his serum acts on the red corpuscles of individuals belonging to the other three groups; and also according to the way in which his red corpuscles behave with the sera of the other three kinds of blood. That, as you see, gives a double check. The result one looks for is what is called agglutination: a clumping together of the red corpuscles rather like the behaviour of people in a street running and forming a crowd when an accident happens."

"I see," said Sandrock, with a trace of scepticism in his tone. "But does it work with blood that's been lying about for a while, sir?"

"It has been found to work with blood-stains fifteen months old," explained Dr. Stangate.

"That sounds good enough," conceded Sandrock. "I didn't know that."

"You have much to learn, Inspector," said Dr. Stangate, with a blandness which almost, but not quite, atoned for the rudeness of his remark. "To make sure that you understand, I'll put the scheme down on paper."

He scribbled for a moment or two, and then handed the sheet to the Inspector.

|                     | Corpuscles agglutinated | | | |
|---------------------|------|------|------|------|
|                     | I    | II   | III  | IV   |
| With Serum   I [AB] | –    | –    | –    | –    |
| With Serum  II [A]  | +    | –    | +    | –    |
| With Serum III [B]  | +    | +    | –    | –    |
| With Serum  IV [O]  | +    | +    | +    | –    |

"The plus sign means that you get clumping of the corpuscles, the dash means that there is no effect," Dr. Stangate pursued. "Obviously, if you have in your laboratory specimens of sera belonging to each of the four groups, and four sets of corpuscles derived from men belonging to the four groups, a few experiments on an unknown blood will serve to show which class it belongs to. For example, if the corpuscles of the sample give clumping with Serum II and Serum IV, but no agglutination with Serum I and Serum III, then the corpuscles must have come from a Group III blood. On the other hand, suppose that Serum I does not produce agglutination, whilst all the other three sera do cause the corpuscles to clump together, then the corpuscles must have been derived from a blood of the Group I type. And so on. You can confirm this by trying the effect of the serum of your blood sample upon the four different types of corpuscles."

"What do these letters in brackets mean, sir?" demanded the Inspector.

"They are the symbols employed nowadays to designate the four classes of blood: AB, A, B, and O. I've used them in my report, you'll find. I shall now proceed to run through the results which I obtained by examining the various blood samples which your people sent to me for examination. You need not make notes. I have set it all down in my report in such a form that even the least intelligent person could not fail to understand."

"The Chief Constable will appreciate that, sir," said Sandrock, goaded out of his normal monosyllabic vocabulary by exasperation.

Dr. Stangate brushed this aside and continued.

"Amongst the specimens furnished to me by the police, I detected four different kinds of blood. In the first place, there was the blood of the murdered man Brenthurst, which belongs to Group O. Traces of the same type of blood were also detectable on the blades of grass growing on the piece of turf stated to have been cut from the border of the path in the garden of Fountain Court; on Mrs. Fairfoot's hands and gloves; and on this man's suit which was submitted to me."

"You mean, sir, that you found Brenthurst's blood on all these things?"

"I mean nothing of the sort," declared Dr. Stangate, with the air of a teacher in despair at the dullness of a backward pupil. "All I said was that blood belonging to Group O was found on all these articles. Thousands of people have blood belonging to Group O. For all I know, *your* blood may be Group O blood. We do not profess to identify the blood of a particular individual. Please make a special note of that."

"I see, sir," said Sandrock. "The blood on the various things is the same kind of blood as Brenthurst had; but for all you can say about it, it might have come from Bill Jones or Jack Wright. H'm! You're not such a help, after all, then."

This last reflection was the Inspector's retort courteous for Dr. Stangate's supercilious attitude. But the expert's vanity was proof against any such thrusts. He simply ignored this one, and continued with his exposition.

"The blood on the gardening gloves and on the knife submitted to me is a mixture. Some of it is human blood, belonging to Group AB; the rest of it is rabbit's blood. The handkerchief embroidered with 'D' and 'T' gives the same result. Finally, there is blood taken from the terrace. It is identical with the blood of the cheetah, apparently, though I have not had the time to establish that definitely, as the process takes a longish period. I can say, at any rate, that it contains no human blood. Thus the samples submitted to me contain, as I said before, four different kinds of blood: human blood of Group O, human blood of Group AB, rabbit's blood, and the blood of the cheetah. That gives you, in the fewest words, the substance of my written report, which I now hand over to you for transmission to the proper authorities. I have sent a second copy to the Coroner, and he informs me that he is calling me as a witness at the inquest."

The Inspector gave Dr. Stangate very perfunctory thanks, collected the knife and other exhibits which had been handed over for examination, and retired without lingering. He felt that he had suffered enough for one day in the cause of education.

When he reached Headquarters, he went straight to the Chief Constable's office, where he found Sir Clinton busy with various routine documents. Sandrock handed over Dr. Stangate's report, and Sir Clinton read it through before asking any questions. When he had finished, he looked up with a quizzical expression.

"I expect you've had an instructive time, Inspector. Dr. Stangate's idea of conversation is a monologue by himself, accompanied by polite noises from his listeners."

"There's too much of this compulsory education about, nowadays, for my taste, sir," said Sandrock, crossly. "However, he seems to have done his job all right, so far as it goes."

"Let's put it aside for a moment," suggested Sir Clinton. "Here's the report of our finger-print expert. On the pistol, the only clear prints he found were Miss Teramond's. He checked them by comparison with some on her hairbrush handle and a hand-mirror from her dressing-table. He could make nothing of that gold pendant, except some fragmentary impressions which seemed to be Brenthurst's and Miss Teramond's. It seems to have been rubbed a bit by Brenthurst putting it into his pocket, and rubbed again by our men clawing it out again when they found his body. You'll have to warn them to be more careful. They left their own prints on it, plain enough."

"Very good, sir."

"We had Mrs. Fairfoot's prints on my fountain-pen, you remember," the Chief Constable continued, "so we were able to check up some others. Our man found quite a number of her impressions, good ones, on the inside of the pagoda door. That tallies with her tale of having held the door for fear of the cheetah. When he came to examine the long shaft of that birch besom we found, he detected at least half a dozen very good prints of hers on it. So she had her gloves off when she was using it. And there was nothing about any sweeping, in her story. So she didn't tell us everything, by a long chalk."

"Well, that pins her, anyhow," said the Inspector, in a tone of satisfaction. "She'll have to explain that bit away — if she can. And what about the pruning-knife, sir?"

"All he could find on it was a print or two, quite sharp, made by Miss Teramond, and some very smudgy impressions from the fingers of Sperling, the gardener."

"Nothing by Mrs. Fairfoot?" said Sandrock, in a tone of some astonishment.

"Not a trace," declared Sir Clinton.

"Oh, of course," Sandrock added, hurriedly, "she was wearing gloves, so she'd leave no prints, anyhow."

"But she had her gloves off when she pressed up against the door," Sir Clinton pointed out.

"So she had, I suppose," Sandrock admitted. "Well, it'll all come out in the wash, by and by, no doubt. Is that the lot, sir?"

"That is the lot," confirmed the Chief Constable. "Now let's take Dr. Stangate's report. We can leave out the cheetah. We know all about it. Take the pruning-knife and the gardening-gloves. They had rabbit's blood on them."

"That tallies with the story about Miss Teramond killing that white rabbit and giving it to the cheetah," Sandrock pointed out. "She must have cut the thing's throat with the pruning-knife and handed the body over to her little pet to eat. That would get the rabbit's blood on to the knife, and on to the gardening-gloves, too, if she was wearing them at the time, sir."

"Yes, but what about the human blood on both these things?" inquired the Chief Constable. "It wasn't Brenthurst's, because his belongs to Group O, whilst the stuff on the knife and gloves belongs to group AB, according to Dr. Stangate."

"I don't see my way through that, sir," Sandrock admitted, frankly. "In fact, I don't see how that second brand of blood comes into the business at all."

"Nor do I," Sir Clinton admitted, candidly. "But I live in hope. It's the rarest of the four blood-types. Only 4 per cent of people have it, as against over 40 per cent with blood like Brenthurst's. But now let's have a look at that suit with the blood-stains on it, please."

The Inspector opened up his parcel and spread out the coat, waist-coat, and trousers on the floor. The suit was of a light slate-blue cloth which showed the ugly stains clearly.

"All the blood's on the front, as you can see, sir," Sandrock pointed out. "The main bulk of it's on the sleeves. The whole of the left fore-arm's been soaked in it. The right cuff's the same, and it's even got all over the inside of the sleeve." He turned back the cloth to show the ominous stains on the sleeve-lining. "There's a light deposit on the outside of the lower part of the lapels and a bit farther down, which looks as if it had got there by the man's soaked sleeve brushing across them. The vest's practically clean; and there's just a drip or two on the trousers."

"H'm! Let's see," said the Chief Constable, thoughtfully. "Just stand as you are, Inspector, please. Now suppose I come up behind you, like this, and clench you round the chest with my left arm — so — and then cut your throat with my right hand. There'd be a bit of a struggle, of course. Throat-cutting is a messy business. It's easy to see how the blood got mainly over the right-hand cuff, and even on to the lining. Then the gush would over-run the left sleeve, which would be across Brenthurst's chest, just below the gash. Meanwhile all the rest of the murderer's jacket and his waist-coat would be protected by Brenthurst's body. If there was a struggle, the legs of the two antagonists would probably be a bit mixed up, which may account for some blood getting on to the murderer's trousers. Then, after it was all over, any movements of the murderer's forearms across his front would leave the light stains on his lapels. That seems to fit, roughly. I shouldn't wonder if it turned out to be near the mark."

He released the Inspector and turned back to examine the suit extended on the floor.

"I suppose you've measured it?" he asked.

"Yes, sir. It would just about fit a man of Fairfoot's build. If we could get him to try it on, we could make sure."

Sir Clinton nodded, and continued his scrutiny of the garments.

"That would depend on whether Fairfoot's weight has kept constant for the last few years," he replied, rather to Sandrock's surprise. "Just look here, Inspector. This suit suggests a thing or two. First of all, the cut of the coat isn't up to date. I'd say that it was in the first flush of fashion three or four years ago. In fact, it's a slight exaggeration of the fashion of that period."

"There's something in what you say, sir," admitted the Inspector, glancing from the clothes on the floor to the suit that Sir Clinton was wearing. "The lapels are a shade different from present-day ones, and the waist-coat opening's different, too. It wasn't cut yesterday, sure enough. But I don't see much help in that, sir."

"No? Here's a suit that must have been bought some years ago, and yet it obviously hasn't been worn much. To judge by the linings, I'd say it hadn't had more than a couple of months' wear altogether, if that."

"Perhaps he bought it, sir, and then didn't like it. That would fit the case, wouldn't it?"

"It would, if you take the case of a man who has the knack of carrying clothes well. But it won't fit Fairfoot. I happened to notice that he's rather hard on his clothes. He hasn't the trick of keeping them new-looking, to judge by the suit I saw him in. His trousers don't exactly bag at the knees, but they give the impression of being well on the way to doing so. Now these trousers don't show a trace of anything like that. Whoever wore them was careful always to hitch them up in the right way when he sat down. And the suit as a whole tells the same tale. It's been worn fairly often, and yet it hasn't been knocked about in the least. In fact, by the look of it, I'd say it had been worn by someone who was anxious to keep up a good appearance, somebody who wanted to be smart-looking. Look at the trouser-creases. They show it's been well cared for. And from the fact that it slightly exaggerates the fashion of its time, I'm inclined to think that the wearer may have leaned towards the flashy side more than good taste would dictate. Now Fairfoot isn't flashy, to do him justice. He dresses, more or less, just as he ought to do, considering what he is."

"Yes, that's so, sir," Sandrock agreed. Then with a faintly quizzing smile he added: "You might look at the tag inside the breast pocket."

Sir Clinton did so, and discovered a slip of white linen sewn inside the pocket. On it were embroidered in red the initials "C.D."

"H'm! So that's why you smiled? 'C.D.' — Clinton Driffield, eh? A queer coincidence, but I shouldn't advise you to build too much on it, Inspector," the Chief Constable declared, with a smile rather more pronounced than that of Sandrock. "When I take to crime, I hope I'll have enough wits left to scatter no clues of that sort about."

"I wasn't suggesting anything of the sort, sir," Sandrock affirmed, in a slightly horrified tone. "I was thinking of something quite different. 'C.D.' — Cecil Ducane. I mean that friend of the Garfield girl."

Sir Clinton did not reply immediately, and when he spoke again it was only to ask a question.

"You've checked her statements about staying at the Duke's Head, I suppose?"

"Yes, sir, I did. I asked the Trendon people to check her tale. It's quite all right. She had booked a double room at the Duke's Head beforehand, and she arrived there in a car. She registered as Mrs. Cecil Ducane. She's been there once or twice before under that name. The man joined her, later on. Then they spent the night at the Duke's Head. The man left by some early train, and she came away after breakfast, in her car. I had a suspicion that it might be one of these put-up jobs. A divorce case, sir, with a bit of collusion thrown in, and her acting as co-respondent. But there's nothing of that sort, none of the usual stunts, chambermaid bringing them morning tea and finding them still in bed, and so on. It's just what she told us it was — the pair of them having a night out for once in a while. What I said about Ducane and the 'C.D.' on the tab was just a bit of a joke, sir. At first sight I did note the coincidence in the initials, just as you spotted they were your own. But there's nix in it, so far as facts go."

"Well, if you're satisfied," said the Chief Constable, "that's enough for the present. But Ducane isn't a very common name, and I heard of it in connection with the Brenthurst family some time ago."

"Indeed, sir?" queried Sandrock, pricking up his ears. "How was that?"

"The late Ambrose Brenthurst had an illegitimate sister, Netta Adine," Sir Clinton explained. "She went off to America and married an actor, Reuben Ducane. She, Ducane, and their offspring were all wiped out in the San Francisco earthquake in 1906. So Peter Diamond tells me. Now up pops this Cecil Ducane from America, and I've been wondering if he's one of the same Ducane clan. Say a son of some brother of Reuben Ducane's, which might make him about the right age for our friend of the Duke's Head. You see, Inspector, Ambrose Brenthurst's mother is intestate and likely to die so, from all I've heard. If Ambrose had survived her, he'd have come into her fortune, which seems not inconsiderable. I've been casting about to see whether, now that Ambrose is gone, any relation of Reuben Ducane's could come into the succession under the Birkenhead Act. But, frankly, I can't see how that could happen. As things stand at present, with Ambrose out of the way, Mrs. Fairfoot is the next in the line of inheritance in case of old Mrs. Brenthurst dying intestate."

"I didn't think of that, sir," confessed Sandrock. "That puts a fresh light on things. A very rum light, so far as I can see. If the likely heiress is Mrs. Fairfoot, then there's a motive all ready. And a motive was what I couldn't see in the thing. That's a trump card, sir. Now I begin to see my way. You think Mrs. Fairfoot did the job? To clear the way for herself to get the cash?"

"Now did I say anything of the sort?" demanded Sir Clinton, with a laugh. "I wish I saw through the business as clearly as all that, Inspector. But I don't. One thing I do feel fairly confident about, and that is that Mrs. Fairfoot's evidence was like white coffee, about half of one thing and half of another."

"You didn't charge her with being an accessory, I remember," said the Inspector, scratching his chin.

"Because I don't want to run any risks over false arrest. It's obvious that she lent a helping hand in the business. But just *when* it occurred to her to put her shoulder to the wheel, I can't tell you at this moment."

"It's felony in any case, sir," said Sandrock, ruminatively. "I see your point, though. If she helped to plan the crime, and was on the actual spot when Brenthurst was done in, then she's a principal in the second degree and gets hanged for her pains. If she had a hand in the scheme beforehand, but wasn't present when he got his light put out, then she's an accessory before the fact, and she gets hanged just the same. But if all she did was to help the murderer in his get-away, then she's only an accessory after the fact, and she scrapes off with penal servitude. Humph! It's the point of her being on the actual spot that's worrying you, sir?"

"Yes, to begin with," admitted Sir Clinton. "If her tale about being in the pagoda were true, was she or was she not present at the actual murder? A sharp barrister might make good play with that point."

"M'yes," conceded the Inspector, doubtfully. "I see the snag, sir. But what else had you in mind?"

"That letter she produced," explained the Chief Constable. "Would you take it as evidence of pre-arrangement? It might well look like that, if Miss Teramond were charged with the murder."

"But you're not charging *her,* sir, surely?" said Sandrock, in a surprised tone.

"So far, we haven't charged anyone with the murder," said Sir

Clinton, with a certain levity. "Not even myself, on the strength of those initials. But you never know your luck, Inspector. I strive always to keep an open mind. You may have noticed that trait in my character; if you haven't, just keep a look-out and I'm sure you'll see it. I rather pride myself on it. But we've other things in hand just now. You got your warrant and searched Brenthurst's house? Did you find anything worth while?"

"Nothing that helps in this affair, sir. Lots of evidence about the sort of fellow Brenthurst was, though. A real dirty dog. The only good thing about him was that he kept all his papers tidy. We'd no trouble in finding what we wanted."

"That wasn't hereditary," Sir Clinton observed, with a smile. "His son's desk was covered with papers and letters thrown down at random, by the look of them. Tidiness isn't young Fairfoot's long suit. He must take a day off, once a month, and file the accumulation *en bloc*. Did you find a will amongst Brenthurst's papers?"

"No, sir, not a trace of one. So I tried his solicitors. They know of no will. He never asked them to draft one."

"H'm! So he may be intestate. If so, he's got no spouse or legitimate issue, so his money goes to his parent, Mrs. Brenthurst; and she's got more than enough for her wants, already, if all tales be true. That's no great help to us."

The Inspector seemed to meditate for a while before he spoke again.

"It's just crossed my mind, sir," he began, tentatively, "after what you said about charging the Teramond woman. After she shot him, he was still fit to raise a howl. That might have brought somebody to the scene. Perhaps his throat was cut to stop his row. One can't rule that out."

"I see your point," the Chief Constable replied, immediately. "You think that she may have had one of her lovers on the spot, and that he did the throat-cutting to stifle Brenthurst's outcries? And you're linking that up with the blood-stained suit, aren't you? Let's follow out that line of argument. The suit had 'C.D.' on it. That suggests Cecil Ducane. But Cecil Ducane is Miss Garfield's property. She's kept him out of touch with Miss Teramond, for good reasons of her own. Therefore it follows that the suit was worn by somebody who wasn't Cecil Ducane, but who had the same initials and who was an old lover of Miss Teramond. It seems to me to make things more complicated, instead of clearing them up."

"Well, sir, perhaps the Teramond woman did the throat-cutting herself," suggested the Inspector, rather hopelessly.

"In that case, some blood would have got on to her kimono," declared Sir Clinton, in a tone of conviction. "But there was no blood on it or on her night-dress. No, it won't pass. Cheer up, though. Things are clearing up in some parts of the field. Sergeant Burford seemed a bit out of his depth in a murder case; but he's excellent when it comes to petty larceny and that sort of thing. So I put him on to the matter of the two men with the ladder and the sack, the people Mrs. Fairfoot declared she saw in the garden that night. He's earned a good mark, Burford; for he's got to the root of the thing almost at once. As I suspected, these two gardeners at Fountain Court have been making quite a good thing out of stealing fruit and selling it in the neighbourhood. It was a sack of apples and pears that they had with them when Mrs. Fairfoot came upon them. You've seen Sperling. The other fellow isn't much better. They're a couple of completely stupid egotists. When they found themselves caught in the middle of this murder case, their only reaction seems to have been: 'Lord, save us! This is going to blow the gaff on our little game!' with consternation as a result. If they showed themselves, they'd have to explain a few things. So they decided to look out for Number One first. 'Let murder be done, so long as our petty pilfering isn't spotted.' Sperling's a rank coward in any case; but half his uneasiness when we questioned him was due to the fear of our getting on the track of his larcenies. He's been making quite a good thing out of it, and he didn't want it to stop. We'll have to take action. Burford's got all the evidence together. The main thing is that we can drop that episode out of the main case."

"That accounts for one or two things that puzzled me, I admit, sir," confessed the Inspector. "I'd put a lot down to Sperling being yellow, without thinking why he was in such a state. Humph! He'll get his dose all right. . . . Is there anything else, sir?"

"This Cecil Ducane seems worth further inquiry," Sir Clinton answered. "There's no proof, as yet, that he has any connection with the Brenthurst business, except the 'C.D.' initials; and since 'C.D.' fits any number of names, my own included, it's not very convincing as evidence. Still, we'd better look him up."

"But how, sir?" demanded the Inspector. "All we know about him is that he's here to-day and gone to-morrow — no fixed abode. A bit difficult to trace a bird of that sort."

"There's one possibility," Sir Clinton pointed out. "It was in the U.S.A. that Cecil Ducane came across Miss Garfield; we know that from her story. We know Reuben Ducane and his family came to grief in San Francisco. I'm inclined to give San Francisco a chance first of all, by putting our colleagues over there on to Mrs. Garfield. I got her address by questioning Miss Teramond while I was pretending to test her memory. So I think we'll put a line down there, and see if we catch anything."

"There might be something in it, sir," the Inspector admitted, though his tone was not optimistic. "It's worth trying, I suppose. But it's some years since these women left Frisco, and a lot may have happened since then."

Sir Clinton seemed untroubled by his subordinate's scepticism, but he changed the subject abruptly.

"Miss Teramond's quite got over her shock by this time, hasn't she?" he asked.

"Oh, yes, sir. She seems quite fit again and able to go about as usual. The nurse is off the premises now, and Dr. Winthorpe doesn't call. Things seem to be pretty normal at Fountain Court, from all I gather. Do you want to see her again, sir?"

"No, not at present," Sir Clinton answered. "There's no need to bother them until we've got the San Francisco end of the thing cleared up — if we manage to do that. By the way, please leave the Trendon police report on my desk. I'd like to look over it."

# CHAPTER XIV

## May Sperling

THE DESK TELEPHONE rang, and the Chief Constable picked up the receiver.

"This is Driffield speaking."

"Well, stop speaking, and let me have a turn," said Peter Diamond's voice over the wire. "Can't you discover murders for yourself, instead of leaving it all to me? Wake up and shake yourself, Driffield. It's too early yet to start hibernating. The housemaid at old Mrs. Brenthurst's has been done in, now. Daughter of the Fountain Court gardener."

"Who told you?" demanded Sir Clinton.

"John Borrett, forester on the Rivercourt place, found the body this morning on his way to work. He brought the glad news to me first. . . . Why? 'Cause I pay for scoops and you don't. But he's on his way to lay information, now. I'll meet you on the spot marked with a cross. In fact, I'll be there before you, no doubt. . . . Bye-bye!"

Peter rang off before Sir Clinton had time to ask where the crime had been committed. There was little to be done but to wait for the arrival of the forester and hear his tale.

When Borrett appeared, Sir Clinton wasted no time in reprimands for giving information to the press before going to the police. That could wait. Borrett was a big, lean fellow with steady eyes and a complexion like teak. He seemed wholly unaffected by the tragedy into which he had stumbled only a short time before.

"This is the way of it, sir," he explained, when told to give his story. "I'm a forester on Mr. Rivercourt's estate, and I have the West Lodge to keep. Just now, my job's stripping ivy from some of the trees up in the wood they call Fawnbrake, so I go that way twice a day. Coming home last night, I saw nothing out of the common. This morning I went off to work as usual, taking the path round the south side of Wolf Spinney, which fringes Mr. Rivercourt's ground. Just after you cross the stepping-stones, you go up a bank, and at the top of it there's a stile. It's soft soil under the trees there, with the rain we had the other day. When I got to the stile, I saw some blood about. That hadn't been there when I passed down last night. A lot of blood, there was. I thought somebody had perhaps come by an accident in getting over the stile. That was what I thought first."

"What time was this?" demanded Sir Clinton.

"It would be a bit after half-past eight. I didn't think to look at my watch," explained Borrett. "I looked about, and I saw some tracks on the ground, like as if something heavy had been dragged in amongst the trees. So I followed up. It was easy, on account of the ground being soft. About fifty yards on I came upon the body of a girl with her throat cut. An ugly sight, to come on, unexpected-like, sir. I just took a good look at her to see if I knew her, and it was May Sperling. Her father's an acquaintance of mine, in a way; he works as a gardener at Fountain Court. May had a place as housemaid with old Mrs. Brenthurst. . . ."

"I know about Mrs. Brenthurst," interjected Sir Clinton.

"Well, then, you know she lives not far off, and May used to come up now and again and spend the evening with my wife. And that reminds me — " Borrett's tone changed to one of sudden suspicion — "now I come to think of it, I remember seeing May out with a fellow in the evening. She wasn't altogether an attractive kind of girl, May, and I wondered a bit, never having known her to have a boy-friend before. And the look of him surprised me, too. Dressed up to the nines, he was: nice grey hat, slaty-blue clothes, regular toff by the look of him, and about the last sort of man you'd think May could have picked up for a walk."

"Did you see his face?" demanded Sir Clinton.

Borrett shook his head.

"No, sir. They had their backs to me, and they was a good way off. I just saw the general get-up of him."

"Would you recognize the colour of his suit if you saw it again?"

"I might, sir."

Sir Clinton rang his desk bell and gave some instructions. In a few minutes Inspector Sandrock came into the room, carrying the blood-stained suit.

"Is that the colour?" asked the Chief Constable, turning to Borrett.

"That's it, exactly, sir," declared the forester without the slightest hesitation. "It's one of these colours you can't describe exactly — leastways *I* can't — but that's the very suit I saw this young man wearing when he was with May that night. I'd swear to it anywhere."

"How many times did you see this man and the girl together?"

"Just the once, sir."

"You didn't speak to her about him?"

"I've never seen her to speak to, not since I saw her with him."

"When was that?"

"Just a fortnight ago, sir."

"Go on with your story."

"There isn't any more to tell, sir. I knew I oughtn't to touch May's body, so I came away immediately to give the news."

Sir Clinton turned to the Inspector.

"I rang up for an ambulance, and warned our surgeon. They ought to be here in a few minutes. Then we'll go up to the place. You'll come with us," he added, turning to Borrett. "You can wait outside for the present."

When the forester had gone, Sir Clinton addressed Sandrock.

"Looks like another appearance of our mysterious friend Ducane, doesn't it?"

"It does, sir. But I can't say it makes things any the clearer to me. Why should he pick up a girl and then do her in? Was she a star turn in looks, or attractive on the sex side?"

"Not very, poor girl, according to Borrett's standards," said the Chief Constable. "He rather seemed surprised at the whole business. But he described that suit well enough before he knew we had it in our hands. And he added that the man was wearing a grey hat, which is something that we didn't know before. What strikes me about the business is that we've another member of the Brenthurst family coming into the limelight: old Mrs. Brenthurst, this time. It's suggestive that the girl was in her service, I feel."

"It does seem rum," paraphrased Sandrock.

"What seems rum, too," continued Sir Clinton, adopting the Inspector's phraseology, "is the fact that he dropped in here out of the blue a fortnight ago, and yet Miss Garfield told us nothing about any such visit. If they're so intimate as all that, I'd have expected Ducane to seize the opportunity for a few hours' dalliance at the Duke's Head or elsewhere."

"Perhaps the Garfield woman isn't the only pebble on the beach where Ducane's concerned," suggested Sandrock, crudely. "He may have other fish to fry. This Sperling girl may have been one of them. You can't go by looks, sir, else no one could ever account for some of the marriages one sees."

"I never attempt to account for them," said Sir Clinton, with a smile.

"What strikes me about it, sir," declared the Inspector, brushing aside the marriage question, "is that this girl seems to form a link which joins the whole thing up. Her dad's this man Sperling, and that tacks her on to the Fountain Court lot. She was a maid with old Mrs. Brenthurst, which brings her in touch with the Brenthurst crew. And now we find her mixed up with this Ducane man. One might think she was a sort of lynch-pin in the case, on the face of it. I don't see my way through it yet; but it seems worth keeping in mind from that point of view."

"It may be accidental," the Chief Constable pointed out, with the air of a man keeping an open mind. "No use jumping to conclusions just yet. I admit, on the face of it, that it's curious. But bear in mind that we haven't proved a connection between the girl and Ducane. It may have been somebody else, wearing a suit of that colour. Let's wait a bit, before plunging. But it's time we got on our way. I heard the ambulance drive up a minute or two ago, and now here's the doctor's car."

Under Borrett's guidance, they left the vehicles on the road near Wolf Spinney and made their way on foot, followed by a constable carrying photographic equipment, and two others bringing a stretcher from the ambulance. When they reached the stepping-stones, Sir Clinton and Sandrock took the lead, to examine the tracks in the damp soil of the woodland path, while the remainder of the party diverged off the trail to avoid adding their prints to those already made. The Chief Constable halted for a moment at the stile to examine the small pool of blood which lay on the farther side.

"Not so much as there was in the Fountain Court alley, sir," the Inspector pointed out officiously.

Sir Clinton nodded his agreement, climbed over the stile and examined the tracks which extended beyond it.

"Well, what do you make of it?" he inquired.

"It's easy reading, sir, thanks to this moist ground. As far as the stile, there are three sets of fresh tracks. There's a pair made by Borrett. He came up to the stile; hung about, probably staring at the blood — you can see he shifted his feet once or twice without moving far — and then went over the stile and up amongst the trees to the left, there. After that, he came back again, climbed the stile, and went off to give the news. Then there's a second pair of tracks, coming and going, men's prints. That'll be Ducane coming up with the girl and going back alone after killing her. Did you note, sir, that these prints aren't quite what an English shoe makes? American-built, I expect. Their fashions aren't the same as ours."

"What I noticed was that the shoes are practically unworn," Sir Clinton explained. "Look at the heel-marks, absolutely clean-cut. I doubt if these shoes have been used more than a few times on the road. But go on with your analysis, Inspector, if you please."

"On this side of the stile, there's just the one track of the girl's feet. She didn't come back, of course. Then, on the far side of the stile, there's two pairs of tracks, one pair going out and one pair coming back. As they came back, he fell in behind her to let her get over the stile first. You can see, there, when his footprint overlies hers. It looks as if he'd killed her just when she turned her back to him, so far as I can read the marks."

"He didn't cut her throat here," said the Chief Constable. "Not half enough blood for that. It looks as if he stunned her with a blow from some weapon or other and then dragged her up into the wood. You'll have all these tracks photographed, please; and if you can get casts of the man's prints, be sure to make them. That's a good clean impression just beside that red stone in the bank. But get several, if possible. Now what height would you gauge the fellow to be?"

The Inspector measured the length of pace shown by the man's footprints, made a short rough calculation in his note-book, and then gave his estimate.

"I'd say round about five foot seven, sir."

"I put it roughly at that myself, by comparing his length of step with my own," said Sir Clinton. "Judging from his height, he must be a sparely built fellow. I'm not stout myself, but his prints are a shade shallower than mine. We can check that by asking Borrett, by and by. Just tell these people to follow on, Inspector. The girl's body is up there. We've nothing to do but follow the trail through the undergrowth."

He and Sandrock went ahead, and after about fifty yards they came out into a tiny glade, through the high grass of which the trail led to May Sperling's body. Sir Clinton took off his hat and knelt down by the side of the corpse to make a cursory examination. He got to his feet again in a few seconds.

"She's been struck on the back of the head," he reported. "A fairly small weapon, probably something like a hammer. There's some blood oozing from the wound. And her throat's cut as well. That was done on the spot here, to judge by the blood and the way it has flowed. Will you take a look at her, Doctor, just in case anything strikes you?"

The girl's body lay under a tree, and as Sir Clinton turned, his eye caught a grey mark on the trunk at about the height of his elbow. He stepped over and examined it attentively, then a gesture brought the Inspector to his side.

"Tobacco ash!" interjected Sandrock, after studying it in his turn. "Well, he's a cool devil, knocking out his pipe after killing the poor girl."

"He tried to relight it first," said Sir Clinton, pointing to a couple of spent matches caught in the tall grass spears. "But here's something much stranger."

He bent down and picked up from the centre of a grass clump the headless body of a white cock. Then after a further search, he found the missing head lying a yard or two away.

"What do you make of that, sir?" demanded Sandrock, in concealed amazement.

"I don't make anything of it at all," said the Chief Constable. "Not for the moment, at any rate. But I'll tell you one thing, which might or might not account for it. Miss Teramond was born at Jacmel in Haiti, when Haiti was run by blacks, and white men were at a discount. Jacmel was one of the centres of Voodoo worship. You must have heard something about that, at one time or other. There are various brands of Voodoo, I'm told, some of them harmless, some that get a name for human sacrifice and so on. The killing of a cock seems to be part of one of the ceremonies. They use goats also, I believe. But unless my recollection is wrong, a white cock is associated with the more harmless brand of Voodoo, and not with the crew who practise human sacrifices. Now you know about as much as I do about the subject and you can draw your own conclusions. Personally, I don't propose to draw any until I learn something further."

He stooped down, picked up the body of the cock again, and fingered it thoughtfully.

"That bird wasn't killed within the last twelve hours," he commented, dropping it back into the grass. " 'Curiouser and curiouser,' isn't it?"

He spoke a few words to the police surgeon, who was busy with his examination of May Sperling's body; then, with a gesture, summoned Borrett to his side.

"I want to ask you a question or two. You saw a man with this girl one evening. Can you remember what night it was?"

"She got out on Tuesday evenings, sir, and I remember it was a Tuesday when I saw the two of them together. A fortnight ago, that was. It would be . . . it would be the 22nd of last month, wouldn't it?"

"That's right," confirmed the Inspector. "The 22nd was a Tuesday."

"What height was this man, can you tell me?" asked Sir Clinton.

"An inch or two shorter than me," said Borrett, readily. "Just a good height for a man, say five foot seven or eight. He wasn't anything like a six-footer. I saw him alongside her, when they were walking together, and he was three inches taller than what she was, I'd say."

Sandrock produced a tape measure and went back to the body.

"She's about five foot four," he announced, when he returned, "as far as I could measure without disturbing her position. That tallies well enough with what we got from the length of the man's pace, sir."

Sir Clinton nodded, and turned back to the forester.

"What sort of figure had he? Stoutish?"

"No, sir," said Borrett. "Not thin, exactly, but not fat. Very much of your own build, sir, so far as I can bring to mind."

"Now there's another point," the Chief Constable continued. "This path is on private ground. Do you let all and sundry stroll over it any time they choose?"

"Oh, no, sir," explained Borrett. "Our orders are to keep any strangers off. But there's never been any objection to known people — I mean people we know personally and can be sure about — going for a walk up here, so long as they stick to the paths and don't go wandering near the coverts. There's only a few of them we let in, folk who'll play the game and do no harm. It's not a regular thoroughfare in the evenings, if that's what you mean, sir. Often no one comes near at all for a fortnight on end."

"Rather lonely, then? And was this girl May Sperling one of the privileged ones who could come and go as she pleased?"

"Oh, yes, sir. We knew all about her. Her father's an old acquaintance of mine, as I told you, sir, and I've known her since she was so high. She understood all about the coverts and not interfering with the game."

"You let her bring a friend in with her?"

"Yes, she could bring one friend with her for company on her walks, sir. She was quite able to look after anyone she brought and make sure there was no disturbance."

"How long has she been with Mrs. Brenthurst?" asked Sir Clinton.

"About four months, sir."

At this moment Peter Diamond came in sight, hurrying through the wood. He nodded to Borrett and the Inspector as he came up, and then addressed the Chief Constable rather breathlessly: —

"Well, what is it? Suicide, murder, manslaughter, or what? Tell the press all about it."

"A little common decency, please, Peter!" said Sir Clinton. "You jar, sometimes, with this 'Cheerio, boys!' spirit. Murder isn't so funny as all that, when you run up against it. If you'll come for a stroll with me, I'll tell you a few things."

Peter fell in at his side, and Sir Clinton led him away amongst the trees, leaving the Inspector to get on with his work uninterrupted. The reporter fathomed the Chief Constable's intention, but was wise enough to ignore it. Sir Clinton gave him a concise summary of the facts which he thought could usefully be divulged and wound up with a request.

"I want you to get this wedged into your tale, Peter, at some place where the ordinary newspaper reader can't fail to notice it. We want news of somebody about five foot seven in height, slender build, dressed in a slaty-blue lounge suit and wearing a grey felt hat. Carries a pipe, probably. Sandrock thinks the shoes may be of an American shape, so you can risk that or not, just as you please. The cut of the suit is smart, and it's almost new so far as the cloth goes; but it's not the latest fashion — say about three years behind the times. I want information about this person being seen any time in the last three weeks, either alone or in company with a girl. You can get the description of the girl from Borrett. It's May Sperling."

"Right!" said Peter. "I'll translate that into journalese and put it where it'll do most good. After that, can I spread the glad news? You'll want it noted by my competitors, too, I presume. By the way, have you got a name to put on the figure?"

"The name's Cecil Ducane," said Sir Clinton, with just a touch of reluctance. "But if you print that, Peter, be careful to suggest nothing beyond the fact that we want to interview this person. The law of libel's a queer affair, and you may let your proprietor in for heavy damages, if you aren't careful."

Peter paid but the slightest attention to this caution. His mind had gone off on a different track.

"Cecil Ducane?" he mused, aloud. "Ducane . . . ? Ha! I remember. My sainted great-aunt, of course. Ducane was the name of the actor-bloke who espoused Netta, daughter to Alison Brenthurst. But *his* first name was Reuben, surely. It's mixed up in my mind with the text about 'unstable as water, thou shalt not excel,' which seemed appropriate to a third-rate barn-stormer. But Cecil? No, that doesn't ring any bell for me. I'll consult my great-aunt. But perhaps you know all about him, Driffield?"

Sir Clinton shook his head.

"Very little," he confessed, frankly. "Friend Cecil is a bit of a mystery to me, especially since the murder of this girl Sperling. It beats me to guess what brought those two together, or what's the motive behind the crime. She wasn't a pretty girl. Not even attractive, I imagine."

"Are you linking this case up with the Fountain Court affair?" demanded Peter, sharply.

"There's one marked difference between them," Sir Clinton

pointed out, cautiously. "Brenthurst was a big, gross, heavy brute, and yet his body was lifted and carried out of the garden and dumped on the road. May Sperling was a slim little thing of five foot four, and about half the weight of Brenthurst. And yet her body was dragged along the ground, probably by one arm, since her clothes were hardly disordered at all. You could have done that yourself, Peter, and you're no Goliath. But you couldn't have lifted Brenthurst and carried him twenty yards without wanting a rest."

"A syndicated job, then?" suggested Peter, with a grin. "Ducane and Co. for speedy removals. Write for terms. Strictest secrecy. By the way, I hear that Percy Fairfoot walks abroad. I thought you'd snaffled him."

"We detained him, pending inquiries," Sir Clinton explained. "But you can't detain a man longer than forty-eight hours unless you're prepared to arrest him, so we let him loose again, and his mother also."

"How's the fair Diana?" inquired Peter. "Sitting up and taking nourishment well, I hope. Or is her statuesque friend still sitting by the bedside holding her hand and smoothing her brow?"

"I believe Miss Teramond has got over her shock," Sir Clinton assured him gravely. "But I doubt if she could stand a visit from you, Peter, if that's your idea."

"I did think of dropping in," the reporter admitted. "She might give me a pointer or two on this Voodoo business, since she comes from Haiti. I've been looking up Haiti. Interesting spot. Charming local customs in the old days, such as filling you up with gunpowder and then putting a match to the cracker. I'd like to see that fortress, La Ferrière, that old Emperor Christophe built, the chap they called the Black Napoleon. They say it cost more lives to build than the Pyramids did. A bloody-minded crew, altogether, these Haitians. And this Voodoo stunt's no religion for the nursery, I gather. Unmentionable orgies and human sacrifice. Even in the mildest forms they seem to be death on white cocks, goats, and what not. If the fair Diana would reminisce a bit, I could write quite an amusing article, perhaps."

"No doubt," said Sir Clinton rather impatiently. "Have you anything of more immediate interest to talk about?"

"Well, I have," said Peter, good-humouredly. "It's just crossed my mind that perhaps other people as well as the fair Diana came out of Haiti. Ducane, now. It's not a name I've met before. But I *have* heard of French people called D-u-q-u-e-s-n-e" — he spelled the word—"and Ducane might be an anglified form of that. What do you think of that bright notion?"

"Not much," said Sir Clinton, freezingly. "It would need a lot of polishing before I'd call it bright, Peter."

# CHAPTER XV

## A Quintet of Liars

"HERE's the doctor's report, sir," said Sandrock, as he came into Sir Clinton's office that afternoon with a paper in his hand. "He finds that May Sperling was killed about ten o'clock last night. That's very rough, of course, since it's gauged from the body-temperature. The cause of death he puts down to a blow from a hammer, struck from the back; and he's been able to give us the diameter of the hammer-head. The throat-cutting was post-mortem, just to make a sure thing of it. Not much new in that. I saw as much when I looked the body over. But it isn't one of these sex murders. The girl had the name of being quite straight in that way, and the doctor finds she hasn't been interfered with. So that's not the motive."

Sir Clinton took the report, read it carefully, and put it into a drawer of his desk. Then he turned to Sandrock.

"The only clue we seem to have is Borrett's tale about the man in a blue suit and a grey hat."

"This man Ducane, sir?"

"We don't know even that," said Sir Clinton. "Slaty-blue suits and grey hats are not so very uncommon, after all. Still, since that's all we have, we must make the best of it. Cecil Ducane's only appearance that we know about was at the Duke's Head. That's outside our county, and I don't like trespassing on another man's territory if I can help it; so I rang up my opposite number this morning and asked him to give us a hand. He's to send a man over on a motor-cycle with a report. It ought to be here later on in the afternoon."

He closed the roll-top of his desk and rose from his chair.

"Meanwhile," he added, "we'll go over to Fountain Court. I want to ask these people a question or two."

Rather to Sandrock's surprise, the Chief Constable stopped his car at a chemist's shop and spent a little time there, coming out again with a number of bottles and a cardboard box which the Inspector discovered from the label to contain a fine atomizer.

"You haven't got a cold, sir?" he inquired.

Sir Clinton laughed.

"No, Inspector. And if I had, I'd be chary of blowing these stuffs into my nasal passages: acetic acid, silver nitrate, ammonium sulphide. Ten per cent solutions of these would make you jump, if you sprayed them up your nose. The big bottle's distilled water."

He offered no further explanation of his purchases, but drove on. At Fountain Court he asked to see Miss Garfield, who was at home. In a minute or two she joined them, evidently rather surprised by this unexpected visit.

"How is Miss Teramond?" inquired the Chief Constable, after he had made some apology for his intrusion. "Quite well now, I hope?"

"Oh, yes, quite well," Miss Garfield assured him.

"Able to get about through the house and into the garden? Has she been beyond that?"

Miss Garfield shook her head.

"No, she says she doesn't feel up to much exertion yet. Our doctor seems quite content with her, though; and the only orders he's given are that she must take a tonic and go to bed immediately after dinner and not get up for breakfast. I've been rather a crock myself. I've been losing sleep and I've had to get our doctor to give me an opiate. But all Miss Teramond needs now is rest, and someone to see that she obeys the doctor's directions. I see to that part of it myself, and pack her off to bed when the time comes."

"That must be rather a tie for yourself," commented the Chief Constable. "You can't leave the house in the evenings, after the maids go away."

"No. Not that it would make much difference if I did," Miss Garfield said, unconcernedly. "Still, I shouldn't like her to wake up and find herself all alone in the house, after the fright she had the last time I left her by herself. I don't specially want to go out in the evening, at present, so it's no hardship to keep her company."

"You're quite positive that she hasn't gone outside your grounds?"

"Not unless she's been creeping out of her window at night," said Miss Garfield. "That's hardly likely, is it?"

"Now I want to ask you something else," said Sir Clinton. "An awkward thing to ask, perhaps, but I'm sure you're too sensible to take offence. What I want is a complete account of your visit to the Duke's Head; I mean the main details of it. Can you recall them?"

Miss Garfield made no pretence of misunderstanding him. After all, he already knew the worst by her own admissions.

"Let me think," she answered, without any hesitation. "I drove across there in our car, taking a suit-case with me. I registered at the office and then put my car in the public park round the corner, as I thought we might need it later on. Then I went up to my room. I forget its number, but it was a double room on the second floor, at the other end of the corridor from the lift. I unpacked my suit-case and arranged my things, and in the middle of that, Mr. Ducane came up. I forgot to tell you that he was coming by the London express which gets in at 6:53. He brought his own suit-case up and began to unpack it."

"How was he dressed?" interjected Sir Clinton.

"A lounge suit, bluish-grey, if I remember, with a tie to match. He had a soft collar and he was wearing a grey felt hat, rather light grey."

"I'm sorry to have interrupted," said the Chief Constable.

"We talked about various things, naturally, as we had not seen each other for a good while," Miss Garfield continued. "Then he annoyed me by telling me that he would not be able to dine with me that evening. I hadn't expected this, and I was very disappointed. We see each other so seldom that it seemed a shame that we couldn't have the whole evening to ourselves. But he had a business appointment, he told me, to meet some client of his at a restaurant for dinner. Of course I was disappointed, but there was no help for it."

"Where was your car all this while?" asked Sir Clinton. "The Duke's Head has no garage, I remember."

"In the park just round the corner from the hotel," explained Miss Garfield. "Mr. Ducane used it to go to this restaurant, and then he put it in a garage for the night. After he had gone away, I changed into an evening frock, dined in the hotel, sat in the lounge until after ten o'clock and then went up to our room. Mr. Ducane came back about half an hour later, and we talked for a while. He got a flask out of his suit-case and we had a drink or two. Then we went to bed."

"When did you wake up in the morning?" asked Sir Clinton.

"At eight o'clock. The chambermaid woke me by knocking at the door. Mr. Ducane had left a call at the office, the night before, as he had a train to catch. I must have slept very heavily myself. There's a lot of heavy traffic outside the Duke's Head in the morning; and the motor-buses change gear as they come round the corner, which makes a frightful row. But I slept through all that, though usually I'm a light sleeper. I woke up with a slight headache, I remember."

"And Mr. Ducane, what about him?" queried Sir Clinton.

"He was already up and dressed. I hadn't even waked when he went out to take his bath. In fact, he'd been downstairs and had brought my car round from the garage to the park beside the Duke's Head. He gave me back the keys of the car and told me where he'd left it. We hadn't much time to talk, as he had to catch a train at 8:45. We said good-bye, and he went away with his suit-case."

"You hadn't got up?"

"No, I only got up after he had gone. I dressed and packed up my things, and then I went down to breakfast. I was still head-achy and hadn't much appetite, I remember. That's unusual with me. I'm generally quite brisk in the morning. After breakfast, I brought my car round to the hotel door, got my suit-case sent down, and asked for my bill at the office, but they told me Mr. Ducane had paid it already on his way out. Then I came away."

"Thanks," said Sir Clinton. "I don't usually find myself giving compliments to witnesses, Miss Garfield, but you've got a very clear head. And I quite recognize that it wasn't a very easy story for you to tell."

Miss Garfield shrugged her shoulders slightly.

"At least I've never pretended to be a plaster saint," she said, looking the Chief Constable in the eyes. "The kind of life I lead is my own affair, but I'm not such a fool as to think that I could cover up an episode of that sort, once you began to pry into my doings. Far better to be candid about it."

"Much better," agreed the Chief Constable. "I wish all witnesses were frank about their doings. By the way, has Miss Teramond said anything to you which might throw light on this affair?"

"Nothing whatever," said Miss Garfield, concisely.

"You mean nothing beyond what she remembered immediately afterwards?"

"I meant nothing fresh," Miss Garfield corrected herself. "She recalls the shooting; but she told you about that. Apart from that, her memory doesn't seem to go."

"Has she ever talked to you about her childhood in Haiti?"

"Now and again she has spoken about it," Miss Garfield answered, after thinking for a few moments. "But, really, I wasn't much interested. But I did gather that it isn't a very pleasant place. She once mentioned some things called *zombis,* which seem to have scared her when she was a child. They were living ghosts or resuscitated dead people; I never quite understood what she meant. And her father seems to have got across one of the priests of that affair they have in Haiti, Voodoo or some such name. I have an idea that it was trouble of this sort that led to her family clearing out of Haiti and going to Guadeloupe. But you'd better ask her about that herself. I really didn't bother about it. I'm not a scrap superstitious and it seemed mere rubbish to me."

"I see you're a realist, like myself," said Sir Clinton, with a smile. "I came across one or two queer cases when I was in Africa, but when we got to the root of them they turned out to be poisonings done on the sly by the local witch-doctors. Voodoo's probably something in the same line, since the Haitians are blacks."

He dismissed the subject with a gesture and turned to a fresh topic.

"I wonder if you could do something for me. I don't want to trouble Miss Teramond just now. Do you think you could get me one of her handkerchiefs, the kind with her initials embroidered in the corner?"

Miss Garfield glanced at him shrewdly.

"And if I don't get it for you, I suppose you'll arrange to take it, whether or no? What do you want it for? I'm not going to do anything behind my friend's back if it's going to harm her."

"We need it merely for comparison purposes," Sir Clinton assured her. "And, as you say, we have other ways of getting it, so you'd do no good by refusing."

Miss Garfield pondered for a moment or two, as if undecided, but finally she made up her mind.

"All right. I'll get it for you now."

She left the room and they heard her cross the hall to go upstairs.

"I don't quite get that, sir," said Sandrock in a low voice.

"Never mind. When we get outside, you're to go round and see Sperling. Make him hunt through the gardening tools and see if a hammer is missing. He must have had one for nailing up creepers. If he has any hammers, impound them and bring them with you. And, another thing, ask him about the chickens kept here; how many there are and especially if there was a white cock amongst them. See if it's still there. That's all."

A warning frown prevented the Inspector from asking any questions, and just in time, for Miss Garfield returned almost at once with a folded handkerchief in her hand.

"Here's what you want," she said, holding it out. "You see the initials in the corner."

"Thanks," said the Chief Constable, glancing round. "Now would you mind putting it into one of these envelopes on the desk, please? Keep it flat as you put it in. And then seal the envelope."

"Very mysterious," commented Miss Garfield, with a tinge of irony in her tone.

"Not a bit," retorted the Chief Constable. "I may have to get you to identify it, later on; and I want it to be clear that I haven't been playing any tricks by substituting one handkerchief for another. People credit me with being not bad at sleight-of-hand, so I have to be careful. . . . Now, please stick down the flap. There's no deception? And perhaps you'd better write your name across the back of the envelope, just to make sure you can recognize it again. Here's a pen."

He pulled out the thick-barrelled fountain pen which the Inspector had already seen in use, and handed it to Miss Garfield. She wrote a bold signature across the envelope. Then she glanced up with a smile.

"What's to prevent you steaming the envelope open and making a substitution?" she asked, with a touch of derision in her tone. "Shall I seal it with wax, to make sure?"

"An excellent notion," said Sir Clinton.

He went over to the desk and picked up a stick of sealing-wax which lay on a little tray. Then, returning to her side, he struck a match and watched her seal the envelope.

"And now you'd like me to put my finger-print on the wax?" said Miss Garfield, with an amusement which she hardly took pains to conceal. "Was this what you've been leading up to? I'll do it, if it's any use to you. But usually I seal letters with that stamp on the desk."

Sir Clinton took her rallying in good part.

"You'd better use the seal," he rejoined, lightly, bringing it from the desk. "You might burn your fingers with the hot wax. But really, you give me credit for too much finesse. If I'd wanted your finger-prints, I've got them already on my fountain pen. Simple, isn't it? Actually, all I want is the handkerchief."

Miss Garfield's expression changed to one of half-feigned rue-fulness.

"And I thought I'd caught you out," she said, in mock despondency. "Evidently I underrated you. I really thought I'd seen through your manœuvres, and I suppose you were laughing at me all the time. Now, are there any more little traps?" she ended, with a smile which suggested that she had taken no offence.

Sir Clinton dropped his levity and reverted to seriousness. "You've heard about that unfortunate girl, the daughter of your gardener?" he asked, gravely. "Did you know her?"

"Only by sight, and even so I've only seen her a couple of times. She never came up to the house. When she came to visit her father she went to his cottage. I'm rather disgusted with Sperling. He doesn't seem to be the least sorry. Too wrapped up in his own troubles, it appears. You know that we gave him notice, after we heard about this fruit-stealing. I was inclined to keep him on, when I heard about his daughter. Dismissing him seemed too much like kicking a man when he was down. But his callousness was too much for me. I don't care for him. But that's nothing. Have you got on the track of the man who killed her?"

Sir Clinton shook his head.

"No," he admitted. "We're merely groping in the dark, at present. You can't suggest anything, I suppose, since you've seen so little of her. She didn't bring any men with her when she came to visit her father?"

"None that I saw," said Miss Garfield, after a moment's thought.

Sir Clinton picked up the envelope and put it into his pocket.

"Then that's all I wanted to ask you," he said, formally. "Inspector Sandrock has been taking notes of what you told us, as I expect you noticed. Will you please sign them, after he's read them over?"

"With your pen?" asked Miss Garfield, with a gleam of mischief in her eye.

"No," retorted Sir Clinton, with an answering smile. "You'd better use your own pen. Then you won't suspect a trap."

After the formality had been completed, the two officials took their leave. Outside the front door, Sandrock quitted his superior and went off to interview Sperling, while Sir Clinton got into his car and drove round to the garden gate near the cottage. The Inspector did not keep him waiting long.

"Sperling says, sir, that they kept about thirty chickens. He collected the eggs, and was allowed to do what he liked with the ones that weren't needed up at the house. That's as it may be. They had a white cock, but it's gone. He says he knows nothing about that. I've told him to go over his garden tools and see if any are missing. He's to see me about that, later. By the way, sir, I thought I'd check what that Garfield woman told us, to be on the safe side, so I asked Sperling. He said just the same. His daughter never came across the Garfield woman at any time, he was quite flat about that. Didn't even know her by sight, he said. She *did* know the Teramond one, though, and when they met by chance in the garden they used to have talks. He'd seen them, and his daughter told him that she'd got permission to pick any flowers she had a fancy to. He asked the Teramond woman about that, to be on the safe side, and she said she'd told May Sperling to take a few flowers any time she wanted to."

"That's a useful bit of information," said Sir Clinton, evidently well satisfied with Sandrock. "I thought Miss Garfield was telling the truth, but it's just as well to have the thing confirmed. Now I think we'll go back to Headquarters and see if that report has come over."

As they drove along, Sandrock remembered something.

"I've never been inside the Duke's Head, sir. What sort of a place is it?"

"It's one of those old hotels which have extended without being rebuilt. Whenever it got too small, they just took in some adjacent premises and converted the interior to suit themselves. Naturally, it's not what you'd call well planned. The dining-room, smoking-room, lounge and so forth are all fairly modern, since they were shifted into the new parts of the premises as the place grew. But barring that they put a lift into it, the old hall is much the same as it was fifty years ago: a big, gloomy place, with a mere pigeon-hole window for the office. And, of course, in a place like that, growing more or less at random, they have about twice the number of stairs that they'd have needed if the thing had been built *en bloc,* and the same holds for doors. They've got about five ways of getting in and out, including one that leads direct into the railway station next door. It's a regular warren of a place. The fittings are modern: electric light, lift, hot-and-cold in the bedrooms, wireless wherever it can be stuck in, radiators in the bedrooms, and so on. I'm told that it's very clean and comfortable, and that the service is good. I've never stayed in it, but I've had a meal there once or twice."

"I've only seen the outside of it, sir. But from the look of that, I guessed the inside was just what you say."

When they reached their destination, they found the expected report awaiting them.

"Sit down, Inspector," said the Chief Constable. "We'll go over this thing together while our memories are fresh. You'd better check it with your notes of what Miss Garfield told us."

He seated himself at his desk, unfolded the report, and began to read it aloud slowly.

"'A double room was booked by Mrs. Cecil Ducane in a letter dated 22nd September. At about 6 P.M. on September 2nd, Mrs. Cecil Ducane arrived in a car, the number of which was not noted. She was wearing a grey coat and skirt.'"

"She had a grey coat and skirt on when we saw her at Fountain Court next morning," the Inspector pointed out.

"'She had a suit-case with her,'" continued Sir Clinton, reading from the report. "'No initials were noticed on it. She has stayed at the Duke's Head once or twice in the past few months, and was recognized by the office clerk, Hetty Burns. Mrs. Ducane is tallish, dark, with a good figure and no noticeable accent. After registering, she drove her car away, probably to the nearest park, since she came back again in a few minutes and inquired about the time of arrival of the London express, by which her husband was coming to join her. She asked Hetty Burns to give him the number of the room when he arrived, and to say that she was upstairs. Her suit-case, taken out of the back seat of the car by the hotel porter, had been sent up to No. 63, which is a double room on the second floor, at the end of the corridor, in the west wing.'"

"That's just what she told us," confirmed the Inspector, looking up from his notes.

"'A few minutes after seven o'clock,'" Sir Clinton read on, "'Mr. Ducane came to the window of the hotel office. He wore a lightish blue lounge suit, and had a suit-case in his hand. Hetty Burns recognized him, as he has stayed at the Duke's Head several times this year, sometimes alone, sometimes with his wife. He is of average height, fair-haired, and speaks with a strong American accent. He asked for the number of his room; inquired if his wife had arrived; and grumbled about the London express being behind time. It was actually seven minutes late. He then went up in the lift to No. 63. He and Mrs. Ducane were in their room for half an hour or more. Then Mr. Ducane came down by the lift and went out by the front door, apparently to get his car, for he brought it round to the front of the hotel almost immediately. He left it there and came to the office window, where he inquired from Hetty Burns the quickest way to get to the Monico Restaurant, saying that he was dining there with a friend. She gave him the information, and he drove off in the car.'"

"That tallies with what she told us," confirmed Sandrock.

Sir Clinton nodded and continued to read.

"'At about eight o'clock, Mrs. Ducane came down by the lift. She went to the dining-room. The waiter, Joseph Hart, remembers her, as she dined à la carte, and made some inquiries about the various dishes on the menu. She was dressed in a black evening dress with some embroidery on it, and she carried a black bag. After dinner, she went into the lounge. The waiter in the lounge says she had coffee and a Kümmel. She asked him to get her some cigarettes, and she filled her case. He, also, described her dress in much the same terms. He saw her reading some of the magazines and papers belonging to the hotel. He cannot remember exactly when she left the lounge, but puts it round about ten o'clock, and this is roughly confirmed by the liftman who took her up to the second floor. The liftman, Albert Ridley, noted her specially because he admired her appearance, but he was unable to give the exact time.'"

"She seems to be quite right in her tale, sir," said the Inspector. "There's no flaw anywhere."

"It's sometimes an advantage to be good-looking," commented Sir Clinton. "People notice you and remember you. She evidently made an impression on Mr. Albert Ridley. Well, let's get on. 'About half-past ten, Mr. Ducane came back to the hotel. He went to the office window and asked if any letters had come for him. There was one in the rack, which was handed out to him. Hetty Burns did not notice anything special about it. He left an order with her that he was to be called at eight o'clock next morning because he was catching the London express. He asked her if there was a restaurant car attached to the train, and she looked up *Bradshaw* for him and found this to be the case.' Just check that, if you please, Inspector. There's a *Bradshaw* on that third shelf."

The Inspector took down the fat volume, turned up the page, and returned the book to its shelf.

"That's right, sir. There's 'R.C.' in the column. He'd be able to get his breakfast on the train."

"Well, we'll go on from his inquiry," said the Chief Constable, and he read out, " 'Hetty Burns saw him go up in the lift, after leaving the office window. Next morning, at 8 A.M., the chambermaid, Ray Eppstein, knocked at the door of No. 63. Instead of answering, Cecil Ducane opened the door a few inches and said it was all right. The chambermaid thought he was trying to prevent Mrs. Ducane from being waked up. Cecil Ducane was in the middle of shaving, and had a safety razor in his hand. At 8:25 or thereabouts, he came down by the lift with his suit-case, and went to the office window, where he asked for his bill, saying that he was leaving before his wife. He paid the bill, and the hotel porter took his suit-case to the train. Cecil Ducane found a seat and dismissed the porter. The porter mentioned he was wearing a light blue suit and a light grey hat.' "

"There's nothing about that in my notes, sir, of course," interjected the Inspector, "but it fits with what she told us."

" 'At about a quarter past nine,' " continued Sir Clinton, " 'Mrs. Ducane came down. She was wearing the grey coat and skirt which she arrived in. She bought a newspaper at the stall beside the office. The newsboy, Timothy Bullen, did not know her name, but he remembered a lady in grey, tall and dark-haired, buying a paper from him. She went into the dining-room and sat down at the table where she had dined the night before. The waiter recognized her. After breakfast she went out, and shortly afterwards she brought her car to the front door. She then went to the office, where they told her that the bill had already been paid. She went up in the lift to her room, rang for the chambermaid and tipped her, and the porter carried her suit-case down. She got him to put it into the back seat of the car and then she drove off.' "

"That's a shade fuller than her own account, sir, but it's all the better for that."

"Now we come to a final detail," said Sir Clinton. "Here's the tail end of the report: 'Later in the morning, the chambermaid went to No. 63 to tidy it up. Both beds had been slept in. On the shelf over the wash-hand basin she noticed the gold-plated box of a safety razor, with the razor inside. On the box the initials 'C.D.' were engraved. Ray Eppstein took it down to the office and handed it in, as is the practice with all property left behind in the bedrooms by guests. Hetty Burns was very busy at the moment, and put the razor-case aside, meaning to look up Mrs. Ducane's address and send the property back there, since that was the only address she knew. She seems to have forgotten about the matter, and it was only recalled to her mind by the evidence of Ray Eppstein. The razor-case was still in a pigeon-hole in the hotel office. It was examined. Unfortunately, the chambermaid gave it a rub-up with her duster before handing it in at the office, so there are no finger-prints detectable on it except her own.' "

"Pity that girl was so tidy," deplored the Inspector. "But for that duster of hers, we'd have had that man's finger-prints, and we may need them yet. Is that the end of the report, sir?"

"That's the end," Sir Clinton said. "What do you make of it all?"

"Well, sir, one point sticks out. That man must have had two suits the very spit of each other. One of them got blood-stained, and he threw it away under the culvert. And yet he turns up next morning in a light blue suit and a grey felt hat, according to the hotel porter."

"Don't let's mix up facts and inferences," cautioned Sir Clinton. "The facts are simple enough. Borrett saw May Sperling in company with a grey-hatted man in a light blue suit on August 22nd. A light blue suit with the initials 'C.D.' on it was found in the culvert after the Brenthurst murder on September 3rd. Finally, Cecil Ducane was seen wearing a light blue suit and a grey felt hat during his visit to the King's Head on September 3rd. I grant you that suits of that tint aren't common at present; but a jury would want something more in the way of evidence before they took your word for it that May Sperling's companion, Brenthurst's murderer, and the man at the Duke's Head are one and the same person."

"I suppose they will, sir," agreed Sandrock, "though personally I'm pretty sure it's so. And here's another point, sir. So far as we've got, the only evidence about Ducane's doings between 10:30 P.M. and 8 A.M. that night rests on what the Garfield woman told us. They spent the night together, she said. But she said something else, if you noticed. They had a drink or two out of his flask. And she slept very heavily all night and didn't wake up until he'd got up, had his bath, and the chambermaid knocked on the bedroom door at eight o'clock. And she woke up with a head-ache," he ended, with a meaning expression.

"I see what you're after," said the Chief Constable. "Dope?"

"Dope, sir, as you say. He drugged her when he gave her these drinks. Once she was asleep, he could come and go as he pleased. She'd never know. That gave him a clear run through the night, so long as he got back before she waked up in the morning. And from the way you describe the Duke's Head, anyone could get about in it without being spotted, so long as he didn't use the lift. There are plenty of stairs and exits from the place. And he could get in again in the morning about breakfast-time when everyone was busy. No one would notice him specially."

"That's highly ingenious," admitted Sir Clinton. "And it does seem to fit the facts. Oh, by the way, did you find out if Sperling knew anything about his daughter's doings? Anything that throws light on that affair?"

"No, sir. He declared he'd never heard of her being mixed up with this man. She was rather a secretive sort of girl, it seems."

"Unfortunately, one can't put too much reliance on Sperling's stories," said Sir Clinton. "In fact, nearly everyone who'd given evidence — barring the hotel people — turns out to be a liar. I can count five of them, off-hand."

"It seems a lot, sir. I can spot some of them. Which ones are you thinking about?"

"Well, start at the beginning," said Sir Clinton, checking them off on his fingers as he gave his list. "There's that hop-picker, Sprattley. His sad tale of insomnia cut no ice with me. If Sergeant Burford had had the wit to search him, I've a strong suspicion that he'd have found some house-breaking implements in his pockets. That's No. One. Then there's Miss Garfield. She's quite obviously lying to protect Cecil Ducane. I simply don't believe that she couldn't tell us something about his present whereabouts. She's completely wrapped up in friend Cecil, and yet she has no means of communicating with him. You may credit that if you like. I don't. The third liar is Mrs. Fairfoot. Nobody would swallow her tale as it stands. Obviously her sole aim was to protect her beloved son, Percy. That makes a third liar. And friend Percy is the fourth, beyond any doubt, since we tripped him up in his story about photographing on Hawkover Common. And the fifth is our friend Sperling, who lied to cover up his own little peccadilloes in the matter of garden produce. There's not a straight-forward unbiased witness in that whole quintet."

"And what about the Teramond girl, sir?"

"Well, what about her?" echoed Sir Clinton. "You can't expect much from anyone who's got her particular trouble."

"I suppose not, sir," Sandrock conceded. "Now there's another point, sir. What about tracing Ducane? I don't suppose there's any hope of getting much help from the station people. There's always a bustle there when the London express is in. I've gone by it once or twice and I know. But we might ask the railway people at the terminus. It's just a chance that someone may have noticed him."

"Try, certainly," agreed the Chief Constable. "I'll be surprised if anything comes of it, though."

"What puzzles me, sir," confessed the Inspector, "is this business of the two slaty-blue suits. Here's a man goes and commits a murder in a blue suit. We know that, because we've got the suit itself. Now his obvious line would be to change his appearance at once and put on a suit as different from the 'murder' one as he could. And yet he goes about next day, travelling by train and wandering about the hotel in a suit that's the very spit of the one we've got hold of. It sounds as if he was a bit short in brains, really."

"I suppose he had his reasons," said Sir Clinton, in the tone of a sibyl.

"I suppose he had," said the Inspector, crossly. "But to me they must come out of Bedlam or Colney Hatch, sir. There's no sense in it."

# CHAPTER XVI

## Some Correspondence

In HIS OFFICE next morning, Sir Clinton began to go through the correspondence which awaited his attention. He hated paper-work of any sort, and it was with stifled resentment that he tackled the little pile of envelopes on his desk. The first three letters contained nothing of special interest to him at the moment, and he disposed of them rapidly; but when he picked up the fourth, a faint smile twisted the corners of his lips. The envelope was a cheap unsized one, plentifully finger-marked and wearing a travel-worn look which suggested that it had been carried for a time in somebody's pocket before being posted. It was the address which had amused Sir Clinton.

To the Head Policeman

He slit open the envelope and drew out the contents: several sheets of cheap note-paper covered with an ill-formed and labori-ous scrawl. But at the first words, the Chief Constable's expression lost its touch of amusement; his eyes grew suddenly keen; and he raced through the letter eagerly. Then he reread it with care, too engrossed to waste a smile on the quaint phraseology and quainter spelling.

Dere Sir,
I'm housemaid at Mrs. Brenthurst of Sunnyhill and before That I was with Mrs. Ashworth of 33 Tenterden Road for two years and my father is Gardener at Fountain Court and Has been their for ten years and Mr. Borrett the forester on Mr. Rivercourts estate could

Speak for me to for I know his wife well and he would speak a good word for me.

Now dere Sir I wish to say that a gentleman Mr. Cecil Dewkane — dont know how to spell it — has been Making up to me and At first I thougt he was alright and was quiet Glad to have him for a freind for it never went bayond that dere Sir as I can asure you.

But lately hes been asking me to prie about in Mrs. Brenthursts Cupbords and see if I Can find some old leters which he says Belong to him and when I could not find them Annywere dere Sir he beggan to hint I might let him into the house at night after evrybody had Gone to bed and I could let him in without annyone knowing about it and he could look round for himself amongst the leters that Mrs. Brenthurst keeps locked up in one of her cupbords as I know for ive seen them and a lot of Other papers for she keeps a lot of old papers lockt up.

Now dere Sir when he asked me to do this I thougt to myself perhaps it wasnt Leters he was after but Mrs. Brenthursts jewelry which she has a lot dere Sir. And you must beleive dere Sir that I had no idea of Doing anything wrong when he spoke to me and I dont want to do what he wants me to do for him and if theres anny Reward for catching a burgalar then I ougt to have it dere Sir for giving You this informtion for after thinking on it Im afriad he is not honnest in what hes been teling me and that he Means to get these jewells and Go off with them and leave me to stand the Blame of them dere Sir which would not be right.

I dont know what mister Dewkanes adress is but if you want to get Hold of him and ask him about it then youl have to send somone to the style at the stepingstones in Wolf spiney at ten o'clock at night the day after tommorrow. Its my evening off and well be going For a walk and Ill Fix it so that we get to the style at the stepingstones at Ten o'clock and then youre Man can ask him any questions you want him asked dere Sir at youre convenence. And if their is anny reward then i would like to be sure of geting it and as Quick as posible, which is all for the Present and I remain dere Sir

Yours truly

MAY SPERLING

P.S. I think i ougt to get five Pounds reward at the very leest, becoz misses Brenthursts jewelry is very valuble and it would be worth Five pounds to save it.

Sir Clinton put the letter on his desk and summoned Inspector Sandrock.

"Here's some fresh news in the Sperling case," he explained when the Inspector entered the room. "Just glance through the letter. Then we can discuss it."

Sandrock picked up the sheets and his eyebrows rose as he glanced at the signature before beginning his perusal. He said nothing until he had read, and then reread the ill-spelt scrawl.

"Pity we didn't get this in time, sir," was his first comment.

"A great pity," Sir Clinton agreed. "It looks as if she'd given it to someone to post — one of the Sunnyhill tradespeople, probably — and he put it in his pocket and carried it about for a few days before remembering to post it. The envelope suggests something of the sort," he added, passing it over to the Inspector.

"Not much doubt that Ducane's the murderer, after that, sir," Sandrock declared, confidently. "What a born fool he was to give the girl his real name."

"If it *is* the real name," said Sir Clinton in a faintly sceptical tone. "Whether it is or not, I can see the point of using it. It doesn't sound so bad if you say to someone: 'I only want you to recover some letters written by me.' It wouldn't be so specious if it were called a plain theft of somebody else's letters, would it?"

"Something in that, sir, no doubt. But I'm quite content with Ducane as the murderer, to be going on with. There's a motive in plain sight, for one thing. He must have found out, somehow, that May Sperling was playing the Delilah game on him, and he killed her to shut her mouth. That letter was a dirty bit of work; but she's paid for it, poor girl. If only it had come to hand when it ought to have done, we'd have saved her life and had our hands on the skunk by now, instead of having to hunt for him all over England."

"We may not have to go so far," Sir Clinton suggested. "Ducane didn't let the Brenthurst murder act as a deterrent. There was this reappearance at Wolf Spinney. Perhaps friend Cecil will make a third visit. And in the meanwhile, we'll try to get our hands on these letters, since they seem so important."

"Do it now, sir?" suggested Sandrock.

"In a few minutes," the Chief Constable reassured him. "First, though, I want to hear about something else. Did Sperling find any tools missing?"

"He couldn't find his gardening-hammer at first, sir. It wasn't in its usual place in that pagoda, he tells me. But he found it in the end, tucked away behind a lot of stuff in one of the corners. I'll get it for you in a moment, sir."

He left the room and returned almost immediately with a large hammer in his hand, which he passed over to the Chief Constable.

"You needn't mind touching it, sir. We've been over it already for finger-prints, and there's nothing worth having. Sperling, of course, had pawed it all over; but apart from that there was nothing we could use."

Sir Clinton picked up the tool and examined it carefully.

"You've measured it, I suppose?"

"Yes, sir. The head of it corresponds almost exactly with the wound on the girl's head."

"It's a common pattern," commented Sir Clinton. "I'm afraid there are too many like it for our purposes. Did you happen to ask Sperling when he used it last?"

"Yes, sir. He hasn't used it for the last month, he says, and none of the other men used it either."

"Ah! That's something to the point," said Sir Clinton, evidently interested. "Just look here. A hammer of this sort gets wet with dew at times or it gets left about in the rain, and so it gets rusty. Now there's a lot of old rust on this hammer-head. There, for instance, and there. But let's take a magnifying glass. Do you see some fresher rust round about the place where the head fits on to the helve? And there's a trace, too, inside the fissure of the nail-extractor, down at the bottom of the opening. The colours of the two rusts are slightly different, aren't they?"

"Yes, sir, they are," agreed the Inspector. "You mean . . ."

"I'm only suggesting that if this hammer has been washed recently and dried with a cloth, these are the spots where new rust would form. I don't lay any stress on it. The new rust may have got there by quite different treatment for all I know. It just happened to catch my eye."

"Oh, indeed, sir," said Sandrock, slightly damped by this dismissal of the subject. "Still, we'll keep the thing. One never knows."

"Keep it, certainly," said Sir Clinton. "And you might as well go over it carefully with the glass and make a note of the exact spots where you find new rust. It'll have to be done immediately, or the fresh colour may wear off."

"I'll see to that, sir."

"I've heard nothing from San Francisco yet," the Chief Constable went on, dropping the subject of the hammer. "I suppose we can't expect them to perform miracles, especially as the scent's fairly old by this time. But I wish we had a reply from them, just to make things shipshape."

"You wrote by Air Mail, sir?"

"Yes, but even that takes seven to eleven days in transit to San Francisco, and the same for the return journey. It was too complicated for cabling. We'll just have to be patient. And now, I think we'd better interview Mrs. Brenthurst."

Sunnyhill was a big house in the Palladian style, surrounded by well-tended lawns flanked by flowering shrubs. A neat maid came to answer the door-bell; but when Sir Clinton inquired for Mrs. Brenthurst there seemed to be some difficulty.

"I think you'd better see her companion, Miss Bromley, first of all, sir. Mrs. Brenthurst's been very put about lately, with all this trouble, and I don't know that she'll want to see strangers."

"Very well," said Sir Clinton, "we'll see Miss Bromley, then."

They were ushered into a gaunt, chilly drawing-room which had an unused air, and there, after a few minutes, they were joined by the companion, a thin little woman with the air of being always on the alert for a summons. Sir Clinton explained his business to her in a few words.

"I'm afraid Mrs. Brenthurst will not wish to see you," she said, timidly. "She's given orders that no one but the vicar is to be admitted. She's very upset by this terrible death of her son and then Sperling's daughter on top of that. Would I not do, instead?"

"I'm afraid I must insist," said the Chief Constable, kindly but definitely. "You can tell her that we only wish to ask her a question or two about some letters which are, I think, in her possession. We shan't bother her much. If she refuses, you may tell her that it will merely mean a search-warrant and much more trouble to her as well as to ourselves. It's a matter of important evidence which we must get, willynilly."

"If it's anything to do with letters," said Miss Bromley, "I think I might be able to give you what you want. Mrs. Brenthurst never writes any letters. I've done all that for her for the last fifteen years. She doesn't even sign them. She makes me write them in the third person always, so that she never needs to put pen to paper."

"Do you file her correspondence?" asked Sir Clinton.

"Well, not exactly," admitted Miss Bromley. "She reads her letters herself. Then she tells me what to write in reply. And I take a copy of what I've written and put it into the envelope along with the letter and then I tie up the envelopes in bundles as time goes on and stack them in a cupboard. Mrs. Brenthurst always makes a point of having all papers kept, though she never looks at them."

"Ah!" said Sir Clinton, with relief in his tone. "In that case, we may be able to save her the trouble of an interview, so long as she will give us permission to examine these stacks of letters. I can tell you exactly what we want: a letter or letters from Cecil Ducane. Will you tell her this, please?"

"Cecil Ducane?" echoed Miss Bromley, as though the name had struck some chord in her memory. "I think . . . Oh, yes, I remember now. That's her grandson, isn't it? He wrote from America. Now I remember that quite well, because at the time it seemed to me that she was very hard, almost brutal, in that affair. I'll see what she says."

Miss Bromley withdrew and came back again in a few minutes. She had been successful. So long as the police did not worry Mrs.

Brenthurst personally, they were welcome to examine the letter if it could be found. Miss Bromley would look it out for them.

"That's quite sufficient," Sir Clinton declared. "Now, if you'll show us the way. . . ."

Miss Bromley led them along a corridor and ushered them into a "snuggery" furnished in a style dating from the early years of the century. On either side of the fire-place was a large cupboard let into the wall. Miss Bromley had apparently furnished herself with the keys during her absence, and she now opened one of these receptacles, and displayed shelf above shelf stacked rather untidily with envelopes tied up in bundles of all sorts and sizes.

"That letter came quite a long time ago," she said, musingly. "I remember now. It was just a year or two after I came here as companion to Mrs. Brenthurst. That would be about 1921."

She pulled out a bundle or two, looked at some post-marks, and then settled down to examine each packet in turn. It took her some time, but at last she gave a little exclamation and pulled out an envelope.

"Here it is," she said, showing it to the Chief Constable. "I remember it quite well. It's typewritten, you see, and Mrs. Brenthurst doesn't get many typewritten letters. And there's the American stamp. Yes, this is the right one," she went on, opening the envelope and glancing at one of the enclosed papers. "Here's the signature: Cecil Ducane."

She handed the document to Sir Clinton, who read it aloud for the Inspector's benefit.

> *1144 Avenell Street North*
> *San Francisco, Cal., U.S.A.*
> *5th December, 1923*

MY DEAR GRANDMOTHER,

This letter will doubtless come as a surprise to you, since you are unaware of my existence.

I am your grandchild, for my mother was your daughter, Netta, who left England in 1902 and came to America, where she went on the stage. In 1904, she married Reuben Ducane, an actor in the company which she had joined, and I was born in 1905.

In 1906, both my parents were killed in the San Francisco earthquake of that year; and it is only within the last few days that papers have come into my possession which prove my relationship to you.

I have been dependent for the last seventeen years on the kindness of a lady who has been a second mother to me. But I feel that I should get in touch with my own kin, especially as at the present time I am on the look-out for some fixed position in life. What would please me best is to go back to England and settle down amongst my own family, and perhaps you will bring this about by furnishing money for my passage and making me an allowance while I live with you, as I understand that you are very well-off indeed.

I gather from various things that you and my mother had a serious dissension when she left your house and came to America, though I do not know the cause of this quarrel. But that is a very old story now, and I feel sure that you will not wish to carry this estrangement into another generation, but will be glad to see your grandchild and to let bygones be bygones.

I have all the papers necessary to establish my kinship with you, and shall be glad to go through them with you when I come to England.

I hope you will look with favour on this request of mine and that you will receive me as one of the family and ensure to me the share of your property which would have come to my mother had she lived to profit under your will. I am sure she would have wished that, had she not been cut off by her sudden death, which gave her no chance of effecting a reconciliation with you.

I quite understand that you may not wish to receive me, and in that case may I ask you to give me a little capital to help me to make my way in the world. I have a desire to go on to the stage, like my father and mother, and I think I should stand a good chance of being successful in the ranks of the Profession if I had enough money to tide me over the beginning of my career. But I would rather go back to England and rejoin my own family in the meanwhile.

I look forward to receiving a remittance for my passage, and remain,

Yours affectionately,

CECIL DUCANE

When he had finished reading the letter aloud, Sir Clinton ran his eye back over the sheets before making any comment. Then he put the letter down and glanced at the Inspector.

"It's typewritten, so one can't infer much from that. The signature is a bit juvenile," he commented. "But two things do stand out very plainly. The writer had a very wide eye open for the main chance. And the whole epistle reeks of the egotism of an eighteen-year-old. Seven out of nine paragraphs begin with 'I'; and there are lots of other 'I''s scattered about the text. As to Mrs. Brenthurst, apart from her value as a money-box, she cuts a very small figure. Naturally, one could hardly expect much affection in the circumstances, but even mere tact seems meagrely represented."

"That reminds me of Canning's rhyme," said Miss Bromley, unexpectedly, in her thin little voice.

> "In matters of commerce, the fault of the Dutch
> Is giving too little and asking too much. . . .

"You seem to think young people are like the Dutch, Sir Clinton. But you shouldn't forget that they often get grievous disappointments. Here's the letter that Mrs. Brenthurst made me write to Cecil Ducane. I felt at the time that it was a cruel letter and I tried to get her to change it, but she wouldn't."

Sir Clinton took the paper which she tendered, opened it, and read the contents aloud.

Mrs. Brenthurst has received your letter of 5/12/23 and replies to it merely for the sake of making clear that she has not the slightest desire to receive any communication from you in future.

Her daughter Netta caused her great pain by her conduct. Mrs. Brenthurst strongly disapproves of the stage and will not supply one penny towards helping you to take up any such career; nor will she receive you if you come to England. She wishes to make it perfectly plain that you will get nothing from her, either now or in the form of a legacy.

Any further letters which you write to her will be destroyed, unread.

"Rather a facer," commented Sir Clinton, putting down the paper. "I suppose that ended the correspondence?"

"I think he wrote one more letter," said Miss Bromley, "at least a letter did come which had an American stamp post-marked San Francisco, I remember. But I never saw its contents. Mrs. Brenthurst opened it when I gave it to her, but she just glanced at the signature and said: 'That creature again!' or something like that. Then she put the thing straight into the fire without even reading it through. She's very hard, sometimes."

Sir Clinton nodded thoughtfully, but his expression suggested that he was thinking of other matters.

"We shall have to retain these two documents," he pointed out, "and you may be called upon to swear to them in court. Perhaps it would be well if you put your initials in the corner of each sheet."

When Miss Bromley had done this, she turned to the Chief Constable.

"Have you found out anything about these dreadful murders, Sir Clinton? I'm not nervous, really, but they seem to be coming very close to us: first Mrs. Brenthurst's son, and now our poor maid. I don't care to go out after dark myself, now."

"I think that's very wise," said Sir Clinton, seriously. "In fact, I'll put a man on duty here at nights, to be on the safe side. And perhaps you'd better say nothing about these letters, and ask Mrs. Brenthurst to say nothing, either. That's for your own sake, you understand. I suppose you know the Brenthurst family well, after being so long with Mrs. Brenthurst?"

"No, I don't," Miss Bromley explained, awkwardly. "I've met Mr. Brenthurst once or twice, but I never liked him and I avoided him as much as I could. As for Mrs. Fairfoot and her son, I've never even met them. Mrs. Brenthurst refused to allow them to come here at all. She paid Mrs. Fairfoot an allowance, I believe, but that was done by the bank. I never heard of either of them visiting her in the last fifteen years; and she forbade me to have anything to do with them, from the day I came here."

"You wrote no letters to them for her? No? By the way, have you ever been at Fountain Court?"

"Only once," explained Miss Bromley. "Mrs. Brenthurst is very interested in some religious charities, and when new people come to the district, she sends me to call on them and ask for their support. When these two ladies took Fountain Court, Mrs. Brenthurst sent me to call and see if I could interest them. I wasn't very successful, I'm afraid. Miss Teramond's a Roman Catholic and would not do anything to help. But Miss Garfield was very friendly and gave me a small subscription. She was very nice to me and asked me all about myself. I'm rather lonely, you see, Sir Clinton, and so few people take the slightest interest in me that it was quite a treat to find someone who *was* kind and allowed me to talk freely about my life and my own little affairs for once."

"Very nice of her," commented Sir Clinton. "And now I see Inspector Sandrock has been taking notes of this conversation. Will you sign them, if you find them correct, please? I'll send a constable up to keep watch over you, so you needn't feel nervous; but I think you'd be well advised not to go outside the house at night for the present."

On the way back to the police headquarters, Sir Clinton discouraged the Inspector's attempts to discuss this latest evidence.

"Just give me a little time to think it over," he said in a tone which drove Sandrock back into his own reflections.

# CHAPTER XVII

## Finger-prints

WHEN THEY reached the police station, the Chief Constable seemed to have completed his mental review of the situation and to be more inclined to talk.

"We can't complain of our luck in this business, Inspector. Except for Mrs. Brenthurst's craze for preserving her correspondence, those letters would probably have been destroyed. I had a strong suspicion that Cecil Ducane was a grandchild of hers; but it's been sheer good fortune that gave us definite proof in black and white. Now I think you'd be none the worse for a genealogical tree to help you to see your way through the thing. Here's an abbreviated one. I've missed out all but the essential people."

He took a sheet of paper, wrote for a moment or two, and then handed the result to the Inspector.

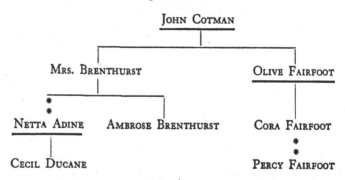

"That's how things stood before Brenthurst was murdered," Sir Clinton continued. "The asterisk represents illegitimacy, the underlining means that the person was dead before the murder. Now take Mrs. Brenthurst. If she makes a will, of course, she can leave her money to anyone whom she chooses. But there's good ground for assuming that she'll die intestate, and in that event the Birkenhead Act of 1925 will apply. Under it, since Mr. Brenthurst is dead and Netta was illegitimate, Ambrose Brenthurst would have come into all his mother's money. But now Ambrose has been murdered, and the cash goes elsewhere."

"Unless he happens to have left offspring," said the Inspector. "He left no legitimate issue, of course. But to judge from what I've heard, sir, he may have left plenty of the other sort."

"They wouldn't come into the money, even if they existed," Sir Clinton explained. "If a woman leaves a legitimate child, and this child dies in his mother's lifetime leaving an illegitimate child, such illegitimate child will have no right to succeed to its grandmother's property. That's due to a little snag in the Legitimacy Act of 1926."

"Is that so, sir? It seems a bit unfair."

"Now look at the state of affairs as it seemed to be, just before the Brenthurst murder," Sir Clinton continued. "Netta's offspring was supposed to have died along with her and her husband in the 1906 earthquake. In these conditions, who would profit by the elimination of Ambrose? The next heir under the Birkenhead Act would have been Mrs. Brenthurst's sister, Olive. But she's dead, and her daughter Cora would take her place. In other words, if Brenthurst died, then Mrs. Fairfoot had every reason to suppose that she would be the heir in the case of Mrs. Brenthurst's intestacy."

"I see that, sir," said the Inspector. "On that basis, the Fairfoots had a financial interest in the Brenthurst murder, over and above the fact that they hated Brenthurst on personal grounds. That's plain enough, and it supplies a good sound motive."

"Yes, but now we find Cecil Ducane turning up alive, after all. Failing Ambrose, the legitimate heir to Mrs. Brenthurst, the next in succession under the Legitimacy Act is Netta Adine and, failing her, Cecil Ducane. Cecil would come in before the Fairfoot clan."

"Humph!" said the Inspector in a speculative tone, "that leaves it about fifty-fifty so far as motives go, for the Fairfoots didn't know Cecil Ducane was alive. The only people who knew it were old Mrs. Brenthurst and Miss Bromley, and by Miss Bromley's tale neither of them can have given the show away to the Fairfoots because they never saw either the mother or the son."

He ruminated for some moments in silence, then suddenly his face lit up as a fresh idea occurred to him.

"I think I see something, sir," he exclaimed. "In that letter of his, Cecil Ducane said that for the last seventeen years he'd been dependent on the kindness of a lady in Frisco. And his letter was addressed from 1144 Avenell Street North, which was the boarding-house kept by Susan Garfield's mother. Put two and two together, and it means that Cecil Ducane was a foster-brother of Susan Garfield. That would account for a lot, wouldn't it? It explains how they came to know each other. It accounts for his influence over her, and her preferring him to all the other men she's taken up with."

"I'm not with you there," objected the Chief Constable. "Very few people marry their childhood's companions. They know too much about them, perhaps, to fall violently in love with them. It's just this tale of an amourette that makes me sceptical."

"Well, she ought to know best, sir, and she quite frankly admitted that visit to the hotel. And besides, we've checked it. You may say it's only once in a hundred times that the boy-and-girl business is the real thing, but this may be the hundredth case. You can't prove it isn't. Now when she came and settled down here, she got in touch with the Fairfoot crew and could worm out of them anything that would be useful to Ducane. And, on the other hand, she would naturally be Ducane's accomplice, if she was so keen on him. It all fits, sir."

"You're barking up the wrong tree, there," Sir Clinton said in a very decided voice, much to the surprise of the Inspector. "If there's one thing I feel sure about now, it is that Miss Garfield is *not* an accomplice of Cecil Ducane."

Inspector Sandrock was completely taken aback by this dictum.

"Very well, sir," he said, "that's as you please. But if you're right, then the only explanation of the hotel business is the one I hit on myself a while ago. He must have drugged her when they had those drinks in their room. It's the only way to make the thing look possible at all."

"I said it was an ingenious idea," retorted Sir Clinton. "I still think so. But let's leave that side of things alone for the present, and turn to something fresh. You're well up in the ordinary finger-print stuff, I know, but we've never yet had any occasion in our local work to use Hudson's method, which came out in 1935."

"I can't say I've heard of it, sir," admitted the Inspector at once.

"It gives one a chance of developing recognizable finger-prints on cloth," explained Sir Clinton. "The principle of it is simple enough. It's the practice that's tricky. But I've been working at it in my spare time lately since I saw a chance of using it, and I think I can bring it off successfully."

He went to a cupboard and brought out various bottles, and a couple of test-tubes as well as an atomizer and some newly made frames. Then from a drawer he took the woman's handkerchief which they had found in the garden, and from which the Inspector had cut a portion to give to Dr. Stangate.

"This bottle contains silver nitrate solution, and this one contains a solution of common salt," explained Sir Clinton, holding them up. "Now we'll pour some of the silver nitrate solution into this test-tube. It's quite clear, just like water, as you see. Here's the common salt solution, clear also. Now I pour some of the common salt solution into the nitrate solution. You see the cloudy white precipitate forming? That's silver chloride, and it's insoluble in water, as you notice. Quite white, isn't it? It's a sunny day, luckily. I'll put this test-tube in the sun. Just watch what happens."

"The white stuff's going darker, sir," observed Sandrock after a few minutes.

"Yes, we won't bother about the chemistry of that," said the Chief Constable. "Now what does ordinary human perspiration taste like?"

"Salt, sir. Anybody knows that," said the Inspector, rather huffily.

"So if you mixed it with silver nitrate you'd get just the result I got just now in the test-tube. Well, that's the principle of the Hudson method of developing finger-prints on cloth. We stretch this handkerchief out on this frame and then spray it with silver nitrate solution to which I've added a little acetic acid. Wherever anyone had grasped the cloth there will be a finger-print left by the perspiration, and the common salt in the perspiration will produce some of that white silver chloride. Of course, there will be a heavy precipitate wherever there's a blood-stain on the handkerchief, because blood contains a lot of salt."

He suited his actions to his description, and then, picking up the little frame, put it carefully away in the cupboard again.

"We'll have to wait till it's dry. Then we'll put it in the sun. The actinic rays will darken the silver chloride and give us the finger-prints in black. After that, all we need to do is to wash away all the unchanged silver nitrate and make the prints permanent by soaking the fabric in a weak solution of ammonium sulphide and washing again."

"Very ingenious, sir," said the Inspector, seizing on Sir Clinton's own phrase.

"You have to learn just how to do it," Sir Clinton cautioned him. "I tried it out with some stuffs that I'd finger-printed myself, for practice, and it took me quite a while before I managed to get the knack of it. Well, once that handkerchief is dry, we can see what luck we've had with it. If we get even one decent print on it, we should be a bit further forward."

"What had you in mind, sir, when you got the Garfield woman to get you one of Diana Teramond's handkerchiefs?" asked Sandrock.

"Well, she handled it, and she probably left some of her finger-prints on the fabric. We can develop them up by the Hudson method if we need them, just to show the jury that the process is perfectly sound."

"I see, sir."

"And while we're talking about finger-prints," the Chief Constable went on, "I got our finger-print ferret to examine that letter of invitation which was found in Brenthurst's pocket. Burford made rather a mess of it by handling it carelessly; but, in addition to his prints, there were three other sets on it. There was a couple of very faint prints of Brenthurst's fingers, evidently left when he was reading the invitation. There were also three rather faint prints made by Miss Teramond, which fits in with her story that she typed it herself. And there were four strongly marked prints made by Miss Garfield."

"Humph!" said the Inspector, injecting satisfaction into the monosyllable. "So evidently, after typing it, the Teramond woman handed it over to the Garfield dame to read. They'd laid their heads together in the matter of the invitation, anyhow."

"You seem to have an explanation for everything, Inspector," said Sir Clinton. "Now there's just one thing further that we might try. You know that young enthusiast in the Templeton Hospital . . . Dr. Wingford, I mean, the one who's raking the district for blood donors to serve in cases where blood-transfusion is required? He tackled me about it, and took a sample of my blood to determine its group. A very winning young man, able to talk the hindleg off a duck, and then persuade the bird to grow a new one. Get hold of him and turn him loose on everyone connected with these two murders: Sperling, Miss Teramond, the Fairfoots, the Fountain Court maids, Miss Bromley, Miss Garfield, Borrett, and anyone else you can think of. You needn't tell him more than's necessary, of course; but if he grows inquisitive, you can explain why we want a classification of these people according to their blood type. But the less you say, the better. I don't want to run counter to medical etiquette. Once he gets the facts entered up in his roll, we can subpoena him, if necessary, and make him produce his list, and that's all we shall want. I doubt if he'll get the lot, for all his plausibility; some of them are sure to refuse. But it's worth trying."

"I'll see to that, sir," said the Inspector. "By the way, there's the matter of that dud diamond. . . ."

"I've been making inquiries about that," said the Chief Constable. "It hasn't been offered to anyone in the diamond trade in this country. Possibly it's gone to Amsterdam or some other of the Continental centres. But my belief is that it's still in the hands of the thief. It's too distinctive a stone to hawk about while there's all this trouble afoot. But I've got on the track of the replica."

"Indeed, sir?" said Sandrock, with keen interest.

"Yes, it was made by Cradock and Tissington, a London firm. Or rather, the order for it went through them."

"And who ordered it, sir?"

"Cecil Ducane," said the Chief Constable, with a smile at the expression on the Inspector's face. "But the trail's covered very neatly. All negotiations were carried out by post. Friend Cecil took rooms within a mile of the Duke's Head, leaving some luggage there as a guarantee of good faith. The landlady thought her lodger was a commercial traveller who went about the country a lot and so could stay with her only from time to time. An account was opened specially at a local bank, in order to draw the cheque for Cradock and Tissington in payment for the replica."

"He couldn't do that without references, surely, sir."

"He gave Miss Teramond and Miss Garfield as references. They both have accounts at this bank, and their affairs have always been in order. Of course, once the cheque was paid and the replica secured, the rooms were given up and friend Cecil vanished into thin air."

# CHAPTER XVIII

## No Past Is Dead

"THAT LETTER I've been expecting from San Francisco came in this morning," Sir Clinton explained to Inspector Sandrock. "We could have moved a couple of weeks ago if we'd depended on news by cable, but it was safer to wait for a sworn deposition sent by mail. There wasn't much chance of things going wrong at this end in the interim. But let's go step by step."

He opened a drawer in his desk and took out some papers.

"First of all, here's a note from young Wingford on the blood donor stunt. He drew blank in several cases. The people wouldn't promise to act as donors. Mrs. Fairfoot and her son wouldn't touch the scheme at any price. But he managed to get samples from all the Fountain Court residents, and here are his results. Olive Hatcham has Group O blood, the same as Brenthurst's. The cook has Group B blood, which turns up nowhere else in this business. Sperling has Group A blood, ditto. Both Miss Garfield and Miss Teramond have Group AB blood, corresponding to the samples found on the pruning-knife, the gardening-gloves, and the embroidered handkerchief which we found in the garden."

"That seems to narrow it down a bit, sir," commented Sandrock. "But the bother is that we haven't got any sample of Cecil Ducane's blood yet."

"We'll come to that later," said Sir Clinton.

He took from another drawer the blood-stained handkerchief, now clipped flat between two sheets of glass.

"We've been lucky here," he said, pointing to two fairly well-defined finger-prints which showed up black upon the fabric. "That Hudson method has turned up trumps. Don't bother about the big black patches; they're merely the places where the salt in the blood left a heavy precipitate of silver chloride."

The Inspector scrutinized the prints with a lens.

"Not much wrong with these, sir. Have you got them identified?"

"I put our finger-print ferret on to them, with the other prints we collected for comparison," Sir Clinton explained. "They were made by Miss Garfield. There's no doubt about that."

"Oh, were they?" said Sandrock, obviously taken aback. "That's a bit rum, sir, but I don't see that it gets us much further. She might have handled one of her pal's hankies by accident. Of course, the blood on it is the same as hers, as you say, sir. But then she's got the same kind of blood as her friend. Humph! I'll think over that evidence. . . ."

"Then you'd better take in some more food for thought," said the Chief Constable. "You remember the invitation to Brenthurst? It has Miss Garfield's prints on it as well as Miss Teramond's. And the S O S message apparently to Percy Fairfoot that Mrs. Fairfoot used has Miss Garfield's prints on it also."

"Very likely the Teramond woman showed them both to her friend, sir, and so they got fingered."

"I admire your resource, Inspector. Let's draw on it further. I ought to add that the S O S letter to Percy doesn't seem to bear Miss Teramond's prints. How do you explain that?"

"Why, sir, you know well enough that you might handle a paper and not leave a print on it, if your skin happened to be quite dry."

Sir Clinton threw up his hand in a gesture of surrender.

"There's no puzzling you," he confessed. "But now here's something more interesting in this report from San Francisco. Never mind reading the covering letter. The affidavit's all that matters at present."

He handed the document to the Inspector, who read it carefully, giving a startled ejaculation at one point in his perusal.

I, Charlotte Catherine Garfield, residing at 1144 Avenell Street North, San Francisco, California, depose as follows: —

In 1900, when my husband died, I started a boarding-house at the above address in order to make a living. My clientele was drawn almost entirely from theatrical people who were birds of passage. I had no permanent guests.

In 1906, at the time of the earthquake, I had staying with me a Mr. Reuben Ducane and his wife, with their twins, Cecil and Imogen, babies of about a year old. They were my only guests at that time. On the date of the earthquake, they had gone to pay a visit to some friends, and took Imogen with them. Cecil was left in my charge on account of a slight illness. The Ducane parents and Imogen were killed in the earthquake, from which my house escaped intact.

I had never heard the Ducanes mention the names of any relatives. In fact, I knew casually that Mr. Ducane had no kin of his own. After the earthquake, I went through their baggage and found some papers which showed that Mrs. Ducane, whose name was Netta, was the illegitimate daughter of a Mrs. Brenthurst, residing in England, though I do not now remember her exact address. It was plain, from the papers I found, that mother and daughter had quarrelled, and that the only feelings between them were those of bitterness. Still, I wrote to the grandmother in England, telling her that her daughter had been killed, along with her husband and child. I got no answer to my letter.

This put temptation in my way. I have always had very strong maternal feelings, and one of my great griefs has been that I had no children of my own. I was very fond of little Cecil, who was an attractive child with very taking ways. I resolved to adopt the child for my own, since it was plain that the grandmother was not the kind of person to whom I cared to entrust the baby, after the way she had behaved. I had something of the sort in my mind when I wrote to England, for I refrained from mentioning Cecil in my letter so that I might judge his grandmother by her reply.

My clientele was a fluctuating one, and as I had no relatives of my own who might have asked questions, I found little difficulty in getting Cecil accepted as my own child. To make things safer, from my point of view, I changed the child's name to Susan Garfield, and gave her to understand that she was my own daughter. She was so young when I adopted her that she soon forgot all about her real parents and regarded me as her mother.

When she had reached the age of eighteen, I gave her the papers which I had found in her parents' baggage, and which I had carefully preserved. As a result of reading them, she wrote to her grandmother in England, but the answer was unsatisfactory, and Cecil (or Susan) made no further attempt to get into touch with her.

In 1932, a French Creole woman, Diana Teramond, came to reside at my boarding-house. She was in the theatrical profession, but she had made no mark in it and was resting for a time, as she could find no one who wanted her services. Although she was some years younger than my adopted daughter, they became close friends, and eventually Cecil (Susan) decided to join this woman in theatrical work.

I strongly disapproved of this project, and it led to constant disagreements between Cecil and myself, which ended in a complete rupture between us. She left my house after a very angry scene, and went off in company with this Creole woman. I have heard from her only once since then and do not even know where she is living at the present date.

Sir Clinton waited till the Inspector had put down the paper. Then he said, with a faint tinge of mockery:—

"It never occurred to you that Cecil is a woman's name as well as a man's?"

"No, sir, it did not," said Sandrock, stiffly. "I suppose I ought to have thought of it when you were so confident that the Garfield woman wasn't an accomplice of Cecil Ducane; but I didn't think of it that way."

"Well, nobody can be his own accomplice, can he?" said the Chief Constable, mildly. "You took things too much for granted, that was all. But we needn't go into these affairs just now. There's something more practical in hand. I've sworn information on the subject before Mr. Wendover. He's a J.P. in this county, and he happens to be visiting me just now. I got him to make out two warrants. Here they are. One is for the arrest of Cecil Ducane, *alias* Susan Garfield. The other is a warrant to search the Fountain Court premises for evidence. I don't know that it is really necessary in the circumstances, but we'll take no chances."

"Very good, sir. We'd better have someone else, just in case. I'll take Sergeant Burford."

Sir Clinton had no high opinion of the Sergeant, but he accepted Sandrock's suggestion.

"Yes, bring him. He was in at the start; he may as well be in at the death. Get hold of him, and Constable Jennings, also, and we'll go now."

When they drove in at the gate of Fountain Court, a car was standing at the front door. Sir Clinton drew the Inspector's attention to it.

"That's Miss Teramond's car. I looked up its number. You'd better note that it's an 18 h.p. Riley Saloon, with a luggage-boot at the back."

"Yes, sir," agreed the Inspector, though his face showed that he hardly saw the importance of the information.

On asking to see Miss Garfield, the three officials were shown into the drawing-room, where they waited for a few minutes before she came in, with a look of inquiry on her face. Sir Clinton gave the Inspector a glance, and in obedience to this tacit instruction Sandrock stepped up to Miss Garfield, tapped her lightly on the shoulder and said in the prescribed form: "I am a police officer and I arrest you on this warrant for the murder of Ambrose Brenthurst." He then read out the warrant to her, completing the little ceremony, and he added the usual caution: "Do you wish to say anything in answer to the charge? You are not obliged to say anything unless you wish to do so, but whatever you say will be taken down in writing and may be given in evidence."

Miss Garfield seemed perfectly cool.

"I don't wish to say anything until I have seen my solicitor."

"Very good," said Sandrock. "I'm going to search these premises. If you have any locked drawers or cupboards, it would be as well to give me the keys of them. Otherwise we'd have to break them open, and there's no need to do damage."

Miss Garfield smiled pleasantly.

"I'll get you the keys in a moment," she said, moving towards the door.

"I'm afraid I can't allow that," said Sandrock, hastily. "You'll have to remain here, in charge of the Sergeant. Just tell us where you keep your keys."

Miss Garfield turned from the door with a slight shrug, as though faintly contemptuous of such precaution. But she had not lost her imperturbability, and her voice was quite pleasant as she gave Sandrock instructions as to where the keys were to be found.

"I suppose you'll search me at the police station?" she asked.

"I'm afraid that's a matter of routine," returned Sir Clinton.

"I'm not objecting," Miss Garfield explained, with complete good temper. "You won't find anything of the slightest interest, I can assure you. But I mustn't waste your time. I can see you are anxious to go on with your investigations."

Diana Teramond burst into the room, evidently in a state bordering on hysterics.

"What are you doing here?" she demanded, turning to Sir Clinton. "This is my house, is it not? Have I asked for the presence of the police? No? Then why are you here, and without asking to see the mistress of the house? You may go, and quicker than that, if you please. I am an American citizen and I will not be treated in this way, as if I were of no account. . . ."

Miss Garfield interrupted her.

"It's quite all right, Di," she said, reassuringly. "They've come to arrest me for the murder of Ambrose. It's just a silly mistake. Don't worry about it. It will be cleared up very quickly."

Diana Teramond seemed completely aghast.

"Arresting you? But it is mere madness! You were not even in the house, that night. Are they crazy?"

"This does no good, miss," said the Inspector, intervening to check a further outburst. "I have my warrant for this arrest. And I've another warrant to search the house."

"To search my house!" cried Diana, in mingled surprise and anger. "You would dare to do such a thing?"

"It's quite all right," said Miss Garfield, soothingly. "Don't make a fuss, Di. It can't do any good. I've no objection to their going through my belongings. They'll find nothing of the slightest importance. Go out into the garden until they've finished. I don't suppose they'll take long over it. You can't prevent them, since they have a search-warrant, and you'll only get into trouble if you try. It's all a very stupid mistake, and the sooner they get through their searching, the quicker we'll be quit of them. Do go, now, please."

Diana seemed unwilling to take this course, but the stronger personality prevailed. She went out through the French window into the garden, ignoring the two officials as she passed. Sandrock watched her go, and then turned to the Sergeant.

"You'll take charge of this lady and see that she doesn't communicate with anyone until we come back," he ordered.

"Very good, sir," said Burford, visibly filled with importance.

Sandrock stepped towards the bell-push, but Sir Clinton's look changed his intention and he followed the Chief Constable out into the hall.

"Hardly fair to bring that maid in to see her in her present position," said Sir Clinton, in explanation of his tacit order. "Just get hold of the girl without ringing the bell."

The Inspector summoned Olive Hatcham, who appeared with a malicious smile on her face.

"Are they being arrested?" she demanded, eagerly. "Are you taking them to the police office?"

Sandrock shrewdly suspected that the girl had been listening at the door.

"Less gab," he said, coarsely. "I want you to show us round the house."

"Where do you want to go first, sir?"

"The box-room, I think," said the Chief Constable, to the maid's obvious astonishment.

As she led the way towards the staircase, Sir Clinton paused in front of the hall table on which some letters were lying, ready for the post.

"I wonder if she's as clever as I think she is," he said enigmatically. "We'll see, later on."

He picked up the letters, thrust them into his pocket, and followed Olive Hatcham up to the first floor.

"This is the box-room, sir," she explained, opening a door.

Some cabin trunks, a couple of hat-boxes, and several suit-cases were lying on the floor. Sir Clinton examined the suit-cases one by one. Some of them had the initials "D.T." on their leather, others bore the letters "S.G." on them, and two were unmarked. The Chief Constable with a gesture drew Sandrock's attention to the fact that on all the luggage, except the two unmarked suit-cases, a faint film of dust had accumulated.

"We'll take those two back with us," he said, putting the unmarked ones aside. "Perhaps some of the people at the Duke's Head may recognize them. We needn't bother with the rest; the dust shows that they haven't been disturbed for weeks. But just open them up, Inspector, please, to make sure there's nothing in them."

Sandrock opened all the receptacles, including the two which Sir Clinton had set aside, but all of them were empty.

"Are those all?" asked Sir Clinton, turning to the girl.

"I think there ought to be another one, sir, an expanding suit-case. I remember packing it once or twice, and I don't see it here."

"Ah! Very smart," was the Chief Constable's comment, which Olive Hatcham took as a personal tribute, though Sandrock suspected that it referred to something else. "Now we'll search Miss Garfield's room. But this searching may be a long job. It would be better, perhaps, to send our prisoner down to the station now, instead of waiting. You might see to that, please, Inspector. Let the Sergeant take her. We may need Jennings. I made all arrangements about accommodating her before we came up here."

In a few minutes the Inspector returned, having carried out his instructions, and bringing Jennings with him. Dismissing the maid, they went systematically through the wardrobe, the tall-boys, the drawers of the dressing-table. Even the bed was searched without result.

"There's nothing here, sir," declared Sandrock, in a tone of disappointment. "I suppose that means we'll have to go over the whole house with a comb, and that's going to be a bit of a job."

"There's a chance that we may save our pains," said Sir Clinton, pulling from his pocket the letters which he had picked up from the hall table. "I wanted to overhaul her room in case anything unexpected turned up in it. But before we go through the whole house, we'd better try a fresh cast."

"These letters, sir? I saw you lift them, and I had an idea you saw something in them."

"When we came into the house," Sir Clinton explained, "I glanced about me as a matter of course. There were no letters lying on the hall table then. But when we came out of the drawing-room, they were there. She may not have put them there; but it looked rather as if she'd put them down as she was coming in to see us. When we drew blank here, it was plain that she'd managed to dispose of all her incriminating stuff somewhere. It's very smart to be able to hide a complete suit of clothes — or its equivalent — in an envelope under our noses. She must have been reading Poe's *Purloined Letter*. Here are the envelopes. Let's try our luck."

He examined the typewritten addresses on the five letters; then, selecting one of the envelopes, he slit it open and took out the contents.

"A blank sheet of paper, you see," he said, holding it out to the Inspector. "And I'm almost prepared to bet that the address on that envelope is completely fictitious. Ditto for these other three. . . ." He opened them, with the same result. "Now here's the real thing, in this last envelope. It's addressed to herself, 'Poste Restante,' at our local G.P.O. And inside it is . . . Yes, I guessed as much. . . . A left-luggage receipt for a suit-case. She's clever, undoubtedly. You see how it is, Inspector? If we hadn't spotted these letters, someone would have posted them in the ordinary course. The four duds would have gone to the Dead Letter Office and disappeared, since there's no clue to the sender and the addresses are fakes. But the fifth one, with that receipt inside, would have been left lying 'to be called for' whenever she wanted the contents. That hid any trace of the suit-case, but still left it available to her any time she wanted it."

"But what good were the duds, sir?"

"If you'd seen one envelope by itself on the table, you might have been inclined to examine the address; but five in a pile looked like ordinary correspondence, and the suspicious one was lying at the foot of the pile, well hidden from a casual glance. I expect she's had these things ready to hand for a while, and brought them downstairs with her when she called to see us. She left them on the table as she passed. If we had called merely on some minor matter, she'd have picked them up again as soon as we'd gone. The point is that the receipt remained in her possession up to the last moment, just in case she wanted to collect that suit-case at a moment's notice; whereas if we arrested her, it ought to have escaped our notice and gone to the G.P.O., ready for her if she was released eventually. Now our next move is to gather in that suit-case and look over its contents. I've a pretty good idea of what we'll find in it."

Leaving Jennings on guard at Fountain Court, Sir Clinton drove to the station with the Inspector. Sandrock procured the suit-case from the left-luggage office, and they returned to Sir Clinton's headquarters. The suit-case was locked, but Sandrock soon produced a set of keys, one of which opened the lock. Inside was a complete man's outfit: a slaty-blue suit, ties, collars, underclothing, socks, studs, sleeve links. On the top was a grey soft felt hat and a wig of fair hair. Sandrock burrowed into the contents and drew out a pair of shoes.

"American, sir," he reported with delight, after examining them. "I was pretty sure of that, from these footprints by the stile in Wolf Spinney."

"Take these things out, carefully," Sir Clinton directed. "We've not got everything yet."

Tucked away in one corner of the case was a tiny packet wrapped in tissue-paper. The Inspector drew it out, unfolded the paper, and disclosed a small pendant with a diamond in the centre. Sir Clinton took it to the window and examined it minutely.

"That's no schlenter," he said, finally. "This is the real thing. Well, it gives one some intellectual satisfaction to have put the last bit of the jig-saw into place."

# CHAPTER XIX

## Compte Rendu

"As you signed the warrant for the woman's arrest, Squire, you have some claim to hear the whole story," admitted Sir Clinton, in answer to a question by Wendover. "Naturally, it's not for publication until after the trial. Here are some of the documents."

He went over to his desk and picked up a folder, which he handed to Wendover.

"It's not exactly a five-act play arranged on classical lines," the Chief Constable continued as he took his seat again. "You couldn't put it on the stage. The construction's hardly up to scratch for that. But, roughly, it falls into five sections. First of all, you have the preliminary stuff which really underlies the whole plot. Second, there's the manœuvring which produced a perfect alibi for the Brenthurst murder. Third, there's the Brenthurst murder itself, which is the keystone of the whole business. The fourth section covers the Sperling murder. And the fifth is still to be played out in the courts, so I can't pretend to tell you how it will go."

"Four sections will be enough for the present," said Wendover. "If you bring the story up to date, I'll be quite content."

"Very well. You remember one night when I had Peter Diamond to dinner, and he told us all about that absurd Thirteen Club? Like Peter, I have a retentive memory, and I docketed a good deal of his yarn in my mind. It was really Brenthurst's doings with his debtors that interested me at the time, but the rest of the facts stuck in my memory as well and turned out to be useful, later on. You may remember that Peter drew up a family tree for us. You'll find a copy of it in the folder. But you may remember also that he warned us that it was complete only so far as he knew from the information which his great-aunt had given him. I noted that qualification; but I really paid little attention to it at the time, because from his tale it seemed certain that the whole Ducane family had been wiped out in the San Francisco earthquake of 1906. But actually, there's a flaw in Peter's table, for there was one child who survived the earthquake and remained unknown for a good many years after that. You'll find in the folder an affidavit by a Mrs. Garfield which tells the story."

Wendover turned to the paper and read it through with care.

"A queer business," was his comment when he had finished, "but not improbable, given the unsatisfied maternal instinct of Mrs. Garfield."

"Try the folder again, and read the letter that Cecil Ducane sent to her grandmother, and the reply she got from Mrs. Brenthurst," Sir Clinton directed.

Wendover read the two documents with a deepening frown on his face.

"Neither of them seems very likeable," he said at last, glancing at his host. "The girl's letter is . . . Well, I never could remember the precise difference between egoism and egotism, but there's a spice of both of them there, I should say. And the grandmother's reply is just a bit of brutality in black and white."

"Quite so," agreed Sir Clinton. "But the important point is to gauge the effect which the reply would have on the girl. At eighteen, a good many youngsters think the world's their oyster, and I guess that Cecil Ducane was one of them. That reply might have hurt and disheartened a weak creature. Sent to Cecil Ducane, who was anything but weak, it had a different effect, I imagine. Wounds in adolescence go deep and take a long time to heal. This one didn't heal. It festered instead. And there you have the root of the whole tragedy. There was no one to explain to Cecil Ducane what the true state of affairs was. All she could gather was that she was repulsed and that help was denied her to which she thought she had a fair claim on the strength of her relationship. From the sequel, it's plain enough that she brooded over her grievance until it became an obsession. She'd been done out of her rights? Well, she'd see about that! Her family had turned her adrift just when she needed a helping hand? Well, she'd see about that too, by and by! And so on."

"That seems to fit," Wendover admitted. "As she saw it, she had an undoubted grievance, and it may well have rankled and grown out of all reasonable proportions."

"Meanwhile, she had to make her way in the world, since she had evidently got tired of living with her foster-mother," Sir Clinton went on. "There, again, I suspect that a magnified grievance may have come in. 'Why did you adopt me and conceal me from my relations at the time when they would have been forced to do something for me, an orphan hardly a year old?' That quarrel with Mrs. Garfield suggests something of the sort. Be that as it may, the quarrel certainly shows that Cecil Ducane was still egotistical and determined to go her own way, regardless of anyone's feelings. She joined hands with this girl Teramond, whom she got to know at Mrs. Garfield's boarding-house, and they ran in partnership in variety turns. Now here again, Peter Diamond was useful. By some chance he had seen the two of them on the stage, and he described one of their turns as a show in which you think there are three men and two women in the cast until it turns out in the end to be two females only."

"I don't see much help there," confessed Wendover.

"No? To me it suggested at once that one of the two women made some sort of fist as a male impersonator. And *that* stuck in my mind, though I saw no immediate use for it."

"Ah! I hadn't thought of that."

"Well, let's get on. You remember Peter, in his description of that Thirteen Club dinner, mentioned a red diamond set in a pendant, which belonged to the Teramond girl? It had been valued at £5,000. By cautious inquiries, I elicited from Cecil that she had been personally in charge of the arrangements for getting the stone valued. And we can prove that she took that opportunity of getting a replica made. The thing was insured, after that;

and it's quite likely that Cecil had some idea in her mind of working a swindle on the insurance company by substituting the replica for the real pendant and then putting in a claim, somehow or other. Actually, she found what seemed to her a better plan."

"What led those two women to settle down in this district?" asked Wendover.

"That will probably come out in the trial when Miss Teramond goes into the witness-box," said Sir Clinton. "I've no evidence on the point at present; but it seems unlikely that they drifted here by mere chance. Of the pair, Cecil was by far the stronger character, and I've little doubt that she influenced the choice. We know how deep a grudge she felt against the Brenthursts, and Fountain Court was a good vantage-ground for observing them without betraying her own real identity."

"I suppose it must have been something of that sort," agreed Wendover. "Go ahead."

"Bear in mind that Cecil had been on the stage as a male impersonator," Sir Clinton continued. "When she left off playing on the Halls, she had two suits of male clothing which she preserved. They were exactly alike. Probably that was intentional, so that if any accident befell one suit, she had the other ready for use in her impersonation turns. She kept them under lock and key; and she was evidently angry when she found her housemaid trying to get into the drawer in which she stored them. Now when it came to arranging for the making of a duplicate of the pendant, she saw obvious pitfalls in the way if she negotiated the affair in the name of Susan Garfield. Replicas of that sort are uncommon and easily traced down. So evidently it occurred to her to use her male attire to cover her tracks. She succeeded easily, and that must have given her confidence in the trick. And for her *Doppelgänger* she chose her own real name: Cecil Ducane. That was a false step. But apart from that, she did the business remarkably well, for she frequented that hotel in Trendon, the Duke's Head, in both characters, posing as Cecil Ducane and also Cecil Ducane's wife, which gave a very good backing to the plausibility of the male Cecil's existence."

"Very neat," grunted Wendover, with a certain admiration.

"Now we come to the verge of the Brenthurst murder," Sir Clinton went on. "You may remember that when Peter Diamond told us his tale of the Thirteen Club dinner, he gave us to understand that Percy Fairfoot was flirting — for want of a better word — with Susan Garfield. Later on, after the Brenthurst murder, Susan Garfield — or Cecil Ducane — admitted this to me quite frankly, and she also explained that Percy had cooled off and transferred his affections to Miss Teramond. She made light of the matter, and seemed to be quite candid in saying that she really did not resent the slight. However, I've learned more about her since then, and I'm not quite so sure of it now. Considering her character, it would be surprising if she had been quite so indifferent as she made out to me that she was. She's not the sort of woman who would see one of her captures snatched away by another woman and be able to take the incident without rancour, even if she showed none. It's only speculation, but I think she bore the two of them, Percy and Miss Teramond, a grudge, though she concealed it admirably.

"Another thing which I can't substantiate by definite evidence is this. She must have gone to some pains to find out just how she stood in the matter of Mrs. Brenthurst's fortune. She had taken up the Fairfoots; and since she was evidently spying out the land, it would be easy enough for her to learn from them about old Mrs. Brenthurst's peculiarities in the matter of signing documents, which Peter Diamond explained to us. She could hardly help discovering that her grandmother was likely to die intestate. And after that, very little trouble would show her that she herself would be an heiress, provided that Ambrose Brenthurst died before his mother. Half an hour spent in any Public Library over the Birkenhead Act and the Legitimacy Act would tell her all she needed."

"As you say, one can't prove a thing like that," said Wendover, "but it sounds plausible enough."

"I doubt if she had enough Latin to construe Cato's favourite remark, *Ceterum censeo, Carthaginem esse delendam*," said Sir

Clinton with a wry smile, "but I've little doubt that she had something like it in her mind: 'Brenthurst must go.' She evidently felt as strongly in that matter as Cato did about the destruction of Carthage. And if the removal of Brenthurst landed Percy Fairfoot and Diana Teramond in trouble, so much the better. Three birds with one stone is quite good marksmanship. Fortunately — from her standpoint, at least — the whole machinery was ready to her hand. Brenthurst had got Miss Teramond into his clutches financially, and you know what Peter suggested to us about girls who got into his claws. Further, Percy Fairfoot had no kindly feelings for his natural father. And Percy was a violent fellow, infatuated with Miss Teramond, jealous, and altogether just the tool that Cecil Ducane needed. Bring Miss Teramond and Brenthurst together in the proper circumstances and one could count on very awkward happenings. Add Percy Fairfoot to the company at the right moment and . . . well, something was bound to fall out. And, if that something wasn't serious enough, Cecil could be on the spot herself to make a certainty of it."

"The idea being to involve both Miss Teramond and Percy Fairfoot in suspicion of having done away with Brenthurst?"

"Exactly. But there's more in it than that," Sir Clinton pointed out. "In Percy's case, there was another object in the scheme. No one knew that Cecil Ducane existed. The Ducane family was supposed to be extinct. Therefore, if Ambrose Brenthurst died, and his mother remained intestate to the end, the next heir was, apparently, Percy's mother, Cora Fairfoot. Which added another possible motive for Percy to get rid of his unnatural parent. Very ingenious. Jealousy on the one hand and hard cash on the other. It put Percy in rather a bad light. She's a clever woman."

"Well, these are the bones of the affair, I suppose," commented Wendover, "but they need some flesh of detail on them before they look very well. Let's hear that part of the business, Clinton."

"Bear two things in mind, Squire. First, Miss Teramond had no clear idea of money. She rather prided herself on that, as she was good enough to inform me. She'd got into a very bad case by borrowing broadcast from Brenthurst. Cecil Ducane knew all about money. I've no doubt that she produced a scheme for Miss Teramond to clear off her debts by pledging that pendant to Brenthurst as security for further advances. Miss Teramond told me the plan; she made no bones about it. And, in the circumstances, it was about the only thing she could do. So she wrote Brenthurst a letter, asking him to come and see her at 10 P.M. one night and bring with him all the IOUs or whatever documents he had in the matter of her earlier debts. She was going to take these back; and in exchange she was going to pawn the pendant with him to cover the old debts and also to raise a fresh advance from him. I've very little doubt that Cecil dictated that letter, though Miss Teramond actually typed it and sealed it up for the post. But letters at Fountain Court were laid on the hall table, so that anyone could take them out to the post. Cecil got hold of that letter, steamed it open, erased 'ten o'clock' and substituted 'one o'clock' instead. Look in that folder and you'll find the document clipped between two cellophane sheets. Just read it, Squire, and consider how a man like Brenthurst would interpret it."

"Pretty black," said Wendover, seriously, after he had finished the perusal. "I see you've been trying it for finger-prints. I suppose that's why you have it protected by cellophane?"

"Yes. The prints on it are Miss Teramond's, which got on to it by her handling the paper as she put it into the machine. Brenthurst's are there also, because he touched it when he was reading it. It was pretty hot weather just then, and people's fingers were moister than usual, in consequence. But the biggest and blackest of the lot, as you'll notice, are those of Cecil Ducane, because she had to hold the paper firmly while she did that erasing and while she fitted the sheet into the typewriter again to insert the 'one' instead of the 'ten' which she erased. That was an oversight. She ought to have worn gloves. But no doubt she'll swear that Miss Teramond handed her the letter to read, before sending it off; and Miss Teramond's memory is in such a rocky condition that there's no relying on it, even if she denies this."

"Well, that arranges for the presence of Brenthurst," said Wendover, "but what about Percy Fairfoot?"

"I ought to explain that owing to a motor accident, Miss Teramond is hardly normal. Her memory's defective in streaks; and she's lost the power of writing to a great extent, although she can manage to typewrite more or less accurately. You'll notice that the typing of the letter isn't impeccable. But she can hardly sign her name with a pen; so it needs no great skill in forgery to produce something that looks like her scrawl. As a matter of fact, she forgets to sign some letters, and people, knowing about her trouble, guess that the letter comes from her."

"That certainly opens a door to all sorts of things," commented Wendover. "I suppose you've got a case in point?"

"I have. Try the folder again, and you'll find a letter beginning *'Brenthurst is coming to Fountain Court . . .'* Got it? Very well. That letter was sent to Percy Fairfoot. I found the envelope of it on his desk when we made a search. It's not signed, as you see; but when Percy Fairfoot got it, he'd guess at once that it came from Miss Teramond. Now, Miss Teramond has no recollection of writing that note; and we can find no trace of her finger-prints on it. But we *have* found a quite clear print corresponding to Cecil Ducane's forefinger."

"Ah!" said Wendover. "And I see the typing is perfect, too. None of the corrections made by striking one letter on top of another, as in the other letter, the one to Brenthurst, which Miss Teramond *did* write."

"Just one more item, and we're finished with the preliminary canter," said Sir Clinton. "We've questioned the porters at the Trendon Left-Luggage Office, and one of them remembers that a few days before the Brenthurst murder, a woman corresponding to Cecil Ducane's description left a suit-case in his charge. He doesn't know who collected it, and the man who must have given it out can't remember who took it away. But we've had an identification parade, and the first porter picked out Cecil without the slightest hesitation as the woman who left that suit-case in his charge."

"I'm never very sure about these identifications," said Wendover, critically.

"This one was absolutely fair," Sir Clinton assured him. "We got some people from exactly the same social class to play their parts, so that he couldn't go by the style of dress, and I took special pains to include two girls who looked rather like Cecil in features. No, there's no doubt about it. The porter was, luckily, a noticing fellow. And you must remember that Cecil is a good-looking woman, likely to catch a man's eye and impress him."

"That sounds fair enough," admitted Wendover.

"That finishes Part I of the story," said Sir Clinton, taking a fresh cigarette from the box beside him. "Now we come to the alibi problem. Obviously Cecil Ducane needed a sound one; and she produced a little *chef d'œuvre* with a double action in it. She not only made an alibi for herself, but she planned the thing so that she could throw suspicion on a nonexistent person, while representing herself as a bit of an injured innocent. And she cooped it up in such a fashion that it looked as if she were dragging herself in the mud by telling the tale at all, since it involved confessing that she'd been spending a night out with a paramour. She told it so well, with so much apparent candour, that she might well have taken me in completely, but for one thing."

"And that was?" asked Wendover.

"That was the fact that I remembered that some names are common to both boys and girls," explained Sir Clinton. "It was really that fact that put me on the alert in the whole business. There are quite a lot of names which will serve just as well for a man or a girl: Hilary, Sydney, Camille, Jocelyn, Denys, Evelyn."

"Yes, that's true," conceded Wendover. "I suppose it was Cecil that put you on the track? It's generally used for boys, but I know three girls called Cecil myself, though Cecile, Cecily, or Cecilia, or Cecilie, or Cicely, are commoner variations."

"It was Cecil in this case — Cecil Ducane," said Sir Clinton. "It just happened to cross my mind that Cecil might be either a man or a woman. And that was the key to the whole affair. It was her one big mistake: using her own real name. But she had a reason for it, which explains her choice if it doesn't excuse it. To put the thing shortly, she meant to unload all her nefarious doings on to the back of a male Cecil Ducane, who, of course, had no substantive existence at all. He was merely Susan Garfield in one of her male impersonation acts."

"And so you people were to be launched on a wild-goose chase after this man, while she sat comfortably in safety? Not a bad idea," said Wendover. "But how did it work out?"

"You'll find a report by the Trendon police in that folder," said Sir Clinton. "You'd better keep an eye on it as I go along. It will probably be easiest to call the two characters in the sketch by the names they used. But bear in mind that Susan Garfield and Cecil Ducane are the same person dressed respectively as a woman and a man. Here's how it goes, and remember that we're dealing with the evening before the Brenthurst murder, to start with. At 6 P.M. Susan Garfield drove up to the Duke's Head in her car. On the seat at the back is one suit-case which contained, we believe, an evening frock, a set of male clothes, and a woman's toilette outfit, etc. In the boot of the car was another suit-case, containing a second suit of male clothing identical with the first lot, as well as some odds and ends. It was an expanding suit-case, so there was plenty of room for all that stuff in it. The hotel porter took the suit-case from the back seat of the car into the hotel. Susan Garfield had written to book a double room beforehand in the name of Mr. and Mrs. Cecil Ducane. At the office she registered. She then drove the car round to a near-by public park where there was no attendant on duty; and she left it in the park. Then she walked back to the Duke's Head; and made some inquiries about the time when the London express was due at Trendon, mentioning that her husband would arrive on it. She then went up in the lift to her room. There, she changed into male clothes. She could do that quick enough, after her practice on the stage that Peter told us about. And so, you see, it was Mr. Cecil Ducane who came out of the bedroom. Do you know the anatomy of the Duke's Head, Squire?"

"I've been in it, once or twice," said Wendover. "Rambling old den, isn't it? All odd corners and stairs. They expanded it from time to time by taking in adjacent premises, didn't they, instead of doing some proper rebuilding? A bit of a rabbit-warren, so far as I recall it."

"That's the point," said Sir Clinton. "It's a rambling place, and one can get to the upper storeys either by the lift or else up the various staircases in different parts of the house. And it has a number of exits in addition to the front door, so that one can come and go without passing the hotel porter at the main entrance. Now what I'm going to give you is our reconstruction of events, so there's some of the story unsupported. But we can definitely prove quite enough for our purpose. Let's go back to Mr. Cecil Ducane outside his bedroom door. He went down one of the stairs and left the hotel by a side-exit, unnoticed by anyone, so far as we can trace. That was about 6:45 P.M. He walked round to the station and mingled with the passengers as they came off the London train. Then he went to the left-luggage office and received the suit-case which Susan Garfield had deposited there, a day or two earlier. Carrying this in his hand, he went into the hotel by the station door and called at the hotel office. He was dressed in a slaty-blue suit and wore a light grey felt hat; and he was also wearing a wig of fair hair. Susan Garfield is a dark-haired woman. Cecil Ducane spoke with a rasping brand of American accent; whereas Susan Garfield speaks with a natural English accent. That was obviously a precaution to cover any similarity in voice. You many remember that the office in the Duke's Head is in a rather dark place, at the end of the hall; so there wasn't much chance of any resemblance being spotted, even if the make-up hadn't been carefully designed to make the two characters quite unlike each other. Cecil Ducane inquired from the office clerk about his wife's arrival, got the number of their room, and grumbled about the London express having been behind time. Then about five past seven he went up with his suit-case in the lift and walked along to No. 63. At 7:45 P.M. Cecil Ducane appeared again and came down by the lift. He brought round the car from the public park and left it at the hotel door. Then he went to the office and asked the girl for directions how to reach a restaurant in the town, explaining that he was dining there with a friend. He next went out, got into the car, drove round to the public park again, and left the car there. After that, he came in by one of the side-doors, unnoticed, and went upstairs to No. 63. He changed his lounge suit for a black evening frock, and now it is Mrs. Cecil Ducane who comes into public notice.

"She came down by the lift and dined in the hotel, taking care to impress herself on the waiters. After that, she sat in the lounge, where she had coffee, and she ordered cigarettes from the lounge waiter just to make him remember her. At 10 P.M. she went up in the lift. The lift-man remembered that, having an eye for a fine-looking woman. When she got up to No. 63, she changed into male clothes again. But so far, you see, Squire, she had given a very good performance, well calculated to persuade the hotel people that they really had a pair of guests and not merely one individual. The nastiest snag was the fact that obviously they couldn't appear together at dinner; but she got round that by this tale of Cecil dining at a restaurant with a business acquaintance. Really, Squire, she's quite a good actress. She played the neglected and slightly resentful mistress quite excellently to me. Such a dreadful disappointment when Cecil declared that he *must* dine with this client of his and leave her alone for the evening! And so on, with a studied moderation which was a first-class bit of acting. She deserved a much greater success on the boards than ever came her way, I'll say that for her.

"At 10:30 P.M. or thereabouts, Cecil Ducane must have come downstairs and left the hotel surreptitiously by one of the unwatched exits. He then walked round to the front entrance. This was meant to represent his return from dining at the restaurant. To impress himself on the staff, he called at the hotel office and asked for letters; and a letter was handed out to him by the clerk. This letter, of course, had been posted a day or two earlier "to await arrival." He also left at the office an order to be called at 8 A.M. next morning as he was going to catch a London train. And he made some inquiries about whether there was a restaurant car

253

on the train, in which he could get his breakfast. He then went up to his room in the lift, having left a very definite impression about himself on the clerk at the desk."

"What about the car?" asked Wendover. "Where was it, all this time?"

"According to Susan Garfield's story, it was in a garage," Sir Clinton explained. "But we combed all the garages in Trendon, and it was not left in any of them. Obviously, it had been in the public park all through the evening."

"That was a serious flaw in the business," said Wendover.

"It couldn't be helped," said Sir Clinton. "And even there, Susan Garfield managed to keep herself clear, for she made her tale about the garage depend on what Cecil had told her; and the fact that it wasn't true didn't directly contradict her own part of the story. That was rather a neat touch, I think. But let's continue. This next part is pure surmise on our part. Cecil Ducane came downstairs again about 11 P.M., unseen, and made his way out of the hotel unobserved. If he had waited much later than that, he would have been conspicuous; but at eleven o'clock there would be plenty of people moving about and he would pass unnoticed amongst them. We assume that he went round to the car park, collected the Riley, went to Fountain Court and committed the Brenthurst murder. His clothes got blood-stained in that affair, so on the way back he extracted a third suit-case from the boot of the car. This suit-case had a complete male outfit in it; and he changed into this fresh suit (which was identical with the blood-soiled one) and threw away the stained suit under a culvert, where it was discovered later and passed to us. Then he must have hung about for a long time, for his next appearance was at the hotel next morning. Evidently he came back, after the murder, put the car in the public park, and sneaked into the Duke's Head unobserved about breakfast-time. By 8 A.M. he was in No. 63, half dressed and ready to show himself with a safety razor in his hand when the maid knocked at the door to waken him according to orders. He opened the door slightly and spoke to her, so that she could not see into the room and spot that there was no sign of Susan Garfield. He took the precaution of lying in the second bed, to leave evidence of two people having used the room. At 8:25 A.M. he went down by the lift with his suit-case. He went to the office and paid the bill for No. 63, as well as for his wife's dinner, breakfast, and incidentals, explaining that he was leaving before Mrs. Ducane, and wished to square up before he went. Then the hotel porter took his suit-case to the London express and was dismissed. As soon as he was out of range, Cecil came away, left his suit-case in some quiet corner, and hurried back to the hotel. He got in unobserved. If he'd been noticed, he could always say he'd forgotten something and so missed the train. But actually he got up to his room unnoticed. He then changed his clothes, and the next appearance is that of Susan Garfield."

"It was just one risk after another," commented Wendover. "He might have been seen by someone who remembered him, during any of these exits and entrances."

"Obviously," Sir Clinton agreed. "But you'll note that even if he had been seen, that isn't evidence against his paramour, who was, according to her story, sleeping peacefully upstairs all night. And here she put another neat little touch to the tale. She wasn't fool enough to say that Cecil drugged her. That would have been inartistic. But she was careful to tell me that Cecil Ducane gave her a drink or two out of a flask before she went to bed, and that she slept like a log all night, and awoke with a bit of a headache. That left us to infer that Cecil had given her a dope of some sort in the drinks; and it also made it evident that Cecil could come and go unwatched by her during the night. I thought that rather a clever stroke on her part. If we went all out to catch Cecil and convict him, she couldn't even be regarded as an accomplice, since she was sleeping her drugged sleep right through all the critical hours of the Fountain Court murder."

"She must have spent a lot of thought on her plans," Wendover commented. "Any other touches of the same sort?"

"One more, at least," Sir Clinton explained. "You remember that the chambermaid saw Cecil, half dressed, and apparently in the middle of a shave? Well, just to reinforce that, Susan Garfield left behind in her room when she finally left it a gold-plated safety razor in its box, and the box had the initials 'C.D.' on it — Cecil Ducane. Fairly good evidence, on the face of it, that a man had spent the night in the room. Add the fact that both beds had been slept in, and you produce a very sound train of evidence."

"A mistress of detail, evidently," said Wendover in a tone of very reluctant admiration. "But go on, Clinton. Let's hear the rest of her doings."

"The rest of the story we can confirm, up to the hilt, because she wanted it confirmed, and took pains to advertise herself," Sir Clinton pointed out. "About 9:15 A.M. she went down in the lift. She bought a newspaper at the stand in the hall. Then she had breakfast, taking care to choose the same waiter as at dinner on the previous night, so that he'd remember her. Notice how neatly she got round the difficulty of Cecil not sharing the meal with her, just as she had evaded it at dinner on the night before. After breakfast, she walked out of the Duke's Head, took her car out of the park, drove round to the station, picked up the suit-case which was lying there and put it into the boot of the Riley, so that the hotel porter would not see it. Then she drove round to the front entrance of the Duke's Head and left the car there. Then she went to the office and asked about her bill. She learned — greatly to her surprise, of course — that Cecil had paid it before he left. And, of course, Cecil was supposed to have got the car out of the garage for her and left it in the park. It was no use our asking Susan Garfield which garage the car had lain in during the night. Cecil hadn't bothered to tell her where he had garaged it, so she couldn't tell us. Which, of course, saved her from a very awkward point. If it was found — as we did find — that the car had never been in any of the town garages that night, what did that matter, so far as she was concerned? It was Cecil's affair, not hers. If the car had been used that night, she knew nothing about it. Very clever. Finally, she went up to No. 63, tipped the chambermaid, got her suit-case put into the back seat of the car, and drove back to Fountain Court, ready with her alibi. That finishes Part II of the story."

"And now you come to the Brenthurst murder?"

"Yes. We can prove a good deal of that because we're going to call the Fairfoots as witnesses for the prosecution. They both lied to me barefacedly when they thought they were under suspicion; but when they found we were after Cecil Ducane, they changed their tune and told the plain truth for once. This is the order of events, as supported by their stories. Evidently Cecil left her car in a quiet spot near Fountain Court and arrived on foot sometime before one in the morning. She had a key of the garden gate and let herself in, dressed in male clothes. I suppose she took cover among the hydrangeas in the alley leading to the tennis-courts. At 1 A.M. Brenthurst arrived, no doubt exhilarated and full of expectations based on the peculiar hour of his appointment. He arrived to find the place dark, so he went up and tapped on Miss Teramond's window. She told him to go round to the terrace, where she let him in through the French window. Meanwhile, Mrs. Fairfoot came on the scene. Percy Fairfoot is an untidy fellow, and it seems that he left the note beginning: 'Brenthurst is coming to Fountain Court . . .' open on his desk. His mother saw it, pocketed it, and decided to join the party without saying anything to him. She was afraid that Percy might get himself into trouble, and she made up her mind to be on the spot, just in case. Unknown to Percy, she set off on a bicycle and waited in hiding until Brenthurst opened the gate. He left it on the latch, obviously to avoid having to fumble with the catch if he happened to fall in with the cheetah by any chance. It didn't love him much, if you remember; and I think he was wise in taking that precaution, just in case he had to beat a hasty retreat. Mrs. Fairfoot slipped in behind him and made for the pagoda, where she expected to find Percy. But Percy wasn't there. He had taken a rather roundabout route, for sound reasons, and had got a puncture which delayed him. Meanwhile, Brenthurst had come to grips with Miss Teramond, and she had loosed off some shots from her pistol, whereupon Brenthurst ran down the path towards the pagoda. The cheetah was after him. Now I had learned that Cecil Ducane had taught the cheetah some tricks, one of which was to round up chickens as a sheep-dog rounds up a flock. She was able, from the side-alley, to give the cheetah orders to shepherd Brenthurst and cut him off from the gate. And, just at that moment, Percy Fairfoot arrived at the gate in his repaired car, coming in response to the appeal in the letter. As soon as Brenthurst was hounded into the side-alley, Cecil Ducane fell on him and cut his throat from behind. We assume so, at any rate. Naturally, Brenthurst made an outcry, which was cut short by even less agreeable sounds when the knife got home. Percy, out on the road, heard this and came in at the gate, to find his mother at the door of the pagoda. He imagined that she or Miss Teramond had killed Brenthurst; and he at once started to get rid of the body by carrying it out on to the road. That left a blood-trail on the grass as he went along. The cheetah followed him, but it was fond of him and didn't interfere. But when he laid the body down on the road, it fell on the corpse and began to tear at the throat, where the blood was. Percy, meanwhile, went back into the garden to get his mother away.

"But Mrs. Fairfoot's a clever woman. She saw that it would be easier for her to escape a murder charge than it would have been for Percy, because it would be hard to prove anything against her, whilst the jealousy motive would come in if Percy were arrested. So she had a short argument with him, and finally ordered him to go, at once. That was overheard by the gardener, who was near by, engaged in robbing the orchard along with his colleague. Percy eventually cleared out and his mother let the lock snap behind him, in case he changed his mind and came back. She's quick-witted, and she remembered that his footprints would show up on the soft sand of the path, so she got a birch besom out of the pagoda and swept up the surface wherever her son had walked. Then she intended to get away. But the cheetah was at the gate. It didn't like her, and she was afraid to face it. So she wandered through the gardens, looking for another way of escape; and in so doing, she blundered upon the gardener and his accomplice. This completely scared her, and she took refuge in an out-house until dawn, when she came out and ran into us as we were looking round. I forgot to say that, with the idea of inculpating herself and so saving her son, she had rubbed her palms over some of the blood and then put on her gloves to delay us in finding out the state she was in. Her idea was to gain time for Percy to get home undetected. You remember what Peter told us about the mutual affection between the Fairfoots? She was evidently quite prepared to take all suspicion on her own shoulders if she could save Percy.

"She told a neat circumstantial tale to us. She must have thought it all out carefully while she was sheltering in the shed. But it didn't quite carry conviction, and we detained her. To complicate matters, we found a blood-stained pruning-knife and a blood-stained handkerchief in the pagoda where Mrs. Fairfoot had been hiding. The handkerchief belonged to Miss Teramond, and the knife was one which she always used in cutting flowers in the garden. That looked bad, at the time. Actually, these things had been planted there by Susan Garfield. We found her finger-prints on the handkerchief. . . ."

"By Hudson's method?" interjected Wendover.

"Yes, by Hudson's method. And the blood on the handkerchief turned out to be the same group as Cecil Ducane's, and was entirely different from Brenthurst's blood-group. Also, there was some rabbit's blood on the knife. Cecil had told us some tale about Miss Teramond getting hold of a pet rabbit and killing it. And there was a white cock which also came to a bad end. That was just to heighten the colour a bit, I think, and to suggest that Miss Teramond has some kind of blood-lust. She also threw out a hint that Miss Teramond came originally from Haiti, where Voodoo is rife, with animal and human sacrifice as part of its programme. My own impression is that Cecil killed both the rabbit and the cock herself. She killed the rabbit to get some blood to put on the knife; and then, finding that she hadn't enough to make much of a show, she probably made her nose bleed and let some of her own blood fall on the knife and also on Miss Teramond's handkerchief. I don't suppose she knew anything about the differences between various types of blood."

"She's not so thorough, then, after all," commented Wendover. "But every detected murderer makes some slip or other."

"Then there's Percy Fairfoot," Sir Clinton continued. "He told us a pack of lies which we had little difficulty in disproving. But once he learned that we did not intend to charge either his mother or Miss Teramond, he changed his tune and told us the plain truth about his doings that night. I can't say I have much liking for him. He's a violent fellow, and his manners leave a good deal to be desired. But he'll be a useful witness, none the less."

"And what about Miss Teramond?"

"It's not worth our while to bring any case against her," said Sir Clinton. "No jury would look at it, since evidently she fired these shots in self-defence."

"Now, I suppose, you come to Part IV of your tale," said Wendover. "What about the murder of this poor girl Sperling?"

"To begin with," suggested the Chief Constable, "you'd better read the affidavit by Mrs. Garfield, of San Francisco. It's in the folder. You see from it that Cecil Ducane (*alias* Susan Garfield) wrote a couple of letters to her grandmother, old Mrs. Brenthurst, in 1923. Now, when the Teramond-Garfield syndicate came to live at Fountain Court, Susan Garfield came across a Miss Bromley, who acts as a secretary-companion to the old lady. Susan Garfield, I think, picked the brains of Miss Bromley, who isn't very bright; and she must have learned that Mrs. Brenthurst preserved her old letters, so that probably these two letters from San Francisco were still in existence. Susan Garfield had a good deal of foresight, and she foresaw that if these letters fell into our hands after Brenthurst had been murdered, they might put us on her track — as, in fact, they helped to do. So she determined to get her hands on them. Burglary wasn't in her line; so, casting about for some other method, she dressed up as Mr. Cecil Ducane and took to sparking that unfortunate girl Sperling. When she had established relations, she suggested to May Sperling that she wanted these letters. That tied her down, of course, to the name Cecil Ducane in her dealings with the maid. May Sperling evidently put difficulties in the way; and finally Susan Garfield suggested that the maid might let her into the house some night, to hunt for the documents herself. Unfortunately, by doing this, she raised a suspicion in the girl's mind that the letters were a mere blind, and that a theft of Mrs. Brenthurst's jewellery was the real thing in view.

"Then came the Brenthurst murder, and things reached a crisis for May Sperling. Susan Garfield feared that the girl would blurt out the fact that this 'man' Cecil Ducane had been after these letters and, once that came out, we would go into the matter and so learn the real identity of Susan Garfield with Cecil Ducane, the murderer whom we were hunting. The obvious thing was to shut Miss Sperling's mouth. And that was done most effectively by luring the wretched girl up to the stile in Wolf Spinney and killing her there with a hammer. Then the body was dragged up among the trees. Just to make things a bit more complicated for us, the body of a white cock was left beside the corpse."

"Why?" interjected Wendover.

"Because white cocks are used in Voodoo sacrifices sometimes, and Susan Garfield hoped that we might suspect Miss Teramond, who originated in Haiti. To strengthen the male impersonation, she brought a half-smoked pipe along with her and knocked out the ash on a tree-trunk just above the girl's body, where the mark couldn't be missed. And she told us a tale about suffering from insomnia and having had to get a sleeping-draught from her doctor. The idea was, of course, to suggest that she was sleeping heavily that night, whilst Miss Teramond got out of the house and murdered May Sperling. We've questioned her doctor about that, but he retired into medical secrecy. That didn't matter, for we got the prescription from her druggist and could prove she had a sleeping-draught in her possession. What she did, of course, was to give it to Miss Teramond that night in the tonic which the doctor had ordered. So Miss Teramond slept heavily and never knew that Susan Garfield had got out of the house to put an end to May Sperling."

"She seems to have been clever enough in establishing alibis," Wendover admitted. "Not that she made a good one in that case. Still, it was a good try."

"When we came to go over the site of the crime," Sir Clinton continued, "one thing gave me a little trouble. Inspector Sandrock declared that the male footprints were made by an American-built shoe. He may be right there. And at the Duke's Head, Cecil Ducane spoke with a marked American accent. Further, a forester, Borrett, had seen May Sperling in company with a 'man' dressed exactly like Cecil Ducane — slaty-blue suit, soft grey felt hat, and so on. And by that time, we were hot on the trail of Cecil for the Brenthurst murder, and naturally Borrett's evidence suggested that Cecil Ducane was also responsible for the death of May Sperling. *But,* in the Brenthurst case, the body had been lifted bodily and *carried* out of the garden; whereas in the Sperling affair the girl's body had been *dragged* along the ground. Now, anyone who could lift Brenthurst, a great fat monster, could easily have carried the body of May Sperling, who was quite a light weight. That bothered me at the time, until it grew clear that the two cases were quite different. Susan Garfield's quite a well-built woman, but she could never have carried Brenthurst's body from the alley out on to the road. But as soon as we began to suspect that Percy Fairfoot had been at Fountain Court that night, it was pretty obvious who had done the carrying, since it could not have been done by Susan Garfield, Miss Teramond, or Mrs. Fairfoot. If he had only been content to let the body lie, things would have been plainer. But he was bent on screening Miss Teramond — and his mother also — so he carried Brenthurst's remains right out of the garden on to the road, closing the gate behind him, so as to make it appear that Brenthurst had been killed on the public highway and not in the Fountain Court grounds at all. The body of the Sperling girl, on the other hand, was dragged away, simply because Susan Garfield didn't want to lift it — even if she had the strength for that — because by lifting it she would have run the risk of getting some blood on her clothes. And she cut the throat of the girl's corpse to suggest a similarity in method between the two murders and so throw more suspicion on Miss Teramond, if we had swallowed her bait in that respect."

"I suppose you've got enough there to establish a good case," said Wendover. "The two suits of male clothing, one blood-stained and the other found in her possession, will be difficult for her barrister to get round."

"Peter Diamond is prepared to swear that he saw the woman wearing a suit of exactly the same colour and cut when she was giving some of her male impersonations on the stage. And we've picked up some stage hands to swear the same," said the Chief Constable. "No, once her alibi at the Duke's Head came apart, she was done for. She can't produce a Cecil Ducane in the flesh, and she can't even show that she and her *Doppelgänger* were ever seen side by side. Whereas we can prove that her own name is actually Cecil Ducane. 'What's in a name?' Shakespeare inquired. But *he* didn't know everything, as Peter would point out. In this case, there's a whole case packed into one name — or two, if you like."

**THE END**

>>> If you've enjoyed this book and would like to discover more great vintage crime and thriller titles, as well as the most exciting crime and thriller authors writing today, visit: >>>

# The Murder Room
## Where Criminal Minds Meet

**themurderroom.com**